"M..."

The view on the ve..... er. Beside her was a bu.... shoulder. "What are your .... asked the reporter.

"Chop the bots!"

"But why?"

"They're obscene! Things! Purify the planet!"

WOODSMAN

DON'T MISS THOMAS A. EASTON'S
SPARROWHAWK AND *GREENHOUSE*

A stunningly original "Organic Future" in which people drive in Roachsters, sleep in Slugabeds, and fly aboard giant Sparrowhawks . . .

"WELL THOUGHT OUT . . . QUITE INTEREST-ING!"

—*Locus*

Ace Books by Thomas A. Easton

SPARROWHAWK
GREENHOUSE
WOODSMAN

WOODSMAN

THOMAS A. EASTON

ACE BOOKS, NEW YORK

This book is an Ace original edition,
and has never been previously published.

WOODSMAN

An Ace Book / published by arrangement with
the author

PRINTING HISTORY
Ace edition / April 1992

ISBN: 0-441-90871-3

Ace Books are published by The Berkley Publishing Group,
200 Madison Avenue, New York, New York 10016.
The name "ACE" and the "A" logo
are trademarks belonging to Charter Communications, Inc.

PRINTED IN THE UNITED STATES OF AMERICA

10 9 8 7 6 5 4 3 2 1

Dedicated to my daughter,
Joellen, whose own children
may live this world.

PART 1

Chapter
One

ONCE MARTHA'S HOME had been as massively solid as her own body. Then she had been banished to the yard outside and forced to watch, morosely pacing while that pile of stone and mortar was torn down and replaced by an oblong concrete rim. Her immense grey sadness lifted only when the construction crew positioned a Bioblimp, a genetically engineered jellyfish, over the rim, glued it down, added braces, killed and cleaned and dried it, and coated it with pungent sprays. The new building was a translucent dome whose thin leather walls trembled when the wind blew.

Inside once more, Martha eyed the buffet with as much interest as the Bioblimp had ever provoked. The pressure of three hundred well-dressed bodies reaching for canapes and plastic cups of punch and coffee and wine was, bit by bit, nudging the long table closer to the bars of her enclosure. In just another moment . . .

"I had *my* eye on that one!" Freddy the pig sounded outraged as he struggled to point with a stubby forelimb. "You can't have it!"

Martha seemed to understand. She showed the modified pig a sheepish, embarrassed eye and extended her trunk toward him. Tom Cross shifted Freddy's weight to one arm to free a hand and accept the small triangle of bread and shrimp salad. Then, as he tucked it into Freddy's upright maw, the elephant dipped her trunk into the punchbowl.

Some of the onlookers gasped in dismay, but Freddy laughed and Tom, his oldest friend, joined in. They were in the zoo's new elephant hall. It held eight roomy cells, three of them occupied; the other elephants were outdoors. Toward the western end of the building was a temporary stage; behind the stage, the setting sun tinted the translucent wall a glowing orange-red. The occasion was a benefit concert intended to raise money to

3

pay the last of the building's costs. The stars of the concert would be Freddy and his wife, Porculata.

Freddy sneezed and muttered, "The place stinks. Somebody should housebreak those monsters. Goddam perfumes, too. I'd stand it better if I had hands. Or even a trunk." The pig wiggled a trotter. Once he had been a garbage disposal; the gengineers had shaped him so, to fit in the dark, cramped space beneath a kitchen sink, with no need for more than vestigial limbs. They had also played on him the cruel trick of intelligence, which Tom had discovered when he was a child of six. Later, the boy had given the genimal a freedom his body did not fit.

Freddy's wife was as crippled, and as intelligent, as he. "You and your wishes," she said now. "They're about as useless as . . . as these." She waved her several legs in the air. There were more than four of them, all hollow tubes through which she could channel her breath. She was a living bagpipe.

Tom's wife, Muffy, reached out a hand to stroke Porculata's tartan hide. "We're working on it," she said. In the crook of her other arm nestled Randy, the giant spider that at one time, when she had been an exotic dancer, had been her trademark prop. Behind her was a broad easel with a display of clippings about Freddy and Porculata and the musical performances that had made them both famous.

A dignified sniff drew Tom's and Muffy's eyes toward a gentleman whose silvery grey coverall matched his swept-back hair. When he saw that he had their attention, he said, "A pig's a pig, and they'll stay that way. If God had intended . . ."

"God!" Freddy snorted.

"But BRA . . ." said Kimmer Peirce. Young and blonde, she stood beside her husband, Franklin, the balding curator of the art museum where the musical genimals lived. He was holding Porculata in his arms.

At the interruptions, the sniffer muttered, "Animals!" and turned away. An older woman, her hair not quite as grey as his, made a face at his back. "The Bioform Regulatory Administration is dominated by the conservatives," she said. Her dress coverall bore the emblem of the Endangered Species Replacement Program. "They don't mind using gene replacement to turn people into animals. And we could go the other way, easy. The technology's just the same. But no, that's . . ."

"We'll persuade them, Calla," said Muffy. Calla Laffiter was the director of the local office of the ESRP. "And then you can . . ."

A gentle chime rang through the hall. "That's our cue," said Freddy. "Come on, let's go!" As the crowd drifted toward the folding seats arrayed across the building's floor, leaving the remaining canapes and punch to Martha, Franklin Peirce and Tom Cross carried their burdens toward the stage. To one side, a brass quintet was arranging sheet music on stands. In the center of the stage, illuminated by a single spotlight, gleamed a pair of chrome-plated support racks for the genimals. Behind them, the building's wall glowed pink from the fading sunset.

The sound of motorcycle engines penetrated the building's walls a moment before the quintet began to play, but no one seemed to notice or to wonder what such antique vehicles should be doing in the pedestrian precincts of the zoo. They were too intent on the stirring brassiness of trumpets and trombones, the throaty wailing of Porculata's bagpiping, and the sheer virtuosity of Freddy's scat-singing, which brought it all together. The audience was rapt.

So too were the three pachyderms still in the building. Martha and her companions faced the stage head-on, swaying on their feet, their trunks curling, flexing. From time to time, one would raise its trunk forehead high and trumpet. Yet no member of the audience flinched or looked around. The voices of the elephants blended into the performance precisely as they should in that setting, precisely as if the score had called for them. The total effect was both weird and marvelous.

Motorcycle engines roared again, closer now. The last glow of sunset cast shadows flickering on the wall behind the stage. The shadows loomed, larger, and yells interrupted the music. Shadow arms rose and fell, and the wall shook and boomed as it was struck.

The music stopped. Someone shrieked, "Engineers!"

A crudely shaped, heavy blade stabbed through the wall with the harsh hiss of parting leather. More blades expanded the single tear to a gaping rent. Yelling figures tumbled through, waving crude swords or machetes that in that frozen instant announced by curve and width and length their origins as ground-down automobile leaf springs. The invaders—unwashed, unshaven, red-eyed—wore blue coveralls with golden cogwheel patches. From their ears dangled brass springs and other bits of technological debris.

The audience screamed as the Engineer terrorists charged. Wild swings of their swords knocked music stands off the stage and battered instruments into uselessness while the musicians scurried out of the way. Not all of them made it. One sword clove Porculata in two and sprayed blood across the stage. The pigs' support racks toppled with metallic clangs. Freddy rolled under a chair and began to wail in terror and instant grief.

The invaders stormed off the stage and into the audience, still swinging their swords. Muffy shrieked as one knocked Randy from her shoulder and stomped the spider into pulp. When she tried to grab the killer by one blood-spattered arm, reaching for his bearded face with clawlike fingers, another impaled her chest on a heavy staff. On the other end of the staff, a painted flag, its colors as black as Muffy's hair, as red as her blood, said, "Machines, Not Genes!" When Tom shrieked as loudly as she and began to raise a chair above his head, a third terrorist buried a sword in his back.

Bowels and bladders emptied in the reflexes of terror. Pungent odors competed with the coppery scent of blood but failed to win. Rivulets and floods spread across the floor, and the terrorists' only casualty came when one slipped and fell. A concert-goer seized the man's sword and thrust it through his throat. A moment later, he too was dead.

The elephants trumpeted in alarm to match the humans' screams. But when Martha tried to do something more by reaching through her bars to seize a grimy neck, a sword chopped through her trunk. Blood sprayed across the hall as she shrieked with pain and panic. Her companions echoed her, and the bars of their enclosures creaked and bent as they strove to come to her aid.

Swords rose and fell. One terrorist cried, "Where's that other pig?" Two or three thrust their blades between the bars and laughed as the elephants recoiled. Most ignored the animals. All seemed to relish the screams of the injured and dying humans.

At last the siren calls of police Sparrowhawks resounded in the sky overhead. One of the Engineers seized a fistful of canapes from the still untoppled buffet table, and all turned to run. Seconds later, their motorcycles roared in flight.

A single banner waved near the center of the elephant hall, its staff still embedded in Muffy's chest. Around it sprawled a scene of carnage, of blood and moans and sobs and screams, both human and animal.

On the stage, Freddy keened in anguished fear and loss, his gaze fixed on the body of his wife. "Porkchop!" he wailed. "Toommmyy!"

The police arrived. With them came the medics, one of whom immediately slapped a sedative-secreting leech on Freddy's neck.

"Forty dead," said Kimmer Peirce. Her eyes were hollow, her blonde hair disarrayed. It was the day after the Engineers' attack on the concert, but she had neither slept nor used a comb. "Fifty more in the hospital."

Freddy stared at the familiar walls of his museum apartment, the mats and pillows, the tub, the fridge, the door to the attendant's booth. The attendant was gone; Kimmer had banished her, insisting on taking over herself.

They had brought him home while he was out. He knew that. He was nestled in familiar cushions, surrounded by familiar smells. But . . . "Porkchop?" he asked, hoping it had all been a nightmare.

It had, but not in sleep. Kimmer nodded, squeezing his forelimbs just above the trotters. "She's gone," she said.

"And Tommy?"

Another nod, another squeeze. "And Muffy." Kimmer's eyes filled with tears; Muffy had been among her favorite people. "Randy, too."

Freddy emitted a shuddering sigh. "Litter. Shit."

She nodded again.

"I'm glad the kids weren't there." Barnum and Baraboo, Ringling and Bailey. They could play in their ways as marvelously as their parents, but they had their own gigs elsewhere.

"They're on their way home."

"But they can't talk." All they could offer was their presence, and that was something. But they couldn't talk. They just weren't equipped for anything but music.

"I can," said Kimmer. "I'm here. You can talk to me." She patted his side and tugged a pillow closer. "Franklin, too."

"He's okay?"

"Thank God." She wiped at her tears. "I don't know what I'd do if . . ."

The door opened, and Franklin Peirce appeared as if they had summoned him. Beside him was Calla Laffiter, the local ESRP chief. She wore a coverall very like the one she had worn at the abortive concert, though it was distinctly plainer in cut.

Franklin's coverall was the light tan of his own position, but that was not all he wore. A heavy bandage decorated one forearm, and when Freddy began to open his mouth, he said, "Yeah, one of them nicked me before I could get out of the way. Reactionary bastards." The Engineers had deified the machine. They wished, they said, to destroy the technology of gengineering and all that had sprung from it—Bioblimps and Roachsters and other vehicles, housing, new food crops, Freddies.

"I wish," said Kimmer. "I wish they'd stuck to litterbugs." That was how the Engineers had begun, by turning their demonstrations into barbecues for the gengineered pigs that served society as street-cleaners. Then they had begun to attack gengineered vehicles. Now . . .

"Still," Franklin added. "There's one good thing coming out of it."

His wife snorted, plainly saying that she doubted that was possible. "It can't be good enough."

"There's a lot of sympathy for you, Freddy. You've lost so much, and it's in all the news. The zoo folks say they think even BRA will soften up a bit."

The pig closed his eyes. He sobbed aloud, and tears ran down his cheeks and neck; the gengineers had made him human in more than mere intelligence. "I wouldn't trade," he finally said. "No way. No way."

Kimmer squeezed his wrist again. Franklin sighed. "No, Freddy. But . . . compensation."

"It's not worth it. It isn't!"

The press conference was being held in the museum's basement auditorium. This was the same room in which Freddy and Porculata once, as musicians, had entertained their public. Their wooden support racks—not chromed, these—still stood on the right side of the stage. On the left, Kimmer Peirce occupied one end of a deeply cushioned sofa. Calla

Laffiter was at the sofa's other end. Between them sat a tall, slender man, round-faced and blunt-nosed. He had not yet been introduced.

The front of the stage bore a podium festooned with microphones. The first few rows of seats held two dozen reporters. From the ceiling hung several veedo cameras, crimson ready lights glowing, all aimed at the man behind the podium.

Franklin Peirce was that man. "You know the background," he was saying. "The Engineers have a lot of sympathizers. Many people yearn for the Good Old Days. They don't like manure in the streets, or doing without their Roachster for weeks while it goes through its molt, or cleaning up leaves the size of bedsheets dropped by their bioform houses. They've heard stories of how neat and clean the streets were in the Age of Machines, of plug-in parts and care-free homes. They forget, if they ever knew, how foul the air was growing, how close we were to exhausting the fossil fuels and ores that made the machines possible, when the gengineers offered us an alternative. They gave us a way to raise everyone's standard of living to what the Machine Age made possible only in a few nations, and then to keep it there.

"It's not really very surprising," he went on. "Not surprising at all, that we should have the Engineers. Dissatisfaction is a basic human trait. It's not something we can legislate out of existence. I doubt we could even *gengineer* it out of existence." He paused to allow a murmur of laughter. "But they went too far when they attacked the concert.

"Freddy was a pig. A pig with a human intelligence and human talents. He was, in fact, a human being stuck in a body designed for immobility. He might as well have been a quadriplegic. Certainly, he was just as handicapped. And he dared to wish for a body, a human body, a freedom that the gengineers had denied him. He dared to say that the technology exists, that a government program even encourages the use of gene replacement to turn human volunteers into members of endangered species.

"Calla Laffiter." He gestured toward the woman, and she nodded, giving the reporters and veedo cameras a toothy smile. "The local ESRP head. She asked the BRA for permission to give Freddy and his wife human bodies. But religious groups, the Engineers and their sympathizers, they said Freddy was just an animal, and a pig at that, a garbage disposal. His

mind was irrelevant. So were his talents. Turning an animal—
much less a pig!—into a human being would be blasphemy."
Franklin Peirce shook his head as if human folly could still
amaze him.

"Tell us," said the reporter from the *Times.* "Animal rights
was a big issue a century ago. People said that we have no right
to exploit animals in research. Some even said that we have no
right to eat them. Certainly, we have no right to manipulate
them for our own convenience. Doesn't any vestige of that
feeling remain?"

Franklin Peirce sighed. "Of course it does," he said. "It even
has a good deal to do with the Endangered Species Replacement Program. Our exploitations, our neglect, our disregard
of the rights of other animals to have their own place in the
world, all that led to the deaths of many species. When we
realized what we had done, and when the technology became
available, our guilt drove us to set up the ESRP. That program
is, in a very real sense, an expiation of our sins.

"It might even have something to do with the idea that we
shouldn't use gene replacement to turn animals into humans.
But more to the point here is the feeling that there is something sacred about the human form. Animals are animals, and
changing them in that way degrades us and defies God."

"Doesn't changing them corrupt their own integrity?" This
was the woman from the *OnLine Herald.*

Franklin Peirce sighed again. "If we made most animals
human, we probably would be doing that," he said. "Animals
are not little, cute, furry people, no matter how many children's
stories and veedo shows and Sunday supplement articles treat
them that way." His questioner tightened her mouth as if she
had been responsible for more than one such article. "They
don't have our sort of minds, and they wouldn't fit in our
bodies. They wouldn't have the faintest idea of how to live
as humans. They would be the equivalent of the profoundly
retarded.

"But those few animals like Freddy," the museum curator
continued. "They do have our kinds of minds. They are human
in all but body. They can talk, and we can ask them what they
want."

"What do they say?" asked the *Times* man.

"Thank you," said Franklin Peirce. He had needed that
question. "*They* say that they are human in the most important

way. *They* say that their integrity is corrupted by unreasonably enforcing their handicap." The man who sat on the sofa, between Kimmer Peirce and Calla Laffiter, nodded at these words.

"It isn't really," said Franklin Peirce, "a question of 'animal rights' at all. In his own mind—and in mine—a genimal like Freddy is as human as one can be. The question is therefore one of *human* rights."

"But he *isn't* human!" said the woman from the *Herald*.

"He is now," said Calla Laffiter.

The man from the *Times* spoke above the suddenly growing murmur. "You mean it worked," he said.

"The technology is quite well established," said Franklin Peirce. "It's only the direction of the change that was new. Of course it worked."

"What does he look like now?"

"He's right in front of you," said Franklin. He turned to face the sofa on the left of the stage. "Freddy? Would you stand up, please?"

The man who had been sitting all this time between Kimmer Peirce and Calla Laffiter stood up. He offered the reporters a slight bow.

Total silence greeted him.

Freddy straightened and aimed his blunt-nosed face at the audience. His nostrils pointed forward just a little more than was usual for a human face, as if the ESRP had been unable to erase all vestiges of his origins. He stepped forward, and Franklin relinquished the microphone.

"Call me," he said when he had positioned the microphone to his liking. "Call me Frederick, now."

"Do you have a last name?" asked the woman from the *Enquirer*.

"Suida. The scientific name of the pig family." A titter of laughter ran among the reporters. "It recognizes my origins, but it is now only my legal name." He stressed the "legal."

"Frederick Suida. But you're still Freddy."

He nodded. "To my friends."

"Can you still sing?"

"Yes! Give us a song! A song for your public!"

For a long moment, Freddy stared at the reporters, his face blank. Franklin Peirce was just beginning to step toward the podium, ready to intervene, when the ex-pig's mouth shaped a curve of pain, he shrugged, and he said, "I haven't sung since . . ."

"Then it's time you did. C'mon."

Franklin looked at the woman from the *Enquirer,* his face grim. "Enough," he said. "He's been through too much to play with him."

"Our readers and viewers will want to know."

Freddy laid one hand on the curator's sleeve. "No," he said. "There's no point in refusing to remember. I can stand it. I'll sing."

Franklin stepped aside. He looked at his wife and Calla Laffiter, who had slid closer together to fill the gap Freddy had left on the couch. He smiled uneasily at them, and then he gave Freddy a "go ahead" gesture with one open palm.

Freddy took a deep breath, said, "There's no accompaniment," and began to sing, "I was born about ten thousand years ago . . ."

Franklin winced. Kimmer began to weep. The woman from the *Enquirer* smirked as if she were satisfied that her prejudices were so vindicated. Several of the other reporters sighed in sympathy, and the ready lights on most of the veedo cameras quietly winked out.

Freddy's voice was not the mellow bass it once had been. It croaked. It squeaked. It wobbled and skittered and scratched upon the eardrum.

Calla Laffiter left the sofa and touched his shoulder. He fell quiet, tears glistening in his own eyes. Into the silence, she said, "He has been profoundly changed. You understand that. It's no wonder that his voice is different, or that he is not yet used enough to it to control it well. Give him time."

The *Times* reporter raised his hand. "Mr. Suida. I'm sorry."

The woman from the *Enquirer* smirked again. "And what will you do now, Freddy?"

He could only shrug. He did not know.

Chapter
Two

BESIDE THE LONG, low building's front door was a small brass plaque that said, "Agricultural Testing Service, Inc." Frederick Suida snorted. The man he had come to see knew as much about farming as he did about mining the moon.

Beside Frederick, a German shepherd with an overlarge head growled as if in agreement with the snort. The man cut him off with a gentle thump and a scratch behind one ear. "Enough, Renny." Then he shifted the dog's collar, repositioning the small lump of the court-ordered radio tracker beneath his throat. The dog had supposedly been named for a star of ancient veedo tales of an even more ancient time when the cavalry had always been ready to ride to the rescue. The cavalry no longer existed. Nor was this an age of heroes.

When the man opened the building's door, the dog pushed past him, tail high and oscillating easily from side to side, sniffing, into a room that held a dust-filmed reception counter, a small couch, three molded chairs, and an arching tangle of bioluminescent vines rooted in a large pot. There was no receptionist, nor any sign of human occupancy. A single door, ajar, confirmed that there was more to the establishment.

Frederick stared at the wall behind the reception counter and called, "Jeremy Duncan?" He winced at the sound of his voice. Ever since his conversion, his voice had been prone to squealing when he shouted.

A sudden thudding bang suggested that someone had heard and dropped his feet from a desktop or windowsill to a carpeted floor. A moment later, a man stood in the room's doorway, one hand holding a bottle of moisturizing lotion. He was short, chubby, and balding, and his chest was bare beneath an open white labcoat. The slits that marked his gills were red lines on the sides of his chest. The skin around them looked inflamed. It also glistened with lotion.

13

"Dr. Duncan," said Frederick, holding out his hand. "I never seem to find you with a shirt on." He did not smile. It had been many years since he had felt he had anything to smile about.

The other shrugged and set his lotion bottle on the reception counter. "Too tight," he said, just as he did whenever Frederick made his ritual comment. "They hurt." Once before, at an earlier meeting, he had explained that he had given himself the gills after he had taken up scuba diving. He had wanted the freedom of the fish; only later had he learned that the reshaped tissue was excruciatingly sensitive to mechanical pressure. When Frederick had asked him why he had never changed his body back, or tried to remove the sensitivity, he had said, "They work just fine in the water."

Now Jeremy Duncan gestured his visitors into the depths of the building and said, "Haven't seen you for awhile."

"Not since I brought the last check." They were passing a door that opened on a dimly lit room equipped with two nutrient-bath tanks and a large freezer. Frederick paused, as he always did when he visited Jeremy Duncan's place of work. The room resembled an operating room, as antiseptic in its gleaming tile and medicinal odors as if it were meant for physical surgery. It was even equipped with cardiac monitors and heart-lung machines. But there were no trays of laser scalpels and hemostats. Instead, there were racks for intravenous bottles. The bottles stood in a cabinet by the wall, together with packets of sterile tubing and needles. The bottles held the nutrients to supplement the bath in its sustaining of the patient while cells gained a pseudoembryonic malleability, tissues and organs reshaped, and the body restructured itself to obey new blueprints. In the freezer, Frederick knew, were more bottles filled with suspensions of tailored viruses.

Similar viruses had changed Freddy's porcine form to the one he wore now. He remembered only too well being laid in a tank filled with a thick, warm fluid they said would nourish him through the weeks of change. But these tanks, here and now, were empty. "You haven't been very busy," he finally said.

Jeremy Duncan was standing in the more brightly lit doorway of his office a few steps down the hall. "You haven't sent me many clients."

"We could send you back to the regular ESRP labs." As he

spoke, Frederick reached into the breast pocket of his green coverall. He held out an envelope.

Duncan took the envelope and shuddered. The viruses the Endangered Species Replacement Program used had been designed to replace, bit by bit, the genes that made a human being human with those that specified an anteater, a rhinoceros, a giant tortoise, a . . . "Turning people into aardvarks and okapi? No thanks." The ESRP had arisen when the technology of gengineering had made it possible for humanity to do something about the guilt it felt for allowing so many wild species to go extinct. It replaced the genes of volunteers with those of vanished animals, enough to turn them into physical duplicates and supply the zoos with exhibits. In time, said the gengineers, perhaps they would make the replacements so complete that they could let the vanished species return to the wild. Whether there would be a wild for them to return to was another question; the world was more crowded with human beings than it had ever been.

"The Engineers trashed my lab twice while I was working for the ESRP," he added. "They haven't found this place yet. There are advantages to being out here in the boonies." He shook his head. "One of these days, they're going to stop playing nice guy . . ." When Frederick looked pained, he said, "I know. I know. Relatively speaking. And I don't want to be there when it happens. I'd rather spend my time twiddling my thumbs." He brought his hands together in front of his paunch to demonstrate. Then he opened the envelope, extracted the check, and waved it in the air. "And letting you pay the bills." He backed up at last, letting his visitors into his office. The room was dominated by a metal desk supporting an ancient PS/4 computer. A stained antistatic pad showed around the edges of the keyboard. The room's walls were covered with shelves that sagged under the weight of books, technical journals, and disks. A stiff-looking armchair sat by the window.

"There aren't that many intelligent genimals." It was illegal to give an animal the genes for human intelligence, but that only limited the number of gengineers who did it. The results were usually turned loose to fend for themselves. Occasionally, they later came to public attention, as Frederick once had himself.

"So I have time to play consultant." Duncan sat down in

the softly padded swivel chair by the desk, tucked the check under the edge of the blotter, and swung toward the window. He gestured Frederick toward the armchair and said, "Is that one?" He pointed at the German shepherd, his expression hopeful. He did not make the mistakes of trying to pet the dog or speaking baby talk to it; experience had taught him that if Renny were indeed an intelligent genimal, he would not appreciate the condescension.

Frederick shook his head as he took the seat, while Renny flopped onto the floor between the two men and barked a laugh. He slapped the carpet twice with his tail. "Bet your ass I am!" Duncan did not seem surprised by the rough but clear voice. He had obviously met many creatures that looked like animals but spoke like humans.

"He seems to be happy the way he is."

The dog nodded, his tongue showing between his teeth. "I know better," he said.

"I'd think you'd want to be like us," said Duncan.

"Huh! Ordinary dogs, maybe," said Renny. "We're pack animals, sure, and they'll take you apes for their pack. But not me. I'm too smart to fall for that con. I'd rather be what I am." He lay down on the carpeted floor and rested his chin on his paws.

"Though he'd like a mate," said Frederick. "I introduced him to a female a few weeks ago. A lab. But . . ."

"Dumb bitch," growled Renny. "Smelled okay, but couldn't say a word."

"I wish he'd change his mind," said Frederick. "That's why I set you up here. Why we fund you. To give genimals like him a chance to escape the limits of their bodies, the persecution of . . ."

"PETA?"

Frederick nodded, his expression grim. "He was working as a guide dog, and someone heard him talking." That was when People for the Ethical Treatment of Animals had reported an illegal genimal and sued to have him destroyed. "They say he's dangerous too. A vicious carnivore. No moral sense. We're fighting it, but . . ."

"A guide dog?" asked Duncan. "For what? Replacing eyes and limbs is easy."

"Christian Scientist," said Frederick. "They still haven't accepted even antibiotics and vaccines."

"So they'll put me down." Renny sighed heavily. "I'm ready, though the boss swore I was the best dog he'd ever had." He paused. "They promise it won't hurt."

Duncan emitted a short, sharp bark that might have been a laugh. "Huh! They're afraid of the competition."

"Maybe so," said Frederick. "They don't like bots either, though they're not . . ."

"Then they shouldn't be complaining," interrupted Renny. "I was doing a job nobody else wanted. None of them, for sure."

"Maybe they're afraid you'll get ambitious," said Duncan.

"Or aggressive," said Frederick.

"They just think I've got too many teeth." Renny grinned to show them just how many he had.

Frederick looked at Jeremy Duncan. "I've talked to a technician who worked in the lab that made him. The word was that they'd designed out all Renny's aggressiveness, but . . ." He shrugged. "It was only rumor. It won't stand up in court. Even if it would, he'd still be an illegal." He shrugged again. "But I'm trying."

"Can I help?"

Frederick shook his head. "Not unless you know the gengineers who made him. I need to track them down and get them into court. With luck, they'll testify that Renny is unaggressive, mild-mannered, and civic-minded, as nice and safe a pussycat as any human being."

The dog barked. "As what?"

When Duncan laughed as well, Frederick let his face turn rueful. "Yes," he said. "There's no denying they have more law than justice on their side." He shrugged eloquently. "But I have hopes."

Bureaucrat though he had now been for years, Frederick Suida had been as happy as he ever got to escape his office on the tenth floor of the Bioform Regulatory Administration's building. The summer was hot, most of his colleagues were less than congenial, and the intensely cloying odor of honeysuckle blossoms penetrated every building in the city. The vines sought the sun everywhere. They choked the city's parks and alleys. They curled around the edges of windows, even crossing sills to invade the pots of house plants. They were, in fact, as all-intrusive as any bureaucracy had ever been.

He had almost smiled when he decided to go. He had then checked an Armadon, a vehicle genetically engineered from an armadillo, out of the BRA parking barn. The genimal was an official vehicle, its two doors each bearing the shield and monogram of his federal employer, but it was also long and low and sleek enough to tell all the world of its enhanced metabolism. Its lines were spoiled only by the essential bulges of its wheels and the strangely cocked angles of the limbs that ran atop them. The passenger compartment in the back was much less conspicuous. The computers that controlled the genimal's nervous system, and thus its movements, were hidden in the dashboard.

Now Frederick stepped out of Jeremy Duncan's lab to face the almost deserted parking lot where he had left the Armadon. A line of shrubbery marked the edge of the lab's lot. Beyond it was a turfed greenway, and approaching on that road was a massive Mack truck. It panted stertorously as it hauled a heavy cargo pod along the road. There were no pedestrians.

For a moment, Frederick came near to smiling. He had once known two truckers, friends of his own best friends. They had gone their way years before and thus survived the slaughter that had let him become the humorless thing that he was. He wondered where they were, what they were doing, whether they still drove their oversized bulldogs.

He shrugged the memory away as the truck passed the building and grew swiftly smaller in the distance, though he turned to follow it with his eyes. As he did so, his eyes swept over the industrial park that concealed Duncan's lab. It was a suburban backwater, half its units empty, the rest unobtrusive in their telemarketing and direct mail and small-scale manufactures. There were few signs, and fewer logo-marked cargo pods awaiting loading or unloading. Most of the businesses here relied on rental Macks.

It was just the sort of place he had needed when . . . His thought paused while he appreciated the blessing it was that the antigengineering forces had not yet found this place. The government, through him, funded Duncan's operation, but it was not an operation he wished the general public to know about. Publicity could be fatal, both figuratively and literally.

The building he had just left was long, rounded, green, its windows opaqued by vertically slatted blinds. The other buildings of the park were just the same, a long file of similar buildings embedded in close-cropped grass. Nowhere was there any trace of the honeysuckle that was doing its best to inundate the landscape almost everywhere. Nor was there any trace of the gengineered vines whose fruit had been dried and carved and fitted out to make the bioform Quonset huts.

"Zucchinis!" muttered Renny with a disdainful sniff. "Let's get out of here."

They had left the Armadon in one of the many empty slots in the turfed parking lot. Now they stepped to the vehicle's front, where Frederick patted its neck and made sure it had had no trouble reaching the water that flowed through the broad gutter before it. Nearby, the heads of a few other bioform vehicles—other Armadons, Tortoises and Beetles, and the ever-present Roachsters—hovered watchfully over the water, waiting for them to leave before returning to their drinking. In the distance, a pair of litterbugs, scoop-jawed descendants of pigs, wandered desultorily about the parking lot as they sought the waste material that it was their mission to remove. Overhead, a wide-bodied Goose carried a pod of passengers toward some distant city. Near the southern horizon, a thick contrail marked the track of a spaceplane bound for orbit.

Frederick opened the Armadon's door. The dog leaped past him to the seat. The man shook his head, climbed in, and turned on the turbochargers mounted in the genimal's throat. Their whine quickly rose in pitch until it became inaudible, and soon . . . For a few blessed hours, he had escaped the office, the honeysuckle, the government that employed him and his thousands of fellows. But such escapes could never last.

Unless . . . Some people did escape. As the Armadon left the industrial park behind, the honeysuckle vines began to appear, covering the banks beside the greenways, wreathing trees, wrapping the walls of buildings. Among the vines, on curbs and benches and steps, sheltered by overpasses and walkways, honey bums passed the waiting hours until they felt again the craving for the euphoric wine the vines collected in their giant blossoms. Buried here and there in the greenery were the living statues, smooth-barked, green-leaved, silent, that the honey bums became if they lingered too long on open soil.

Traffic slowed to a crawl when they finally left the greenways for paved city streets. Frederick swore, and Renny pointed with his nose. "Over there. That's why." The dog was staring toward a Mr. GreenGenes franchise. Behind the glass were Roachsters,

Slugabeds, hanky bushes, pad plants, flytraps, condombers, snackbushes, garbage disposals, litterbugs, fluorescent philo-dendrons, and other products of the gengineer's art. Spilling across the sidewalk and into the street was a milling crowd of people in blue coveralls. Golden cogwheels were embroidered on patches that decorated their chests and shoulders. Many had small brass springs and gears dangling from their earlobes. They carried signs that screamed in vivid colors, "MACHINES NOT GENES!"

Frederick felt the muscles of his neck and shoulders suddenly cramp with tension. There were, he saw, police officers hovering near the fringes of the crowd, with a pair of lobster-clawed police Roachsters waiting on a side street. They were a necessary precaution, and he wished that the Engineers' threat had been appreciated so well when he had been a pig.

He sighed with relief when he left the scene of the demonstration behind and traffic speeded up.

Chapter Three

SAM NICKERS WAS basking in his living room when the doorbell chimed.

He was naked, his green skin exposed to the array of sunlamps mounted on the ceiling, his chloroplasts churning out a flood of sugar that he found more satisfying than any pre-dinner drink had ever been. The greengenes had been his wife's third anniversary present, just the year before. He had given Sheila a similar outfit, ornamented by a sleek cap of feathers that replaced her hair.

He lay on a padded lounge. Beside him, a second lounge lay empty, separated from his by a narrow benchlike table. A flatscreen veedo hung on one wall, its face half obscured by leaves and branches; a forest of small palms and other tropical vegetation filled the room with green. Orchids and bromeliads furnished splashes of color, as did the three small birds that perched and sang among the foliage. New droppings and older stains marked the short-piled carpet, a geometric array of brown and green; he told himself that it was time again to scrub; vacuuming never did the trick. The walls were painted white.

One of the birds swooped through the air and a buzzing he had not noticed suddenly became conspicuous by its absence. He stared toward the open window. The birds routinely tried to escape, but all they managed was . . . The half-drawn drapes revealed three bee-sized holes in the screen, and beyond them a sky grey with both clouds and twilight. It was the end of the day, a time for themselves alone, free of the hordes of kids they faced at work. "Are you coming back?" he called.

"As soon as this casserole is in the oven," she answered him. "But I'll have to get dressed soon. Finca's putting out a mailing this week." Sheila was a volunteer campaign manager

21

for a city councilwoman, directing the stuffing of envelopes
and the collection of signatures and the delivery of voters
to the polls as the seasons of the woman's terms demanded.
Others wrote the press releases and newsletters and coached
the councilwoman on the issues.

Sam shifted on his lounge. He volunteered his services to
the community in another way. He taught history, but he had
trained as well as an emergency medical technician. At least
two evenings a week he assisted the ambulance crew at the
local fire station. There was never any danger of boredom.

On the table by his side sat a small mail terminal, its
screen glowing with a letter from his father. Mike Nickers
had recently retired from his position as a recruiter for the
Daisy Hill Truck Farm, and he was bored. He was thinking
of traveling, of moving, of finding a replacement for his dead
wife, Sam's mother, of . . .

The doorbell sounded. The birds fell silent. Sam swore.
Sheila appeared in the doorway, grinning, her green skin glowing in the bright light. He stared at her, struck as always by her
beauty, and by what the genetic changes had done to enhance
it. Her nipples and lips were so dark a green that they seemed
almost black. The dark brown and orange of her feathers, the
black and yellow of the small butterfly-wing inserts over her
cheekbones, the pink and gold of the snakeskin along her
jawline caught the eye like the organic jewelry they were.
He swore again. She laughed and held out his robe. "Here.
I'll get mine."

Sheila was behind him when he opened the door to face
a clean-cut young couple. The man was dark-haired, slim,
with the lines of his muscles cleanly limned beneath the cloth
that covered them. The woman was blonde, red-lipped, wide-
hipped, her nipples little spires on the broad domes beneath the
fabric of her coverall. Together, they seemed designed to rivet
the attention of whoever might answer their knock.

Yet as soon as they saw the Nickerses, their eyes went
suddenly wide, their mouths opened, their torsos leaned back,
away, their hands full of pamphlets jerked upward as if to
erect a paper barrier before them. They were so fully human,
with no slightest trace of genetic modification, that Sam hardly
needed their shocked recoil, nor their blue coveralls and golden
cogwheel patches, to tell that they were Engineers. Nor did he
wonder that they seemed surprised to find that the Nickerses

were not quite the traditional model of human being. Most of the apartment building's tenants had no genetic modifications or, at least, none that showed.

Behind him, Sheila blew a short blast of air through her nose. He felt just as disgusted. "You're wasting your time," he said.

"No!" The man stepped forward, his pamphlets still raised. Then, "Yes!" he said. "Gengineering is Abomination! It's all in here." He held out the pamphlets, one of the many jutting forward as if he were offering to perform a card trick. Sam Nickers did not take one.

"Especially the bots," said the woman earnestly. She meant the plants to which the gengineers had added human genes, giving them something in the way of human appearance and intelligence. "And the genimals," she added. "Especially the ones that think they're so smart."

"We need to get rid of them all," said her partner. "Then we can get back to the Golden Age." He tapped his cogwheel as if it were a religious emblem. For him, it was. "Utopia," he said. "The Age of Machines."

They held their heads so that, for the first time, reflections of light from the apartment at his back drew Sam's attention to the single tiny, gold-shiny gears they wore in their right earlobes. The gears might have come from an antique watch.

"No more Macks," said the woman. Now she offered her pamphlets. "Read, and you'll see. No bots. No Roachsters or Bioblimps or . . ."

"No green . . ." The man fell silent, as if he had suddenly realized the threat he was about to offer the two he was trying to sway to their cause.

"Skins?" said Sheila from behind her husband. "Greenskins" was what the Engineers called people like her and Sam.

"But you can be repaired!" cried the woman. Yet already the missionary enthusiasm was fading from her face. She knew that she and her partner would find no converts here, no demonstrators, no soldiers for the revolution the Engineers claimed was essential to save humanity for its true, mechanical destiny.

Sam said nothing more to them, nothing about shortages of fuels for the machines, shortages of steel and other minerals, nor of the problems of chemical, industrial pollution that human civilization had largely left behind when it chose a more organic path. He simply shook his head and closed the door.

When Sheila said, "It wouldn't help much if we were, would it?" he shook his head again. As always, throughout history, converts were suspect. If the Nickerses had the gengineers undo their changes, that would only mean that they were once more consorting with the enemy. They would not be rejected—the Engineers would happily enlist anyone and everyone they could to achieve their ends—but later . . . Once they were in power, the Engineers, like all the other extremist groups that had gone before them, would surely purge all those allies who happened to be, or ever to have been, "contaminated."

Would they ever be in power? Sam prayed that they would not, but their numbers, the numbers of their sympathizers, the volume of their protests and demands, the influence they exerted on governments and courts and media, all grew year by year. He feared . . .

The school was much as schools had been for centuries: a housing for hallways linking rooms full of chalkboards, books, desks, and young people, walls hidden behind lockers and posters and trophy cases and displays of student art. There were computers too, enough for all the students, although, as if in obedience to educational tradition, the technology was a little out of date: inset in the surface of each desktop was an electronic screen and keyboard from long before the days of the gengineering revolution.

Sam Nickers looked out over his class of eighth-graders. Forty faces of all the shades of human skin—no green like his, but black, brown, tan, pink, red, and yellow—stared back at him, eyes bouncing between his face and the clock on the wall behind him. He checked his screen; everyone had finished. He moved his mouse-gloved hand, clicked the button set on the side of his index finger, and the machine graded the quiz and displayed each student's score, both on his and on the individual student's screen. There were smiles, groans, shrugs, another mass glance at the clock.

A buzzer echoed in the hall. He too shrugged. "Class dismissed."

The room promptly emptied, and silence fell. He was putting papers into his briefcase when the speaker on the wall grated, "Mr. Nickers?"

He faced the little box, feeling just as he always had, ever since he had been a kid in school himself, and the squawk of the annunciator had meant that some mischief of his had been found out. "Yes?"

"Would you stop by the principal's office before you leave?"

"Of course," he said. "I'll be just a minute."

"Thank you." A click confirmed that the conversation was over. What, he wondered, had it been about? What could the principal have to say to him? He didn't think it could have anything to do with his work, for his evaluations were good. They always had been. Still, he could not help but worry.

The worry only increased when he met Sheila in the hall outside the school's office. She taught another grade, another subject. What could the principal possibly have to say to *both* of them?

The answer was not long in coming.

When Sam and Sheila stepped into the office, they found the door that normally bore on its closed face the sign, "Lillian Bojemoy, Principal," standing open. The principal herself, a short, grey-haired woman who wore a loose robe instead of the usual coverall, was standing in the doorway, delivering stern instructions to the school librarian. When she saw the Nickerses, she turned, gestured, and said, "Go right in. Sit down." She did not smile, but that was not alarming. No one had ever seen her bend her tight-pressed lips in any friendly way.

A moment later, she was standing behind her desk and saying, "I felt we had to have a little talk. I wouldn't want you to misunderstand."

Sam looked at his wife. Her eyes were widening in alarm, just as, he was sure, were his own. He turned back to the principal. "What is there to misunderstand?"

She pushed a litter of papers aside to reveal a keyboard. She tapped keys, stared at the screen set to one side, and said, not quite as if she had not been studying the same information for hours or days, "Your record is fine. Your students do well on the achievement tests. And you yourselves . . ." The principal gestured as if to indicate their skin color. "You're good examples. You show the kids what progress means. You demonstrate the silliness of prejudice."

She paused. Sheila reached for her husband's hand and squeezed it. Both their hands were damp. "But . . ." said Sheila.

"Yes." The principal nodded. "But. *I* don't have any problem with what you've done to yourselves."

"The parents," said Sam. His worry vanished. Now he knew what was coming, and it was as bad as he might have guessed.

She nodded again. "The district has a lot of Engineers and Engineer-sympathizers. And they don't want their children learning tolerance, or the value of progress. They don't want their children coming home and questioning their parents' values or attitudes."

"They don't want their children exposed to us," said Sheila.

The principal nodded. "So. I'm afraid . . ." She sighed. She turned one hand palm up, mutely imploring them not to create a scene. "I'm afraid we won't be able to renew your contract for next fall. You can finish out the year, but . . ."

"Unless we return to normal?" asked Sam.

She nodded. "That would help, I'm sure."

"No," said Sheila. "Ask the Nazis. Once a Jew, always a Jew." Her voice was tight, almost choking.

When the principal looked blank, Sam added, "Or the Ku Klux Klan. It didn't matter what you looked like, once you—or your ancestors—had touched the tar brush. Once a nigger, always a nigger."

When their boss still didn't seem to get it, Sheila said, "We'll start looking for new positions immediately, of course."

"Of course."

Later, walking home, Sam said, "Dr. Ohmigod!" The nickname had come from another teacher, one who knew a little Russian. He spat toward the gutter, prompting a patrolling litterbug to dart from behind a passing Tortoise. When it found nothing worth retrieving, it returned to its station in the stream of traffic.

"You'd think they'd learned something in school," he added. "But no. They'd rather believe wishes. And there just aren't the resources to . . ."

"Bigots," said his wife. "Shortsighted, hidebound, reactionary bigots!"

They were passing a small neighborhood park separated from the sidewalk by a low brick wall. Behind the wall rose a billow of honeysuckle vines, their pink and yellow blossoms swaying upright, like wineglasses, on their stems. A number of men and women leaned against or sat on the wall, and one of them, blue-clad and golden-patched, lurched into their path. He stopped and raised one fist, a honeysuckle blossom crumpled in it. His features sagged as if he had left, somewhere, a trail of other blossoms. His breath reeked of honeysuckle wine.

"Who you callin' a bigot, greenie?" he said.

The Nickerses stopped. Sam tightened his grip on the handle of his briefcase—solid metal and wood, and heavy with books and papers—until his knuckles blanched. He glared. He put all the anger he was feeling, all the menace he could summon up, into his voice as he said, "Get out of our way."

Surprise or shock made the other's face go even slacker. He turned toward his friends along the wall as if to ask for help in cowing his prey, but they did not move. One shrugged and pointed toward the road with a stubbly chin. Sam snatched a look in that direction and saw a long-clawed police Roachster moving slowly in their direction. When he looked back, their accoster was no longer in their way.

When they reached home, they stopped first in the building's basement stable. There they fed and watered their Beetle. A vehicle with a strong resemblance to one of the twentieth-century internal combustion automobiles now visible only in museums and parades, it had been gengineered from an insect by enlarging the body and legs, reinforcing the exoskeleton with an internal framework modeled on—but stronger than—that of mammals, and creating a passenger compartment in the abdomen. Its shell was bright red.

"We should have driven today," said Sheila, patting the Beetle on its bristly brow.

Sam shook his head. "It wouldn't have changed a thing. We still would have heard from Ohmigod."

"But that bum!"

"The harm was already done. He just underlined it." He put a hand on her elbow and turned her toward the building's elevator. "Let's get a little sun and check the mail."

But the day's trials were not done. Taped to the door of their apartment was a crudely rendered drawing of a tree, its trunk warped into a demented face, its branches twisted. Facing it, a man with a cogwheel prominent on his back raised an axe. "It's a photocopy," said Sheila. "They must be spreading them all over the place."

"Nothing personal, you mean?" She grunted an assent that

did not seem entirely confident.

He activated the living-room mail terminal then, and said, "Something from the squad." A moment later, he said, "*That's* personal. Shit."

He stepped aside to let her see the screen. The glowing characters spelled it out: The emergency medical squad to which Sam had volunteered his time for years did not need him any more. There had been complaints, concerns that the viral vectors used in his greening might invade an accident victim through a wound, threats of lawsuits if that should indeed happen.

Sheila's arm wrapped around his waist. She leaned her head against his shoulder. His own arm circled her, his head leaned on hers. "Ignorant bastards. Cretins. Bigots."

Two days later, Sheila left Sam on his lounge, this time combining the effects of the sunlamps with those of rum, to attend a strategy session for Finca d'Antonio. She did not take the Beetle, for Finca's ward was small and the meeting was within easy walking distance. When Albert d'Antonio let her into the townhouse, Sheila went directly to the spare bedroom that was the councilwoman's headquarters.

Finca never had installed gengineered lighting or snack-bushes. The room was brightly lit by overhead fluorescents. On a table to one side sat an electric coffeemaker and a tray of miniature Greek pastries. Half a dozen people sat at the larger table in the center of the room. Sheila Nickers knew all but one. There were no empty chairs.

"Sheila, dear!" The councilwoman stood up and crossed the room, her arms open for an embrace. She was black-haired, dusky-skinned, short, and, like many politicians, somewhat over her ideal weight. Her eyes were black and lively, and her voice was bright.

"I want you to meet," she said, gesturing toward the stranger, a young man who was now looking at the tabletop. "Adrian Bartlett. He'll be handling the petitions and mailings from now on."

Those were two of Sheila's jobs. She looked again at the table. It finally registered that the lack of an empty chair was deliberate. She said, "Voter transportation . . ."

Several heads shook slowly back and forth. Finca nodded her own vigorously. "Yes, that too."

"Then . . ." Her throat seemed to swell, and her voice choked off.

"I'm afraid so, Sheila. I'm sorry." Her expression did not match her words. "I have to adjust my positioning a bit, you understand. There are more and more conservative voters out there, and . . ." Her sweeping gesture said it all. She herself and all the others in the room, all except for Sheila Nickers, were unmodified humans. Sheila was the bright green standout, the conspicuous liberal who would surely cost Finca crucial votes.

"Is there anything . . . ?"

Finca d'Antonio simply shook her head. There was no place for Sheila Nickers on the politician's staff. Nor was there anything the teacher could do to change her mind.

Sheila got home much earlier than usual. Sam was still on the lounge, still basking, still drinking, though the level in the bottle had not really gone down very greatly. Sheila entered the room, swore, seized his glass, and drained it.

"Get one of your own, honey," her husband said. He was just drunk enough to speak his words slowly and carefully. "What happened?"

The liquor cabinet hid behind one of the room's palms. She got a glass and a bottle of the sherry she preferred when she drank. She told him what had happened. "She doesn't want me," she said at last, the tears bright in her eyes, the pain thick in her voice. "She doesn't want me anymore, not at all, not anywhere in the campaign. Not even licking envelopes. My spit might contaminate the voters. Turn them all green! I wish it would!"

She was stripping as she spoke. Now she sat down beside him. When he laid a gentle hand on her thigh, she said, "You've had enough sun. Make you fat."

"Need a cuddle, huh?" He set his glass down, closed his eyes, and sighed. "So do I."

She nodded, groped for his hand, and squeezed it. Minutes later, she was squeezing the control node on their Sluga-bed, and the genimal's warm flesh was curling around their bodies, sheltering them from a world that was turning crueler every day.

A few days later, they found their Beetle dead. Someone had used an axe to sever its legs and head and cave in the side of the passenger compartment. Green paint had then been sprayed over the seats and dashboard.

The police were unsympathetic, though they did not quite tell the Nickerses it was their own fault. They did say, "What did you expect? You must have known that what you did to yourselves would draw attention. So it did. It got them mad. And now . . ." Yes, there were laws, but . . .

Fingerprints? On the Beetle? The cops were sure they must have been there, but the corpse had already been fed to the city's buses. Not that it mattered. The crime was only vandalism, after all.

"And," said Sam as they walked wearily home. "I'll bet there isn't a judge in the city . . ."

"In the state," Sheila interrupted.

"The country, even," he said. "Not one who would convict an Engineer. They wouldn't dare."

"It's too bad we're not covered by the discrimination laws."

"They cover only race, religion, sex, and handicaps. Not liberalism, not rationality."

"Not us." Sheila led the way into their building, past the neighbors who now, for the first time in memory, refused to meet their eyes, past the super who . . . He would not let them pass. "Here," he said, and he held out a long white envelope.

"We're being evicted, right?" Sam spoke sourly. When the super gave a tight grin and a shrug, he added, "That's all that's left to happen."

The eviction notice was spread upon the table. It expressed regrets, but the message was plain enough: Their sunlamps were ruining the apartment's paint. They themselves were attracting unwelcome attention. They were thus a hazard to their neighbors. And there were rumors that the viral vectors the gengineers had used to make their changes could be contagious. The company that owned the building trusted that they, the Nickerses, understood why they had until the end of the month to move.

Sheila pointed at the wall. "The lights aren't doing any harm at all," she said.

"The unwelcome attention is real enough," said Sam. "And if it gets bad enough . . ." He pushed several ragged-edged pieces of paper toward their old friend. "Look at these, Alice.

They were on the door. Under the door. Even in the elevator. What the *hell* can we do?"

The crude drawings, some of them photocopied, some of them original, were not pretty. The words, block-printed, scrawled, pieced together from scraps of this and that, were worse. They were hatred and venom and prejudice, all distilled from millennia of fear of strangers and change.

"The worst of it," said Sam, "is that the building has a security system. A good one. People can't just come in off the street. It has to be other tenants."

"We didn't show them to the cops," said Sheila. "They weren't any help before, and we didn't expect . . ." Her posture slumped dejectedly. They had told their visitor about the Beetle and the school. They had also told her of how their volunteer work had ended.

Alice Belle's sigh was the sound of wind over tall grass. Sam thought that he should not feel surprised. Her ancestors were far more truly, more completely, plants than his. They had been amaryllises; to them, gengineers had added human genes. Over many generations, they had become progressively more humanlike. Now they had legs and could walk, though they wore bushy ruffs of fibrous roots around their shins. They had torsoes, though they were sheathed in long, bladelike, spiralling leaves. They had heads and eyes and mouths and lungs. They had brains, though a smaller secondary brain was housed in the bulb they carried between their legs. They did not have hair; their scalps were covered instead by lawns of tiny blossoms. Alice Belle's blossoms were orange with veins of scarlet on their petals.

Alice Belle was a bot, a botanical. Sheila had first met her when she was trying to recruit outsiders to visit her classes and explain their work. She had been fascinated to learn that some bots occupied high-level positions as administrators, scientists, and even gengineers. Alice Belle was an administrator with a small research lab.

Over the bot's head buzzed a small bee. Sam did not know whether it had followed her into their apartment or discovered her there. Bees often orbited bot heads; for all he knew, they even fertilized the bots' flowers, though he had heard that when bots wished to mate, they bowed to each other and let their blossoms touch to exchange pollen. Both parents then set seed; there were no separate males and females.

At last, she spoke: "You will have to move, I think. Even if you could fight this eviction, and even if you could win, you would not want to stay. The environment would be too hostile. You would expect awful things to happen, as indeed they did to your Beetle. You would turn paranoid." She shook her head. "I would hate to see that happen. Paranoids are not very pleasant people."

"I wish we had a place to move to," said Sam. "But there aren't many empty apartments in the city, and those we've tried to see . . ." His face was crystallized frustration.

"As soon as the agents see us," said Sheila, "forget it. It was just rented. Or it's being renovated. Or the rent is suddenly sky-high. Or—once! as blatant as can be—it's not for greenies. Or bots."

"The suburbs?" asked their friend. "The Engineers aren't as strong there."

"You'd be surprised," said Sam. "We've looked there too."

"There aren't even any jobs for us," added Sheila.

Alice Belle sighed again. "I wish I could help. I wish I could share . . ."

Sam snorted. "Outdoors? We're not so close to nature. We need a roof." From time to time, there were veedo specials on how the bots lived, working at night and returning by day to fenced enclosures in the city's parks where they could unfurl both roots and leaves and feed from soil and sun while they gossiped, told stories, and sang songs, some of them the ancient spirituals of another race, another age.

"You don't understand." Alice Belle scowled at him as if he should know better, as if he were being no better than the Engineers who persecuted him. She waved an arm to encompass the apartment, its walls, its bright lights, its greenery. "I work during the day, like you, on a human schedule. I rest at night, and I need lights, like these. Photosynthesis is much more important for us. So I have to have a place much like this. And there are others like me. We even have our own building. We own it."

"In the city?" asked Sheila.

"Any vacancies?"

Alice Belle opened her mouth to speak, but then she hesitated. Finally, she said, "Yes, there are, but . . ." She took a deep breath. "It's just us, you understand? Just bots. It would be perfect for you, and you're good people. You deserve a safe place to live. But . . . but there's a rule."

Sam slumped, defeated. Sheila stared at the bot, their friend, for a long moment. "Is there anyone you can speak to?"

Alice Belle slowly nodded. "The management committee."

"Would you? Please?"

She nodded again. "Yes," she said. "I will."

There was another moment of silence. Sheila broke it at last by picking up the worst of the papers they had found pinned to their door and offering it to Alice Belle. "Maybe it would help," she said. "Show them this."

"I will."

Chapter
Four

"IT'S A WASTE of money." Salamon Domenici was one of the Bioform Regulatory Administration's senior program managers. Now he was glaring at Frederick Suida, leaning aggressively over his portion of the conference table. "Let 'em *have* the mechin' dog!"

The woman beside Frederick stretched an arm in his direction. He did not try to avoid it. He knew what was coming, for she had done it before. When she touched his head and patted, he stiffened; he successfully suppressed the glare he wished to give her, and all those who dared to smile. "Freddy can't do that, Sal. You're forgetting—"

"Of course," said another of Frederick's BRA colleagues. "He's not exactly unbiased."

"He's an axe-grinder. The way he bulled that conversion lab through on us . . . We should shut it down before the public hears about it."

"They *should* hear about it," said Berut Amoun. His dark skin and heavy-lidded eyes spoke of Near Eastern ancestors. He was one of the very few BRA staffers Frederick counted among his friends. "If they thought their new boss might have been the dog they kicked last year, they might act a little more civilized."

Someone laughed. "More like, we'd have a mob kicking down the door."

"And it's bound to leak."

"It's a waste of money too."

"Enough." Judith Breger, the agency's Assistant Director, was slender, dark of skin and hair, her coverall a silvery sheath whose metallic finish proclaimed efficiency. She did not speak loudly, but her voice was firm enough to halt the jabber of rivalry and condescension and outright enmity. "Of course Mr. Suida is biased. That's why he has the responsibility for protecting gengineered sentients. It's also why you, Mr. Domenici, do not. Frankly, I have trouble imagining that you would give the assignment anything like the same amount of energy."

There was laughter. Salamon Domenici was well known in the agency for his long lunch hours and padded expense vouchers.

Frederick clenched his teeth and sighed. He should have expected this reaction to his progress report on the attempt to save Renny from PETA's short-sighted protectionism. Even within the Bioform Regulatory Administration . . . PETA and other animal-rights activists had once named the attitude "speciesism." Now it was just specism. His colleagues were specists. The worst of them held his origin as a gengineered pig, a garbage disposal, against him. Despite his sentience, despite the human form the gengineers' viruses had given him, they did not see him as fully human. They called him "Freddy" as if he were a child, or a pet. They sneered at him for trying to pass for human. They tried to block his efforts to help others to pass, or to avoid persecution.

The Assistant Director interrupted with, "Now, we have a number of permits to decide on."

"Do we really need any more bioform gadgets?"

The Assistant Director's sigh did not stave off Domenici. "I move we table them."

"No," she said. "You've tried this before. Let's get on with it."

The meeting had not begun until near the end of the afternoon, and it had run late. Now the building was empty, its lights dimmed, its hallways quiet. But Frederick had not yet left. He had retreated to his office, his mind continuing to churn with anger. Even in BRA, he told himself. Not just on the streets. Not just the mad Engineers. "Specists!" he muttered aloud.

"Idiots," said Renny. The gengineered German shepherd was stretched on the carpeted floor near his feet.

Frederick nodded. Even in BRA, he repeated to himself. It did not seem possible. Ideologues who wanted to restrict gengineering, and not just by holding up permits for new prototypes or production models. The next item on the agenda had been licenses for those new graduates of gengineering programs who had passed their qualifying exams. There had been a move to hold those up as well, on the grounds that society had quite enough gengineers already. He suspected that some of his colleagues had put their true sympathies with the Engineers.

Bioluminescent vines covered his office ceiling, glowing as brightly as fluorescent fixtures. By the window sat a snackbush; its small, cylindrical fruits tasted like sausage. Around the window's edge hovered the leaves and blossoms of the honeysuckle vines that climbed the building's exterior; a few tendrils crawled over the sill. A shelf held a small, boxy veedo unit, its screen accompanying the soft music the unit was bringing into the room with a constantly changing display of random blobs in pastel hues.

Frederick's office computer was a state-of-the-art bioform. A pot full of dirt erected a thick, woody trunk beside his desk. Branches held broad, stiff leaves before him. One leaf, covered with touch-sensitive spots, served as a keyboard. Four others hung side by side to serve as a monitor, currently displaying the file on Renny's upcoming court hearing. A box of oblong gigabyte floppy-cards, each in a protective sleeve, sat to one side. One of the sleeves lay empty on the desk. Its floppy lay like the filling in a sandwich between two specialized leaves that could read the pattern of magnetization that encoded all the information the floppy held. The floppies themselves were manufactured; the rest was grown.

Distant sounds, not quite covered up by the music from his veedo unit, caught at his attention. Rattling metal, squeaking wheels, humming machinery, voices. The evening cleaning crew had arrived to vacuum hallway floors, tidy offices, wash windows, water plants. Frederick sighed. He didn't usually stay so late, even after a meeting. But he made no move to leave.

The voices drew nearer. They were high-pitched, feminine, and there seemed to be three of them, bantering cheerfully back and forth. Frederick felt his anger fade to be replaced by a deep wistfulness. "I wish . . ." he said, and he stopped.

"*What* do you wish, Freddy?" asked the dog. His tail was wagging gently.

What he really wished was the same sort of camaraderie in his own life. Once he had had it. He had had friends. He had had fans. He had been happy. But the Engineers had killed them all. And then he had let the Endangered Species Replacement Program try to console him with a human body. That had distanced him from other people more than his original body ever had.

The dog had called him Freddy, and it hadn't stung the way it had in the meeting. Perhaps Renny . . . ? He dismissed the urge to say anything other than, "I wish I could make out what they're saying."

The dog snorted. "Singing in the cotton fields, Freddy." He pricked his more acute ears toward the door. "One's asking, 'When you goin' to set a little seed, honey?' " He changed his voice: "The other says, 'We know you're sweet on her. There's bees all round your head all day.' " His voice shifted again: " 'That's why you wear that kerchief. Save that pollen!' " And then again to sing, " 'Shakin' my anther for you!' "

Frederick sighed. "They're bots, of course."

Renny didn't answer. Instead, his tail went stiff and he growled softly as a heavier tread sounded in the hall and a rough voice said, "Haven't you got started yet? Enough goofin' off!"

The man winced. Such a tone had never been aimed his way, but those that had were bad enough. Too few humans—full, natural-born humans—were not overbearing, abusive, disdainful, condescending, rude. He wondered if the bots were any happier than he in their dormitory ghettoes, away from their human masters and supervisors, their overlords.

Frederick got out of his chair with a grunt. He stepped to the window, looked out at a sky with a thin band of light still hovering on the western horizon. The city's lights were on, marking windows, streets, and flowing traffic. He shrugged and turned toward the snackbush at his elbow. He picked a sausage. He looked at the dog and half smiled to see his ears pricked toward him, his face expectant. He picked another, tossed it, and turned again to the window.

He stared at the sausage in his hand. Once, he thought, he had had no hands. His mouth had been aimed at the underside of a sink, and later at the ceiling. Someone else had had to put food into his mouth. He hadn't even been able to feed himself.

And now he worked for BRA. He shook his head at the irony and put the sausage in his mouth. His wife had been in the same fix as he. So had their kids, the calliope shoats. Now Porculata was gone. The kids? He would have liked to send them to

Duncan, but Barnum was dead, poisoned by an attendant who had turned out to be an Engineer sympathizer. The other three, Ringling and Baraboo and Bailey, had permanent gigs playing circus music for a New Orleans disney. And when he had offered, they had refused. They were happy where they were. He sometimes thought they were smarter than he, though they had never been able to speak.

The rattle of his office doorknob drew his attention back to the room behind him. He watched the door open, a hand appear, holding a cloth and a pump-bottle of cleaning solution, a figure, her scalp covered with small yellow flowers, her trunk as green as grass and remarkably feminine in the contours that showed beneath the green sheath of her leaves, her face intelligent and sensitive. She wore only a short apron rather like a carpenter's around her waist; its pockets were weighted down with cleaning equipment. He watched the eyes widen as the bot realized the room's lights were still on. He heard Renny's chuff of inquiry, almost as if he had cleared his throat, and he actually, if briefly, smiled at her startled jump.

"Excuse me!" said the bot. "I didn't know . . ."

"Come on in," said Frederick. "You can work around us, can't you?"

She nodded. "But . . . We're not supposed to. Will you be here long?"

"A while." The truth was that he had no idea how long he would linger in his office. There was no work that needed doing, but then there was nothing he could do anywhere else either. "What's your name?"

After a moment's hesitation, the bot murmured, "Donna Rose." She stepped all the way into the room and let the door close behind her. Her eyes searched the room, lighting first on the veedo, source of the quiet music that warded off utter silence, then on the computer, on Renny, his face aimed like a sword at her midriff, his ears sharply erect, his tail furiously active. Finally, she sprayed her cloth with cleaning solution, turned her back, and reached for a nearby shelf.

Frederick and Renny continued to watch her. Her movements slowed and stopped. Her hand still on the shelf, she turned back toward them. "I . . ."

When she faltered, Renny said, "Been doing this long?"

Her eyes widened at the dog's words. "Ever since I started working." She did not seem very old. "Always this building."

"Do you know what we do here?" asked Frederick gently.

She shook her head. "I've wondered."

"This is the BRA building," he explained, and she nodded slowly, uncertainly. That much she had heard. "The Bioform Regulatory Administration. The government set it up when gengineering was still new. It was supposed to keep people from making anything that could get out of control. Like diseases, or genimals that might destroy crops, or plants that would take over forests and fields."

"Like honeysuckle," said Donna Rose. She abandoned her cloth and bottle on the shelf and stepped nearer to him.

Frederick nodded. Once there had been a plant called kudzu that had done its best to smother the landscape of the American south. The honeysuckle had replaced it with unsurpassable vigor; the new plant was now found even in Canada, while kudzu was scarce. "BRA wasn't very successful, was it?" he said. "The technology got too easy to use. It became available to too many people, even in children's gengineering kits." He watched her as he spoke, but she seemed oblivious to his reference. One of those kits, he had learned years before, had led indirectly to her kind. A teenaged boy had played with himself as young gene-hackers often did, and . . . "Now our job is to try to help the world adapt to the inevitable. Sometimes that means fighting—we've got gengineers trying to develop a virus to kill honeysuckle." He snorted.

"Is that what you do?" Did she seem suddenly wary? Was she afraid that he might have a virus that would kill her?

He shook his head as Renny growled, "Tell her, Freddy. You're just as futile as the honey zappers." The dog looked at the bot. "As soon as they release a virus they think will kill the stuff, it stops working."

The man sighed. "I'm supposed to protect those genimals that turned out to be smart." He gestured at the dog. "He's been hanging around this office too long. He knows more than he should."

"Too many human genes," said Renny. "Too nosey."

"That's what he's got," said Frederick. "So do you, though you're not a genimal. You're a plant, a plant with as many brains as me."

"He's a genimal, though," said the German shepherd.

When Donna Rose looked surprised—Wasn't he human, truly? How could he be a genimal?—Frederick explained how he had gained a human body. Then he said, "But appearances don't really count, do they? There are too many humans who don't want us around." Donna Rose nodded, and he described Renny's plight.

"The enemy," she said. "They hate us. They want to kill us all."

"I'd like to think it's not that bad," said Frederick. "But I'm afraid it is."

"Litterheads!" said Renny. "They want the Good Old Days back. The Machine Age, when all us plants and animals knew our place! And they'll wreck every bit of gengineering if they get the chance."

Donna Rose stared at Renny, saying nothing, as if she had never before seen a genimal talk back to a human being, even if that human was only an artifact, a product of the same technology that had made the dog.

As if, thought Frederick, being human was a matter of appearance only. And perhaps it was, to his fellow artifacts. To true humans, born humans, however . . . He sighed. "You may be right," he said. "I don't want to believe it, but . . ." He had seen the Engineers progress from demonstrations and picket signs to streetside Roachster bakes and terrorist massacres. He had seen news reports of murdered bots, stripped of roots and leaves and flowers. And he had seen the Engineers' numbers swell. He had seen them gain sympathizers, even within BRA. The trend was there to be seen, though he prayed that it would not go as far as the bot and the dog clearly feared.

"We do the best we can," he finally added. Briefly, he described Jeremy Duncan's secret lab. "We keep it quiet," he said. "We don't want any attention from the Engineers."

"There's a lot more of us," said Donna Rose. Her voice bore a plaintive note. "I wish you could make *us* human."

"Someday, I'm sure," said Frederick. "The principles are just the same. Though that's not necessarily the answer."

The veedo music stopped, and a voice announced a special news program, "Coming up right after we hear from . . ."

Renny got to his feet, stepped nearer to the bot, and licked her hand sympathetically. "It wouldn't help," he said. "It doesn't help *him*."

Frederick shrugged and sighed. "There's another office for the bots. It sets up the dormitories in the parks. And it's planning to set up more of them, on rooftops, on islands in the bay. They'll be harder for the Engineers to get to, safer from whatever they might do."

There was nothing he could do, Frederick knew. Not for Renny, though he would keep trying. Not for the bots. Not for anyone. The Engineers would rise up on a tide of prejudice and persecution and sweep everything away. His mood was so bleak that he barely noticed when the veedo began to speak of Engineers marching on the bot dorms in the city park.

"Oh!" cried Donna Rose. "What's happening?"

"Turn it on," said Renny, his ears pricking toward the veedo set. "Let's get a picture."

Frederick obeyed, tapping at the keyboard of his computer. He did not use a mouse-glove, though one lay forgotten in the drawer, because such interfaces worked best with electronic computers. They did not interface well with bioforms.

The small screen replaced its random colors with a long shot down a major avenue. The street was filled with people, and the picture flickered with the flames of torches. Many of the marchers, but by no means all, wore the blue coveralls and cogwheel patches of Engineers. Visible in many hands were kitchen knives, axes, machetes, crude swords of the sort that still haunted Frederick's nightmares. The narrator was saying, " . . . heading toward the park. They gathered in the streets less than an hour ago. There was no apparent provocation."

The view jumped to an outdoor reporter, standing beside the mob of Engineers, a building facade at her back. Beside her was a burly Engineer with an axe over his shoulder. "What are your plans for tonight?" asked the reporter.

"Chop the bots!" was the reply, punctuated by a shaking of the axe in the air.

"But why?"

"They're obscene! Things! Machines, not genes!"

Donna Rose moaned. Renny crossed the room to the window, where he reared up on his hind legs, scanned the city-scape outside, and said, "You can see the glow from here."

Frederick and Donna Rose joined him, ignoring the veedo screen for the moment. "See?" said the dog, and yes, they could. The crowd itself was not visible, but despite the street-lights the torches they carried did indeed cast a noticeable glow against the overcast.

"And there," said Frederick. Where he pointed they could see a street end-on, vehicles excluded by the press of bodies, the pavement obscured by the sparks of a host of torches.

"What are they going to do?" Donna Rose's voice trembled on the verge of tears.

"Chop the bots," said Renny. "Just like they want to dock this dog. Purify the planet."

Together, they turned back toward the veedo screen. It now showed a daylight scene, and the announcer was describing the Engineers' target: "Every dawn," he said. "Every day, they leave their jobs just like everyone else at the end of a long day." The screen showed the weary workers walking, boarding subways, Bernie buses, trains, going home.

"They work in factories. Night shift." A view of assembly lines, staffed almost entirely by bots, the blossoms on their heads making long rows of color interrupted occasionally by the smoother heads of humans. "In office buildings." A cleaning crew like that of which Donna Rose was a member. A human supervisor stood by, idle. "Stores." A discount store, an all-night diner.

"Going home." The gates to the dormitories in the parks, the bot ghettoes, the gardens in which they slept and chatted away the days, stood open wide in welcome. They streamed through, found the small plots of earth they called their own, and stopped. The roots that bushed around their shins unraveled, stretched, kissed the earth, and burrowed in. The leaves that coiled around their trunks unfurled to drink the sun. Faces tipped like flowers toward the light. There could not possibly have been a less threatening scene.

The scene changed and changed again until the screen held a group of bot pedestrians striding toward their bus, a Bernie, a greatly enlarged Saint Bernard with a passenger pod strapped to its back. Nearby were three humans, well dressed, prosperous, on their way to their own jobs. They sneered, stepped aside as if to avoid contamination, and passed on. The bots took a few more steps and passed a shabbily dressed human who extended a cane to trip the nearest. As the bot picked herself up, the man grinned and spat. In the background, a grimy face peered from the tangle of honeysuckle that choked the mouth of an alley.

The narrator said, "Prejudice is widespread. The worst comes from the poorest. They blame the bots and the gengineers for stealing their jobs. The poorest, however, say nothing at all. They can't be bothered. They are the honey bums."

The camera jumped back to the park to show the high chain-link fence around the dormitory area, its harsh lines softened by the leafy mass of honeysuckle growing thickly around its base. Honey bums lounged near the vines, never far from the drug that consumed their lives. "We try to protect them." Security guards stood near the entrance to the dorm.

"But security is not perfect." The scene turned dark once more as the view returned to the present and night. The mob of Engineers had reached the park and begun to spread out, approaching the fence on a broad front. The guards were now conspicuous by their absence, while axes, machetes, and bolt-cutters made short work of the vines, of the fencing, and of any honey bums who happened to stand in the way.

The veedo cameras spared no detail of the slaughter that followed. The mob used its steel weaponry on every bot who had not, for whatever reason, gone to a job that night. Some, like the human poor, were unemployed. Some were heavy with seed. Some were young, not yet even able to draw their roots from the soil and attempt to flee.

Renny lay down on the carpet and whimpered. One forepaw twitched as if he would like to cover his eyes.

"Lily," screamed Donna Rose as one slender bot was hewn down. "Mindy Alder. Hyacinth. Angelica. Rosa Lee." For a moment, she hid her face in her hands, but that could not last. She had to see. Her hands moved aside to clutch at her cheeks, the fingers digging into her temples, the nails tearing blossoms loose, blood flowing.

Her blood, the blood on the screen, the blood on the ground, none of it was the colorless or green-tinged or latex-white sap of plants. It was red, as red as that of any true human, as red as that of the Engineers themselves.

The city's riot police did not arrive until a forest had been laid low. When they did come, riding Sparrowhawks and Roachsters, equipped with tear gas and riot shields and sonic grenades and rubber bullets, the Engineers faded away, flowing back through the gaps they had made in the security fences, returning to their homes, their faces, brought to the veedo screen by long-range lenses, full of righteous satisfaction.

The announcer's face filled the screen. Beside him sat a hastily assembled panel of experts, ready to comment on what had just happened, just as if it were some upheaval of nature, an earthquake or a hurricane. Ignoring him, Frederick turned

to look at Donna Rose. Her eyes were swollen, her cheeks
wet, her nose red. Blood was clotting on her cheeks. Yes, he
thought, bots can cry. They can grieve, and mourn, and even
hate. They are as human as I.

"That was my . . ." Donna Rose choked on her words. "My
home. My dorm. Mindy Alder was my sister. The rest were . . .
were friends." She sobbed. "They're dead."

"Not all of them," said Renny. "Most were at work, right?"
She nodded. "But . . . I can't go back. I can't."

Frederick hesitated. "I wouldn't expect you to," he said.
"No one should. It wouldn't be safe, now that . . ." Now that
the Engineers had broken all the bounds of civilized dissent,
he thought. Broken them more thoroughly than ever they had
before. There was no telling what would happen next. It might
well be just as bad as the dog and the bot had suggested just
a little while before.

"They must have planned it," said Renny. "For night, when
most of the bots would be gone. That way, there wouldn't
be much possibility of resistance. And they could be sure of
getting on prime-time veedo."

The office's doorknob rattled again, as it had at Donna
Rose's entrance. The door creaked, and words interrupted
them: "There you are! I been looking all over for you! C'mon
now. Let's get back to work." Frederick recognized the harsh
voice even before he turned toward the door. It belonged to the
cleaning crew's supervisor. Now he saw a paunchy, red-faced
man wearing a sand-colored coverall. The thin ruff of hair
surrounding the bald top of his head was grey.

"Haven't you heard?" asked Frederick. "The Engineers just
raided her dorm. They killed her friends. She's too upset to
work."

Renny said nothing, but he did growl, and the fur on his
neck bristled.

The supervisor's eyes went wide, but he clenched his fists
and ignored the dog. "Who cares?" he said. "She's got work
to do, and it won't wait for her to stop crying. And she'd better
not tell any of her friends about it. The last thing I want is a
bunch of mechin' weepers." He leaned backward just enough
to see the nameplate on the door. "Mr. Suida, right? Freddy.
I've heard of you." His expression plainly said what he dared
not put into words: Jumped-up genimal, less than human, don't
shove your do-good interference in my face.

Frederick sighed. "She's working now," he said. His mouth twisted as if he had bitten into something bitter. "Helping me understand what hap—"

"She's a stupid bot," the other man interrupted. "She don't know enough to help you with anything. C'mon, Rosie. You're holding up the whole crew."

Frederick said simply, "No. She can stay if she wishes."

"She ain't got any wishes. She's dumb as a post."

Frederick stared at the other man for a long moment. Renny growled louder, deep in his throat. The supervisor took half a step backward before quelling his instinctive reaction. "Of course," he said. "If you want her . . ."

"You mean she's property."

"Damn near."

Renny got to his feet, still growling. The fur over his shoulders rose even further than it had already. "Then I'll keep her," said Frederick. "As a pet."

The silence that followed was broken first when Donna Rose let her equipment apron fall to the floor by her feet. "Attagirl," said Renny. His fur was still bristling.

Donna Rose's supervisor glanced again at the German shepherd with the swollen skull and swallowed. "Sure, Freddy." He hesitated, and then he began to seem relieved, as if Frederick had finally put matters on a footing that he understood. "Right. Lots of folks do that. They say they're lotsa fun."

There was a long pause while Freddy wondered what must be going through the man's mind. Finally, he thought he had it figured out. Deliberately, though without the humor that had vanished from his life years before, he grinned. He winked. He said, "I've heard the same."

The supervisor laughed and bobbed his head. "Right, Freddy. You'll both enjoy it, I promise. And it won't hurt her a bit." He backed up into the hallway. "I'll bring a pot of dirt for her, eh?"

As Frederick crossed the room to the door, the other began to sidle apprehensively to one side. He stopped when he saw Frederick's hand reaching for his wallet, and when a bill emerged, his eyes narrowed greedily. "Just let me know when you're tired of her." He did not refuse the bribe.

When the door was closed once more, Renny said, "I hope you didn't mean it."

"It's all right," said Donna Rose. "If that's what it takes . . ."

Frederick shook his head. "No," he said. "Let him think whatever he likes. It's not unheard of. It's not even rare. And if the word gets out, I don't see how it could make people think any worse of me."

"You *do* have friends," said Renny.

The man shrugged and returned to the chair behind his desk. "I'm not worried about them," he said.

Renny laughed doggily, his tongue lolling. "You'll be out on your ear in a week." Then he looked at Donna Rose, said, "Want a sausage?" and crossed the room to help himself.

Chapter
Five

FREDERICK SUIDA YAWNED and flipped the long leash that linked Renny to his hand. A wave traveled down the leather strap and made the metal clips and rings at its end jangle together and rattle against the side of the radio tracker fastened to the collar.

Another dog, a German shepherd much like him except for its smaller head and lighter coat, was being walked on the other side of the street. Renny stared stiffly toward it. Then he wagged his tail and growled, "Mechin' leash!" just loudly enough for the man to hear.

He got no answer except another yawn. Frederick had not slept well. Old nightmares—monsters tearing through the walls of the world, bleeding snakes, friends impaled and split and torn and dead—had returned as they always did, whenever he heard or read or saw on the veedo reports of Engineer atrocities. Sometimes the dreams were mild. Only rarely were they as bad as they had been this time. He wondered if the reason were the severity of the slaughter in the park, or the simple fact that Donna Rose gave him a personal, if slight, connection to it.

Renny tugged as if to test the restraint Frederick had laid on him. The man yawned once more and said, "So I'll move a little faster. Will that suit you better?" He looked up at the tall structures that surrounded them. They were old apartment buildings of corniced stone, their lower windows embraced by iron grills. High above, the domelike blisters of floater garages clung to the stonework. Here and there, stained masonry and eroded carvings peeped through the honeysuckle vines that traced their every line.

The leash, like the radio tracker, had been PETA's idea. When Renny's case had landed on his desk, Frederick had been appalled to learn that the dog was being kept in a kennel

49

pending the outcome of PETA's lawsuit. One of the first things he had done was to petition the court to have Renny released in his custody. PETA had objected, claiming the genimal had to be kept under lock and key. It had escaped the permitting process, its modifications were unexamined, and the public deserved protection from this potentially savage beast.

The court had granted his petition, although it had let PETA demand the radio tracker and the leash, at least when Frederick had the dog outdoors. The court had refused PETA's demand for a muzzle as well when Frederick had pointed out that such a thing would interfere with Renny's ability to speak.

Frederick had ignored the leash requirement on his trip to Jeremy Duncan's lab. But now he could not. The long stroll from his apartment to the BRA building took him past too many witnesses, and if one of them were linked to PETA, it would not matter how well behaved the dog was being.

The dog growled again. "Mechin' conservatives. No freedom. No choice. Nothin' but control! They don't trust people."

"Are you people?"

"Isn't that what you're supposed to prove?"

Frederick had read enough history to recognize the truth of the dog's complaint. Conservatives were paranoids, given to seeing threats everywhere they looked. They were the inventors of all the conspiracy theories of history, the ones behind all the witchhunts and pogroms and wars of extermination.

"Wait till we get to the office," he said. "Left, here."

"Wrong way!"

"It'll take us by the park. Wouldn't you like to see?"

But they were still two blocks from the park when they were diverted by a line of blue-and-yellow-striped sawhorses that blocked the street. A single police officer, watched over by a massive Roachster parked on the sidewalk, gestured traffic away from the obstacle. When Frederick and Renny grew close enough, they could make out the officer's constant patter of instruction, explanation, and comment. No one was being allowed to enter the park until the bodies had been removed and the fences rebuilt. No rubberneckers. No press. No gloating Engineers. Not even dog-walkers on their way to the park. Only local residents could pass the roadblock.

Frederick wondered whether the bots had been allowed to return home to their dorm that morning, when they had left work. But when he asked the police officer, he learned nothing.

"Haven't seen 'em," the cop said. "Maybe they took 'em out in the country. Plenty of dirt there."

"Frederick!"

The main entrance to the BRA building was only a few steps away when the hail rang out behind him. He turned, and Berut Amoun was striding hurriedly to catch up.

"Did you hear about the massacre?" asked his friend.

Frederick made a disgusted face and said, "We were watching the veedo, Bert." Renny growled. "They went nuts."

"I hear," said Bert, gesturing Frederick out of the flow of other pedestrians and into the recessed entry of an abandoned genetic tattoo parlor. Only a few weeks before, its owner had been using a small airgun to shoot microscopic gold beads coated with pigment genes into her customers' skin cells. Frederick had stepped in once, to watch as the woman had used the gun like a pencil to draw dark designs on white skin and light designs on dark skin; she had told him she could erase her work just as easily. But now the windows were shattered, the samples of artwork intended for display were splattered with paint and blood, and she was gone. When he turned away from his contemplation of the wreckage, Bert said, "I hear there won't be any arrests."

Frederick looked surprised. The dog yelped, "What? They've got pictures!" A passerby eyed the leash skeptically, decided it was strong enough, glared, spat, and raised one hand to touch the silver gear that dangled from one earlobe. He did not wear the blue coverall of the Engineers.

Bert shrugged. "Policy decision, the news said. 'Heat of the moment.' 'Carried away.' 'Not responsible for their actions.' And that was a lot of voters in the park last night."

Renny growled, and Frederick bent to stroke his head. "I'm not surprised," he finally said. "I'm really not. I only hope . . ."

When he opened his office door, he was for a moment surprised to see the tall plant silhouetted by the window, long leaves spread to the eastern sun. But before the sound of the latch had finished rattling in his head, the plant's leaves whipped around its trunk and it turned to show itself as Donna Rose.

"Good morning," said the bot. Her eyes were dull with fatigue. Her face was drawn. Her cheeks were marked by wet streaks surrounded by lines of salt that showed where other tears had dried.

Frederick stared at her while he thought: She is half plant, perhaps more than half. Yet she is human enough for tears. Then, silently, he unsnapped Renny's leash. The dog trotted toward the metal tub in which the bot stood and sniffed Donna Rose's legs. "So you're still here," said the genimal.

"Where else would I go?" Donna Rose looked at the man.

He made a face and said, "They're not letting anyone into the park. I don't know where your friends are now." He gestured toward the window, which was open about a centimeter. A branch of the honeysuckle vine that climbed the outside of the building had taken advantage of the opening and entered the room. Its tip had found the soil of Donna Rose's tub and seemed already to have taken root. "Did you open that?"

The bot nodded hesitantly. "Shouldn't I? I'm used to the outdoors. I wanted a little air, and . . ."

"It's all right," said Frederick. "I open it myself sometimes, and even when it's closed, it's impossible to keep the honeysuckle out." He showed her the fine tendrils that had squeezed under the window the day before; they still clung to the sill. Then he ran a hand down the new branch, gripped it firmly just above the soil of her tub, and said, "Damned weed. I'll just . . ."

"No!" said Donna Rose. When he looked up at her, puzzlement plain upon his face, she said, "Please. I like it there. It's lonely in here at night."

Renny flopped on the carpet near Frederick's desk. "After last night," he said, "she needs company. Companionship. A pet, and what's a better pet for a bot than a plant? Let it stay."

Frederick felt a memory tickle at the back of his mind. It came from another and a simpler time of his life, a time before he had lost his friends, and he wished it would jell. But it wouldn't, though he knew it concerned the honeysuckle and its relation to the bots, and then even the tickle vanished in still another of his yawns.

With a "Tchah" of exasperation—some things were like that, whenever he tried to look much beyond the events that had marked his conversion to humanity—he let go of the vine, grunted, and got to his feet. "I understand," he said. "Can we get . . . Do you need water?" But the soil around her ankles was not dry, as if the vine had shared with her its sap, and she did not answer. Instead, she turned wordlessly back toward the window. Her leaves once more uncurled from her trunk, revealing smooth, pale skin, tinged with green, and the nippled breasts of a human woman. The breasts were useless on her, for bots did not suckle their young; they had come with the human genes that made her what she was. There was no navel.

The man sighed. There was nothing he could do except give her space, a bit of dirt in which to root, a place of safety, if that were truly possible. He crossed to his desk, chose a floppy-card, set it between the leaves of the bioform card-drive, and booted his computer. "We still," he told Renny, "have to find someone who can testify about your gengineering."

The German shepherd stared toward Donna Rose, who was still ignoring them, presumably communing with grief, mourning the friends who had died in the Engineer attack the night before. "Then you should try for the boss."

"It would help if you could tell me where Hannoken disappeared to." The chief of the gengineering lab that had made Renny sentient was Alvar Hannoken. If Frederick could track him down, if he could be persuaded to show up in court, he could testify to Renny's harmlessness. He could confirm the technician's claim that the dog's natural aggressiveness had been curtailed.

"No idea," said Renny. "He was still there when they passed me on to the Seeing Eye program."

"How much longer will there even be such a program?" Frederick was willing to chat as he worked. He had already learned that Hannoken was not listed in the national computerized phone directory. BRA's own records revealed that he had not renewed his gengineering license in the last two years. He was no longer on the rolls of his professional associations.

"As long as anyone's left who doesn't want their eyes or nerves or visual cortex regrown." In a world that could change a pig into a man, there was no need for any blind person to stay blind for more than a few days. Yet there were those who had learned how to deal with a world of darkness many years before the gengineers learned how to repair their damage. As they grew old and died, their numbers dwindled. There were also those, like Renny's erstwhile employer, who rejected what the gengineers might do for them.

Now the man keyed in a request for access to the Internal Revenue Service's database. A moment later he was typing furiously, and then . . . "They're searching," he said. For some things, such as sheer calculation, bioform computers were slower than the older electronic machines. But biological memory was superb at searching out and retrieving small chunks of information hidden in large databases. Still, the IRS database was among the largest in the world. It would take a few minutes to learn whether that arm of government had any record of Hannoken's current whereabouts.

"Do you know," he said to the dog while they were waiting. "I'm surprised it took so long to make a sentient dog. The techniques were there, and they were used." He pointed a thumb at his own chest. "But . . ."

"Maybe the gengineers liked dogs just fine the way they were," said Renny. "Fawning slaves. Sycophants. Ass-lickers."

"Or it was too obvious. A sci-fi cliche." The computer dinged to catch his attention. Frederick peered at the leafy screen. It held a view of Hannoken's latest tax return. "There," he said. He pointed at the top of the image. "We've got him. He's on Probe Station."

There were many surveillance and communications satellites and a number of space stations in orbit around the Earth and its moon. There were even two small LaGrangian habitats, hollow cylinders each holding several thousand technicians, engineers, and workers dedicated to building solar power and other satellites, sharing the lunar orbit sixty degrees ahead of and behind the moon. They had been named Hugin and Munin, as if the Man in the Moon were the Norse god Odin. The names had once belonged to the pair of ravens that flew around the world each day to keep Odin informed of all that happened.

Probe Station was also in the moon's orbit, but nowhere near a LaGrange point. As a result, it needed to expend relatively large amounts of reaction mass to hold its unstable niche. What justified the expense was that the LaGrange points were, though stable, too polluted with dust, gas, and debris, both natural and the products of the habitats' activities, to permit Probe's large telescopes to explore the cosmos effectively. The station also held labs for assorted other disciplines.

Renny stood up, stretched, curled his tail over his rump, and put his forepaws on the edge of Frederick's desk. "He makes enough money, doesn't he?"

"And no dependents," said Frederick. "I wonder what he's doing there."

"So call him."

"I will." He tapped his keyboard, and the image on the screen was replaced with a specialized orbital communications directory. He chose a number and told the computer to dial it. After a pause while the call routed through a comsat to its destination, the four leaves that comprised the computer's monitor lit up with a line-drawing of the satellite in space, its name spelled out across the bottom of the screen, and the StarBell logo. A moment later, the drawing was replaced by the computer-generated image of an exceedingly buxom redhead. With a few more taps, he put a duplicate of the image on the screen of the veedo unit on the shelf.

"May I help you?" Frederick turned up the volume, identified himself aloud, and named the man he wished to speak with. Three seconds later, the image responded to his words by nodding and switching to an internal communications line. The office's two active screens flickered simultaneously, and Frederick was looking at the face of a man whose heavy jaw, bladelike nose, and thick mat of iron-grey hair spoke of an ancestral blend of Scandinavian and Slav.

"Dr. Hannoken?" Because he did not wish to wait upon the three-second time delay before Hannoken could answer him, he immediately introduced himself. Then he laid one hand on Renny's neck. The dog was still leaning over his desk. "Do you remember this genimal? He came out of your lab a few years ago." Renny opened his mouth and panted doggily; his tail wagged eagerly.

The camera that sent images from the office toward Probe Station was mounted inconspicuously in the veedo unit near the wall, and Hannoken's image on the veedo screen aimed the gengineer's broad smile accurately toward the two faces leaning over Frederick's desk. The image nearer their faces, because its viewpoint was not the same as the camera's, seemed subtly askew.

In a moment, Hannoken added to his smile, "Of course I do, Mr. Suida. We called you Renny, didn't we? Rin-tin-tin. You're looking well."

"But maybe not for much longer," said Frederick. He explained the situation. "To save him, we need to be able to prove he's not a threat to the public. I understand you removed his aggressive instincts, and I'd like you to come to Earth long enough to testify to that effect."

The distinguished face fell as Hannoken shook his head. "It doesn't work that way," he said. "A dog's aggressive behavior is linked to its senses of territoriality and hierarchy and, yes, we weakened those senses. Renny isn't very turf-conscious, and he won't fight to be top dog. But any animal has to be able to defend itself and those it cares about. And he will certainly fight if he feels threatened."

Frederick hoped that Hannoken's words would make as much sense to the judge as they did to him. "Then there's no danger that he would attack people on the street."

"Not unless someone threatens him. You say he was a seeing-eye dog? Or if they threatened his employer. A mugger, say."

"PETA." Renny's rough voice made the comment sound like a curse.

"They're certainly a threat," said Frederick, glancing at the dog. He sighed. Their lawyers might well point that out and claim the dog could attack them right there in the courtroom. "The court date," he added. "It's—"

But Hannoken was already shaking his head. "No. I'm sorry, but no. I came up here to get away from the Engineers and their craziness. They were picketing the lab, breaking in and wrecking equipment, 'liberating' our research animals. It was only a matter of time before something like that riot . . ." He broke off, paused for a moment while he seemed to scan what he could see in the screen before him. His eyebrows thickened as his face turned serious. "That was horrible, horrible. Obviously, you're all right. And Renny. But . . . Is that a refugee behind you? Or . . . ?"

Frederick turned to see Donna Rose still in her tub, leaves open, staring out the window. She did not seem to be paying any attention. "Yes," he said. "She didn't have any place to go."

Hannoken sighed. "We don't have any bots up here. And I'd love to get her into my lab. Her genetic structure must be fascinating."

Frederick interrupted as best he could in the face of the three-second time delay. "I didn't realize there was any genetic research at Probe."

Hannoken shrugged. "If I'd stayed down there, I'd eventually have had to give it up completely, that or go into hiding. Here, at least, there's no harassment. Though it's barely a hobby. They made me director of the station, and that keeps me too busy." He shook his head. "Too busy for your court hearing."

The dog growled. His tail stopped moving.

Hannoken shrugged again and looked aside as if he could not stand to meet the German shepherd's large, dark eyes, nor to think that he had been quite right to say that the dog could be aggressive when threatened. "I'm not coming back."

"Not even—"

"No. Not even to save him."

Frederick knew, and he knew that Hannoken knew, that a subpoena would be useless. The distances and the times and the expense of travel were so great that the orbital community was in many ways like an independent foreign nation. Congress had not yet recognized this fact of modern life, but the courts had. They usually refused to subpoena orbital workers, knowing that such orders could all too easily be ignored.

The silence of thought stretched well beyond the time delay inherent in any conversation across a third of a million kilometers. Finally, Frederick said, "Is there anyone else?"

"No. Not that I know of. But . . ." Hannoken turned back toward the camera that captured his image for the veedo set. "Perhaps . . . He'd be safe if you could send him here, wouldn't he?"

"What do you think, Bert?" Frederick turned the mug of coffee in his hand. For half an hour after his talk with Hannoken, he had paced his office, muttering about the selfishness of human beings. Renny had chimed in from time to time. Donna Rose had been silent, her mind dwelling on her own tragedy.

Eventually, he had closed his eyes and dozed for a few minutes. Then, feeling somewhat refreshed, he had left the room to the bot and the dog, locking them in while he walked down the hall to Berut Amoun's office. The room was identical to his own, with a veedo unit on a shelf and a bioform computer by the desk. There was even a snackbush by the window, though this one produced clusters of crunchy, salty twigs, as much like potato sticks as pretzels.

"Forget it," said Amoun. "PETA would scream like hell. And the court would never go for it."

"Then he's doomed."

"You knew that already."

Frederick shook his head. "No!" That was, he thought, the whole point of his assignment: to defend the genimal, to find some way to ward off the doom PETA wished for him. He had thought that meant fighting PETA in court, and he had been optimistic. But then Hannoken had offered a far surer path to safety, even as his refusal to testify made the court fight seem far less promising.

"Yes. With the mood the world is in right now . . ."

"He said he could put through a requisition for an experimental animal. Route it here instead of NSF's purchasing department. Then we take it as approved and authorized and ship him the only animal we have. He called it creative mix-up, and he thought PETA wouldn't mind it."

"Maybe not. But what the hell would they do with him?" Both men knew that Renny had no training for space, and without hands, even with training, there couldn't be much for him to do. And space had little tolerance for idlers or parasites.

"The only pets they have up there are little guys," said Amoun. Usually that meant tropical fish. Mice were rare, said the Sunday supplements. So were gerbils and hamsters and crickets. They were all small enough, and they could all be kept in small cages that did not get in the way in cramped quarters. But if they got loose, they could all too easily get into crucial equipment and short out circuitry, chew wires, or plug small ducts.

"Or they have roots." The favorite plant-pets were goldfish bushes and pussy willows.

"Renny's too smart to be a pet," said Amoun. "He's also too big, and too mobile. They'll have to move him to a habitat." The two LaGrangian habitats raised the meat and milk and eggs that made their people the envy of the other satellites from plants, not animals, but they did have room.

"He needs more than room," said Frederick. Only after he had hung up on Hannoken had he thought to ask himself just how happy Renny would be on Probe Station. He would be alive, with no threat hanging over him. But he would be useless, and he, as much as any human being, prided himself on being useful to the society of which he was a part. Frederick did not think he would be happy as a pet.

When he returned to his office, he found Donna Rose out of her tub and pacing about the office. Renny greeted him with, "Hannoken called back. She didn't have any trouble at all with the download, and . . ." The dog was behind the man, sounding surprised, using his nose to push him toward the desk, where the computer's leafy screen displayed a short block of text:

"Yes, we can do it," Hannoken had written. "We have a group that has been working on a new space drive. They'll be ready soon for a test flight, and they'll need a test pilot. They have a human volunteer already. But a dog would make a perfect copilot. They said it would remind everyone of the Russian Laika that was the first living thing to leave the Earth back in the 1950s. And it even makes sense to route the requisition through BRA, since there is a possibility that the new drive may change living material in unforeseen ways."

"Sounds great, doesn't it?" said Renny. "I've always wanted to be a rocket jockey."

"Laika died," said Frederick as he erased Hannoken's message. The thought made him feel surprisingly apprehensive. He had not known Renny long, but he had become quite attached to him.

"But this way I get to be a rocket jockey *first*. If I stay here . . ."

No one said that if he stayed on Earth PETA or the Engineers would surely kill him, legally or illegally. There did not seem to be any truly desirable choices among his possible futures.

Frederick used his keyboard to put through another call to Hannoken. Once the orbiting gengineer was on both computer and veedo screens, he said simply, "Huh?"

Three seconds later, Hannoken laughed, set aside the floppy-card in his hand, and said, "What do you mean, 'Huh'?"

"A new drive?" said Frederick. "I haven't heard . . ."

"You wouldn't," said Hannoken with a grin. "I hope. We've kept this Q-drive quiet, though they tell me it should simplify things a bit." Frederick was not surprised when the other man failed to go into detail. Defense departments and intelligence agencies played a much smaller role in the world than once they had, but they still existed, and they still coveted technological monopolies. There was no telling who might be eavesdropping on the communications signals from a known research satellite. "Sound good?"

As they spoke, Donna Rose stepped back into her pot of dirt, spread just the tips of her leaves to the sun, touched a honeysuckle leaf with one hand, and assumed a thoughtful look. Frederick glanced toward her but did not wonder what she was doing. Instead, he asked Hannoken what he had meant when he said the drive could change living tissue.

The other man shrugged lightly and said, "I don't think it's serious. As the station chief, I have to know about any project like this. But I'm a biologist, too, and that got me involved a little deeper, as a consultant." He hesitated before continuing. "Nobody really understands how the biohazard would work. Some of us don't even think it's all that serious a risk. I don't."

"But some do," said Renny. As before, he was leaning on Frederick's desk, staring intently at the man who had made him what he was but would not come to Earth to help him now. His tail was twitching slightly, as if he were not sure how to feel toward the man.

Hannoken stared out of the screens at the dog, not at Frederick. "That's right," he said. "Just as some physicists thought the first nuclear tests a century and a half ago might trigger a planetary chain reaction. But they tried the experiment anyway. It was the only answer, the only way to find out who was right."

"But the risk . . . !" cried Donna Rose from her place by the window.

After the inevitable pause, Hannoken shifted his gaze toward her. "Yes," he said. "But the ones in charge thought the pessimists were wrong."

"Couldn't they have done it in space?" asked Renny.

Frederick was the first of the two men to shake his head and say, "Not then. No rockets, no space travel." Then Hannoken continued with, "That was even before Sputnik. Though it would have been a good thing if they had been out here like us, eh?"

"And not down here." Donna Rose was withdrawing her roots from the soil and stepping back onto the carpet.

When Hannoken's eyes turned back toward Renny, the genimal said, "I'm willing." When Frederick grunted as if in surprise, the dog glanced in his direction and added, "I haven't got much to lose, Freddy. Have I?"

"You don't have to," said Hannoken. "Remember, we do have that human volunteer."

Frederick felt a sudden wave of relief as he guessed that much of the message Hannoken had left on his screen must have been meant for other eyes than his, eavesdroppers, chasers of those records that had once, before computers achieved their omnipresence, been called paper trails.

Renny showed his teeth in a doggy grin. "You need to justify that requisition, right?" Without waiting for Hannoken's agreeing nod, he said, "And if it'll get me away from PETA, I'll do anything."

After Hannoken's image had blinked off the office's two screens, Frederick leaned over his desk, his hands bracing his head at the temples. What was he getting himself into? He would save Renny from PETA, yes. But his BRA superiors would have words for him, he was sure. He might save Renny only at the cost of his own pigskin hide.

Was the saving worth its price? Should he, perhaps, ignore the sneaky, underhanded, roundabout solution to Renny's problem, that "creative mix-up" that Alvar Hannoken had offered him? The philosophers claimed that doing wrong for the sake of good never worked. Saving Renny was good. Of course it was. But saving him in this way, by subterfuge and lies and misdirection? Was there any other way?

He felt a hand on his shoulder. Slowly, he let go of his head and turned. Donna Rose stood beside him now, gazing at him sympathetically. Automatically, he covered her hand with his own and squeezed lightly.

"Can I go too?" she asked.

Chapter
Six

SAM NICKERS STOOD on the crest of a small rise in the city park, his hands deep in the pockets of the coat he had put on over his coverall. The sky was overcast this evening. The breeze was unseasonably chill on his neck and face.

"Sheila," he said. She was beside him, wearing a long cloak. Ahead and to either side, the landscape of lawn and thicket and flowerbed and path was dotted by other couples, singletons, and small groups. The tennis courts were quiet, and no one at all was on the softball field. All were there to confirm the news reports that the park was open once more, the damage to the bot dorm had been repaired, and the bots were back in their home. Some of the watchers were surely Engineers; perhaps they had even been part of the murderous mob that had done the damage three days before, come to feed their dissatisfaction with the temporariness of their impact. Some, like the Nickerses, fed fears of another sort. Only the honey bums lurking in the shadows where clumps of trees struggled to emerge from tangles of honeysuckle did not seem to care.

"Look at the nursery," he said, pointing. They had been here before, in better times, when there had been neat rows of infant bots, rooted in the rich soil near the little duck pond, unable to move until their legs had shaped within their trunks and their nervous systems had matured enough to command their muscles. Until the age of two, they were little more than plants.

Sheila's breath caught in her throat as she said, "There were hundreds of them." The bots were fertile creatures, as they needed to be to maintain their numbers. Few lived more than a decade.

"And now . . . A dozen." They had not been transplanted to some more sheltered garden. The small stumps still jutted from the ground.

63

She shuddered. "It looks like a prison camp." The guards were armed. The honeysuckle had been cleared from the ghetto border, leaving a strip of bare earth beside the fence. In that strip, mounds of dirt marked where dead honey bums, rioters, and bots had been buried. The fence itself was higher, though admittedly the barbed-wire top angled outward, not inward. Most ominous of all, the bots within the fence seemed wilted. They milled about and chatted as they always had, but their movements seemed subdued, their voices were quieter, and there was no sound of song. Their leaves spread as before to the sun but seemed to remain closer to their trunks, as if in apprehension.

"It may become one yet," he said. They had months to go before the school year and their contracts ended. But they had still not found new jobs. No one wanted to hire greenskins. No one wanted to draw the attention of the Engineers and their friends. The forces of reaction were strong. He thought they would grow stronger yet.

He was a teacher of history, historian enough. He knew there was nothing unprecedented about the situation, nothing abnormal, nothing strange. It had happened before, many, many, many times throughout humanity's span of time.

What he felt as he contemplated the future had been felt before, he was sure. By pre-21st-century American Blacks, 1940 Japanese-Americans, Bulgarian Turks in the 1990s, Jews in the England of the 2060s or in 19th-century Russia or 1930s Germany or medieval Spain . . . The minority, ethnic or racial or religious, called less than human, feared, demeaned, mistreated, persecuted. He felt sure the killing had only begun.

And there was not a thing he could do about it. He could not even tell the killers how much they depended on the bots, who worked at jobs and for pay scales no human would accept, or on the gengineers, who had appeared just before the vaunted Machine Age must have used up the resources it required.

He stepped sideways, closer to his wife, and wrapped an arm about her. He felt bleakly reassured when her own arm put an answering pressure on his lower ribs. Together then, supporting each other, comforting, praying to whatever gods they sheltered within their hearts while the lower edge of Sheila's cloak flapped against their ankles, they stared over that piece of the world that had once been a peaceful, happy dormitory for the bots. The lower ones. The menials. He imagined that in due time the upper bots, the ones Alice Belle had said owned their own building and had apartments and worked by day, would join them there. And then . . .

Humanity was too sweet to waste on the lower orders.

They watched as armed guards yelled and gestured the bots into a long line before the gate. Some distance off, near the park's main entrance, someone laughed and yelled, "Line 'em up!" The source was a group of young Engineers in blue coveralls; they were hurriedly forming a double line on either side of the drive.

The dorm gate swung open, and the column of bots began walking toward the city's streets and their jobs. Guards walked at the head of the column and along its flanks, peeling off at the park entrance to press the Engineers gently, courteously back. That gentleness seemed oddly diffident, as if the guards were not sure whether the Engineers were friends or foes, or the bots were wards or prisoners. It did nothing to stop the heckling, the pokes and prods and grabs at blossoms that—Sam could see, even from his distance—left scalps red with blood.

The bots speeded up their pace as they approached the park entrance, rushing to escape the gauntlet. Yet their faces grew ever bleaker. The gauntlet, they knew, did not end there.

Sam could feel Sheila shivering at his side.

It was warmer behind the walls of an apartment building whose windows glowed strangely bright, as if the lights that dispelled dusk from the rooms within were miniature suns.

In a way, they were. This was Alice Belle's home, a building owned by bots and adapted to their comforts, of which the bright lighting was only one. The floors had been waterproofed and covered with garden loam, just deep enough in most areas to ease the barefoot souls of strolling bots, a little deeper under the brightest lights, where the sentient plants would root and rest at night. Overhead, pipes served a sprinkler system that could mimic mists, showers, and driving rainstorms. The honeysuckle vines that arched over the windowsills and rooted in the soil were so thick that it was obvious they were welcome visitors. No one had ever trimmed them back. No one ever would.

The room's single occupant did not seem to be a bot. It stood in the room's best bed, where the soil was deepest and the light the brightest. It was as tall as any bot, and its leaves were as green. But its head and face seemed to be sculpted from a single massive flower, its color the deep red of an amaryllis, and its trunk was a simple, slender cylinder. There was the merest trace of human curves. There were no arms, nor a division of the lower trunk into legs. A single massive bulb swelled from the surface of the soil.

The room's door opened. Through the portal stepped a number of conventional bots. One by one, they paced barefooted across the soil and bowed their heads to the room's strange occupant, almost as if it were their king or queen. Then they found positions in a ring around the object of their deference, scuffed their feet, let down their roots, and anchored themselves in the thin layer of loam. A smaller bot then entered the room, moving stiffly, and took up a position within the ring, close to the rim but facing the center. Her head was small, and the bulb between her legs was nearly twice as large as those of the others, as if it held a greater proportion of her brains; certainly, it was large enough to account for the awkwardness of her movements.

Finally, Alice Belle appeared, one hand holding tightly a crumpled sheet of paper. She did not join the ring, but instead rooted herself a little to one side, not far from a window.

The bots in the ring were what the papers they had filed with the city's bureaus and the Internal Revenue Service called a "management committee." Yet they were not quite that in truth. Yes, they managed the building, its maintenance and financing and tenanting. But they also managed the residents themselves, acting as a sort of governing council, and in this function their influence actually extended well beyond the building's walls, largely because of what occupied the center of their circle.

Membership on the committee was a function of intelligence, ability, and energy. The members therefore tended to have in the world outside the building positions as high as society would allow a bot. They were executives and researchers. One was an artist. Others were gengineers. Many had surpassed the ten-year life expectancy of the average bot.

The gengineer's name was Cindy Blue, and her scalp blossoms were a pure and snowy white. She turned toward Alice Belle. "You have asked us to let humans move into this building with us. Why should we, even if we do have a vacancy?"

Alice Belle glanced out the window, turned, and eyed the members of the management committee. Her gaze lingered longest on the strange figure in the middle of the ring. "We're bots," she said at last. "Plants the gengineers have moved toward being human. They—the Nickerses—are humans who have moved toward being plants. At least, they have chloroplasts in their skin, they photosynthesize, they love bright light."

"But that doesn't really make them very much plant," said the bot named Shasta Lou. Her blossoms were pale blue with yellow centers. "Skin them, and they're still just meat."

"Our blood is just as red," said another.

"They love the future. They're like us that way," said Alice Belle. "Change and difference."

"They're neophiles," said Cindy Blue. "Technophiles. Not conservatives."

"Not Engineers," said someone, and there was a rustling of antipathy, as if a gathering of Catholics had crossed themselves in unison at mention of the devil.

"And they're my friends," said Alice Belle. "I like them. And . . ." She smoothed the paper she had been holding against her thigh. "I've shown you this."

"They are hated," said Cindy Blue, nodding. "And feared. Discriminated against. Even persecuted. That is plain."

"But they are not bots," said Shasta Lou. "No one threatens *them* with axes and torches. No one promises to destroy *them* for the crime of what they are."

"Yet," said Alice Belle, but before she could either go on or indicate that she was done, a gust of odor struck the ring of bots. All turned toward the figure at the center. "Eldest," they said in unison, for that was who they faced, the last of their ancestors still alive, a relic from so many generations before their own time that she had only a few human genes, just enough for size and brain and thought. Their answer was a flexing of the Eldest bot's trunk, a bending of her leaves, and a flow of perfumed pheromones, an ever-changing mixture of floral and other odors.

The small bot just within the ring finally spoke: "We too are human now. Just as smart as they. But we are different too. We cannot save them. We should not try."

Alice Belle stared at the Eldest, for she knew whence the words had really come. Once her kind had been able to sense and interpret the communicative pheromones directly. But the continuing admixture of human genes to their genome had canceled the ability, distancing them from their roots almost as completely as would shaving their calves. Fortunately, there still remained a few survivors of those generations that had been able to communicate in both ways and could therefore translate from scent to speech. This one bore the title of Eldest's Speaker.

"But they are friends!"

"Too different," said the Eldest through her Speaker. "This building, others too in other cities. They are our refuges, refuges for us, our kind. Not humans."

"But they *are* our kind!" cried Alice Belle. "They have more human genes. They have added plant to human, not human to plant. But they too are part plant, part human."

Shasta Lou jerked one hand dismissively. "They are human base," she said. "They are therefore evil."

"They are not Engineers!"

"But they are apt to be converted," said another bot. "And then we would have enemies, spies and saboteurs, among us."

"No!" cried Alice Belle. "That's how their troubles started, when they said no." Briefly, she then related what the Nickerses had told her of the Engineer recruiters at the door with their pamphlets. "That's when they lost their jobs as teachers, and—"

"Teachers?" said Cindy Blue.

Alice Belle nodded. "They're human base," she said. "But not all humans are as deranged as the Engineers and their sympathizers. The Nickerses aren't, I know. Sam and Sheila are *good* people."

"And so are we," said the Eldest, the words coming on the heels of the gust of pheromones. "We try. We do. But we must also live. Survive. Protect and shield and isolate us from our enemies."

"Could they help us as we help them?" asked Cindy Blue.

Alice Belle was silent for a long moment. Perhaps good deeds should not be traded like goods in a marketplace, but they were. She had seen it often in the world outside this brightly lit enclave, and this was hardly the first time she had seen it within. But what could the Nickerses offer in exchange for a place to live?

Finally, she recognized the interest Cindy Blue had shown once already for what it truly was. "They're teachers," she said again. "And we cannot send our children to the local schools." Quite aside from the question of whether the kids would survive the inevitable persecution, their lives were simply too short. If they were forced to learn at the human pace, they would be dead of old age before they finished high school. If they were forced as well to abide by human notions of age and readiness, they would never make it out of the elementary grades.

"We have our own ways of learning," she added. "But they could help, I'm sure."

"So." Shasta Lou constricted her leaves tightly around her trunk, a gesture of rejection. "We give them a home, and jobs as well. And then they will put our blossoms in vases, and our leaves in salad, and—"

"No!" sent the Eldest. "They need. We need. That is truth, it is. It is also true that we can help each other. But should we? Dare we? Dare we trust the strangers?"

"They are kin!" cried Alice Belle, and the others stared at her, their mouths open in shock. The Eldest was never interrupted.

Yet the Eldest did not seem to mind. "No," her Speaker said. "They are greenskins. Not kin. Not enough. They are too human, closer kin to Engineers."

Again a collective shudder ran through the group. "We should be thankful," said Cindy Blue, "that humans are not that unified. There are those who oppose the Engineers, those who could help." She fell silent for a long moment before adding, "And we may need all the help we can find in the days to come."

"The situation is not *that* bad," said Shasta Lou.

"Perhaps it is," said the Eldest. "Listen to the honeysuckle . . ."

Obediently, the others let the tendrils of their roots find those of the honeysuckle that wove throughout the soil beneath them. The same gengineer who had taken the first step toward the bots had designed the honeysuckle as a way for sentient plants like the Eldest to communicate over larger distances than scent could carry. It had soon become something more, for, equipped with sensors for vision and sound and other senses, it could gather information from any place where its vines grew and pass that information to any bot who wished to receive it. Now the sensory data gathered by the honeysuckle flowed to the Eldest, to Alice Belle, and to the members of the management committee.

It was a collage of bits and pieces drawn from a thousand viewpoints, in this city and others, in other nations, in other continents, all labeled "NOW" despite the differing times of travel:

—A parkland dormitory, a horde of Engineers, these equipped with cans and bottles of flammable liquids; the police stood idly by.
—A dozen city sidewalks, a dozen isolated bots being stripped of leaves and blossoms, being chopped to pieces with heavy blades.
—A Roachster bake, with several burly Engineers laughing uproariously as they watched the vehicle sputter on the coals.
—Bioform houses, an orange pumpkin, a purple eggplant, a stucco-coated squash, set afire, while sharp blades and sticks kept the residents from escaping through the windows.
—More traditional homes torched as well, apparently because their residents, their bodies visible on their lawns, bore too many genetic modifications.
—A zoo, all those exhibits bearing "Endangered Species Replacement Program" signs destroyed.

As one, the younger bots shivered in reaction to the horrors they had seen and withdrew their roots from the honeysuckle. Only the Eldest did not seem to react.

"We must do *something*," said Cindy Blue.

"There is nothing we can do," said Shasta Lou. "Nothing. Nothing at all. The enemy is at the gates, and we are doomed."

"We can try," said Alice Belle. "We can help others, and thus deserve whatever help may come our way."

Shasta Lou snorted, but there were nods of agreement. The scenes the honeysuckle had shown them had impressed them all with the danger that surrounded them, the danger that threatened even non-bots if they had been gengineered. Yes, the axes did await the Nickerses.

"Listen," said the Eldest. "I have stayed with the vines. Not all the news is bad. One of ours has found a promise. A hint of refuge. She will travel soon. Learn of possibility and potential. And if and if and if, then just perhaps . . ." Her scent and the Speaker's voice trailed off together.

"Yes," said Alice Belle, sighing. "We can hope. But in the meantime, we should also help."

Even Shasta Lou nodded in agreement now, though her movements were stiff, clearly reluctant. Cindy Blue said, "The enemy is those who kill, those who hate change, those who crave the stasis of the past. There are people who share our form and minds, who favor life and novelty and the changes of the future. And to them we really should offer what protection we may hold."

The debate was over. Alice Belle had won her point. The Nickerses would be invited to move into the building.

Chapter
Seven

FREDERICK SUIDA STARED at the tub of dirt by the window. It was empty except for the branch of honeysuckle vine that had crossed the windowsill to invade it. The bare surface of the dirt seemed freshly tilled around two slender footprints, broken and churned where Donna Rose had withdrawn her roots that morning. He supposed he should call maintenance and have the tub removed.

He turned in his seat to stare at the Fat Bag commercial on the veedo. The gengineers had modified the virus that caused skin tags so that the once tiny tabs of flesh now grew larger, filled with fat preempted from the body's normal depots. To lose weight, one now needed no more than a pair of scissors, a dab of antiseptic, and a bandaid. No more diets! No liposuction!

He snorted and blinked and sighed. The patch of carpet by his desk where Renny had liked to sprawl was bare. He sighed again. The dog too was gone. He looked at his watch. In just a few more hours, the genimal would be beyond the reach of PETA, safe from Engineers, safe from persecution, legal or otherwise.

He glanced toward the leaves of his bioform computer screen. The requisition was still displayed there. A window showed that he had approved it and arranged the necessary spaceplane tickets, one for a cargo crate containing one experimental animal, dog, invoice number 98-2377742, one for an animal handler, non-federal, ID number B-701-33-2047. The B prefix marked the ID numbers of all bots.

He hadn't had to lie very much at all. In fact, Donna Rose had already had all the identification she needed to support his claims on her behalf. For tax purposes, the cleaning service pretended it was a broker for a horde of subcontractors, and each individual cleaning bot was suitably defined in the government's computers. He had just had to ask the Civil Service computers to change her assignment. Fortunately, he had enough authority for that.

Frederick had known he could never keep Renny. He had known that if PETA won its lawsuit, the court decision would take him away, put him away; if PETA lost, he would go off on his own. Either way, the genimal would be gone. He wasn't a pet. But Frederick had grown used to having Renny around. He missed him already.

Somewhat to his surprise, he was realizing that he missed Donna Rose as well. He hadn't known her as long, but she was attractive and sympathetic. And she aroused his own sympathy, just as did Renny. He supposed his history must have something to do with that. He too had been persecuted, had lost friends and loved ones, had—

"Mr. Suida?" He had not heard his office door open, but the fact that there had been no knock was enough to tell him who his visitor was. He did not need her voice.

"Dr. Breger." He turned toward the BRA Assistant Director. Her coverall was as metallic in its finish as it had been the other day, though it was now bronze, not silver. With her dark skin, she looked almost robotically efficient. Her expression was a narrow, tight-lipped smile, almost like that of a mother amused by her child's mischief.

"What have you done now, Frederick?" she asked. As the door clicked behind her, she pointed at Frederick's computer screen. "Didn't you know the system would flag that sort of expenditure? It was the first thing on my screen when I got back after this morning's policy meeting."

He *had* forgotten, but what could he say other than what he had rehearsed to himself a dozen times already? Deliberately, he shrugged. "I didn't think there would be any problem."

"But there is." Breger leaned over his desk, supporting her weight on her hands. She was precisely as intimidating as she intended to be, although the touch of red in Frederick's cheeks came not from that, but from the narrow gape of her coverall and what it showed. "Tell me about it."

"They called yesterday to say they had a new spacedrive that might do funny things to living matter . . ."

"What sort of funny things?"

"I don't know. They didn't say. But apparently they don't want to take a chance on a human test pilot." He was careful to look her in the eye as he lied. "They wanted an animal."

"And you had one."

He nodded jerkily. "I suggested they go through NSF, but they said the biological effects . . ."

Now it was the Assistant Director's turn to nod. "Made us seem more appropriate." At the same time, she relaxed, straightened from her dominating stoop, and walked around his desk to stand beside him. "I suppose you're right."

"And then this morning . . ." He gestured at his screen. "There it was. So I went ahead and approved it. And bought the tickets."

She stared at him. "And the bot 'handler'?"

This, he thought, was the weakest point. "It's a long trip, and I thought the crews wouldn't have much experience with animals." He shrugged again. "I decided to send someone to look after him."

Her stare did not relax. "Is she coming back, Frederick?"

He shifted awkwardly in his seat and added, "She's a cleaner. Part of the night crew." He looked away, toward the window, and knew she was noticing the empty tub of dirt. "I took her in after the Engineers trashed her dorm."

The Assistant Director grunted and nodded as if she understood what had moved him. "So you've moved two out of harm's way," she said thoughtfully. "I wish I could think it would make much difference." But then she scowled, her smile vanishing as if it had never been, even in the rudimentary form he recalled. "Do you realize what a mechin' mess you've made?"

The question was not one that needed an answer. Frederick sat rigidly still and said nothing.

Breger groaned theatrically. "There are channels, you know. It's not your place to approve such things." She spun away from him, clutched her hands behind her back, and strode to the window. "Honeysuckle!" She bent, yanked the vine from the dirt it had claimed and hurled it out the window. "You've made us all look like mentally defective twits who care nothing at all for public opinion. PETA will get its judgment quite automatically, just as soon as the judge finds out. We—or you, just you, I hope—will be up for contempt of court and favoritism and conflict of interest. The Engineers will be on the sidewalk down there, screaming for your blood."

She spun. "Why?" She glared. After a moment, she said, "I know why. Judgment or no judgment, the dog is safe. But you, sir, are not. You're . . ."

"Fired?" Frederick's voice shook. He hadn't expected this severe a reaction, though he was already telling himself he should have.

"No." Breger let out a gusty sigh. "No, dammit. You're suspended, with pay, until we find out . . . If I'm right, we'll have to be able to show we've taken steps. Then we'll schedule the disciplinary hearing." She moved toward the door. When her hand was on the knob, she turned toward him once more. "Maybe," she said, "we can convince the judge to say experimentation is a more useful form of disposal than execution, that by shipping Renny off in this way, we have capitulated in a way that he can simply rubber-stamp. But I doubt it. PETA would certainly object." She shook her head. "We all have our natural sympathies. I should have known yours would make trouble."

He was alone again. Staring at the tub of dirt, empty now of honeysuckle, though the window was still open and surely the vine would invade again. Staring at the carpet, the veedo, the requisition still on the computer screen. Feeling sorry for himself. He had blown it. Disgraced himself. Meched himself out of his job. Yet he did not feel that he had done the wrong thing.

What now? he asked himself. And then he realized. Breger had said nothing about canceling the tickets. She could have. Renny and Donna Rose would still be in the airport, waiting to board their spaceplane. So she must be going to let him get away with it. She too had her natural sympathies, and if she couldn't bring herself to act on them, she could let him. PETA's lawsuit would be moot, for Renny would be safely out of reach. So, for that matter, would be Donna Rose, though Breger had hardly reacted when he had explained who the bot was. And all the blame was his. He guessed that she would simply throw him to the wolves. A scapegoat. Scapepig. He shouldn't feel surprised, though he did.

But if she hadn't canceled the tickets . . . He turned to his bioform computer, tapped the sensitive spots on the specialized leaf that served as the keyboard, and . . . The tickets were still good. Donna Rose was still on the passenger roster, Renny still listed among the cargo. And there were empty seats on the spaceplane.

The cab was a Yellow Hopper, a gengineered version of a grasshopper. It had never succeeded as a civilian vehicle because, even though the city's streets were maintained far better than they had been in the Machine Age, it jounced constantly, as if the wheels it didn't have were slamming in and out of potholes. Frederick gritted his teeth against the rattling gait, clung to the strap that hung from the wall of the passenger compartment, and watched the streets. Honey-bums peeked from their sheltering vines. Blue-clad Engineers stared insolently at bioform vehicles and modified humans and bots. A mother stood by, smiling, a small dog straining at a leash, while her child used a small metal shovel to pick up a lump of dog excrement and hurl it at a Mack.

Frederick shuddered. He had done the right thing. This city, this country, this world was no place for a sensitive, intelligent being, genimal or bot or, indeed, even human. He had done it again when, before leaving his office for what might well be the last time, he had used his computer to spend most of his savings on a third, round-trip ticket on the afternoon spaceplane to orbit.

The Hopper stopped at the door to his apartment building. "Wait," he told the driver. Then he let himself in and packed a small bag. After a moment's hesitation, he removed from the wall three holos, one of his late mate, Porculata, the living bagpipe, one of their children, and one of his old friend, Tom Cross, and his wife, Muffy. He tucked them into the center of the bag. Then he carefully watered his two house plants, a traditional coleus and a goldfish bush, even though he thought it might well be a futile gesture—he expected to return, but he had no idea whether it would be in hours, days, or weeks, by which time the plants would be withered sticks and dust.

"The airport."

The cabby, though he wore the colorful headwrap of some Southeast Asian tribesman, was clearly Caucasian. For a moment, Frederick wondered whether he had been adopted by the descendants of immigrants, his ancestors included Asians, or emigrants to Asia, or he just thought the headdress handsome. But he did not say anything after giving his simple instruction, and the cabby said nothing in return. The Hopper lurched through the city streets toward the greenways that led toward the suburbs and the airport, and Frederick stared glumly out the vehicle's window.

Frederick scowled as a trio of Roadrunners sped past the cab, honking, their red-clad riders bent low over their necks. When he had been a garbage disposal, when Tom had been a child, long before he had learned what pain meant, there had still been a few internal combustion automobiles and trucks on the roads, antiques, status symbols. Now they remained in storage, in museums, in the garages of collectors, emerging only for parades and similar special occasions. Motorcycles had remained in use the longest, for they had appealed to the Engineers despite the high cost of their fuel and the difficulty of finding parts except by cannibalizing other machines. They had succumbed within just the last few years. Now the Engineers used bicycles or took the Bernies.

He peered at the sky. To one side, a column of smoke marked a fire. He wondered if the Engineers had torched a house. Ahead, a web of contrails radiated from the airport. Jet-liners—Alitalia Cardinals, American Eagles, China Air Juncos, each identifiable by coloring or wing configuration—circled, waiting for their turns to land. Outlying hangars began to show beside the road, and he could see jets on the ground, with workers cleaning and restocking the passenger or cargo pods strapped to their backs and mechanics working over the engines strapped to the roots of their tails. The engines were essential because the great birds could never fly under muscle power alone. The advantage of gengineering was that it made the jets largely self-manufacturing, though they needed skeletal reinforcements, and if their engines failed, the muscles could provide at least some emergency control.

A distant roar and an arrow-straight contrail, growing louder, closer, faster than any gengineered jetliner could possibly manage, even with strap-on assistance, marked the arrival of a spaceplane from orbit. "There," said Frederick. "The Yonder terminal."

It was commonplace to find Engineers picketing the air-line terminals with their "MACHINES NOT GENES" signs. Frederick had not expected to find them also protesting at the gateway to space, holding signs that said "UNFAIR" and "BRING THE MACHINES HOME." Here if anywhere the

Machine Age still lived in all its most glorious aspects. Rockets, spaceplanes, satellites, habitats, Moonbases. All were as mechanical as could be, as dependent on machines, as rejecting of bioforms as any Engineer could wish.

Nor had he expected to see an Engineer bent over a sheet of cardboard flattened on the sidewalk. He was carefully painting a new sign. A finished version leaned against a pillar nearby. It read, "KEEP SPACE CLEAN. NO BOTS." Frederick told himself that Donna Rose must have been noticed.

The Engineers, he thought, did not appreciate how much of the world around them was still based on mechanism. There were still electronic computers, engines for Bioblimps and jets, strap-on passenger and cargo pods, and a thousand other things. The bioforms had been developed to fill all the roles they could, to replace mechanical devices wherever that was possible and thus to ease the strain on energy and mineral resources. One result had been that in many respects, mechanical technology had stagnated. Innovation had followed the bioforms and left spaceplanes and their kin much as they had been a century before.

Yet bioforms could not do everything; space technology was simply the most blatant testimonial to that fact. Certainly bioforms were not suited to the harsh environment of space, airless, subject to extremes of heat and cold and solar radiation. Frederick did not think the pattern would ever change, nor would it need to, for the space environment, though harsh, held all the resources a mechanical technology needed or could use. It also held plenty of room for mechanical innovations.

Yet that only taunted the Engineers, as if they were children above whose heads someone dangled candy. The Machine Age wasn't dead, but it was definitely eclipsed by the dominant technology of gengineering. The machines remained gloriously strong only where they were far out of the Engineers' reach, in space. And they would remain out of reach as long as the Engineers continued to echo the religious fundamentalists of another age who had refused to accept the discoveries of science. Their attitudes were such that no space-related operation would hire them. Their lack of tolerance for the new disqualified them for the very world they craved.

The woman at the ticket counter wore a jet black coverall with silver piping and a golden sunburst above her left breast. When he handed her his National Identification Card, she

slipped it into the slot of an electronic card-drive much like
that of the bioform floppy reader in his office computer. The
NIDC, or niddic, carried embedded in its magnetic surface all
the data it needed to serve as both a passport and a checkbook;
bills remained in use only for smaller purchases and bribes
such as he had had to offer Donna Rose's foreman.

When the ticket clerk eyed him carefully, he knew that she
was comparing his face with the picture the niddic had thrown
onto the screen of her terminal. When she placed a form on the
pressure-sensitive surface of the counter and said, "Sign here,"
he knew her computer was comparing his signature with that
recorded in the niddic.

He accepted his ticket and checked his bag. "Gate Seventeen," the clerk said. "It takes off in twenty minutes."

The Yonder terminal jutted farther from the main building
than any other, and Gate Seventeen was at its far end. He
walked, following the corridor through weapon scanners and
bomb sniffers and past plate glass windows that offered views
of feathered jetliners being fueled from truck trailers filled with
meat gengineered to grow on sewage, of litterbugs cleaning up
the jets' waste deposits, of luggage carts drawn by small Macks
to and from the jets' cargo compartments. Only when he was
passing Gate Twelve did he glimpse the spaceplane that was
his destination, its needlelike prow stabbing the sky above the
runway. As he drew closer, he could see more of its snow-
white ceramic-coated metal hull, gleaming in the sun, long
enough and high enough to dwarf any of the flying genimals
he had passed already.

A single black-clad attendant stood by the door to the spaceplane's boarding ramp, glancing at his watch. Beyond him,
Frederick could see a single pair of legs climbing toward the
plane's entrance hatch. "You're the last," said the attendant.
"Just in time."

As soon as Frederick entered the surprisingly small passenger cabin—most of the spaceplane's bulk was devoted to fuel
tanks—he spotted Donna Rose's distinctive yellow blossoms.
The sight of an empty seat beside her tempted him to smile, but
when he realized that the seats in front of and behind her were
also empty, he scowled instead. The plane was by no means
full, but still, there were no other clusters of empty seats as
large. He hoped that most of the passengers were grounders
on business trips; he expected more tolerance of habitat and

station residents. Under his breath, he muttered, "Bigots!"

He slipped into the seat beside the bot just as, behind him, the hatch chunked closed and, ahead of him, the "Fasten Seat Belts" signs above all the seats came on.

"Mr. Suida!" she said. The tips of the long leaves that sheathed her chest drew away from her skin for just a moment.

"Frederick," he answered. "Call me that, please. Or even Freddy."

"But . . ."

"They caught me," he explained. "The boss got pissed when she found out what I'd done. And then she kicked me out, at least temporarily. So here I am."

"I'm glad," she said. "I mean . . ." She laughed awkwardly and looked away. "Not that you're fired, Frederick. That you're . . ."

"Here?" Frederick allowed himself a small smile, the first in longer than he wished to remember that had not been a purely mechanical social gesture, not that there had been many even of those. "So I am. That's what I said. I've always wanted to visit a station."

The spaceplane's engines rumbled, and the great vehicle began to move away from the terminal. In the reflections on the terminal's vast windows, Frederick got his first glimpse of the plane's narrow, swept-back wings.

She was looking at him once more. "I was confused," she said. "It took forever to find the terminal. I've never been here before."

"But you made it," he said. "That's what counts." He hesitated, hoping that she would not take his next words as insulting her competence. "Where's Renny?"

"He's okay," she said. "They said they'd put his carrier in the warm hold." Now it was her turn to hesitate. "I'm glad you're here," she finally added. "I was lonely."

"And so am I." The spaceplane swung into position at the end of its assigned runway, the engine roar grew so loud that speech was impossible, and thrust pressed them into the backs of their seats as they began to move. Donna Rose clutched the arm of the seatrest between them with one hand. He laid his own hand over hers, yawned, and closed his eyes.

A spaceplane was a hybrid vehicle. It began its journey from the ground as if it were an ordinary jet plane, burning fuel with air. As it gained speed and altitude, it became a ramjet, forcing air down a funnel throat, compressing it to maintain the flow of oxygen needed to burn the fuel. As the speed became too great and the air too thin for any ramjet to function, the plane's carefully shaped underside came into play, channeling and compressing air into a channel where a spray of fuel could keep the thrust building. Only when the spaceplane had reached such a high altitude that there was too little air to exploit at all did it begin to function as a rocket.

The advantages of the multimode propulsion system were two: First, unlike a pure rocket, the spaceplane needed to carry relatively little liquid oxygen with which to burn the fuel it used within the atmosphere; it could therefore carry a heavier payload to orbit. Second, the thrust never became oppressive; the passengers were pressed into their seats with only a little more force than they might have experienced in a rapidly climbing jet.

The changes in the spaceplane's mode of action revealed themselves in changes in the notes the engines sang. When it was a jet, the note was low, bass. As a ramjet, it sang higher, tenor, the note vibrating through the plane's very frame as exterior sound was left behind the sound barrier. As a scramjet, the note was highest of all, a screaming operatic soprano. As a rocket, it dropped back to a bass that vibrated in the passengers' bones, and shortly after that, it quit entirely. The spaceplane had achieved orbit. Now it could coast, adjusting its course if necessary with only small bursts of rocketry until it approached the long cylinder of Nexus Station. There any passengers going beyond to other destinations would have to change to local spacecraft.

"Mech," said Frederick. He was holding one hand over his mouth as if . . .

"Do you need this?" Donna Rose reached into the pocket on the seatback in front of her and offered him a bluntly labeled "Barf Bag."

He shook his head. "I can control it. I think." He accepted the bag, laid it in his lap, and swallowed. "Give me a minute. Never been in zero gee before."

"It doesn't bother me," said Donna Rose.

He looked at her skeptically. She seemed to be trying very hard not to smile at his discomfort, and though he knew that such smiles were more of relief than of amusement, he grew irritated. He made a growling noise.

"In fact," she said, "it feels nice, like when I let my roots down and spread my leaves and soak up sun. Like floating."

"We *are* floating," said Frederick. He was used to feeling the pressure of his seat against his butt. Now there was nothing, not even the opposite pressure of his seatbelt on his stomach, the vestibular apparatus in his middle ear was stubbornly insisting that he was falling, his stomach was floating, twisting, turning, fluid was churning, sloshing, lapping at the base of his esophagus, his stomach muscles were clenching, now slowly, now faster, his mouth began to water, and . . .

He got it all in the bag.

"There's a pill," said Donna Rose, pointing, and he saw it in a blister fastened to the base of the bag. He extracted it, swallowed it dry, closed his eyes, leaned back in his seat, and clutched the armrests, forcing himself into the cushions as if he could by sheer will supply the missing force of gravity. Within moments he could feel the pill begin to work.

Thrusters made soft thudding noises. The spaceplane lurched, slowing for its approach to the Nexus dock. There was a clank of metal latches, a hiss and ear-pop of equalizing pressures, and the plane's hatch opened once more. Following the other passengers, Frederick and Donna Rose pulled themselves from seatback to seatback, propelling themselves into the station's receiving hall where their attention was seized by a dozen corridor mouths so ringed by signs that no one, no matter which way their feet were pointing, could fail to read them. They did not notice the pair of black-clad attendants waiting at the entrance until one said, "Where you going?"

"Probe Station," answered Frederick, and four hands seized and hurled him toward a corridor to the left. Two more attendants halted his flight, said, "Shuttle to the right," and turned away to catch Donna Rose.

The luggage must have traveled by some other route, for when they reached the shuttle's berth, marked by a single circular opening in the wall and beyond that what was clearly the interior of a small spacecraft, Frederick's bag was waiting for them. So too was a large plastic crate with a metal grill on one end. "Renny?" said Frederick.

"I wondered if you'd make it, Freddy," said the German shepherd. He sounded as if the trip had had no more effect on him than it had had on Donna Rose.

A woman dressed in a pale green coverall with white chevrons down the sleeves emerged from the shuttle's hatch. Her auburn hair was cropped short. So were her legs, which stopped at mid-thigh. If they had been intact, she would have been no more than a meter and a half tall. "What's this?" she said. "It talks?"

"Yes." Donna Rose nodded. "We're taking him—"

"Then what's he doing in that box?" She promptly unsnapped the catches that held the crate's grill in place, and Renny pushed himself into view, his tail wagging furiously.

Frederick immediately noticed that though Renny still wore his collar, the radio tracking device PETA had convinced the court to order was gone. Donna Rose caught the question in his glance at her and said, "I left it in a waste can at the airport."

"Nice dog," said the woman in green. "I hear the boss did him himself."

As the German shepherd drifted across the corridor, he thrust his forelimbs straight out and curled his tail over his back as if he wanted to stretch, but the lack of gravity made the effort futile. The woman grabbed a handhold and pressed Renny toward the nearest wall.

When his feet touched, Renny pushed, bowing his back until the joints popped. "Ahh," he said. "Thanks. I like you."

Donna Rose laughed, while Frederick answered the woman's own comment. "Years ago," he said. "But they don't want him down there." Silently, he wondered at the woman's lack of legs when the gengineers could easily stimulate their regrowth. Then he realized that the ticket clerk on Earth and the attendants who had helped him and Donna Rose on their way through Nexus Station had shown no signs of genetic modifications. Yet he had seen no signs of prejudice other than the zone of empty seats around the bot. Perhaps, he thought, it was simply that these people thought more in terms of controlling their environment, of metal and machines and externals, than of controlling their internal flesh.

"Of course not." The woman turned away, pulling herself back into the shuttle with one arm, keeping the other curled around Renny's chest. The lack of legs offered no handicap in zero gee. Over her shoulder, she said, "I'm Lois." She gestured toward her thighs. "An accident. Nothing to do with my piloting. And are you coming? There's no one else."

As they entered the small spacecraft, Frederick asked, "How'd you know about Renny?"

"It's a small station," Lois said. "Most secrets we don't even try to keep, except from outsiders. I heard from the com tech who monitored your call."

The shuttle was little more than a small cylinder whose stained and padded walls were equipped with straps for fastening passengers and cargo into place. Toward one end was a large veedo screen that let the pilot see in any direction she chose; beside it was a small porthole. Set in front of the screen was a padded bucket seat whose broad arms were covered with pressure and slide switches, the spacecraft's controls.

"Strap down," said Lois. "It can get a little bumpy." Hardly was she in her own seat before she showed them what she meant. The shuttle's thrusters separated the craft from Nexus Station gently enough, but then the engine fired and the sudden acceleration was enough to stagger anyone who wasn't anchored.

The shuttle was not a fast ship. The trip to lunar orbit and Probe Station took most of the next day, for the distance was far greater than that between Earth's surface and Nexus Station. Frederick and Renny passed part of the time napping, while Donna Rose asked the pilot to position the shuttle so that full sunlight shone in the small porthole and then spent the hours basking and photosynthesizing. "I have never," she said, "felt such *thick* sunlight. It's delicious."

When the station finally came into view, it proved to be a slowly rotating cylinder whose ends had been stepped in toward the center. It looked like a pair of tin cans, one short and fat, the other longer, thinner, tucked inside the first so its ends protruded. Docking ports and communications antennae were visible on the ends. A radio telescope several kilometers in diameter, its supporting framework seeming impossibly delicate to eyes accustomed to gravity, hung off to one side, as did several smaller cylindrical stations. When Frederick asked what the latter were, their pilot said, "Research labs. We don't do the messy stuff in the living room."

A moment later, she said, "Brace yourselves. The docking collar's an elastic sleeve, and . . ." There was a click as the

shuttle's hatch met the docking port, the sound of sliding
metal, and the snap of closing latches. Then the shuttle began
to turn as the docking collar confronted and conquered the
ship's inertia.

Alvar Hannoken was waiting for them inside the station, his
rugged face beaming as he spotted the dog he had gengineered.
"Renny!" he cried.

The German shepherd barked his own greeting, and Frederick
said, "Dr. Hannoken." He looked at the other curiously.
Gengineers had a reputation for modifying themselves in
strange ways that only later showed up in the populace, and
there was something he could not quite identify about the man's
body. Certainly, the legs of his coverall were looser than they
were on most people, but . . .

"Frederick. I didn't expect to see you too. But you're
welcome, of course." When he turned toward Donna Rose,
Frederick introduced the bot. "She's a refugee," he said.

Hannoken's face sobered instantly. "We get the news. I'm
sure we can find a place. And besides, we can always use the
oxygen. If more bots follow the drinking gourd up here . . ."

"Actually, sir, I use more oxygen than I make."

"That's all right. Don't worry about it." He turned to Renny,
smiling again. "And you, sir, are the first dog I've ever seen
with a portable tree. Come on, now. Let's get you some
weight."

"I'd like that," said Frederick, and in a moment the three
new arrivals were following Hannoken and Lois down a corridor, pulling themselves along with handholds fastened to the
walls. They had not gone far before Frederick realized what
was peculiar about the station director's body: His coverall
knees were creased, not smooth. His legs bent backward.
In fact, the "knees" were really ankles; true knees made the
fabric bulge near the hips. Hannoken had redesigned his legs to
resemble those of a goat. The thighs were short and powerful,
the feet elongated. There were no hooves, but the man wore
black stockings as if to mimic their appearance and he would
clearly walk upon his toes when they reached those parts of
the station where its rotation provided a centrifugal substitute
for gravity. Frederick supposed that Hannoken's modification
might actually offer some advantage in low or zero gee, where
so much movement was by jumping.

Chapter
Eight

Testimony from a hearing of
The Senate Committee on Agricultural Policy
Transcribed from GNN (Government NewsNet)
for the *Federal Register*.

The Honorable Cecil D. Trench (DemSoc-NC), Committee Chair: Gentlemen and ladies, agricultural subsidies have been a tradition in this fine nation of ours for the last century and a half.

In my own state of North Carolina, the tobacco crop was supported in that way for many years. In the Midwest, subsidies have seen thousands of corn and wheat and hog farmers through years of drought and flood and foreign dumping.

Dairy farmers saw difficult times when new technologies such as bovine growth hormone came along. That was a product of the earliest of the genetic engineers. Later the udder tree came on the market. Both of these developments increased productivity enormously. So enormously in fact that the price of milk seemed bound to decline to virtually nothing. The farmers would have starved and gone bankrupt. The dairy industry would have collapsed entirely. And then the nation's children would have been without their necessary and essential nutrition and the nation itself would have gone the malnourished and therefore brain-damaged way of Ethiopia and Bangladesh and Brazil. All that, and more, except for the price supports that kept the price of milk high and kept the dairy industry in business.

But now, ladies and gentlemen, some people are claiming that this noble tradition is no longer necessary. They say we can do away with crop subsidies. They say that the forces of our traditional free market system should be given free rein. They say that if farmers go out of business, that is only a sign of their superfluity. The gengineers, they say, will provide. For years, in fact, new crops have been in the fields. Some have been mere modifications of traditional crops, ones that make their own fertilizer and pesticide. Others have been new kinds of plants—house plants with edible fruit or flowers, pie plants, and more. Still others have been strange hybrids of plant and animal—hamberries, potsters, sausage bushes, the udder trees, more. Yields have reached new heights, and the price of food has reached lower levels than any human being now alive can remember.

Yet—Yet!—some say this very boon for the consumer is a curse for the farmer who cannot get enough money for his unprecedented bumper crops to pay his mortgage or his taxes or even his seed bill. Some say the subsidies are more essential than ever before.

And some say the new crops are more profitable than ever were any of their predecessors. Some say those farmers who have embraced the new technology are banking more money than ever before, even as those who turn their backs on the fruits of gengineering go wailing to the wall.

That is what we are here today to discuss: Do agricultural subsidies remain a desirable way for our government to spend its tax revenues? And if so, who should get those subsidies?

Catherine Dubuque-Kinshasa, Ph.D., Deputy Assistant Secretary for Agricultural Demographics, Department of Agriculture: Senator Trench, gentlemen, ladies. Yes, there are people who favor continuing our system of agricultural subsidies. They argue that those farmers who accept the benefits of gengineering monopolize all the money to be made in farming, leaving only scraps for the few farmers who prefer more traditional crops and methods and thereby forcing the latter to abandon their farms and find other lines of work.

These people are, of course, absolutely correct. Gengineered agriculture is the dominant form of agriculture in this country today. It is dominant because it is more productive, more cost-effective, and more environmentally benign. If it forces traditional farmers out of farming, that is no tragedy. Traditional farming depletes the fertility of the soil. Constant plowing leads to erosion. The use of pesticides and fertilizers leads to water pollution and air pollution. Traditional agriculture demands heavy use of scarce energy and material resources. And its costs are a burden on the consumer, the taxpayer, and the government.

Gengineered agriculture needs very little in the way of fertilizer and pesticides and, last but not least, very little labor. Every crop that once had to be planted anew every year can now be produced on trees and shrubs that continue to bear for decades. Every crop that once required vast farms far from the consumer can now be grown in a family's yard.

We should be delighted that the traditional farmer is virtually extinct. With him has gone any need for subsidies. Those modern farmers that we still need are profitable enough not to need them. As for the traditional farmers—soon, there will be none left to demand or receive the subsidies.

Oscar Pembroke, farmer, Upton, VT: Senator Trench, I'm here to tell you! Old-style farming is *not* extinct. No way is it extinct!

(Waves thick paperbound book in air.) This book, this one right here in my hand, it's *The Guide to Organic and Mechanical Farming.* It's a manual on how to make that kind of farming work! It used to be that mechanical farming, all that sod-busting and chemical fertilizing and pesticiding, wrecked the soil, yeah. But if you plow and plant and use *organic* techniques, if you use lots of manure and predator bugs to eat the pests, it's *good* for the soil. It *builds* the soil!

The Honorable Earl P. Mitchum (LabRep-ME), committee member: Isn't that still a form of biological engineering?

Mr. Pembroke: But it ain't *genetic* engineering. Gengineering is the devil's way. It's not the way God meant for us to raise our food. There's no denying that it's good to the soil, and it's productive, right enough, but it's the path to hell. It puts farmers out of work. And because it means there's not so many farms anymore, it means kids can't go see where their food comes from. It puts people further and further from their roots, from the soil. Senator Trench, we need those subsidies!

Dr. Dubuque-Kinshasa: I should think gengineering would put people in *closer* touch with their roots. After all, they don't have to visit farms when they have pie plants and sausage bushes growing in the living room and two-meter green beans or squash blossoms hanging on their house plants.

Arnold Rifkin, M.D., Ph.D., M.B.A., President, Foundation for Economic Trends: The health of the American farmer is not really the point. Genetic engineering is the most insidious form of pollution—of the human genome, of the biosphere—that human beings have ever had the temerity to devise. The foundation I have the honor to represent here today has been fighting this genetic pollution ever since the first gene was spliced. I hope that you will seize the opportunity before you today to ban the technology, the gengineers, and all their products. There are more environmentally benign ways to ensure human survival!

Senator Trench: Dr. Rifkin, our concern here today is agricultural policy, not the desirability of genetic engineering.

Harriet McKenzie, Ph.D., Professor of Agricultural Science, University of Kansas: Senator Trench, ladies, gentlemen. I must say that I agree with Mr. Pembroke, although for different reasons. The subsidies remain at least useful and perhaps even essential because they keep alive a form of agriculture that may be all that stands between us and catastrophe.

We have not analyzed these new gengineered crops thoroughly enough at all! The Bioform Regulatory Administration is far too ready to grant permits and licenses. Worse yet, many products of gengineering are released without any pretense of regulation. And we have no idea what their long-term effects on the environment—

and on us!—may turn out to be. In fact, there is no
reason to think that the honeysuckle that has displaced
the infamous kudzu and so vastly extended its range may
not be the least of the curses hidden in the Pandora's box
of gengineering!

Senator Trench, continuing the subsidies gives our
society an insurance policy. I do not say that gengineering is bound to turn sour. But it may. And if it does,
we will need those who are skilled in the traditional
modes of survival.

In addition to the subsidies, I would like to see a firm
moratorium on any further gengineering for agriculture.
This would give us a chance to study carefully and
thoroughly what we have done already. Only when we
know what the long-term effects of all these new organisms
may be should we permit any more gengineering. When
that time comes, of course, we should analyze each new
proposal to gengineer a plant or animal just as carefully
and thoroughly. Only in this way may we hope to avoid
disaster.

Andrew Gilman, M.D., Ph.D., M.B.A., Director, Research
and Development, Neoform Laboratories: Senator Trench,
gentlemen, ladies. Technology is not something whose
undesirable side-effects can be foreseen except in the
most general of ways. For instance, it was fairly easy,
when gengineering was new, to predict that unscrupulous
gengineers would use it to make drugs available in
new ways. I'm thinking of "hedonic parasites," and
of the cocaine nettles and heroin-producing jellyfish
that came later, and of the snakes with drugs in their
venom.

If we go back to the dawn of the age of automobiles,
we can see a parallel example in the way people were
predicting the mechanization of warfare. People were
also complaining, even then, of the machines' stink, and
a prediction of air pollution problems was an entirely
logical extrapolation.

But no one predicted traffic jams, or suburbs, or shopping
malls. Similarly, the first gengineers and their regulators
could not have foreseen the bots and their domination of
the menial labor market. Once that had been managed,

however, it would have been no great trick to predict the resentment of human low-level laborers and the resulting protests.

I have some sympathy for Dr. McKenzie's go-slow attitude. Unfortunately, that attitude is grossly unrealistic. If we wish not only to survive but to thrive in the future, we have to take risks. We cannot embrace the no-risk ideology of the Engineers and their nostalgic sympathizers. That is a recipe for stagnation and decline.

And the fact is that orgamech farming, with subsidies or without, simply cannot support the world in the style to which it has become accustomed. It requires too much fertile land, when past generations have permitted the loss of topsoil to erosion, covered the land with pavements and buildings, and emptied the underground aquifers of the water necessary for irrigation. And speaking of irrigation—that all by itself has ruined millions of hectares of land by the build-up of toxic salts in the soil.

The only way the orgamechers could do the job would be if we reduced world population to a fraction of present levels. As things stand, there are just too many of us on the planet. We need too much food and clothing and housing. And the resources needed to maintain simultaneously both a mechanical agriculture and a mechanical civilization do not exist any longer. We do not have enough liquid fuels or metals for both tractors and jet engines, not to mention spacecraft.

The Engineers and their fellow travelers yearn for the "Good Old Days" of the Machine Age, when there was plenty for all. They forget that that "plenty" existed only in the industrialized countries of the world. Everywhere else, for the vast majority of humanity, poverty and misery were the norm. Today, gengineering is raising the standard of living for all.

If we turn our backs on gengineering, we will therefore have a world poor in resources, potential, and human happiness. It will be a world doomed to a "Good Old Days" of subsistence farming, of the inevitable crash of the world population to a level supportable by our ruined soils, of mass starvation and death.

Only far too late will we realize that it was the gengineers who made possible the continuance of civilization past the time when the resources needed for mechanical civilization became scarce. Those resources will still exist, but not in great quantities. There will remain, as now, just enough to fool reactionary ideologues into believing that they can retreat into the past successfully.

We can see the reactionaries trying to begin that retreat now. They are trying to ban, destroy, or hamstring all possible alternatives—such as gengineering—to their vision of the way the world ought to be. They ignore the way the world *is*. Tragically, if they have their way, they will have no destiny except disaster.

I hope the committee will see the path of wisdom and recommend that Congress end all agricultural subsidies. They are no longer necessary. They are even dangerous, for they encourage the reluctant to continue in their refusal to accept reality, the future, and gengineering, with all its present benefits and future promise.

Senator Trench: I see that we're out of time for today. We will reconvene next week.

Thank you all.

PART 2

Chapter
Nine

THE ROOM WAS about twice as long as the shelflike bunk in one end and not much wider. The bunk, covered by an air-filled mattress, folded out of the wall. When down, it left only a narrow aisle between its edge and the walls. The aisle was so narrow that Frederick Suida found it difficult to walk beside the bed. Alvar Hannoken had much less trouble. His goatish legs and tip-toe gait were better fitted for tight spaces.

The room's brushed-aluminum walls were studded with the doors of small cupboards and the fronts of drawers, each one painted a different color. There were many more such storage spaces than Frederick had needed for the few possessions he had brought with him.

A thin curtain divided the room a little past the foot of the bed, setting off a space onto which opened a door. Above the door was mounted a small communicator grille. At the far end was a tiny closet of a bathroom much like those that had once graced the small trailers that vacationing families had dragged behind their automobiles: Even without the toilet seat—most of the station's quarters had not been designed for use in zero gee—there was barely room in it for Frederick to stand up and turn around.

"I'll have to sit to shower," said Frederick. "I'd expected . . ."

The station director shrugged with almost Gallic eloquence. "Fresh water," he said, "is cheap in space. Space isn't."

"What's so cheap about water?" Renny cocked his head curiously. "Don't you have to haul it up here?"

"But only once," said Hannoken. "After that, we've got all the sun we need to distill it from any wastes we make. Even bodies. We make compost out of the residue."

"Then you must grow plants," said Donna Rose.

"Of course," he said. "For oxygen and food." He looked at her with much the appraising eye some men turned upon attractive women. "And psychic ease," he added.

"And the space?" asked Frederick.

"It's expensive because the larger a station is, the more it leaks and the more often it gets hit by flying rocks. The construction materials are cheap enough. They're from the Moon. Our air is cheap too, and the energy to heat and cool the station. But every seam is a risk."

The bedless portion of the room held more cupboards and drawers, a fold-down desk, and several fold-out seats. There was also a porthole before which a work crew had set a metal trough half full of compost diverted from the station's gardens. The trough itself might once have been a piece of rocket casing. The porthole, of course, did not look directly out on space. It was the room's floor that, as the station's hull, faced vacuum; mirrors linked the porthole and its view, which changed constantly as the station rotated. Periodically, light flashed blinding bright despite the filters that betrayed their presence in sudden dimming.

Renny lay on the thin carpet, his head on his paws, staring at Hannoken, who was standing in the room's doorway, one hand on the frame, the other scratching at his scalp. The way the thick, grey hair resisted his fingers suggested the use of a stiffening agent. Hannoken was saying, "It's yours while you're here. It's a little roomier than most, but our people have desks in their offices. They usually need only enough room for a bed."

"I don't need that much," said Donna Rose. Stubby legs had been welded to the trough's rounded bottom to keep it from rocking, but still she stepped carefully onto the surface of the rich soil. Her roots unfurled and sank into the dirt. She uncoiled her leaves and spread them unselfconsciously to the light coming from the overheads and through the porthole.

Frederick smiled when he realized that Hannoken was trying to pretend he did not notice the femininity of her form. Yet the Station Director's sidelong glances were hardly subtle.

Donna Rose sighed contentedly. "Nice," she said. "There wasn't even sand on the way."

"I'm okay too," said Renny. "A patch of floor, a dish of water, a bone. That's all I need."

Hannoken seemed startled for a moment. "I'd take you into my own room, but it's really too small. If you want one of your own . . ."

"Uh-uh." The German shepherd's tail thumped the floor. "I'm used to Freddy now."

Hannoken looked faintly hurt as he handed Frederick an electronic keycard. He was, after all, the dog's "father" in as real a sense as ever actual parenthood could provide. He had made Renny what he was, given him his intelligence, and Frederick thought he could not help but feel that the dog owed him some loyalty. And if anyone suggested that his unwillingness to come to Earth to help Renny had amounted to abandonment, had forfeited the loyalty he wished to see, he would have seemed surprised.

"You can lock up if you wish. Some do." Hannoken dismissed his hurt and Renny's lack of loyalty with a blithe wave of one hand. "I don't bother. And now, let's get you to the dining area. You can have a bite, meet a few people."

Donna Rose reluctantly began to extricate herself from her trough. Renny sighed and got to his feet. Frederick nodded, and Hannoken opened the room's door to reveal the unbroken pastels of the corridor walls. The dining hall and many of the station's offices, he said, were near the station's rim, where near-Earth-normal gees kept food on plates and papers on desks. The communications and control center was at one end of the station, near the axis, where the lack of gees minimized fatigue and the equipment could be near the antennae.

He paused where two open doors faced each other across the corridor. The rooms beyond both held tables, comfortable-looking chairs, computer screens and keyboards; one held as well a pool table and a rack of cues. "The game room," said Hannoken, gesturing. "We have over three hundred people here. It gets used a lot." He pointed at the other door. "So does the library." No one was in sight in either room at the moment, although creaks and clicks suggested that if they were to enter and turn a corner or go around a rack of shelves, they would find . . .

The sounds of moving air and distant people, of quiet machineries and flexing metal, kept them company as they moved. They passed doorways and cross-corridors that Hannoken said led to laboratories, workshops, storerooms, and maintenance areas. They nodded at those members of the Station's complement they happened to see at work or in the corridor. They passed by the elevators that offered access to the smaller interior decks. What equipment was visible, much as Frederick had expected, was almost all mechanical. There were very few bioform devices in sight.

"We can't have them," said Hannoken. "If we get hit by something—and that's always a possibility—a mechanical or electronic gadget will keep right on working. At worst, it will work again as soon as we plug the hole, restore the power, and replace the air. A bioform would be dead. If we depended on bioforms, so would we. We have enough food and oxygen in storage to last us, if necessary, until new crops can grow."

The station's corridors had been arranged to strike the eye as level. Only those that paralleled the station's axis ran long and straight. Those that circled the axis, following the curve of the station's skin, jigged and jogged and bent, never offering a view so long as to reveal the skin-curve. The result was an illusion, a sense that one was in a building much like any building on Earth, even though, Frederick knew, here one could lose weight simply by riding an elevator closer to the station's axis.

The illusion shattered when they entered the dining hall. This room was so large that its floor, the inner surface of the station's hull, showed a disconcertingly visible curve, rising in the distance. The tables and chairs and people in it seemed, for just an instant, distorted as in a funhouse mirror. But the familiar odors of food and bodies, the sounds of voices and cutlery on china, the vision of long rows of snackbushes and conventional crop plants, of tomato, lettuce, onion, pepper, carrot, cabbage, and broccoli plants, of herbs and flowers—even a gengineered amaryllis or two with their facelike blossoms— all growing in knee-high planters stretched along the walls and extended through the room as dividers, all quickly restored the sense of the familiar.

"Go on," said Hannoken. "You can find your own way around here. We can talk some more later on. I've got to get back—" As if to underline his words, a soft chime issued from a communicator grill set in the wall beside the door to the dining hall, and then a feminine voice: "Doctor Hannoken?"

"On the way," he said, and he was gone.

Faces turned their way. Conversation and clatter halted. Someone said, "A bot!" There were scattered frowns, more smiles, a "Haven't seen one of them since I came up here," a "Visitors? Or refugees?" And a watchful silence, until Renny walked up to the nearest occupied table, stood on his hind legs to put his forepaws on the table edge, sniffed, and said, "How do we get something to eat around here?"

The table's occupants were an older man and two young women, his skin as dark as their hair, his hair a spring-coiled cap, tight and grizzled. One woman was a little taller than the other, whose Mediterranean heritage showed in larger bosom and darker, honeyed skin. All three were wearing patterned coveralls. When Frederick looked around the room, he realized that people here seemed to wear whatever they liked. There was no suggestion of station or job uniform other than the white labcoats worn by a few. Certainly there were no blue coveralls or gear emblems.

The women at the table Renny had addressed smiled at the dog. The man laughed and said, "I will be damned. Corlynn? Show them where the food is? And then bring them back here." Then he held out one hand, accepted the paw Renny offered in exchange, shook, and said, "I'm Walt Massaba. Security."

Frederick was sipping at a cup of tea and watching the room. The word had spread. More people had come into the dining hall while they were eating, and food did not seem to be more than an excuse. Hands held small snacks and beverages, yes, but the eyes kept converging on the table that held the security chief, his companions, and the station's newest visitors. The room was not silent, but softly abuzz with conversation and speculation.

If he had remembered how to smile, he might have. The eyes kept sliding past him to settle on Donna Rose and Renny. There were twitches as if people wished to come to them, introduce themselves, ask questions, but did not quite dare as long as they were with Massaba. The security chief was, after all, the station's voice of discipline and control, and while Frederick detected no hint of official repression, the station's people did show a definite reserve.

Frederick was telling Massaba about the antipathies that had prompted him to send Renny and Donna Rose to space, and Massaba was listening intently, when two men approached the table. Their manner was diffident, tentative, though both had the muscles of manual workers. One had a face plentifully adorned with scars, the pocks of ancient acne, the lines of fights, the broken blood vessels of too many drinking bouts. The other's face was almost childishly smooth. Side by side, they hovered, staring in turn at Donna Rose, Renny, and Frederick.

Walt Massaba's female companions, Corlynn and the shorter Tobe, pushed their coffee cups toward the center of the table and looked watchful. Frederick realized then that they were not just friends but members of the man's staff, security agents, keepers of the peace, protectors of the station. The thought that they presumably carried weapons somewhere on their persons relieved him.

Finally, the smooth-faced stranger spoke: "You gonna send 'em back where they come from, Walt? We got enough trouble with the mechin' plants, we don't need 'em walking around."

"Cool it, Chuck," said the scar-faced one.

"Right," said the security chief. "There's nothing wrong with bots. They're smart, and they're good workers. And if they make it up here, we'll take all we can manage."

The scar-faced man nodded. "You saw the news, Chuck," he said. " 'S not fair to kill 'em, is it?"

Chuck grunted and turned away, propelled by his friend's hand toward the door to the room. Massaba said, "We don't have too many like that up here."

"I'm surprised you have any," said Renny.

"Someone has to do the muscle work."

Frederick looked at Donna Rose. "And he's afraid the bots would push him aside."

"As long as there's work to do, he'll stay busy. We've never believed in unemployment. We can't afford to feed deadwood." Massaba made a face as if to say that, of course, there were exceptions. "It's only when someone can't work. An injury, say. If he's permanently disabled, we send him down again. We'd do the same if anyone refused to work."

"Then I'd better find something to do," said Donna Rose. "But not cleaning, not just muscle work. I've done that, and we do have brains. You'd be surprised how well we're taught."

Walt Massaba showed his teeth in a smile as he shook his head. "You have a while before we get huffy. And we may not. I think we're going to have to find a way to fit refugees into our world up here."

"Then tell Chuck," said Frederick. "Refugees are unemployed, and any unemployed who hate the thought of Earth . . ."

Renny snorted. "There shouldn't be any employment problem," he said. "You'll need to build new quarters, Q-ships . . ."

Massaba suddenly leaned forward, his eyes intent first on the gengineered German shepherd, then on Frederick and Donna Rose. His companions pushed their seats back and moved their hands off the table, nearer perhaps to whatever weapons they had. The room around them hushed as others registered the sudden tension. "What do you know about Q-ships?"

"Is it a secret?" asked Frederick. "Dr. Hannoken told us a little, just enough to justify shipping him"—he nodded toward the dog—"up as a test passenger. He also told us there's no real need for an animal test; you already have a human volunteer."

Massaba and the women relaxed. Hands returned to view.

"How does it work?" asked Donna Rose.

Walt Massaba simply shrugged. He did not know or he would not tell, no matter what his boss had already revealed.

Frederick had noticed that communicator grilles seemed to be everywhere. There was one in his quarters. They marked the corridor walls at regular intervals and were mounted by every doorway. In the dining hall, he could see them on both the walls and the ceiling. The idea seemed to be to have at least one always within hearing range of everyone on the station. Now the nearest chimed and the same voice that had summoned Hannoken said, "Chief Massaba? The director is ready to see the visitors again now."

Massaba nodded and looked at the shorter of his companions. "Tobe? Show them the way?"

The first thing that struck the eye in Director Alvar Hannoken's office was the broad picture window in the wall, the view of the distant radio telescope that did not change as the station rotated, and the steady flood of sunlight that struck the plant in the pot upon the floor. The plant was a severely trimmed kudzu vine, its stub-cut branches covered with rich green leaves and purple blossoms.

"Mirrors," Hannoken said when he noticed Donna Rose's stare. "Just like in your room."

"But it doesn't . . ." she said.

"There's a suntracker outside." He opened one hand to reveal a small, silvery implement that resembled a short, fat syringe. "Do you remember when I said I'd like to study your genetic structure?" When she nodded, he went on. "I meant it. I'd like a tissue sample, if . . ."

"Of course." She took a step in his direction. "What do you need?"

"Anything," he said, holding up the tool in his hand. "This will punch out a bit of skin and underlying tissue. A few thousand cells. Hardly noticeable."

Donna Rose held still while he applied the tool to her side. When he was done, she stepped closer to Frederick and asked, "Could I have a suntracker too? I need the light, just like . . ." She pointed one hand toward the kudzu.

For a long moment, Hannoken's eyes measured the distance between the bot and Frederick. He was clearly considering whether he had any chance of attracting Donna Rose and as clearly deciding that her own attraction lay elsewhere. When he finally nodded, Frederick let his attention move to the room's other features. A slablike desk occupied the side of the room across from the picture window. Its surface bore several slots that suggested the availability of thin screens for computer and com displays. There was also an inset keyboard and a slender stalk, a microphone that indicated the director's computer could be activated by voice alone and that it must therefore be a fairly powerful AI system. He wondered just how powerful it was. Could it, for instance, keep track of precisely where everyone was and use the nearest communicator to speak to one person alone?

The room was large enough to express the director's status. Its carpet was noticeably thicker than that in the dining hall. However, the walls, as elsewhere, were a patchwork of colored panels set in brushed aluminum. One panel, on the wall to the right of Hannoken's desk, was entirely obscured by a large flatscreen veedo. A few other panels bore photographs. There was one of a brick-and-glass building that might have been the research institute at which Hannoken had done his gengineering work. Another showed a puppy that might have been Renny. A third showed a woman's pale white head sitting on bare dirt. Behind it was a gravestone.

"*What* is that?" asked Frederick.

Hannoken laughed. "A bomb," he said. "One of our researchers developed a fungus. You put a spore in someone's mouth just before you buried them. It sprouted, developed a mass of tendrils—mycelium—all through the brain, and extracted the strongest memory, the last to go, the one that presumably was most basic to the dead person's personality or identity. Then it shaped itself to match that memory."

He turned toward the desk. "I still have one of the brochures we made up when we tried to market it. Here."

The picture on the brochure's cover was the same as that on the wall, with the addition of a woman, her face a sorrowful duplicate of the one on the ground, gazing at the grave. Across its top was the legend, "Give your loved ones the Last Word!"

"It didn't work," said Hannoken. "The 'Last Word' was hardly ever what the loved ones expected."

"But . . ." He took the brochure from Frederick's hands and tossed it onto his desk. "I understand you met Walt Massada."

"You set that up," said Renny.

A shrug. "I had to. He's not terribly officious, but he does insist on vetting all new arrivals."

"He seemed a bit alarmed that we'd heard of the Q-drive," said Frederick.

"Hmmph. We *are* trying to keep that quiet, but it can't last. The test flight is too close, and then . . ."

The director sighed. "We're looking at constant acceleration at one gee, or more. Your trip from Nexus Station would take only an hour or so. We'll have colonies on Mars, not just research bases, stations among the asteroids and looking down on Saturn's rings, and the furthest of them only days from Earth. Given more time for acceleration, we should even be able to come near light-speed."

"And that," said Frederick, "will put the stars within reach."

"We won't be able to go faster than light," said Hannoken. He waved one hand to dismiss that shortcoming of the Q-drive. "But close enough so that time dilation will make the trip seem short. No lifetimes on the way."

"Except back home," said Donna Rose.

Hannoken looked startled, as if he had never dreamed that a bot, an animated plant, could even begin to grasp the complexities of relativity. "That's right," he said. "If we were to go very far, there wouldn't be much point in coming home. We would be long forgotten."

"You sound like you intend to go along," said Renny.

"If I'm still here when the time comes. I wouldn't miss it."

"If you leave for good, though," said Donna Rose, "won't you need something bigger than a spaceship? Even something bigger than this station?"

Hannoken nodded and pointed toward one corner of his picture window. "There," he said. "Athena, magnify." His office computer system obeyed the order and the window revealed itself as much more than a mere window. A small frame popped into place around a tiny speck, and frame and speck enlarged until the speck was clearly the fat disk of a distant habitat. There was no indication of whether it was Hugin or Munin. "We'll need something more like that. And in fact we have our eyes on a certain asteroid. We've already named it *Gypsy*. There are over twenty thousand of us here in orbit, and it would hold us all with room to grow. If the Q-drive tests pan out, then we'll begin to make more solid plans. We'll have to hollow it out first."

"That will take a while," said Frederick.

"We have time."

Renny growled. "Not as much as you think."

"Hmmph," Hannoken snorted. "We haven't even tried the drive yet, except on drones. Maybe we *will* use you for the test pilot. We still don't know it won't scramble the passengers' brains or genes or anatomies." He paused. "Want to see the test ship?"

A little later, Frederick was fighting the urge to vomit while Donna Rose looked at him with an expression he could only take as amusement. *She* didn't get spacesick, whether they were free-falling within an enclosed spacecraft or, as they had just done, passing through the low-gee core of a rotating space station, riding a taxi that was little more than a tank of compressed air attached to a plastic bubble, and stepping aboard a spherical satellite station, much smaller than Probe Station itself. "We keep everything that might be hazardous at arm's length," Hannoken had explained as he used his caprine legs to propel himself to a suitable vantage point within a cavernous construction bay. He had halted his flight by grabbing a cable with one hand and swinging to a stop.

Donna Rose followed the director, one arm wrapped around Renny's middle. A moment later, Frederick won the struggle to control his stomach and joined them.

The cable to which their hands anchored them was one of many that formed a spiderwebby maze that secured a bundle of cylinders in the center of the bay. The half-dozen cylinders on the outside of the bundle were dome-capped tubes about ten meters long. Projecting from their middle was a somewhat longer cylinder whose bulging tip bore an access hatch and a row of three portholes. Painted beneath the ports was the ship's name, *Quoi*.

"Not fuel tanks," said Arlan Michaels. Director Hannoken had introduced the short, slender man as the head of the project, a physicist and engineer. Now he held to a nearby cable, facing them, holding himself carefully upright to their point of view, while he described the center of his life. Grease streaked his blond hair and emphasized the strong Oriental cast to his features. He shifted his grip on the cable from one hand to the other. "Reaction mass," he said now. "Powdered moon rock. The Q-drive vaporizes it to make a high-energy plasma. It's vastly more powerful than anything we've ever had before."

The ship was much smaller than anything designed to claw its way out of a gravity well, even one as shallow as the Moon's. Yet it was also larger than orbital transfer vehicles like the shuttle that had carried Frederick, Donna Rose, and Renny between Nexus and Probe Stations.

Michaels led them around the ship, pointing at detail after detail of its structure. "If it works the way we hope it will," he said, "this thing has the reaction mass to go to Mars and back in less than a week. It could even land there, a classic tail-down landing. A bigger model could even land on Earth."

"The drive's in the central cylinder?" asked Frederick. They had reached the swollen nose of the spacecraft.

"It takes up most of it," said Michaels. He pointed at what they could see through the portholes. "That's why the pilot has so little room."

Frederick had once visited the National Air and Space Museum in Washington, D.C. There he had seen a Mercury capsule that had carried one of the first men to leave Earth's atmosphere. The Q-ship gave its pilot very little more room to move about.

"It wouldn't be too tight for me," said Renny. His tail was wagging.

"But you're not going," said Frederick. "That was just a ruse."

"Here's the pilot now," said Alvar Hannoken. Ricocheting toward them, her hands shifting smoothly from cable to cable as she propelled and steered, was the shuttle pilot who had delivered Frederick and his companions to Probe Station. "Lois McAlois."

The pilot landed palms down on the nose of her ship. "We've met," she said. Then she slapped the nearest port. "See why I'm keeping my stumps?" she said to Renny. "For a while anyway. It's the only way I can fit in there halfway comfortably."

"If it works," said Michaels, "we'll build the bigger model I mentioned."

"And I'll let the gengineers at me."

"What if it doesn't work?" asked Donna Rose.

Lois simply shrugged. Michaels said, "That's a chance we take. *She* takes. But she volunteered."

"Why?" asked Renny.

She shrugged again. "We needed someone. I've got the training. I happened to fit the box. And we all wanted to see this thing work. It will mean so much to everyone."

Renny chuffed as if he were trying not to bark. "I suppose I could fit in there with you."

Lois smiled at the big-headed German shepherd and opened her mouth as if to speak, but Michaels beat her to it. "Uh-uh," he said. "We only need one test pilot."

"I've heard a lot," said Frederick, "about what this thing will be able to do if it works. But how does it work?"

Michaels's face showed some relief at the change of subject. "Do you know," he asked, "that a vacuum can produce particles spontaneously, out of nothing?" Hardly waiting for Frederick's nod and Donna Rose's puzzled look, he continued: "They come in matter-antimatter pairs, so there's no net production of matter, and they usually annihilate each other immediately. This can yield energy, though normally in vanishingly small amounts. What we've done . . . Well, lab work here at the station turned up a way to 'stress' space and make the necessary quantum fluctuations much more likely."

"Blew the wall out of a lab," said Lois. "And vaporized the researcher."

"Fortunately, his work was in the computer," said Hannoken.

Michaels nodded. "We can get enough energy that way to run the Q-ship. That's what the Q stands for: quantum fluctuation. Unfortunately, the 'stress' alters quantum probabilities in many ways, not just in the drive but in the whole ship, and even for some distance around it. Lois? Would you turn the stressor on? Keep it low."

He turned in the air of the construction bay until he faced the wall a few meters away. "No blast at all," he said. "We're safe." Frederick noticed a square of dark blue fabric on the wall. On it, as unmoving as if they were glued in place, were six large dice and a lidded bucket. "Velcro," said Michaels as he swung toward the wall. "Watch."

With a rapid series of ripping sounds, he peeled the bucket and the dice from the fabric holding patch. He put the dice in the bucket, held the lid in place with one hand, and shook. Then he hurled the dice toward the fabric. When they struck, they froze in place.

"Four threes," said Frederick. He sounded surprised.

The next three throws produced five fours, three sixes and three ones, and six twos. When Michaels had Lois turn off the Q-drive and rejoin them, the throws became more mixed.

"You're warping probability," said Donna Rose.

Michaels nodded and tossed her a Velcro-coated die. "Right. And the probability 'warps' will be much stronger when the drive is going full blast. They may even be strong enough to affect living matter. To cause cancer, or to cure it. To mutate genes, or . . ." He shrugged. "Though they don't seem to hurt mice. On the other hand, the pilot—and eventually passengers—will be exposed for much longer times."

"On the third hand," said Lois, "we have great hopes for the warps."

"Tunneling?" asked Frederick.

Arlan Michaels grinned at him, appreciating the sign of understanding. "We need more control, but yes," he said. "Subatomic particles can appear, quite suddenly and without moving through the intervening distance, on the other side of a barrier. They have a certain probability of being anywhere, and sometimes they are. Larger objects have such probabilities too, but they are infinitesimal. Useless. We hope to make them larger, and then . . ."

"The stars," said Donna Rose. "Faster-than-light travel."

"A warp drive," said Renny.

"Exactly," said Lois McAlois.

"But we do need control," said Michaels. "So far, all we can do is warp the probabilities in a general way. That's enough for generating energy, but it won't let us pick a destination or a distance. And we wouldn't want to leap several light-years in some random direction. We have to be able to steer."

Donna Rose looked at the die he had given her. She turned it over in her hands. She reached out and pressed it back onto the fabric that had held it first. "Steering doesn't matter," she said quietly. "Not if all you want to do is flee, to go elsewhere."

"The Engineers," said Frederick quietly, though he would have been surprised if Michaels were not aware of what was happening on Earth.

"Yes." The physicist nodded his head. His expression was sympathetic, his tone wry. "But we would like to be able to test such a drive and get word about the results back. If we can't know whether it works, using a tunneling drive to flee the Engineers might amount to no more than an expensive way to commit suicide."

"Huh!" Renny's exclamation was nearly a woof. "Staying within their reach might be cheaper, but it would still be suicide."

"It can't be that bad, can it?" Director Hannoken's face and voice both seemed skeptical, and Frederick remembered what he had read of history: In the twentieth century, when the German Nazis had been slaughtering Jews and other minorities by the millions, the world had refused to admit that such things could happen. Only when the death camps had been liberated by opposing troops had the evidence become inescapable. And before another generation was past, scholars had been writing books that claimed to prove that the death camps were only propaganda: There had been no poison-gas "showers," no ovens, no mass shootings, no mass graves, no multiple decimations—decimation meant the death of one in ten, and fewer than that had survived—of the innocent.

The news reports, he thought, were clear enough. No one would fake veedo footage such as that which had shown the attack on Donna Rose's dorm in the city park. And Hannoken had said the station got the news, had offered her sanctuary when Frederick called her a refugee, had suggested that more bots might seek freedom in the sky. Walt Massaba had indicated that they would be made welcome to the extent that the station—perhaps even all the stations in orbit around the planet—had the room and resources to support them, and surely his words had been directed by his boss.

Had Hannoken forgotten? Or did he think that what was

going on on Earth was nothing more than the sort of persecution American blacks had endured for more than a century after
the Civil War? Not the program of extermination Renny had
just suggested?

Chapter
Ten

ALICE BELLE AND her two friends were a cluster of green on the side of the street, staring across the stream of Roachsters, Hoppers, and Armadons, Macks and Bernies and coveralled pedestrians that was the city's traffic. For her that green was the green of long leaves coiled around her torso. For the Nickerses, it was the green of genetically modified skin. For all three, it was the green of chlorophyll, the green of grass and tree that stand unmoving while the noisy tides of animal life and conflict flow past. Brighter colors entered the picture with Alice Belle's blossoms, Sheila Nickers's feathered scalp and ornamented cheek and jawbones, both her and her husband's patterned clothing.

"There it is." Alice Belle gestured toward the building across the way.

There was nothing about the building's exterior to distinguish it except that it bore no floater blisters and on its roof there was a small greenhouse. It did not have, as some buildings did, the slowly pulsing green bulge upon its roof that was a Bellows, part plant, part animal, a lunglike supplier of warmed or cooled, dried or moistened air. Central heating remained, but mechanical air-conditioning was an extinct luxury.

Like many of the city's buildings, it was an old structure of reinforced concrete. Once its window openings had been sealed with glass against the outside air. Many decades ago, the seals had been broken and more traditional windows had been installed, ones that could be opened to permit cooling cross-breezes or closed to conserve heat. The result was a gridwork of window frames and sills to which clung honeysuckle vines enough to add a layer of cooling shade.

"I like it already," said Sheila Nickers. "It looks like home." Many of the windows were closed off by louvered grilles, but she was able to point at one, another, another, that were not. The lighting that glowed within was far brighter than in most of the city's apartments.

Three concrete steps led up to a flagstone platform and the building's entrance, a pair of high glass doors. Mounted above and behind the doors was a camera. Beyond them sat a pair of computers, one bioform rooted in a pot and one electronic device. "Image recognizers," said Alice Belle as she stepped into the camera's field of view. "They back each other up. The bioform's immune to power failures, the other one to poisons or diseases. If they both fail, steel shutters fall down to cover the glass."

Sam Nickers gave the bot a sidelong glance. Paranoia? But what had happened to them, to him and Sheila? What had happened to those bots who lived in the dormitory in the park? Were similar outrages happening elsewhere, in other cities, other nations? Disquieting rumors suggested that the news reports of violence were being downplayed, and that some outrages were being hushed up entirely.

He looked up at the slot that held the shutters and thought the steel looked thick enough to stop bare-handed rioters but not the impact of even a small Mack truck. But he said nothing as the door's lock clicked, Alice Belle pushed, and they entered. "We'll give them a look at you later on," she was saying. "The bioform will need a sniff as well."

The entranceway smelled of soil and growing things, and a few feet past the doors the flagstones gave way to bare dirt. Alice Belle removed her shoes. "You don't have to," she said. "But we do like the feel of dirt on our feet."

"So do we," said Sheila, and she and Sam followed suit. "Though we don't get many chances."

To himself alone, Sam smiled. He hadn't gone barefoot on bare dirt since he had been a sprout. He remembered that the luxuriously cool feel of soil on his feet had been marred by the awkward, sometimes sharp projections of twigs and rocks. When he realized that such things were nearly absent from the soil that covered this building's floors, he let his smile reach his face.

"Your place will be on the third floor." An elevator took them there, and Alice Belle led them along corridors whose doors, many of them open, exposed apartments whose carpets of soil swelled into mounds beneath bright lights. Honeysuckle vines crept over the sills of windows, both those open to the outdoor light and those blocked by louvers, and rooted in the soil. In some of the rooms they passed, mist was spraying from overhead pipes. A resident, stepping slowly across her apartment's floor while her roots sifted through the soil like fingers searching through piles of coins, caught Sam's eye. He paused to watch, and when he saw her roots heave a pebble to the surface, her green torso bend, and her hand pitch the small stone out the window, he understood why the soil was so soft and fine.

Alice Belle and Sheila retraced their steps to join him at the door. "Narcissus Joy," said Alice Belle. "She works in our gengineering lab."

A trio of bees hummed above Narcissus Joy's scalp blossoms, creamy white with orange rims. She straightened, looked toward her visitors, and said, "Our new neighbors. May I help you?"

"They're curious," said Alice Belle. "They've never been here. No humans have. It's all new to them."

"Why do you . . . ?" asked Sam with a gesture toward Narcissus Joy's roots and the trail of sifted earth behind her.

"There's no need, really," the bot said gently. "It's a way to think, to meditate."

"Gengineering?" asked Sheila.

Narcissus Joy swung to point toward the window. "You see the honeysuckle? It's as old as our kind, and the roots interconnect, everywhere. We use them as our grapevine, a way to communicate. And the humans think the vines are a nuisance."

"BRA keeps releasing viruses to destroy them," said Alice Belle.

"And it's a full-time job designing the genefixes to keep the vines alive. We need them badly. We depend on them."

"Most people," said Alice Belle, "think we're barely more than walking plants. Janitors and other menials."

"*We* don't," said Sheila, aiming her voice toward the gengineer. "We know Alice Belle, and I'd heard that some of you were scientists. But I've never met a botanical gengineer."

"We don't parade our higher talents. And we do try to keep that one fairly quiet. We don't apply for BRA licenses and permits. But our gengineers are good, and we have several labs."

"There's one in this building?" asked Sam.

Alice Belle and Narcissus Joy both nodded. A few minutes later the Nickerses were standing in the door of another apartment. "Yours," said Alice Belle. She gestured toward the workers who were trimming back the honeysuckle around the windows. "You won't be able to use the vines, so . . ." Other workers were raking the apartment's soil level and covering it with a conventional, fabric carpet. "And you can't root." She reached overhead to check a valve on a pipe above the doorway. "Your furniture can't stand the rain we make."

The workers in the apartment might have been menial bots brought in from outside the building. They might have been residents, doing a stint of "community service." There was no way to tell, for they wore no uniforms and no identifying badges like the patches many humans wore on their coveralls. The green leaves that curled around their torsoes were all the clothing they needed other than belts and aprons for their tools.

The soil beneath the carpet gave the apartment's floor the softness of a well-kept lawn. Sheila discovered this first and, grinning, invited her husband to join her in a little dance that wound up near one of the room's windows. Sam took the opportunity to peer outside and immediately said, "Look." They were above and to the left of what could only be the building's service entrance. A large Mack had backed a cargo trailer against the lip of a loading dock, and a crew of bots were moving familiar furniture into the building. These bots wore tunics that swung as if they were made of some heavy fabric; Sam supposed they must need the protection against the scrapes and bruises that must be a mover's occupational hazards. Their human supervisor was visible in the Mack's cab, arms folded over a prodigious paunch, his chin tucked into the top of his chest, a billed cap pulled down over his eyes.

"We were followed."

The apartment was now as nearly identical as it could be to the one the Nickerses had been forced to leave. The living room had its lounges and low table, its veedo and potted plants. The kitchen had its cupboards filled with dishes, pots, pans, and small appliances. The bedroom had bed and dressers and a closet full of clothes. There were pictures on the walls. There were no birds; they had been released, since the new apartment had no screens and the Nickerses had not wished to keep them caged.

The movers were finished, and their chief, a battered-looking bot whose arms and legs were thick with muscle, was holding an electronic invoice deck. She spoke as Sam Nickers inserted his niddic into the deck's slot.

"Followed?"

"Yeah." She pressed a button, and her deck spat Sam's card back at him. He caught it deftly. "There was a couple of Engineers outside the building. One of 'em stayed there. The other one caught a cab. He was watchin' us unload."

When she pointed one thick hand toward the window, Sheila Nickers followed the gesture with her feet. After a moment of scanning the sidewalk opposite, she said, "He's still there." Sam joined her at the window and soon spotted the distinctive blue coverall in the shadows at the mouth of an alley. He could make out no distinctive glint of metallic ornaments—of earrings, patches, or pins—though the honeysuckle that choked the alley behind the lurker was plain to see.

When they turned away from the window, the movers were gone, but Alice Belle was still there. In the doorway behind her stood another bot. Sam thought he recognized her as Narcissus Joy, the gengineer. With her was another whose scalp blossoms were a pale blue with yellow centers.

"It's no secret," said Alice Belle. "We can't hide the fact that this building is full of bots, and we've never tried."

"But . . ." said the stranger, staring at the Nickerses.

"Shasta Lou," said Narcissus Joy by way of introduction.

"But," said Shasta Lou. "Now it holds humans too, even if they are greenskins, and that may provoke the Engineers more than ever."

"Why?" asked Alice Belle. "Bots and humans mingle all the time, on the streets, on the job . . ."

"But not like this. And they hate the thought of fraternization. Worse yet, they're bound to build unfounded fantasies. Of conspiracies, miscegenation, perhaps even worse."

Sadly, wishing that he did not feel forced to agree, Sam nodded his head. "They're like the ancient Ku Klux Klanners." When Shasta Lou and Narcissus Joy both looked puzzled, he added, "Humans too. Whites. They thought of blacks in just that way."

Shasta Lou's voice was quiet. "What did they do?"

"Jailed them on slight excuse. Hung them. Shot them. Burned them, and their homes." He paused, turned toward the window, and said reflectively, "But they weren't the worst."

"Who was?"

Sam was silent, trembling as he realized the similarity of this conversation to the last one he and Sheila had had with Lillian Bojemoy, the principal of their school, when she had told them . . . But Sheila seemed oblivious. "The Nazis," she said. "They slaughtered Jews. And others. Anyone they didn't like. And they did it very efficiently. They killed millions."

"That's what we are," said Sam when he was able to speak again. His voice was bitter. "Bots and greenskins. Niggers and kikes. Wops and wogs and gooks."

All three of the bots were shuddering, even though he had said nothing they did not already feel in their souls.

The lurker near the building's loading dock was still there the next day, or another Engineer much like the first. No one supposed that Engineers needed no sleep, or that they were not sane enough to work in shifts.

The day after that, a pair of Engineers appeared across the street from the building's main entrance. Others took up positions where they could watch the single door that opened from the basement onto a side street, the end of the fire escape, the second-story sundeck that was never used. Two even appeared on the roof of the building across the alley to the rear, as if that too were a potential escape route.

But they did nothing. They did not interfere with the comings and goings of the building's residents. They waved no signs. They did not heckle. They simply watched, though they could not see past the doorways and windows. Certainly, they could not see the Nickerses settling into their new apartment, accepted by beings who were like them in color yet as unlike them in basic design as it was possible to be and still share genes, free of the prejudice that had plagued them in the outside world. Nor could they see Alice Belle bringing up the possibility that the Nickerses might work as teachers in the building's school, nor the greenskins' eager response and the ensuing meetings with elder bots and teachers, nor their introduction to a classroom unlike any they had ever seen before.

The children were old enough to be free of the nursery's soil, and they were as active as the young of any species.

Like kittens or puppies, they tumbled and wrestled and tangled in the honeysuckle vines that entered the room through every window opening. Like calves or colts, they kicked and galloped and rolled on the ground. Like young monkeys, apes, or humans, they poked and pried inquisitively at anything that seemed pokable or priable. Like flowers, they ignored the bees that wandered through the room.

They ignored also the opening of the classroom door. Only when their teacher, an older bot whose scalp blossoms were a deep honey color, cleared her throat did the movement and the noise stop. Then, as the children took their places in orderly rows and columns, she crossed the room to a still-blaring veedo unit, turned toward the class, said, "The knobs?" caught what some anonymous hand tossed her way, put the veedo's knobs back in place, and eliminated the last source of noise.

The Nickerses still stood in the doorway, watching, smiling, recognizing familiar dynamics, appreciating the evidence of a teacher whose control of her class, while not absolute—as it should never be—was certainly unquestioned. Her name was Mary Gold.

"There," she said at last. "My class. Come in and meet them, and then we'll have a lesson to show you how we do it." Her face and tone still carried some of the skepticism she had voiced earlier. How, she had asked, could humans possibly teach her students anything at all? Or even help in the teaching process? The short bot lives dictated a pace of learning that a human could never match, neither as student nor as teacher, and the mode of that learning must be forever inaccessible to those who had no roots.

The Nickerses had not understood, and Mary Gold had been unwilling to explain in words. "I will show you," she had said. "And then you will go find someplace else to meddle."

Now, a dogged determination plain upon her face, she turned abruptly to her class and said, "Roots out, now." Some of the students groaned in protest. A few looked apprehensive, as if they dreaded what was coming. But all obeyed, and very shortly all were rooted in the room's floor of soil.

Mary Gold unfurled her roots as well. As they penetrated the soil, she said, "I mesh my roots with those of the honeysuckle. So do they. Then I select the lesson, some part of what I know, and pass it to the students. The honeysuckle roots link our nervous systems together, and the knowledge flows from my brain to theirs."

Sheila Nickers asked, "Can you link directly to them, without the honeysuckle?"

"Just to one or two. The vine lets me work with a whole class at once."

Sam breathed a sigh. "Direct transfer," he murmured to his wife. "We've wished for that for ages. Painless education."

Sheila stopped his words with a touch upon his arm. "No," she said. "Not painless. Look."

They both looked, watching, staring, and they saw the children's faces contort, some only lightly, as if they suffered a headache, some in agony, as if some brute were pummeling their naked brains with clubs.

"Oh, stop!" cried Sheila. Her eyes were full of tears. But there was no response. The teacher did not seem to hear.

Fortunately, the lesson did not last long. Mary Gold withdrew her roots from the soil, gasped, sighed, and said, "You see?"

They saw. The children too were gasping. Some were sobbing, quietly or not. All were pale and sweating.

They also saw that Mary Gold hated what she had to do to her young charges. That it was necessary was no consolation.

"The brain," said the teacher, "does not store information in any organized way. I can send what I know to the honeysuckle, but it goes as a jumble, and it reaches them"—a nod indicated her students—"in the same way. The pain is worst for those who cannot tolerate knowledge without understanding."

Sam shook his head in sympathy. "And those who are comfortable with rote learning feel the least pain?"

She nodded sadly. "Many of them," she said. "They learn quite well, but . . ." The tips of the leaves that embraced her torso unfurled to reveal the upper curves of her quite human bosom. "We need understanding, the ability to use knowledge creatively, to build. Those who cannot think that well become the menials." She hesitated, facing her suffering class, and added, "And yes, sometimes they catch on late."

Then she left them, moving among her students, speaking soft words of empathy—once, when she was young, she had gone through the same ordeal herself—touching, hugging, wiping at tears, comforting. She paid the most attention to those who seemed to be in the greatest pain.

Eventually, she returned to the head of the classroom. "What I just gave them," she said to the Nickerses, "was everything I know about our bioform computers. Would you like to ask some questions? To see how much got through?"

Sam accepted the gauntlet and asked how the bioforms could possibly process information. Hands waved. He picked one. And the answer was that in their stems and roots, bioform computers had nerve cells based in part on those of animals. How did they make pictures on their four-leaf screens? Single cells, glowing with bioluminescence or, in some models, darkening with pigment, formed single pixels. The disk drives? That was simple; the sensors were single cells containing grains of magnetite, genetics courtesy of certain bacteria which could orient on the Earth's magnetic field. Could a bioform computer's roots interface with those of the honeysuckle vines the way their own did?

No hands rose into the air for that one. The young faces, perplexed, turned toward the teacher who had not given them that bit of information, of understanding, who had not known the answer. In reply, she shrugged in quite a human way and said, "We can find out. Let's go down the hall."

They soon found an apartment with a computer rooted not in a pot but in the soil that covered the floor. A waterproof box stood beside the card-drive, both beneath a small canopy that shielded the floppies from the showers that periodically must descend from the pipes overhead. Mary Gold sank her roots into the dirt, closed her eyes, and laid a contemplative expression across her face. On the other side of the computer, one of the students did the same.

Mary Gold's eyes snapped open. "Jackie Thyme! Not yet!" There was a pause, and then, though the child had said nothing aloud, she said, "Why not? . . . A memory dump might burn out your mind . . . But you're doing it, aren't you? You really are."

Sam sat down in front of the bioform's keyboard and quickly found the commands that could let him route information to and from the computer's roots. He then used the bioform to ask Mary Gold, root to root, for a small sample lesson.

Her eyes snapped open when she realized how he had spoken to her, but she said nothing. Wordlessly, she obliged,

and the computer had surprisingly little trouble accepting her
memories of growing up in a dormitory nursery into its memory. Its designers had long ago solved the problem of translating
the language of neurons into that of human language for pres-
entation on a screen or transfer to an electronic machine. And
if the resulting computer file was precisely as jumbled a
mess as Mary Gold had indicated earlier, the necessary links
were indicated within the morass, and Sam was able to use
a standard utility to rearrange and simplify, to impose some
order. When he was done, he sent the file to Jackie Thyme.

The child winced at the onset of the transmission, but as
soon as it was done, she smiled and said, "That was fast. And
a little smoother."

"It's just as you told us," Sam said to Mary Gold. "You can
progress much faster in your own way than you ever could
in the public schools. And of course, you have to, with your
lives as short as they are. But you could progress even faster.
You've been ignoring pedagogy."

When the bot looked puzzled, Sheila Nickers said, "I think
I know what he means. Any textbook, whatever its form—
paper book, computer file, or bot brain—should move from
the simple basics to the complexities."

"That's all I did," said Sam. "I organized the material. Put
it in sequence. And I can do it better. Some of it Sheila can
do better yet. And we can record the lessons."

The Engineers had crossed the street. Now they paced back
and forth on the sidewalk before the building's entrance. They
carried signs emblazoned with their standard invective. They
harangued the passersby who crossed the street to avoid them.
They spat on bots who dared to leave or enter their home.

Inside, Sam and Sheila Nickers struggled with the bioform
computer that had been assigned to their efforts. They adapted
indexing and sorting and organizing routines devised over
more than a century of computer experience. They learned
that the mind embedded its own organizational links within
its memory structure and that though those links could not
necessarily be passed directly to another mind, they could be
exploited to organize the material of any lesson. They learned
what speed worked best for transmission to a student's mind.

For half of each day, Mary Gold stood by, her roots embedded
in the soil, her class assigned to entertain itself. On the other

side of the computer stood Jackie Thyme. Their jobs were to test whatever the Nickerses could persuade the machine to do.

And finally . . .

Sam and Sheila were walking barefoot down the hall. "Jackie said that last was the smoothest ever," said Sheila. "The merest twinge of headache. Very short recovery time. Mary Gold said that she could give twice, three times, as many lessons in a day."

"We're ready," Sam agreed. "Our new job didn't last very long, did it?" The door to their apartment stood open before them. On a small table just inside, the bot who handled that chore had dropped their mail. Sam began to sort it through.

Sheila laughed. "We're not done. Mary Gold will record her lessons on the floppies, and we will collect lessons from all those bots who lack the talent to shape their memories even as much as she used to do." When Sam looked puzzled, she added, "Most bots, she told me, have such jumbled memories that all they can give students is agony. Good teachers are rare."

"Look at this." He held out a sheet of paper much like those they had seen before. It was hate and ugliness. It named them horrors, damned them to eternal flame, promised doom.

"We will!" said Sheila. "We *will* do good! We will make it easier and faster for them to educate their children. We will make that education better, deeper, broader. We are *not* what the Engineers call us with their twisted minds!"

They abandoned the mail, moved deeper into their apartment, and saw the blinking light by which their phone announced a waiting message. When Sheila triggered the playback, she blanched.

Alice Belle had entered the apartment behind them. When Sam heard her soft step and turned, she waved that hateful piece of paper, or one just like it, and gestured toward the phone. "We're getting them too. It's not just you."

The bullhorns woke them.

"FRANKENSTEINS!" someone was screaming. "MONSTERS! Unholy prideful gengineers have tampered with life. BOTS are their blasphemous offspring, horned and forktailed fruit of their rotted loins! THIS IS THEIR DEN!"

"Oh, no," moaned Sam. "Oh, Jesus, no." He shuddered with rage, with outrage, with sudden fear.

"THIS IS THEIR DEN!" the strident scream repeated. "Where human Judases have joined them. Greenskins, yes. But they were human once. Now they have betrayed their kind. They have betrayed US. They have betrayed all humans. And they have done it twice. Once by letting the unholy gengineers pollute their very genes! And once by going over to the BOTS!"

Sheila gripped his hand so tightly that he knew that if he were not one of those greenskins about which the Engineers were raving his skin surely would have blanched. "They didn't do enough already?" she asked the air. She too was shuddering. "The mail wasn't enough? The phone calls? The signs on our door? Getting kicked out of—"

"GOD ONLY KNOWS WHAT THEY DO IN THERE! They won't let us in. But God DOES know! And He knows it IS abomination!"

The sound of sirens growing nearer filled the silence left when the ranting Engineer paused for breath.

"Someone called," said Sam with a sigh of relief. "One of the bots, or a neighbor." It didn't matter who. It mattered only that blessed silence, peace, would return, for a while. That the mob would not storm the building to stamp out abomination. That the pogrom would not—not yet—begin.

He wished there were something he could do.

Chapter
Eleven

LIKE MOST PEOPLE on Probe Station, Lois McAlois had a tiny box of an apartment just large enough for her bed to fold down and leave a narrow aisle. Unlike most of the station's residents, she lived in the low-gee zone. She also had more than enough room in her bed. The missing two-thirds of her legs left a broad expanse of blanket as flat as if the bed were empty.

Yet that legless portion of her bed was not going unused. Curled atop the blanket lay Renny, his overlarge head pointed toward her own, his eyes open as hers were not, watching.

A soft click sounded from the wall near the head of the bed. Music began to play. The woman's eyes opened. She grinned. "Hey, Renny," she said. "It's nice to have company in the morning." One hand snaked from beneath the covers and reached to scratch the German shepherd's ears.

Renny followed as she slid out of bed and stood on the stubs of her thighs. "I couldn't do this in full gee," she said. With one hand, she flipped the switch that folded the bed back into the wall.

She stretched, eyeing the dog speculatively, and stripped off the shift in which she had slept. Renny cocked his head, stared deliberately at her breasts and belly, whined, wagged his tail, and laughed. "You wouldn't do that if I was a man," he said.

"Maybe I would." She stepped into the bathroom, leaving its narrow door open. "I like you." Only after she had brushed her teeth did she dress. The coverall she chose was dark brown with a pattern of light green and yellow maple leaves.

Renny's repeated whine suggested that the feeling was mutual, and that he was not concerned that he was missing anything by no longer accompanying Frederick and Donna Rose where they went. He had found in the pilot another focus for his attention.

125

After breakfast, she took Renny with her to the Q-ship simulator. This was a room about twice the size of her apartment and even nearer the station's axis. Jointed arms mounted on its walls supported a rectangular metal box on whose side a metal hatch hung open. Inside, it looked identical with the cramped interior of the Q-ship prototype. The odors of stale sweat and fatigue surrounded it like a cloud.

Arlan Michaels was standing beside the hatch, scratching in his blond hair with one hand. "Ready for another run?" he asked.

"In that sweatbox? You sure we need it?"

"Can't afford any mistakes."

With a grunt and a roll of her eyes, the pilot agreed. Michaels's grin told Renny that her protest and concession were a ritual they played through at least once for every training session. Once, perhaps, the words had been empty. Now, with the first flight almost upon them and the training having lasted for months, they bore more weight.

"The dog going with you?" Michaels asked.

"He'll fit." With a wave of one hand, she gestured Renny through the hatch. He lay down where her feet should have gone. "See?"

Michaels nodded. "You plan to take him with you?"

"Why not?" She pulled herself into the simulator's small cabin. "Company's nice to have."

The clang of the hatch cut off whatever reply Michaels might have made.

"NORSAT 816. We have the feed."
   "EUROSAT 153 . . ."
   "AUSSAT 32 . . ."
   "NIPPOSAT . . ."
   "SINOSAT . . ."
   "MOSSAT . . ."
   "PYRASAT . . ."
   "MECCASAT . . ."
   "CANSAT . . ."
   "LAPSAT . . ."
Hands embedded in mouse-gloves twitched, pointed, gestured. Switches mounted in palms and along the sides of fingers clicked subliminally. Curses muttered. Keyboards rattled. Images appeared on veedo screens. The cloud-veiled outlines

of continents and islands and peninsulas took shape, enlarged, and disappeared as views zoomed in on evidence of climate change: coastlines studded with drowned buildings. The world had warmed under the influence of carbon dioxide released by the Machine Age's fossil exhalations and forest clearings. Yet the warming had had good effects as well; without it, it would never have been possible to have, even in areas once famous for frozen winters, genimals based on insects, reptiles, and tropical mammals.

Further inland lay farmlands thick with gengineered crops; forests; broad tracts once fertile, now turned to dust or marsh, the outlines of abandoned fields and homesteads still visible. Cities sprawled, surrounded by suburbs, their thick ranks of homes a random mix of traditional wood and stone and brick and modern bioforms, pumpkins and eggplants and squash and bean plants and even plants in the guise of massive human heads, squatting on the landscape like the leavings of some mad executioner; in most, the bioforms dominated. In time, they might restore the climate to what it once had been, for the houses drew carbon from the air, while elsewhere forests grew less raped of lumber than they had been in centuries.

City streets streamed with bioform traffic, Roachsters, Macks, Bernies, Beetles, Hoppers, and more. Pedestrians—bot and human—were not quite distinguishable on the sidewalks. Here and there, larger groups surrounded smaller ones, contracting and expanding like the irises of eyes or cameras.

Several operators were scanning newscasts and other signals, the sound turned low but audible. Frederick could hear snippets of politicians' speeches, weather forecasts, crime reports. There was footage of fires and floods, an earthquake, an announcement that the government had decided to retain its subsidies for traditional agriculture a little longer, a report that someone had poisoned a squadron of Air Force Warbirds, another that a Warbird had bombed a tank farm, killing fifty of the rhino-based genimals. Occasionally he heard brief mentions of "local disturbances." There were no explicit admissions of any widespread trouble, no suggestion that Engineers throughout the world were giving up their signs and slogans and becoming more demanding, more aggressive, more violent.

With delicate gestures, someone tried to tweak the enlargement on a satellite image just a little greater. When the image did not improve, another technician said, "I've found a minicam signal. No broadcast, but . . ." The image changed, and several of those in the room gasped at the evidence of what governments were keeping from the news. Alvar Hannoken pointed his prow of a nose toward the veedo screen and said, "It's *that* bad."

Frederick Suida uttered an involuntary tsking noise. He was not surprised to see Engineers in the outer ring of an iris, nor bots and gengineered humans in the inner, nor knives and clubs and unzippered blue coveralls. He sighed. Murder and rape. Rape and murder. The traditional sports of reactionaries, revolutionaries, and other idiots. One of them the sport that had once cost him nearly every friend he had ever had. A smile was further from his face than ever.

A bearded Engineer noticed the cameraman and waved a crude sword threateningly. The picture centered on the sword and remained steady as its wielder advanced. The weapon rose and fell, and the picture went dark.

Frederick stood, his feet held to the deck by Velcro slippers. He was in Probe Station's broad, low-ceilinged, low-gee communications center near the spin axis. The room was filled with perhaps two dozen electronic consoles and veedo screens. At each one sat an operator. At the nearest, beside his hip, the operator was Donna Rose. Her screen was one of those that did not display some view of the planet from which they had escaped.

He shifted his attention to Donna Rose and spoke codes and passwords. Smoothly, rapidly, her fingers moved upon the keyboard before her. Three seconds later, time eaten by the passage of light from station to Earth and back, the screen bloomed with acknowledgements. She had logged onto the computers of the Bioform Regulatory Administration. Now she should be able to access any of the various government networks that anyone on the station could think of.

"State?" asked Hannoken.

Frederick gave Donna Rose the access code for the State Department's intelligence net. Within minutes they were downloading reports of Engineer riots, lists of dead and injured, and analyses that identified the Engineers' targets as anyone in any way connected to gengineering—bots, of course, and greenskins, and other gengineered humans, but also gengineers and their employees and the owners of bioform houses, vehicles, computers, and appliances. A research laboratory had been burned, a university gengineering department trashed. There were complaints that even embassy personnel were being attacked. There were requests for official protests to those foreign governments that turned blind eyes on Engineer activities. They found no sign that any such protests were filed. Nor did they see any sign that Washington was prepared to restrain the Engineers within their own nation's borders.

The screen blinked, wiped clean, and displayed a message:

ACCESS TERMINATED.
PLEASE INSERT YOUR NIDC IN YOUR CARD DRIVE.

IDENTIFY YOURSELF
BY CLEARANCE NUMBER
AND ACCESS AUTHORIZATION.

"Do we have enough?" asked Frederick. Donna Rose glanced up at him, the tips of the leaves that covered her chest twitching away from her skin just enough to reveal her collarbones.

Hannoken nodded jerkily and made an abrupt, chopping motion with one hand. "Close it down."

The bot obeyed.

As her screen cleared, however, another caught Frederick's eye. The view it showed was familiar, horizontal, not sky-eye vertical, but . . . He pointed. "Turn up the sound."

It was a newscast: "Firefighters quickly extinguished the flames," the announcer was saying as the camera centered on a broken window from which a tendril of smoke escaped.

"But the damage had been done." Another camera moved through an open rotunda, past a rubble of smashed souvenirs and filigreed grillwork that marked what had been a gift shop. The walls overhead still held, intact but soot-stained, antique WPA bronzes. The mouth of a corridor was partially blocked by the crushed and tattered remnants of biological sculptures and other products of the gengineer as artist.

"The mob destroyed almost everything before the police arrived." On the steps outside, bodies. In the auditorium where Frederick and his wife and their children had once entertained audiences with the music only they could make, more bodies. In an office . . .

"Even the museum's director. They found his wife in another part of the building." The bodies looked small, the near-white hair stained with blood, the faces smoothed of wrinkles.

"No," said Frederick. Franklin and Kimmer Peirce had been his friends almost as long as Tom Cross. They had survived the massacre that had cost him Tom, and Porculata, and . . . They had helped him become what he was. And now . . .

He hadn't seen them in weeks. Not since before Renny's case had landed on his desk. He should have visited them before he left for Probe Station. But he hadn't had the time, and he hadn't dreamed that they would not be there when he returned, and . . .

He wanted to scream, to hit something, to burst out in tears. But he felt stunned, frozen. The tears refused to come. All he could do was turn away, head down, and stumble from the room.

This time, the elephant—what had been her name? Martha?—had not been in the nightmare. But Tom and Muffy had been, and they had died as messily as they had in reality. So had Franklin and Kimmer, who had survived the massacre that had helped Frederick into manhood but now, in the dream, joined the others in death. Porculata, his wife, had died more messily. In reality, an Engineer's sword had simply cut her in two. In his night-dark mind, she was cloven, stabbed, hacked, burned, boiled, dead a hundred times, a hundred ways, and more, and worse.

When Frederick drew back the curtain that divided his quarters, he found Donna Rose facing him. Her eyes were closed, her back arched to thrust her breasts forward, her arms by her sides, their lower portions angled outward. Her leaves were unwound from her torso and draped over her forearms to soak in the beam of light that shone through the porthole behind her. The light was constant, steadied by the mirrors Hannoken had ordered installed. As in the director's office, a filter reduced the sun's searing brightness to a near equivalent of a summer noon.

For a moment, he stared at the spot where a navel would have been if she were human, or even truly mammalian. Then, suppressing the catch in his breath that her pose invited, he grunted morosely. "Are you trying to cheer me up?"

Her eyes opened. Languidly, she refurled her leaves. She grinned. "I was just getting a last bit of sun before going back to work."

He grunted again. "I need some breakfast. Down there . . ." He gestured toward the porthole as if Earth were just outside. "Down there, I could just pick a sausage. Here the bushes are all in the cafeteria."

"Bots eat too," she said. "Sometimes. And I'd like something now. So let's go." She drew her roots from the soil, shook her feet daintily to remove the crumbs of soil that clung to her soles, and stepped toward the door. He stood, leaving the bed down, unmade, and followed her. But before they could leave the room, the communicator spoke: "Frederick? Donna Rose? Director Hannoken would like to see you as soon as you've eaten. In his office."

When they reached Hannoken's office, the station's director was facing his picture window, his hands clasped behind his back, his face turned into the light. His kudzu plant stood nearby, a simple nonsentient decoration. Withered purple petals had fallen to the floor around its pot.

He turned to greet them and said, holding Donna Rose's hand, "I knew you'd found a slot in the com center. I didn't know how good you were until yesterday. I just hadn't seen you in action." He faced Frederick. "She's good," he told his guest. "She worked that console like a pro. And you say she was a menial. A cleaning bot."

Frederick nodded. When Hannoken added, "But why? That's an utter waste. And how'd she learn?" he shrugged. He didn't know how she had learned. He did know how to explain the waste. "People keep them out of every job they can," he said. "Some are good enough to escape that, but most . . ." He shrugged again.

"Ahhh." Hannoken sighed. "I know, really. But . . ." He shook his head. "I thought I was doing something good," he said. "When I became a gengineer. I saw what others had done before me. I thought I would benefit society, that it would welcome whatever I came up with. Not . . ."

He turned toward Donna Rose. "That tissue sample I took," he said. "It's growing fine. And your genome." He shook his head. "Anyone I know would have pieced it together in a very different way. But it works. Of course it does. And very nicely, too." His eyes added another meaning to his words.

"And they reject you too." he said. "Look at this. Athena, veedo on. Play that last recording." All three turned to face the veedo on the wall. The recording was that of a newscast, and it showed a street littered with bodies. Most showed green leaves or skin.

"Ahhh!" Donna Rose's wordless cry shook with pain. Frederick said nothing at all.

"One of those 'local disturbances,' " said the station director as the tape reached its end and began again. "For some reason, they put this one on the news."

"Can't you . . . ?" She fell silent, staring at the veedo and its recording of blue-clad Engineers and others—others in more varied clothing, not uniforms, others who were not Engineers but sympathizers, fellow travelers, perhaps just ordinary people who wished to be left alone and therefore allied themselves with what seemed the most threatening force in sight—as they walked among the scattered bodies, hacking with Engineer machetes, axes, kitchen knives, removing flowered scalps, the bulbs that hung between bot legs, and other trophies, smearing their clothes with blood as if it were some badge of honor. "They'll be killed, won't they? They'll all be killed. Can't you save them? Some of them? Bring the bots up here? To the stations?"

The ensuing silence, though it did not last long, not even long enough for the recorded excerpt from the veedo news to begin once more, seemed oppressive. Finally, Alvar Hannoken raised one hand to his nose. He pinched the bridge and drew his fingers down. He sighed. "I wish we could," he said. "But this station could hold only a few. The habitats could do better, but even they are pretty close to their design capacity already. We just don't have the room for many."

"The lifeboat problem," said Frederick. When the others looked puzzled, he explained: "When people used to travel across the ocean in ships, the ships would sometimes strike a rock or an iceberg and sink. The passengers would get into smaller boats, the lifeboats. But the lifeboats could only hold a few, and the ships often did not carry enough for everyone. And if too many crowded into a lifeboat, that boat would sink too."

"Yes," said Hannoken. "Not enough stations. Not enough habitats. And not enough spaceplanes or shuttles even if we did have places to put the ones we rescued."

"But can't you try?" cried Donna Rose. "Can't you save a few? As many as you can?"

There was silence again while they stared at the recording, each absorbed in thought. Finally, Hannoken said, "Would it really help? Or would it hurt? Raise false hopes? Shouldn't they work out their problems down there?"

"Can they?" asked Frederick. He did not sound optimistic.

"I should go back," said Frederick. It was evening. He was sitting on the edge of his bed, his hands cradling the sides of his head, facing Donna Rose in her rocket-casing trough of compost. "That's where I belong, and I can't do much here."

Donna Rose held her unfurled leaves toward the light that still streamed through the port, unfaded by Earth's diurnal rhythms. She turned to put her breasts in silhouette, but Frederick barely noticed. "You can't do much there, either," she said. "No one can. We're doomed."

"But I should try," said the man. "That was my job at BRA, to try. The agency was supposed to protect the environment, people, from reckless gengineering. But it had begun to realize that some of the gengineering needs protection too. Intelligent genimals, that's what I dealt with. Now it's obvious we need to do more for the bots. And greenskins, and gengineers, and . . ."

He fell silent. The bot said nothing. There was nothing to say, for his words were only truth. If BRA, or some other agency, did not act to protect gengineering and its fruits, licit and illicit, deliberate and inadvertent, the technology would be lost. And civilization would tumble across the thin line that was all that separated it from utter savagery.

Finally, he added, "I'm sure I could get into the nets better from down there. Keep better track of what's going on. Maybe even . . ."

"It's too late for them," said Donna Rose softly.

"I know." He stared at the floor, his voice thick with unshed tears.

"You shouldn't go," said Alvar Hannoken. "It's futile. One man can't halt the tide." They were standing beside the small office in the full-gee zone that handled bookings for travel to Earth, the Moon, and the other stations and habitats in orbit. Just beyond the open door, a single clerk sat before a terminal, looking bored.

"I have to try," said Frederick. "I don't know what I'll do, but . . ."

"Stay here," said Donna Rose quietly. There were tears in her eyes, as there had been when she watched her friends being slaughtered. "Please, Freddy."

He shook his head. "I can't."

"Then you're an idiot," said Renny. In a lightweight wheel-chair beside him, one hand on his shoulder, sat Lois McAlois. She alone said nothing.

"Then I'm an idiot," said Frederick. He turned, stepped into the booking office, and held his return ticket toward the clerk. "Can you get me on the next trip down?"

The clerk tapped his keyboard and stared at a screen of glowing characters. "Not many going in that direction. There's empty seats," he said. "Now let's make your reservation." He copied a string of numbers from the ticket. "Just a sec."

Frederick was standing close enough—he would have been close enough even in the corridor—to see the screen wipe itself clean and display three lines:

TICKET CANCELLED
MESSAGE WAITING
MR. SUIDA, PLEASE INSERT
YOUR NIDC IN THE CARD DRIVE.

Vaguely, Frederick was aware of noises behind him, but he paid no attention. He felt stunned. His ticket cancelled? Had Judith Breger fired him after all? But then why . . . ? Had PETA sued him, and the court frozen all his assets?

The clerk shook his head. "I've never seen that before. You want the message?"

Frederick didn't dare to try to speak. Mutely, he produced his niddic and handed it over.

The clerk inserted it into his machine's card drive. Immediately, the screen displayed a new message:

YOUR NIDC HAS BEEN CANCELLED.
MESSAGE WAITING

"Mechin' litter," growled Renny. "That's a nasty trick. What's going on?"

"I haven't got the . . ." said Hannoken.

"He'll have to stay here, won't he?" said Donna Rose. She sounded relieved.

The clerk simply shook his head and touched his keyboard's Enter key. A moment later, the screen displayed the message file:

You have been fired.
> Your severance pay has been credited to account # QW-47033 on Probe Station.

Your airline ticket has been cancelled.
> Its price has been refunded to account # QW-47033 on Probe Station.

Your apartment lease has been cancelled.
> The security deposit and pro rata rent refund have been deposited in account # QW-47033 on Probe Station.

Your National Identification Card (NIDC) has been revoked.
> You no longer have permission to cross national borders.

"You're stuck," said Renny.

"I am," said Frederick. Earthly governments, including his own, viewed low Earth orbit as marking the upper border of all nations. His future travels were now limited to visiting other space stations, habitats, the Moon. Earth was off limits. "Dammit. I didn't dream they would go that far."

"They're probably doing you a favor," said Lois McAlois. "That's no place to be, down there, not now."

"But why?" asked Frederick, though he knew there could not possibly be any answer. Not one of his companions, nor anyone else on Probe Station, was privy to the thoughts of those who could fire him and banish him. "I stuck my neck out," he said. "I went outside channels to send Donna Rose and Renny up here. I expected to catch some litter for it. But this much?"

"It does," said Hannoken, "look like overreaction."

"You're an administrator," said Lois. "And you wouldn't do something like this."

"What about my ticket?" asked Donna Rose as the station's director shook his head, and Frederick remembered. Renny's ticket had been one-way; supposedly he had not been intended

to return. The bot's had been round-trip, to support the pretense
that she was on official business. He had not expected that she
would ever use the return half.

"Do you have it with you?" he asked.

"I remember the numbers." She recited them, the clerk typed
them into his machine, and the screen revealed that she too no
longer had a valid niddic. Her ticket too was cancelled, its
value credited to a Probe Station account even though the
money had not been her own, but BRA's.

"I don't get it," said Renny with a low growl.

Together then, they turned away from the clerk and his
perplexing machine. Hannoken's office was not far away,
nor a small rack of bottles and glasses. When those with
hands—even Donna Rose, to the surprise of those who thought
botanical beings could not tolerate or welcome alcohol—were
all supplied, the director said, "Perhaps the Engineers brought
pressure on your bosses, Frederick. Being what you are, defend-
ing Renny, working for BRA, you are a symbol of all they are
against. As soon as you were off the planet, assuming they knew
about it . . ."

"They knew," said Frederick, thinking of the Engineer at
the airport, the one with the "NO BOTS" sign.

"Then they could have moved immediately to make it permanent. Certainly, they have the clout. And who else could
it be?"

Indeed, who else could it be? But that was a question
no one could answer. Each time Frederick used Hannoken's
office facilities to try to call Judith Breger, he got only the
computer-synthesized voice of StarBell telling him that all
satellite circuits were busy, all ground lines were busy, the
ground station was down, the number was busy, the number
was out of order.

"Athena, query," said Hannoken. "Is anyone else on Probe
Station having any similar communications difficulty?"

The answer came immediately in the same voice that
Frederick had heard from the communication grilles in the
dining room, the corridors, his own quarters: "No, sir."

"That," said Renny, his lips wrinkling into a suggestion of
a snarl and his ears flattening against his skull, "sounds like
someone doesn't want you talking to your boss. Or maybe she
doesn't want to talk to you. Is there anyone else?"

He tried to call Berut Amoun at the office, but with no more success. Nor did he get through when he called Bert's home. He knew his friend had an answering machine, but he wasn't being allowed to reach even that.

"Let me try," said Hannoken. "I have a friend who might . . . Athena, get Lou Polling." As promptly as anyone could wish, a young man with swept-back blond hair was on the office screen. Hannoken and Polling exchanged greetings, and then the director described the problem. "Can you help, Lou? Relay a call to BRA for us?"

"Just give me the number," said the other as he pulled a bioform keyboard into view. But as soon as he had typed out the number, the screen went blank except for two stark lines of type:

LAND LINE FAILURE.
PLEASE TRY AGAIN.

"We launch the Q-ship in just five days," Lois had said. "I need to get in a lot of time on the simulator before then."

"Me too," Renny had said. "I'm going with her, and I want to learn everything I can, even if I don't have hands."

"And I have chores as well," Hannoken had said.

Frederick had left the director's office, almost too dejected to notice that Donna Rose was by his side, one hand on his shoulder, comforting, an ear if he wished to talk, a presence if that was all he wished. He was grateful, though he said nothing.

When they reached their quarters, Frederick lay down on the bed. Donna Rose sat beside him. When he rolled to his belly, she leaned over him and began to knead the tense muscles of his neck and shoulders.

"Do you remember?" she asked. "That first night? I walked into your office, and we watched . . ." Her hands clenched a little harder than necessary. Frederick grunted. "And then my supervisor—Ladysmith was his name, Mr. Ladysmith— wanted me to get back to work. You let me stay, though you had to let him think . . ."

She had been offering him nonverbal signals almost from the start. He had carefully ignored them. Frederick grimaced into the pad beneath him as she paused. He could guess what she was about to say, what comfort she was about to offer.

Her hands now lay flat and gentle on his back. "It's possible, Freddy. That's not how we reproduce, but we do have . . ."

He rolled over. "See?" she said, and her leaves peeled away from her torso, revealing her chest and belly all the way down to where her foliage emerged from the flesh of her hips and groin. The cleft she was referring to was visible among the bases of her leaves, revealed by their extreme unfurling; below it was the small bulb that held a portion of her central nervous tissue, a second, smaller brain. She bent her head to follow his gaze with her own. "That doesn't get in the way," she said.

He looked away. "No," he said. "I can't."

"Is it because I'm not really human?" Her expression fell, and her leaves curled once more around her.

"No. I'm not either, after all. But . . ." He paused, sat up, put an arm around her to offer what comfort he could after spurning her own. "Years ago," he said, "when I was still a pig, I met your ancestors. They couldn't move like you. They didn't look like you. And they used their odors, pheromones, to make men mate with them. That's how you got your human genes."

"But we don't do that anymore!" Donna Rose protested. "We can't even make pheromones. We lost that ability generations ago."

Frederick nodded sadly. "I know," he said. "I do. And you're lovely in a very human way. If I didn't have the memories I do, I could easily respond. But . . ." He shrugged and shook his head.

"Is there someone back on Earth?"

"No." He shook his head again. "There never was."

Chapter
Twelve

HE KNEW IT shouldn't. He knew better. But still it never failed
to surprise him, that a bot's blood could be as red as his own, as
wet, as sticky. Only the smell was different, for it was touched
with the earthiness of a fresh-sliced beet.

Sam Nickers was kneeling over one of his new neighbors,
wrapping a bandage around the hole in her upper arm, tsking
when the clean fabric touched the soil of the apartment floor.
Whenever he tsked, Jackie Thyme raised a little higher the roll
from which Sam drew the bandage he needed. But the young
arms were tired, and they sagged. The cycle repeated again
and again.

Just a few days before, Jackie had been helping Sam and
Sheila develop the bioform computer as an interface between
teacher, honeysuckle, and students. Now she was a medical
orderly, fidgeting with an impatience that had not shown when
the wounds had been new and fascinating. She stared at a
nearby bioform computer, its screen and card-drive torn and
useless. She half turned to face the honeysuckle vines that hung
in the window to her right, most of their leaves still green,
many blossoms still upright and filled with wine despite the
tattering effects of gunfire.

Alice Belle stood to one side, her blossoms a splash of
orange and pink against the shadowed wall, watching Sam
work. She had come to the small, windowless room he had
set up as his aid station, where he had picked splinters of glass
from scalps and bandaged simple wounds and dispensed slings.
She had said, "We've got a bad one, Sam. She's bleeding and
screaming, and she won't let us move her."

Sam never knew his patient's name. He knew nothing about
her except that she had been injured and that her skin was pale
and her leaf-tips and petals were limp with the shock of her
injury. A tranquilizer leech had taken care of the screaming.

139

Antibiotic and clip-stitch and bandage were taking care of the rest.

"There," he said at last, in as soothing a tone as he could manage. "It didn't hit an artery. It didn't hit the bone. You should be able to use the arm. But stay away from the windows."

"Right, Doc."

"Doc!" he snorted, rocking back on his heels as she struggled to her feet. The bots had been calling him that ever since he first unwrapped his paramedic training. They had already had the tools of his trade—bandages, drug-secreting leeches, bottles of saline and glucose, stands and rubber tubing and rubber gloves—but none of them knew more than the rudiments of first aid. He did, and he knew that he had saved lives that would otherwise have been lost.

"You're the closest thing we've got," said Alice Belle. The patient was gone, moving—even trotting—back to whatever task the Engineers' bullet had interrupted. Now Alice Belle left as well, returning to her own work.

Shots echoed from the building across the street. Dark spots and cracks appeared in the wall before Sam's eyes as slugs smashed into the plaster. He sighed wearily and wished . . .

Some of the windows in the bots' apartment building faced alleys, offsets, decorative panels, and the scars of blisterlike floater garages. The snipers across the streets therefore could not see straight in and had to fire at angles that left much of the space within the apartments to which those windows belonged quite safe. On two sides, where the building rose above its neighbors, there were even windows snipers could not reach at all, unless they were content to shoot holes in the ceiling.

It had begun with the demonstrators. At first they had simply marched and picketed and waved their signs and screamed their slogans. They had slaughtered and roasted a Roachster on the street in front of the building. They had beaten and chased those bots who had dared to leave the building.

Sam jumped as something touched his shoulder. He tipped his head up and back and recognized Jackie Thyme. For a moment, he had forgotten she was there. "You should be in the shelter," he said. They had been moving as many bots as possible, but especially the very young and the very old, to the basement.

"Uh-uh." She shook her head. "I want to help," she said. "And if I can't help you . . ." She let the tips of her leaves part in a gaping botanical shrug. "Then I'll just be a gofer." She paused, and then she added, her voice touched with plaintiveness, "Why did the roaches leave?"

"I don't know. Maybe the mayor turned Engineer. Or the chief of police."

At first, the police had tried to help. They had come whenever the bots or Sam or Sheila had called to complain. They had dispersed the demonstrators. Then they had begun to swing by on their rounds, but their patrol had proved regular and predictable. Whenever the official Roachster had been due, the Engineers had vanished into doorways and alleys and basements like the roaches whose name they—and kids of all kinds—used for the police. Only a few remained in view, now quiet and peaceable and waiting for the police to turn the corner, when they would call back the others, as obstreperous as ever.

And then, the afternoon before, the police had vanished completely.

As if their leaving had been a signal, and perhaps it had, Engineers had swarmed into the neighborhood. They had expelled most of the residents of all those buildings that faced the bots' apartments. Shots had suggested the fates of those who resisted or who bore genetic modifications such as green skins or cosmetic inserts or even genetic tattoos. The remnants of a few bioforms—garbage disposals, computers, flycatchers, floaters—had been thrown to the street below. The largest pieces had once belonged to the bubblelike garages that had clung to the outer walls of those apartments whose tenants owned floaters. The Engineers had pried them loose and watched them fall, yelling in destructive glee.

Once the neighborhood had been properly cleansed of all modern technology except for the roof-top Bellows, half plant, half animal, that kept the buildings bearable in summer, the Engineers had moved in. Now they sat by darkened windows, rifles and pistols in their hands, sniping at whatever bot dared to make herself visible. The shots had died down the night before, when the bots had turned off the lights that fed them. They had resumed when morning sunlight began to illuminate their rooms.

"We don't use such things ourselves," Narcissus Joy had told him. "We have our own devices. But those weapons are no less effective because they're so traditional. Guns are elegantly simple as machines go. They even consume few resources of material or energy, especially if they reload their cartridges. And they take a long time to wear out."

Sam had been puzzled. "How can you admire their guns when they—?"

"It's not the tool that matters," Narcissus Joy had said. "But the aim of its user."

It was a cliché of history and philosophy and ethics, Sam knew, that a good end could never justify evil means. She had seemed to deny that, though he had had to agree that a bad end could befoul good means. Yet he had not tried to argue. He had said only, "I'm glad their aim isn't any better."

Now he said to Jackie Thyme, "Let's get into the hallway." Windowless and shielded by interior walls, that was the safest place on most of the building's floors. It was not, however, completely safe, as the holes in wooden doors and plaster partitions insistently reminded him. At least, the snipers couldn't see them there.

"This," gasped Sheila, "is a helluva way to get to talk to my husband."

"Hush," said Sam. "We've both been busy." He positioned a light blue leech on the side of her throat. Then, while he waited for it to secrete its dose of pain-killer, he used a scrap of clean bandage to wipe blood from the snakeskin along her jaw. When the pale green of her skin—it would have been white with her pain if she had been an unmodified normal human—began to darken toward its normal hue, he stroked her cap of orange and brown feathers and began to work on the damage.

"So have those snipers." Her wound was low on her ribcage, a tear in the skin, a broken rib, blood. By the time the bullet had penetrated the corridor wall to find her, its force had been more than half spent.

The children she had been leading toward the elevators to the basement squatted quietly by the wall, low, below the level of the windowsills in the apartments to either side, so that bullets would be less likely to find them as well. The youngest children, still too young to withdraw their roots from the soil and walk, even too young for their stalks to begin the changes that would give them legs, had been transplanted into earthenware pots that now rested on children's wagons shaped like miniature Tortoises, Armadons, and Beetles. The older children held the wagons' handles; until their guide had been shot, they had been pulling them down the hall.

Except for Sam's mutterings as he worked, the few words he exchanged with his wife, the noises that bullets made as they punched holes in walls and plaster fragments rained upon the floor, the hallway was silent. The younger bots in their pots could not yet speak. The older ones did not.

Sam finally looked up from his wife's wound. "Jackie," he said, "get these kids downstairs. And stay down there yourself."

"Uh-uh," said the young bot. "I'll be back." But she obeyed his first command, gesturing to the others, starting the parade once more moving down the hall.

When the last of the wagons had passed, Sheila stared yearningly after them. "They're making shields," she said as her husband applied a last clip and began to wrap her chest in yards of bandage. "For the windows, you know? They're using doors. Some are steel. Most are just wood, and there won't be enough, but that's my next job. As soon as all the kids are downstairs. Gotta get the adults down there too. All except the marines."

"The marines?"

"They have a few . . ." She gasped as he tightened the wrapping that would help her rib heal. "A few who have studied war. No experience, but they've read a lot. They've got weapons. And plans."

"Good," said Sam. "I hope it works, but . . ."

Sam began to notice differences among the bots who passed him in the building's halls. Some, the majority, kept their heads ducked while they carried dismounted doors toward the windows and equipment such as bioform computers toward the elevators, as if that would keep them safe from the Engineer snipers. Others, the marines, Sam thought, held their heads higher and moved with an air of brisk determination.

Not all the bots he treated could walk away from him. They needed stretchers and stretcher-bearers. Unfortunately, no such luxuries were available, and when he tried to commandeer a door, Shasta Lou stepped from a doorway to shake the pale blue blossoms of her head and say, "No. We have to seal the building."

"And let her die?" He stared pointedly at the bandages he had tied in place over the injured bot's abdomen. He hoped she had some notion of how easily his crude patchings could come loose. "I don't dare carry her myself, or let anyone else. She needs support, and even with that, she could bleed to death internally."

"The group comes first," said Shasta Lou.

With a quiet shudder, the patient rendered their argument moot. Sam sighed and bent and carried the body to the wider patch of corridor onto which the elevators opened. He had just laid it on the floor when a door sighed open and Jackie Thyme emerged.

"I thought I told you to stay down there."

The young bot's shrug belied her serious, determined expression. "I want to help."

"Think you can handle this one? Don't take it to the shelter. The first floor should do."

Another shrug, and the small bot grasped the body's ankles and began to pull. The corpse slid obediently into the elevator.

As it did so, Alice Belle stepped out of the next elevator to the left, waved one hand, and hurried off down the corridor. Behind her appeared Narcissus Joy. From a belt around her waist hung a radiophone. She was carrying a heavy pot from whose top grew a leafy bush covered with compact fruit. Curious, as soon as Jackie Thyme had disappeared with her burden, Sam followed Narcissus Joy into the nearest apartment and watched her set the pot on the floor to one side of an unshielded window. She noticed him behind her, nodded, and said nothing as she leaned toward the window and peered outside.

Sam noticed that her scalp blossoms, normally a creamy white, were now limp and bedraggled. Their orange rims seemed dirty. Fatigue, he thought. No time to stand beneath one of the building's artificial rainstorms, nor to stand, rooted and sunlit, photosynthesizing, resting, recharging.

A shot chipped paint from woodwork near her head. She withdrew and picked one of her plant's fruit. A long, hairlike tendril continued to link the fruit to the branch that had borne it. She found a grip on the fruit's skin and peeled it back like that of a banana. As soon it was exposed to air, the inner fruit darkened in color and spread birdlike wings. It stepped onto her wrist, fluttered, preened, and looked at Narcissus Joy, who looked in turn at Sam and said, "A botbird."

She flicked her wrist toward the window, and the botbird flew through the opening. Behind it trailed a continuation of the fiber that had spanned the break in its stem. "Fiber optics," said Narcissus Joy. "So we can see what's going on out there. It's easier than using the honeysuckle."

She turned toward the plant she had brought into the room and began to poke and pat at its uppermost leaves, until they formed a flat surface like the screen of a bioform computer. On that surface there appeared a view of the streets and buildings outside their walls and below the botbird.

The view blanked out. "The fiber broke," said the bot, even as she reached for another botbird fruit, peeled it, and released it. The landscape outside once more began to slide across the screen, and in a moment they could see what the buildings hid from their eyes: a street, a block away, dotted with groups of Engineers. "More guns," said Narcissus Joy. "And . . . Litter!"

"What?" asked Sam. She pointed at the image, and he stared at the heavy tubes that rested on three blue-clad shoulders. He knew what they were; he had seen them in old veedo movies and in occasional newscasts of foreign wars whose disputants could afford nothing more modern than the small missiles these tubes would launch.

A gasp behind him announced that someone else had recognized the old-fashioned weaponry as well, and probably for the same reason. He turned his head and saw Jackie Thyme leaning forward, wordlessly intent on the view. As silently, he put one arm around her shoulders.

Narcissus Joy had her phone in her hand, punching digits in a blur of motion. "They're getting ready for the main assault," she said, staring at the screen that showed the botbird's view. "No, I don't think they'll have much trouble getting in. Yes, get things up here." On the screen, the Engineers carrying the shoulder-fired missile launchers were beginning to trudge toward the nearest intersection. "And hurry."

The phone went back on her belt. She continued to stare at the screen, gauging the enemy's progress. Finally, she said, "We only want the fighters up here now, Doc. You'd better go down now." She looked at Jackie Thyme. "You too, and stay there this time. You'll be safe as soon as they seal the doors. The Engineers will never find you."

"What about . . . ?" Where was Sheila? Was she upstairs? Downstairs?

"We have a few minutes," said Narcissus Joy. "Don't worry. We'll send all the noncombatants down."

Voices rang in the halls. Feet sounded in the hallway outside the apartment. Shasta Lou entered the room, followed by two bots carrying bushel baskets full of what looked like large fruits and seed pods. "And you?" asked Sam.

"You're the rear guard," said Jackie Thyme. "I—"

"No. You're too young." Narcissus Joy gave them both a mirthless, toothy grin.

"And so are you," said Shasta Lou. She was pointing to show the other bots where to set their burdens. "Get out of here. Go with them."

"We've got a war to fight."

"I can sell myself just as dearly as you can. And a lot more dearly than any mechin' Engineer. And we only need one of us at a window."

When Narcissus Joy finally and reluctantly nodded, Shasta Lou turned to Sam and Jackie Thyme. "See?" she said. "She developed the botbirds herself. Others did these." She held up one of the seed pods, brown and patterned with lines of small bumps. "Grenades. Mother Nature already had small ones, for spreading seeds. They beefed them up and grew them right here."

A cry of alarm, echoing from another room, brought their attention to the window. Forgetting for a moment the risks posed by the snipers, they looked out and saw, kneeling on the sidewalk across the street, a missile-man. The streak of smoke and the explosion downstairs seemed to be simultaneous.

The building shook. There was the groan of stressed masonry, the rattle of falling walls and ceilings, the screams of the wounded and the dying. Sam prayed that Sheila was safe in the basement shelter, or higher in the building and on her way to safety, anywhere except within reach of the explosion.

Shasta Lou picked up a fruit whose pink and purple skin bore an unwholesome sheen. "And gas bombs," she said. "It will cost them a lot to get into this building. Now go! Before they seal the shelter."

They went, all three, leaving Shasta Lou to throw her grenades and gas bombs at the Engineers. In the hall they joined a steady flow of others toward the basement. An elevator door hissed open, and two bots elbowed them aside. They were carrying what seemed to Sam no more than a large plant, rooted in an oversized pot, and he wondered why they were bothering with their pets at this late moment. But other bots stepped out of the way, clearing an ample path into the elevator, and Jackie Thyme whispered an awed, "The Eldest! She wouldn't leave until the last minute!"

"Let's take the stairs," said Sam. That word was enough to make him realize that he had finally seen one of the ancestral bots. It was as large as any member of the current generation, but it was legless, armless, more profusely leaved, its bulb embedded in the soil, its head a massive flower. Scent accompanied it, and a sense of mingled panic and resolve.

Chapter
Thirteen

"SOMEONE . . ." SAID ALVAR Hannoken. He was standing
before the broad picture window in his office, facing outward, his hands clasped behind his back. His fingers worked
obsessively at a twist of leaves he had taken from the kudzu
plant beside him; they were green with plant juice. From time
to time his elongated, goatlike feet shifted restlessly on the
carpeted floor. He was as frustrated as Frederick. "Someone
doesn't want you talking to anyone at BRA. You can't call
your boss. You can't call your friend. Not at the office. Not at
home. You can't even call BRA employees you don't know,
and no one else here can call for you."

"It's like they built a wall between you and them," growled
Renny. His tail thumped the floor.

Frederick Suida sat backward on a long-legged stool the
Probe Station director had produced from a cupboard in his
office wall. His arms were crossed on its backrest, his chin
propped on his forearms, and his eyes fixed morosely on the
room's blank veedo screen. Two steps away, Donna Rose
stared worriedly at his back. Neither spoke.

"Between *us* and them," said Hannoken. "Probe Station
can't get through to BRA. No other station can get through
unless it's on their own business. If we ask them to call for
us, boom! the circuits go out. Or so StarBell tells us."

"They're wired right into the computers," said Lois McAlois.
She was in her wheelchair, as she was whenever she ventured
out of the low-gee zones in which her stump-legged body
functioned most efficiently. One hand rested on Renny's back,
just behind the collar. "They have to be," she added. "There's
no other way they could stop us *every* time."

Renny pointed his nose at Frederick, jerking it upward
almost as if he were trying to lift him out of his depression.
"You're not doing any good whining about it." He added a

149

small whimper as if to show them what he meant. "Maybe there's a reason, and we'll find out in due time. In the meantime, give Freddy something better to stare at than a blank wall. Turn on the news."

Hannoken pivoted on one foot to look at Frederick, who continued to stare blindly at the empty screen. He did not seem to have heard a word, but still Hannoken said, "Athena, veedo on, news."

The picture that came to life before them showed an aerial view of: an apartment building most of whose windows had been blocked on the inside; brief openings and arms hurling round objects that promptly vanished in clouds of vapor and shrapnel; snipers firing from windows across a street; pavement littered with blue-clad bodies; Engineers crouching behind shards of floater bubble to fire antitank missiles from shoulder-mounted launchers; gaping holes where missiles had penetrated walls; the shattered glass of the apartment building's main entrance. Close-ups added detail: the arms that threw what could only be grenades were green; the snipers wore the same blue as the bodies in the street, with patches and medallions and ear ornaments that proclaimed their allegiance to the Engineers; within the holes the missiles had blasted were green bodies, red blood, wreckage. The sound was rattle and boom and shriek, the sound of gunfire and explosions and painful dying.

From time to time, the veedo showed them a glimpse of media Bioblimps, each one marked with the logo of a different network. The sky beyond was the blue of a summer day, flocked with small clouds, pierced by climbing jets, pocked by distant Bioblimps and floaters. It was nature's disdain for human folly.

There was no hint of any official attempt to quell the violence. No police. No National Guard. The Engineers seemed far too free to do whatever they wished.

"Where's the Army?" asked Renny. "Or the Marines?" They were the traditional back-ups when local forces proved inadequate to the task of restoring order, but there was no sign of them either.

"Most of their tanks are dead," said Hannoken. "There are apparently a lot of Engineers and sympathizers in the armed forces, and they've bombed the farms and depots, turned the tanks on each other, poisoned the birds. We don't even have a Navy anymore. They scuttled the blowfish subs."

"They're disarming their enemy," said Lois, shaking her head. "They're not planning to stop with—"

"I *know* that building," said Donna Rose.

The others' words had not been enough to penetrate Frederick's depression. The veedo picture, though he was staring directly at it, had not even made him blink. But the pain in her voice, which was much like that the slaughter at the park had elicited, made him turn and ask, "What is it?"

She said nothing. She did not need to, for the newscaster finally spoke. "The Engineers," he said, his voice sounding awed, excited, and alarmed together, "seem to have declared war on what they consider the enemies of civilization. The building you see on your veedo is owned and occupied by white-collar botanicals. As you can see, they are offering considerable resistance."

The view zoomed in on the street just as a pair of round objects arced from a fourth-floor window toward the surface of the street. They were clearly vegetable in origin. "Grenades," said the newscaster. "One sprays seeds with lethal force." The close-up showed a knobby brown seedcase as it disappeared with a sharp bang. Immediately, the screen filled with a noxious-looking fruit through whose split side a misty vapor was billowing. "The other emits a poisonous gas."

Yet the bodies in the street must have accumulated in the first few moments of the bots' return fire. Even a strong arm could not throw the grenades far, and it was not difficult for the Engineers to stay out of range, remaining within the facing buildings, gathering toward the ends of the block. Meanwhile, their guns and missiles continued to batter at the building, punching aside the barriers that blocked the windows, pruning away the arms that hurled the explosive fruit, blowing ever-larger holes in the street-level walls.

The newscaster sounded fearful when he spoke again: "There is little doubt of what the Engineers will do when the resistance to their attack ends. They will search out every botanical they can find and . . ." Slowly, with the rhythm of a dirge, the veedo screen pulsed with images taken from the recent past, images that had, till now, too rarely reached the news: killing at the park, raping greenskins in an alley, butchering Roachsters and litterbugs, chasing, hacking, burning . . . "And for that . . ." he said. His in-drawn breath was clearly audible. "For that display of anti-Engineer propaganda, I am surely doomed."

He fell silent. In tribute to his courage, the audience in Hannoken's office said nothing to break the speechless quiet. They could only watch as . . .

The screen flickered, and a new voice spoke, jovially avuncular: "We shouldn't be alarmists, folks. The Engineers say they represent the will of the people, and I can't believe the people could be that destructive. The Engineers are single-minded, but they're not monomaniacs! Surely they know how essential gengineering is to modern society, and . . . Why, look! The firing is dying down already."

Nothing moved in the building's windows. The snipers were falling silent. The missile-men were setting down their launchers, standing, stretching. No one was making any move to cross the street and invade the bots' ravaged preserve.

The new voice resumed: "Only a few of the bots in the building were actively resisting the will of the people, as interpreted by the Engineers. They have given up now, and all that remains to be done is to round them up and bring them out for trial. The rest of the bots in there are surely innocent. They will be left unharmed. Just watch."

The veedo screen showed three figures rounding the corner of the block. Two of them were carrying a heavy crate in a sling. The third was gesturing, pointing toward the nearest missile-man, stopping his porters beside the launcher, removing a pair of knob-headed, phallic missiles. When the trio moved on, the missile-man loaded his launcher and knelt, awaiting the command to fire.

That command came as soon as every missile-man was armed with the new missiles. Together then, simultaneously, they fired. The missiles smoked across the street and into broken doorways and windows. The ground floor of the bots' apartment building erupted with smoke and flame.

"Incendiaries!" Hannoken's voice was shocked.

The newscaster who had replaced the alarmist said nothing at all.

The missile-men reloaded and fired again, this time at the third-floor windows. Minutes later, the entire building was an inferno in which nothing could possibly be alive. Flaming lengths of honeysuckle vine were falling from the walls, landing in the street and even on the doorsteps of those buildings that had harbored the Engineer snipers.

The crackling sounds of burning wood and the roar of the flames themselves covered any special sounds that burning flesh might make, but the smoke from the fire had a greasy look to it. "I'll bet it stinks," said Renny.

Only then did the sound of sirens come over the veedo's speaker.

Only then was there any sign that society recognized any responsibility to protect its members from catastrophe. Sadly, "catastrophe" did not seem to include what society, through its members, could do to itself. Only fire, and the danger that the flames might spread to other buildings.

The fire trucks arrived, immense, walking water bladders from which grew muscular hoses; their ancestors had once been elephants. A few police Roachsters accompanied them. Even though there seemed no attempt to pursue the Engineers, the latter melted away, around corners and into alleys. The camera followed them as they regrouped a block away, and then as they began marching down the street.

"Where are they going?" asked Lois McAlois.

"Oh, no," said Donna Rose.

Frederick sighed and rested his forehead on his arms where they crossed his seatback. "The park," he said. "That's the way to the park. Again."

The view on the screen lifted to show several logoed media Bioblimps, all following the parade. No one, not even on the veedo, said a word until Hannoken finally broke the silence with, "Athena, com center."

The voice that answered sounded shaky. "Yes, Director?"

"You were watching?"

"Yes, sir." There was no hesitation, no question of what he meant.

"What's happening elsewhere? Have they really stopped the news embargo?"

"Here's the feed."

The veedo flickered, showing other cities in their own land: nothing so bad, just riots and *small* massacres. But elsewhere: In Europe, a bot ghetto lay in ruins while military bombers circled overhead, their booming cries the sounds of demented, bass gulls. In England and Italy, green figures dangled from lampposts. In Asia, Tokyo, Singapore, Beijing, Seoul, and Ulan-Bator were all aflame.

Frederick could not stand it. He left his perch so abruptly that the stool toppled. He turned off the veedo set. The room was suddenly dominated by Renny's panting, Donna Rose's sobs, Alvar Hannoken's and Lois McAlois's and his own harshly syncopated gasps.

For long moments no one spoke. Hannoken stamped one black-stockinged foot as if he had the polished hooves of the goats he had modeled his legs on. He turned once more toward his window as if he could indeed stare directly into space, as if there were no glass and no mirrors between him and the void. He reached toward one side of the window's frame, touched a control, and the distant radio telescope began to drift toward one side. He had turned off the mechanism that kept the outside mirrors tracking a stable view. Now the rotation of the station showed. Earth rolled into sight. He and the others stared at the world that had given them all birth, down at chaos and pain and death.

As abruptly as Frederick had knocked over his stool, Hannoken spun on one foot, stepped to the wall, and opened his liquor cache. He grabbed a bottle and glasses. He poured. "Here," he said. "It's my only single-malt Scotch, but . . ."

Frederick sipped and choked. "No water?"

Hannoken shook his head. "No. Never. 'Whiskey' comes from the Gaelic, you know. 'Uisgebeatha'. 'The water of life'. And life . . ." He paused. He lifted his glass as if in a toast. He tossed its amber contents into his throat as if he were a Russian with a tumbler full of vodka. "We'll have to do something," he said. "I wish I knew what."

Lois McAlois imitated the station director's gesture. So, with a skeptical expression, did Frederick; this time he managed not to choke. "We have to get them up here," he said. No one asked him who he meant. "As many as we can."

Hannoken nodded jerkily. "I'll talk to the other station directors. See how many that is. And what else we can do." Setting his glass on his desk, he walked out of the room.

Donna Rose was standing beside the trough of soil that was her bed. Her arms were folded tightly across her chest, her head bowed, her blossoms awash in sunlight.

Frederick stood beside her, staring at the limited view of the universe that their porthole provided. The sun, its brilliant fire softened by filters, filled most of the glass, and the stars were invisible, but still there was a sense of vast black distance beyond.

He was thinking: His first glimpse of the Engineers, the very day Tom Cross had trundled him down the road and into the city, had revealed them as greedy, short-sighted, destructive, violent. He and Tom had come upon them barbecuing litterbugs, and they had seen him, the pig from under the sink, as no more than a second course. He and Tom had only just escaped.

Later, years later, other Engineers had slaughtered Tom, Tom's wife, his own wife, and more. The public's horrified reaction had helped get Frederick his human body. But now? He shook his head silently. The public was no longer horrified by Engineer atrocities. It joined in. Reactionaries persecuted sentient genimals such as Renny. Sympathizers carried weapons to the city park and helped to slaughter bots, or they looked aside when Engineer troops marched on an apartment building. Anyone who objected, like that newscaster who had dared to forecast a massacre, was silenced.

Donna Rose must have been having similar thoughts, for her shoulders shook and a small moan escaped her lips. Frederick reached out and laid one hand on her shoulder. He squeezed. She turned. Her arms went around his chest, desperately constricting. Her tears soaked his coverall and were warm upon his skin.

Her blossoms were just below his nose. He looked at them. They were pale yellow, the central pistils paler, the tiny anthers darker, almost orange, the fragrance subtle but warm, musky, hinting of violets and cherry blossoms. He let his own arms fold around her, feeling for the first time the fibrous texture of her leaves, the firm meat beneath, the knobs of bone, the warmth.

Neither of them ever knew how long they held each other, except that it was long enough for Donna Rose's tears to slow and finally stop.

That was when Frederick spoke his first words. "I'll have nightmares tonight," he said. "If I even sleep." Such things, such atrocities, whether he was involved as he had been when he had given Donna Rose refuge after the massacre in the park, or only saw the slaughter on the news, always left his mind roiling with the pain of memory. Rest came late or not at all.

The bot only squeezed his chest more tightly and murmured something into the wet cloth of his coverall.

"What?" he asked.

She shifted her head, freeing her mouth. "I won't sleep either. I know it. How could I?"

A long moment later, she added, "Maybe. If we just held each other. Like this, Freddy."

The muscles of his legs were protesting, informing him that he had been standing far too long. He sighed and watched the petals of her blossoms flutter in the breeze of his breath. "All right," he said. "Let's lie down."

They turned together toward his bed.

It was not long before they sought a comfort deeper than simply holding tightly to each other could provide. As Donna Rose had promised, her bulb did not get in their way. Nor did the way her roots twined involuntarily around his ankles or her leaves enfolded them both in a green cocoon.

Just before he fell asleep, Frederick wondered whether their mating could possibly be fertile. The bots themselves relied on their head-top flowers and seeds for reproduction. But their human genetic component was large, and they might well, he thought, have more animal apparatus than met the eye. Ovaries. A uterus.

What might their child be like?

"We launch this thing tomorrow," said Arlan Michaels. His short figure straddled one of the cables that held the *Quoi*, the first crew-carrying Q-ship, the prototype, in its bay, his legs holding him in place. He gestured toward Lois McAlois. "The tanks are full. Make sure it's ready, and let's get it outside." Three technicians leaned over open panels in the ship's long central spine, bracing themselves in the gaps between the tanks of reaction mass that girdled the spine. They were making final adjustments to the Q-drive itself.

"What's the rush?" asked Renny. Both he and Lois wore vacuum suits, the faceplates of the helmets open. His had been tailored especially to fit his nonhuman form. Lois held in one hand the end of a tether clipped to his belt, and when she let go of her own cable, the two of them began to drift toward the ship's cabin hatch.

"Director's orders," said the pilot. "He said we need it now."

"It can't help them down on Earth, can it?" asked the German shepherd. "Even if it works. It's too small."

"It'll work. Never doubt it."

Michaels grimaced. "It's a machine. Maybe he figures, if it works the way it's supposed to, it'll calm those Engineers down a little."

"Huh!"

"Maybe he'll offer it to them. A bigger model, a trip to the stars, a hunt for a world with enough resources to let them live the way they want, at least for a while."

"It'll take too long. They're not that patient. And there's too many of them to move." Renny was growling his words.

"What else can we do?" said Lois. She did not sound hopeful, but now the hatch was open and she was pushing the dog into his niche, the space her missing legs would not occupy. She slid in behind him, strapped herself into her seat, and began the process of bringing the controls to life. A computer ventilation fan began to hum. Indicator lights lit up. A computer-synthesized voice said, "The hatch is open."

Metallic noises from behind the cabin suggested the closing of access hatches. Lois touched a control and the cabin hatch swung shut, sighing into its airtight seal. She closed her helmet and reached toward Renny's. As soon as they were both thus shielded against any loss of cabin pressure, Michaels's voice came from speakers beside their ears. "The techs are clear."

"Power on," said Lois, and she fed the necessary commands to the Q-drive. Probabilities shifted. Particles materialized from the vacuum, and a digital meter spun out its report of available energy.

Renny twisted, more awkward than ever in his suit, to position his head near her truncated thigh, where he could watch her face. She did not look at him, for the controls demanded all her attention. "Just like the simulator. Is everyone out of the way?"

"The bay is clear."

"Release the cables." Someone obeyed the command, but the cables did not let go of the ship quite simultaneously. The *Quoi* lurched and began to drift toward one side of the bay. She fed the merest trace of lunar dust to the drive, routed the mildest possible thrust to the appropriate side, and recentered the ship.

"Pull the air." The throb of air pumps faded rapidly as the air that carried the sound grew thinner.

"Open the bay." The great door that closed one end of the bay irised open. She fed more dust to the drive, and the *Quoi* moved slowly out of its shelter, into the environment for which it was meant. Black filled the ports, and stars, and the bulk of the construction shack, and further off Probe Station itself, the separate research labs, the radio telescope, the Moon, and Earth. The sun was not in their field of view.

"No problems."

"Then bring her around," Michaels said over the radio.

The other end of the construction shack held a dock, an elastic tube with a mouth like that of a lamprey. Carefully, Lois swung the ship. The ports darkened as they came to face the sun. They cleared again as the *Quoi* swung its nose still further. A touch of thrust, the merest feather, then pushed the ship. More feather touches, more swings, and finally the dock's lamprey mouth could fit over the cabin's hatch. Then, at last, she could shut down the controls once more and say, "Tomorrow, Renny."

When Frederick opened his eyes that morning, he found Donna Rose staring at him. He blinked, and he almost smiled. "No nightmares," he said.

"None at all?" She did smile.

"None."

PART 3

Chapter
Fourteen

THE PLACE WAS like a gravel pit or crater, its high walls marked with the strata of civilization, its floor a day-baked, night-chilled puree of dust and sand and small stones and fragments of garbage, studded except near the working face with the shacks of the imprisoned workers. The air reeked of a thousand stinks, of rot and sweat and smoke and ordure and ancient chemicals. The only moisture lay in small, glistening puddles, oily, acrid, plainly toxic, that no one dared to touch. There was no trace of green plants, not even of the ubiquitous honeysuckle, though there were within the crater a very few skins marked by chlorophyll. Most people whose modifications were so obvious had not survived to be confined in the camp.

One side of the crater was open to admit a road, though it was blocked by chain-link fence and armed guards. More guards patrolled the crater rim. Beyond the fence, their cinderblock barracks sheltered in its lee a few small, dusty shrubs. Trees were visible in the distance.

Naked except for a strip of tattered cloth wrapped around his hips and a pair of crude sandals cut from rubber tires, Jeremy Duncan crouched in the sun beside the shadow cast by a fragment of pumpkin shell. He sniffed at his arm, detecting in his sweat the odor of malnutrition. There was food, but it was not enough to maintain both life and strength. To make up the deficit, he had already used up all his fat; now he was using protein, muscle, and the wastes he generated in the process accounted for his body odor. When all the muscle he could spare was gone . . . He stared alternately at the ruins of his home and at his neighbor, as naked as he, as naked-ribbed scrawny, though he didn't have the festering sores that marked the edges of Duncan's gills.

What he did have was a small, smoky, reeking fire, its fuel bits of ancient, punky wood, organic pulp, and his own manure, all dried in the sun. He also had a shack, a hovel, pieced together from bits of ancient plywood, a rusty automobile door, a tattered shower curtain. It was barely more than a burrow, but it helped to contain his body heat at night and it provided a minimum of shelter against the wind and rain.

Duncan had had a shack like that himself, but he had made the mistake of using a piece of pumpkin shell for one wall. That morning, early, dawn barely in the sky, three guards had come to roust him from his sleep and chide him.

They wore tan shorts and shirts, polished black shoes, black socks, broad-brimmed hats. The smallest had stood to one side, an automatic weapon held ready in his arms. The other two had carried heavy sticks.

"You know better, genny," the one with the mustache had said, backhanding him, kicking him, striking him on the gills with his stick. "No more gene shit. Never. I should even rip these things out of you. With my bare fingers, or an axe, or . . ."

While the guard raved, while he cowered, hiding his face with an arm as much to conceal his defiant, hating glare as to protect his eyes, another guard, the largest of the three, had torn the shack apart. He had kicked the rusty doorposts until they fell. He had peeled the roof off and hurled it sailing through the air until it sliced into a nearby shack; a shriek marked protest or pain, though it cut off immediately, as soon as the victim peeked through a crack and saw what was happening. He had pushed at the walls until they fell, and then he had stomped, shattering ancient glass, crumpling rusty sheet metal, breaking half-rotten wood. Finally, all that was left was the piece of pumpkin shell, jagged-edged, too heavy to hurl, too thick to break with feet or hands alone.

"Don't use it again," the one with the mustache had said. "We'll bust *you* up next time." He had grinned as if he would enjoy the job.

As soon as the three guards had left, the camp's other prisoners had emerged from their crude shelters, kindled their morning fires, and stood beside them, warming their hands, carefully not looking in his direction. The desultory mutter of complaint and argument and memory had resumed as if it had never quit the night before, but no one had said a word to Duncan. It was as if the others feared that if they came too close to one who had attracted such unwelcome attention, they too might suffer.

When Looby and his small entourage appeared, the voices paused for only a moment. They too were a threat, but they too were prisoners. They were also the only ones who had anything to grin about as they were grinning now. Alone among the camp's inmates they wore shorts and shoes, filthy but intact, and carried both sticks and extra flesh. All but one wore shirts as well; the one without was too furry to need such a garment.

"Aww, Jerry," said Looby. He was a greenskin whose ability to photosynthesize a few extra calories had in the early days given him an edge over other would-be bullies. His other modification—his thumbnails had been replaced by retractile talons—had also helped. Now the other bullies danced attendance on him, and the group kept its informal status as chief thugs by dispensing the meager rations, trading food and drink to the other prisoners in exchange for what they pulled from the ground. It was not surprising that Looby and his friends were the best fed, nor that they protected their privileges by beating and starving those who dared to protest and by informing on those who spoke of escape or riot.

"Aww, Jerry," said Looby again. No one knew his last name. "They wrecked your house! And I can use that piece of wood, those posts, that . . ." Extending one thumb claw as a mute warning that Duncan should not object, he used it to point at the few still usable bits of wreckage. "Mickey, Stanley, Bess," he said. The indicated aides picked up the pieces. When they had everything that was salvageable, and Jeremy Duncan had nothing left at all, Looby said, "Amy! Give the man a potster."

The woman he indicated bore a large scar on her cheek, where some Engineer had sliced away a genetically implanted decoration. Fragments of healing, reforming tissue revealed that the original had been a patch of butterfly wing and that Amy might once have been beautiful. Now, however, she was as scabby, string-haired, and filthy as anyone in the camp. Not even the chief slaves could wash. But she had a cloth sack over one shoulder, and now she produced what looked like a withered potato. Duncan's mouth watered at the sight. When she tossed it on the ground in front of him, he seized it eagerly. He had expected nothing, for the guards brought food only once a day, in the evening. That, they said, was when the slaves had earned a meal.

Potsters were one of the gengineers' earliest successes. They grew in the ground like potatoes but tasted much like lobster. Duncan thought it little wonder that the Engineers tolerated their existence despite their principles, but he said nothing. He was not about to give Looby a chance to change his mind. He was already chewing when the gang turned toward their own huts not far from the guardhouse, there to use what they had taken to make their rooms larger and their walls tighter against the wind and their roofs less likely to leak when it rained.

When he had eaten half the potster, Duncan folded the rest into his hand. Then he sat back on his heels and stared disconsolately at the little that was left of the wreckage. It had been all he owned. There was nothing else. No book. No rag. Not even a shiny bit of stone or metal. Nothing. They were allowed to build their shacks, if the materials they chose were worthless enough, or if they were ideologically pure, though if they were that they would not be here. Everything else they found was taken away.

He stared at his neighbor. He was a lucky man. He had no genetic modifications, at least none that showed. The guards therefore did not abuse him as badly. He had a little more pigment in his swarthy skin, and the sun did not burn him. Duncan glanced at his own cracked and peeling hide. And was he also chewing? Could he possibly have saved a crumb of their meager rations? Or was he simply gnawing on his tongue, or a bit of plastic or rotten leather?

"Bert?" He held out what was left of the potster, offering to share.

"Yah," said Berut Amoun, accepting the trade, biting, chewing. "I suppose there's room. You can squeeze in here tonight."

"We're slaves."

"Tell me something new."

"I hate them. They're dumb. They're stupid. Idiots." He kept his voice soft. He had seen what happened to those who insulted their masters too loudly. "I hate them. If I ever get the chance . . ."

The Engineers had triumphed. Through elections and coups and riotous rebellions, they had taken over every government that mattered. They had slaughtered gengineers and gengineered, the owners and sellers of Slugabeds and garbage disposals and Roachsters, greenskins and bots. And when their frenzy had calmed, they had marched the survivors into the labor camps. Duncan no longer remembered how long he had been here, in this camp. Nor did he remember whether he had already been here when Bert arrived, or whether Bert had been here first. He did remember that they had arrived only days apart, and that they had quickly discovered that they both knew Frederick.

"I wonder where Frederick is," said Duncan now. "And that dog."

"He sent Renny up there," said Bert, not for the first time. He bent his gaze toward the sky, too hazy with the smoke of burning garbage to be blue. At night, they could not see even the brightest of stars or satellites, and the moon was blurred. "Probe Station. Oughta be safe enough, eh? And then he went up too. I hope he had sense enough to stay there."

Duncan nodded gravely and stared at his hands. They were calloused, stained, cut by shards of metal and glass, red and swollen and oozing pus where the cuts had become infected. It would only get worse. One day, as he had seen happen to others, he would be unable to use them, unable to work. Looby would stop feeding him then. The guards would ignore his pleas. They would beat him. And he would die. He had seen it happen to others.

A horn blew, and the camp stirred. Duncan groaned. Bert crawled from his shelter. Looby screamed from somewhere, "Back to work! Move, you loafers!" He had chosen to make his occasional show of directive energy, as if to convince the Engineer guards of his value; most mornings he remained undisturbed in his hut. His henchmen appeared and began to chivvy the Engineers' prisoners toward the wall of the camp and the leavings of the Machine Age.

The place had once been a sanitary landfill, a dump where layers of earth had shielded from rats and seagulls and other vermin each day's accumulation of empty cans and bottles, steel and aluminum and glass, the plastics of outworn shoes and clothes and broken toys, scraps of foil, electric motors full of copper wire, cast-off refrigerators and microwave ovens, all the discards of an age far richer in material resources. The aluminum and copper and glass and plastic were still there. The larger chunks of steel had sound, unrusted cores. And it was the prisoners' job to separate anything and everything of value from the dross.

The gate in the fence opened, and an ancient front-end loader, red with rust, belching smoke, rattling, creaking, threatening imminent collapse, roared into the crater. When it reached the working face, it dug its bucket into the compressed layers of garbage and dirt, wrenched, and tore. Its job was to loosen, to make what was there available to sorting, stacking fingers. Whatever they found they would hand over to Looby and his crew in exchange for food. Later, they would pile it all in bins near the gate, and later still in the wagons that hauled it away to be used as the raw materials for a new Machine Age. The wagons were drawn by horses, cows, and even people, slaves as much as those who mined the dump.

Only the sodden lumps of cellulose that had once been newspapers and magazines and books and solid wood were not immediately salvageable, although they were tossed to one side to dry in the sun. Eventually, the prisoners burned them.

"Move!" A stick landed on Duncan's back, poked at his gill slits. He gasped at the pain. He lurched. He looked over his shoulder and saw the furry back of Stanley, Looby's chief side-kick. The man's upper arms were naked skin, decorated with a Roachster head, a Warbird, "Mother," genetic tattoos drawn in lines of melanin. Now he was swinging at a woman not far away. He wore a ferocious scowl, but his lips were quirked as if he enjoyed his role. The woman screamed, drowning for a moment the roar of the machine. Stanley hit her again.

Duncan did not know her name. He knew only that she was too scrawny to have breasts. Most of the women were, and sex was not part of life in the labor camp, except for Looby and his bullies.

"Nooo!" Someone else screamed, high and agonized yet unmistakably male. Duncan peered toward the sound. Bess, Looby's mate, had a prisoner on the ground. He rolled and flailed. She kicked at his crotch and poked at his face with the end of her stick. Spatters of blood suggested that she had stabbed at least one eye.

"Nooo! Tige! You killed my Mack! Juulie . . . !"

There was a sudden crunch. The screaming stopped. Bess struggled to pull the end of her stick from the eye socket.

Beside Duncan, Berut Amoun began to pant. "Jimmy," he said. "I knew him." He moaned, bent to pick up a rock, and began to run toward the murderer. He was staggering with the weakness of his malnutrition, but still he ran.

Bert's scream of rage was interrupted by the short, sharp sound of a shot. He crumpled in mid-stride. He fell. And Looby yelled again, "You! And you! And you! Pick 'em up. Put 'em in the pit." The pit was the hole, not far from the entrance to the camp, where all the bodies went. "The rest of you! Move it! Work! Or you don't eat!"

As the prisoners silently resumed their movement toward the working face of the landfill, Duncan bent his gaze upward, toward the edge of the cliff ahead. A guard stood there, above the layers of garbage the prisoners—the slaves—were about to burrow into. He had a rifle in his hands, its butt still against his shoulder, its muzzle sweeping over the scene below.

Duncan did not even feel shame at the thought that now Bert's shack would be his, if only he hurried when this shift was done, if only he reached it first. Nor did he feel shame at his lack of shame, though somewhere within his mind a flicker of uneasiness did struggle for life. Far stronger was his intent to survive, to persist. If, he thought, he was very, very lucky, he might someday gain the power to avenge himself, his friends, his civilization.

It was dusk. The day's labor was done. Duncan squatted in the doorway of Bert's hut, held his hands in the light, and stared at them. They were filthy, bleeding from fresh cuts and gashes, stinging where he had let the black liquid that oozed from the ground touch them. There was no way to wash. There hadn't been since . . . He thought of the day's deaths and shuddered and did not feel any safer to know that his back was sheltered by walls and roof that Bert had pieced together. He was, he knew, at the mercy of fate as embodied by Looby and the guards.

The horn blew again. He peered toward the fence at the mouth of the crater he and the other slave-laborers had carved in the landfill. The gate was open. The guards were pushing into the crater a wheeled bin of the sort the slaves loaded with glass and metal and plastic. It was empty now of garbage but filled with buckets of gruel and water and baskets of potatoes and cabbages and turnips and the fruits of sausage bushes and pie plants and . . . Most of them would be overripe, soft and moldy. But they were dinner.

Jeremy Duncan thought the food must come from local farms, where it spoiled in the field for lack of transport to city markets. The Engineers would not be starving, though. They had destroyed the world's Macks, but they had slaves who could haul wagons toward the city. The substitute transport would be slow, and it could not haul vast tonnages, but it could haul enough to keep the city fed, even if it left as much in the field to rot. It helped that they had killed so many that demand was not what it once had been.

The prisoners moved eagerly toward the dinner cart. The first to reach it, as always, were Looby and his henchmen. They surrounded it, barring access. As each of the rest arrived, they doled out the food, first putting what they wanted for themselves, including any unusual delicacies such as potsters, in the sack Looby's Amy carried. Some, who had not worked hard enough or found rich enough treasure, got nothing. No one got enough to feel full.

Like all the rest, Duncan drank his cup of water and wolfed his food as soon as it was in his hands. Unlike the rest, he felt a little more satisfied than usual. The potster the rubble of his shack had earned had been small, and he had shared it with Bert, but it had still made a difference.

The gate in the fence had been shut as soon as the garbage bin had passed. Now a trio of guards stood before it, their guns over their shoulders. Other guards overlooked the scene from the barracks roof and the rim of the crater.

The three by the gate were clearly bored. They were passing a small potted plant back and forth, holding it in one hand, stroking it with the other, pressing its leaves to their cheeks, even licking it. Duncan was too far away to make out any detail, but he knew they held a cocaine nettle, as much a product of the gengineering labs as his gills or pumpkin houses or litterbugs. He grunted wryly at the thought that the Engineers were so selective in their condemnations. He grunted again when he saw the sense in that selectivity: They rejected what replaced the machines of their dreams. If it was only another version of something—food or drugs—that had always grown, always been biological, they might accept it. They still rejected pumpkin houses and bots.

The prisoners dispersed as quickly as they had gathered, returning to their shacks. A few stood or squatted in twos or threes, talking quietly. Most huddled in their doorways, leaning over their small fires, adding fuel, much of it still damp with ground water and toxic chemicals, letting the smoke and fumes obscure their vision of the present and the feeble warmth combat the growing cool of the night, mindlessly awaiting the next day and its renewal of labor, perhaps remembering happier times, when the Engineers had seemed too trivial, too out of step with the reality of the day, ever to be a threat.

Jeremy Duncan gathered the splinters and fragments of wood that were all that remained of the hut he had built himself. He piled them by what had been Bert's shack. Then he sifted through the ashes of the fire Bert had had earlier, looking for a tiny coal. When he found it, he added a scrap of carefully dried paper, splinters, larger bits, and blew as gently as he could. If this did not work, he could fetch a coal from someone else's fire. Even rain rarely extinguished them all; someone always sheltered the flames and kept a supply of fuel dry. Only when the rain lasted for days did all the fires and coals go out. Then all the prisoners shivered until the sun returned and dried more fuel. The trick was rekindling the flame. Some of the prisoners made do with bottles, filled with water, to focus sunlight, but that worked only in the day. Sometimes there were matches, but the guards were stingy even with something so cheap.

When his fire was finally going, he added chunks of nearly dry pulp. They would dry and burn, smoking, stinking, but also warming. In due time, he would let it die, cover the coals with ashes, retreat into Bert's—now his—shelter, and curl himself into a ball to sleep. He would be cold, but he had learned to stand that.

In the meantime, there was memory . . .

He had not met anyone who had failed to see the burning of the bots' apartment building on the veedo. Many had not realized what it meant, but he had. He had thought of returning to his lab, at least long enough to make it impossible for anyone to use his files to track down any of those genimals he had helped to become human. But he had not. He had told himself that they would be able to take care of themselves. They would have to, as he would have to. And besides, he dared not take the time.

He had wrapped his torso in painful cloth, wrapped a sleeping bag around his speargun and mask and knife, and packed a small bag with a change of clothes and as much as he could of the food he had had in his cupboards. Then he had gotten into his Armadon and taken the greenway south. He had hoped he could reach the Gulf of Mexico. There, with his gills, he would be safe.

He should, he thought, have gone to the nearest river. The news reports on his vehicle's radio should have told him that. The Engineers were massacring all who embodied what they hated: bots and gengineers and Macks and Buggies and more. But he had only leaned over his tiller, straining to hasten his Armadon along the road to safety. He had never once thought of the streams and rivers that passed beneath his wheels every few kilometers as what they truly were: other, safer paths. The water would have been colder, but it would have let him swim invisibly toward his goal. The trip would have taken longer. But . . .

He had had a map. He had planned a route that would avoid all the cities between his home and the Gulf. It would even avoid most small towns, and the few he could not avoid he had planned to pass at night.

He had not expected to find a roadblock. The Armadon's legs had been running tirelessly atop its wheels, driving it steadily southward toward the border between Indiana and Kentucky. He had rounded a curve, and the Engineers had been waiting for him behind a windrow of dead Macks and Tortoises and Buggies. They had opened fire immediately, and when his vehicle was dead too, they had taken his bags and patted him down. When they felt the irregularities on the sides of his chest, they had stripped him. They had called him genny then. They had beaten him. They had tied his hands and beaten him again and forced him to march and beaten him once more.

When he came to, he was lying on the hardwood floor of what could only be a high-school gymnasium. The wood was stained with blood, much of it too dry and crusted to have come from his own wounds. Around him lay perhaps a hundred others, all of them genetically modified. There were ornamented faces and green skins and furry scalps and altered limbs. There were normals who, he later learned, had sold or owned gengineered products or worked in gengineering labs or objected to the Engineers' tactics or beliefs. There were those who, like Bert, had worked for public agencies and been involved in regulating or inspecting or licensing the gengineering industry. There were even police officers, guilty of no more than using Sparrowhawks and Roachsters in their work.

Day by day their numbers grew. So did their filth and their stink. They waited in that gymnasium for weeks, helpless beneath the guns of their guards, with no soap or water for washing, with only plastic buckets for toilets, with just barely enough food to remain alive. Eventually they were herded into antique livestock trucks and driven north and east to an abandoned landfill.

How long ago was that? He did not know. But it had been long enough to enlarge by half the crater in which they lived and labored. More weeks. Months. Long enough for slaves to be worked and neglected to death. Long enough for more prisoners to be delivered, for the camp to grow, for a barracks to be built for the guards, for hope to vanish.

Yet thought remained, and the very disasters that had stricken Jeremy Duncan and his fellow slaves told him something of the troubles the Engineers must be having as well. At the beginning of the revolution, the cry had been, "No quarter!" The Engineers had taken no prisoners when they attacked the bots in their dormitory in the park and later in their building. They had killed them all.

But he had been taken prisoner. He had not been butchered. Nor had his fellow prisoners.

He thought he knew what that meant. Someone, someone high in the Engineers' councils, had realized the difficulties they faced. They wanted the Machine Age back again. But they had no machines other than museum pieces and junkyard wrecks. They had none of the raw materials needed to make new ones, nor the factories, nor the skills, and it would be many years before they could possibly rebuild the necessary infrastructure. Worse yet, the ores that had once been plentiful had been exhausted by the Machine Age that had been. There were none but poor, low-grade ores, usable only with the application of large amounts of energy and labor, for its reincarnation. And the fossil fuels that had powered the Machine Age, either directly as fuels for engines or indirectly as fuels for electric power plants, were gone. Coal remained, but it could be mined and transported only with the aid of the machines they did not have.

The answers must have seemed obvious. The people of the Machine Age had been notoriously wasteful. Their dumps were full of metals that could be retrieved and melted down with no expenditure but labor. Of plastics that could be burned for fuel or converted back to something like the petroleum from which they had been made and then used for fuel again or as the raw material for new plastics, fabrics, pharmaceuticals. And if gengineering was anathema, its sentient products and proponents could still be exploited. Theirs could be the labor that mined the dumps for raw materials. Theirs could be the animal energy needed to process and build. And when they were worn out, dead as surely if more slowly, they would have atoned in part for the sin of their existence.

The leaders of the Engineers must, he thought, have regretted the initial purges. Human labor, slave labor, was slow and inefficient. But enough of it could do the job. It had built the pyramids of Egypt and Mexico, after all. And as it made possible the construction and operation of machines, of bulldozers and trucks and factories, it could be replaced. As it was replaced, the pace of reconstruction could accelerate. Eventually, it would no longer be necessary. Nor would the slaves.

Jeremy Duncan thought they were fools. They did not realize how pervasive the products of gengineering had become, or how much machinery would be necessary to maintain civilization, or how much fuel. They would struggle for a while. They would make him labor for them, and he would be a slave for as long as he lived, which he did not think would be very long.

He wished he could live. He wished he dared to hope that he might someday be in a position to bring vengeance upon his tormentors, the murderers of the technology he loved and served, the destroyers of his world. But he knew better. He himself had no hope of bringing the Engineers down. And though they must inevitably fail, he had no hope of seeing that failure. He would not see their dreams founder, the cities they now owned die, the world return to the poverty of subsistence farming without tractors or fertilizer or pesticides.

He wished he could laugh at what he saw for the future. But it was too bleak for that. Too bleak for him. Too bleak for all his species.

The fire was almost out. Using a fragment of broken glass, he scraped ashes over the last flames, hoping the coals would last until the morning. Then he backed into his small shack, his burrow, his hide, to sleep.

Chapter
Fifteen

DONNA ROSE HAD turned her back to the keyboard and array of small screens at which she worked as Frederick Suida's assistant. Bolted to the deck beneath her was a trough of soil much like that in her and Frederick's station quarters. Its surface was covered with a porous membrane that kept the dirt in place despite the lack of gravity; the pores were large enough to let her roots penetrate to the soil.

"Why can't we? Why? The tests were successful. The drive worked perfectly. It didn't scramble Lois's genes. It didn't hurt Renny. The physicists say there shouldn't be any problem handling heavy loads or flying close to stations. And there they are!" With the hand that did not wear a mouse-glove, Donna Rose gestured furiously at the larger wall screen that showed the skeletons of six new Q-ships being built outside the construction shack. They drifted in vacuum, tethered to the shack's hull with cables, while suited workers crawled over their frames, welding and fitting and slowly bringing them toward completion. They would be much larger than the *Quoi*, which would be able to fit inside just one of their reaction-mass tanks. They were designed not just to test whether the drive would work, but to carry passengers and cargo.

"Why *can't* we save them, Freddy?" she added.

The object of her fury hovered near one wall, not far from a handhold, and shrugged helplessly. "You know why," he said.

"But they're killing them all!" Donna Rose slumped as if she were indeed a plant, wilting beneath a desert sun. While they lasted, the newscasts from Earth had been a constant litany of murder. More buildings had been attacked and destroyed. Outdoor dormitories had been laid waste. Those bots and genetically modified humans who had survived the initial massacres had gone into hiding but the Engineers had searched them out, imprisoned them, enslaved them in labor camps, and slaughtered them mercilessly. There was no hope of escape, for by now most of the world's spaceports and airports had been wrecked, and nearly all of the world's spaceplanes were scrap.

Worst of all, the tone of the newscasts had changed. At first, some newscasters had been appalled. They had called the destruction folly and madness and error. Some had tried to sound more neutral, but within days, even they, as voices of the old order, had been replaced by people who could echo the dogmas of the Engineers: Machines were better than genes, more in tune with human needs, less of a challenge to the natural way of things. The gengineers and all their works must go, and if it was unfortunate that blood must be spilled, it was nevertheless necessary.

In time, even those half-apologetic reservations had been silenced. Now there were no newscasts at all. Veedo and radio were dominated by entertainment programs and official exhortations.

Only a handful of refugees had made it into space. As far as Donna Rose knew, there had been no bots among them.

Frederick spoke more gently. "The Orbitals," he said. That was what those who lived in space had begun to call themselves. "The Orbitals have begun to build extra living quarters. More were opened up when the *Gypsy* workers left. But the ships aren't ready yet. Look at them." He pointed at the screen, and then at the large, reinforced window on its right. The window overlooked the half that remained of the bay that had once held the *Quoi*. The office they were in, as well as other offices and workshops and labs where Arlan Michaels could design new drives and ships and physicists could strive for improvements in the technology, had been carved from the rest of the bay. Beyond the window were scattered several Q-drives in various stages of assembly. Beyond them was the broad iris that could open onto space.

The bot straightened as if she were summoning energy from the air. "There are others down there, Freddy," she said. "We've seen the camps, the graves. And we have the spaceplanes!" Her torso jerked as if she would like to pace, to turn and stomp and emphasize her protests with every motion at her command. But her roots were embedded in her trough of soil.

She did not withdraw those roots. She only jerked and gestured. Her leaves lashed. She pointed past the half-finished Q-ships toward Earth's rim to indicate the low-orbit stations where several spaceplanes had been mothballed. They had not dared to return after they had delivered their pitifully few refugees. "The spaceplanes!" she said again.

"Which would have to be refueled on the ground."

"Give them Q-drives!"

He shook his head. "No. They would need too much refitting to handle the mass tanks. It's simpler to build the new ones. They should even be able to handle the round trip. But . . ." He shook his head again. "Even if they were finished, we couldn't use them. Their pilots are still in training."

"We have Renny!" As soon as the *Quoi*'s test flights had proved successful, the dog had decided that he wanted to be, like Lois McAlois, a Q-ship pilot.

Before Frederick could answer her again, Arlan Michaels swung through the office door. "We've got a problem," he said as he stopped against a wall.

"Pilots or drives?" asked Frederick. Michaels was still in charge of pilot training as well as drive design. Frederick's responsibility was overseeing the construction of the new Q-ships. He handled paperwork, saw to it that the project had what it needed, dealt with the conflicts that inevitably arose among the workers, and did his best to solve whatever other problems arose. He also learned, and if he was no Q-flux engineer or physicist, at least he could now understand some of what those specialists were saying.

At the moment, what Michaels was saying was not hard to understand. He was drifting toward the window that overlooked the drive assembly shop, pointing, saying, "We've got a batch of superconducting ribbons that won't superconduct. Not at anything over 400 K, anyway. Someone cracked the casing and let air in. That let too much oxygen diffuse into the ceramic, and now it's shot."

"Minerva," said Frederick. His computer was a near duplicate of Alvar Hannoken's Athena. "Spec sheets, high-temp erbium superconductor." To Michaels, he said, "Can you fix it?"

"If I could heat it just right, in a vacuum. That would drive the oxygen off."

"Vacuum we've got." Frederick indicated the spec sheet on the screen. "And the processing temp seems to be within reach."

"But how do I know when to stop it?" With hardly a moment of hesitation, he answered his own question. "Run a current through it, of course. As soon as the resistance drops to zero, stop heating and seal the casing." Such procedures had been impossible when superconduction happened only at the temperature of liquid nitrogen or below.

"Was it sabotage?" asked Donna Rose.

"I don't think so," said Michaels.

"Was what sabotage?" The voice from beyond the door was so nearly a yelp that the sudden appearance of Renny's pointed nose was hardly necessary.

Frederick explained very briefly what had happened. Then Michaels said, "I'll see what we can do," and turned to leave. As soon as he was gone, Renny pulled himself through the doorway, positioned himself near the screen, and folded his hands beneath his chin as if they still were forepaws.

"I wish she'd get back," the German shepherd said. His tail pumped twice. For a moment, he seemed to be staring at the half-formed Q-ships outside the construction shack. The first of them to be completed would be his. He had finished his training. He had done as well as Lois on the simulator. And Hannoken himself had done the work that gave him the hands he would need.

Then his gaze shifted, his focus moving outward, his mind quite visibly pursuing Lois. She was headed toward the Belt, towing a chain of cargo pods loaded with supplies and equipment and crew. She had taken the first such train when Renny was still growing his hands. Workers had been burrowing into the asteroid that would become the *Gypsy* ever since. The rock they removed in the process was processed to remove its metals. The remaining slag was ground and set aside for later use as reaction mass. Meanwhile, the workers smoothed the forming *Gypsy*'s rough contours, hollowed out corridors and chambers, installed cables and plumbing. Others gathered and powdered smaller asteroids, for the *Gypsy*'s own excavated mass would hardly be enough to propel the vast ship everywhere that it might go.

Toward one end of the immense ovoid, workers were preparing the cavern that would be the new ship's drive chamber. When it was ready, the largest Q-drive yet imagined would be assembled within the cavern and the *Gypsy* would move under its own power to lunar orbit. There its conversion would be finished. It would acquire computers and furnishings, desks and kitchen ovens, all the paraphernalia that would be necessary if the *Gypsy* ever went, as some intended, elsewhere. Eventually, it would acquire its crew and inhabitants.

"She'll have legs, you know," said Renny. She had finally let the gengineers treat her stumps before she left.

"Three more weeks," said Frederick.

"She has to stop at Mars," said Donna Rose. Several of the pods Lois was hauling were destined for Chryse Base. Several more held cargo for the Saturn outpost, though she would not take them all the way; instead, she would bend her trajectory just so and then release them to fly a tangent course. They carried retrorockets just sufficient to slow them at the end of their journey.

"But she'll be at *Gypsy* in ten days," said Frederick. "Three more days to refill her mass tanks and hook up the return pods." Some of the construction workers were rotating home, back to families and friends, but Lois's return cargo would be much less massive than what she had hauled from Earth orbit. "She'll make better time on the way home."

In many ways, the Q-drive was free of the restrictions inherent in normal rockets. Still, what the *Quoi* could do did depend on the reaction mass she could carry in her tanks, and she was a small ship. She could handle heavy cargos, but like a tugboat with a line of barges she had to strain. The necessary acceleration came much faster with smaller loads, and her peak velocity was higher.

Renny stared outward for long moments. Frederick finally broke the silence by saying, "Do you think you could land one of the new ships on Earth?"

The answering snort was distinctly doggy. "You've got rescue fantasies."

"It's safe enough, isn't it?" insisted Donna Rose.

"That's what Michaels says. The drive didn't hurt Lois or me, and he's confident enough to have us building those." Renny gestured toward the skeletal, half-completed ships outside the shack.

"Doesn't it need a vacuum?" asked the bot.

Renny nodded. "That's not supposed to be a problem," he said slowly, as if he were thinking his way through lessons that had struck him as less than central to learning how to pilot. "For maximum power, it needs a vacuum even purer than that of the space out there." He gestured toward the screen. "If the vacuum isn't that good, the Q-flux generates less power, but then the flow of energy drives out any particles in the drive chamber, just as if they were fuel particles. That improves the vacuum, and then the power increases. It should therefore work just as well in an atmosphere. It might even work better, for the air itself could be used as reaction mass. The ship wouldn't have to carry extra."

"Then . . . ?"

"But you haven't got the foggiest idea of who to rescue. Or where to find them."

"Anybody!" cried Donna Rose.

Renny shook his head. "The Engineers are in power everywhere," he said. "The spysats don't lie. There's nobody left to rescue."

"There are the labor camps," said Frederick.

The dog shook his head again. "That's just fishing," he said. "Half the slaves are probably Engineers on the outs."

Later, when Renny had returned to his training and Frederick and Donna Rose were once more alone, Hannoken called. Minerva chimed, Donna Rose worked her fingers in the mouse-glove above her keyboard, embedded circuitry responded, and the image of uncompleted Q-ships on the wall screen was replaced by the face of Probe Station's director. His picture window was visible behind him. Before it sat a pot much like the one that had held his kudzu vine. This one, however, was empty except for a tiny shoot.

"What's that?" asked Donna Rose.

"Your tissue sample," answered the station director. He turned and gestured. "I made some changes, and . . ."

"What?" The bot's voice was outraged. "I didn't—"

"What's up?" Frederick cut off her protests with a placating gesture.

Hannoken turned back toward his veedo pickup and grimaced. "I thought you'd like to see what the com center just picked up. It seems to be a government situation analysis." His face faded from the screen to be replaced by text. "See what you think."

"Hunh," grunted Frederick. "He didn't say much about it."

"His face did." Her tone was sour, as if she had much more to say about becoming a mother without her knowledge or consent.

"Let's see . . ."

The document was straightforward. It said:

At the height of the Machine Age, there were over five billion people on the planet. Our ancestors knew that this population was greatly above Earth's so-called carrying capacity. That is, it was much too large to be sustained indefinitely. The world population would have to be much smaller if it was to require no more resources—food, fuels, solar and hydroelectric energy, wood, ores, etc.—than natural processes made available each year. They were forecasting that when the population exceeded the resources necessary to support it—whether because the fuels and ores were used up and soil fertility lost, or because the population simply grew too big—billions of people would die. The world would, quite inevitably, reduce the human population to or below the carrying capacity defined by the simplest of all the laws of nature. In simple, human terms, that law is: You cannot spend more than you earn; if you try, you will empty your bank account, exhaust your credit, and wind up facing that law again, only without whatever cushion you had the first time around.

Unfortunately, the gengineers were able to forestall the balancing of nature's equation. Population grew until, just before our Revolution, it had more than doubled. The last worldwide census put it at 12.3 billion.

As our ancestors were beginning to realize when gengineering first appeared, the technology of the Machine Age cannot support such numbers. Fortunately, we have already removed over two billion bots, greenskins, and other social contaminants.

Yet, if we are to succeed in our aims, we will have to cleanse the human species of many more of its members. Recent estimates indicate that we do not have the resources to support more than two billion.

Our present difficulties in obtaining sufficient food, fuel, and materials may prove to be a blessing in disguise. By this time next year, the world population will be lean and trim, and we will be the healthier species of which we have long dreamed.

"They are mad." Donna Rose's voice was hushed. "They won't have time to do anything but bury people."

"Or eat them," said Frederick with a shudder. "They'll lose too much. Starvation means a generation of brain-damaged children. They may not have the intelligence to rebuild until centuries from now. But there'll be disease, too, plague, and that will cost them even more. They'll lose whatever technicians they have, or most of them."

"Savages," said Donna Rose. "The survivors will be hunters and gatherers. Subsistence farmers if they're lucky."

"Is there any more?"

Donna Rose touched a key on her board, and four more lines scrolled into view:

Unfortunately, our numbers may be so much reduced that it will prove difficult to maintain a mechanical technology unless we appeal to the Orbitals for raw materials and technical assistance. At the very least, they must keep their power sats in service. They cannot keep diverting the beams for their own purposes.

"Would they help, Freddy?" asked Donna Rose. They were together on Frederick's bed, the lights dimmed, the softest of music in the background. "The Orbitals."

"I don't know." Frederick sighed and tightened his arm around her shoulders. "I don't think so. They destroyed the ground facilities. They rejected everything the Orbitals stand for."

"Not machines."

"But the new. New tech. New ideas."

They were quiet, then, until Donna Rose said reflective-ly, "My child. I never set the seed, but . . . What will she be like?"

When Frederick had no answer for her, she said, "I need some sun." She drew away from him, tugged a cover over him, and crossed the room. She uncovered the porthole, drew the curtain that kept the bright light from interfering with Frederick's sleep, and stepped into her trough of soil.

Frederick watched quietly until the curtain hid her. Then he sighed deeply and closed his eyes. But he did not sleep.

He thought he had come to terms with his firing, his barring from Earth. He had told himself months before that it was for the best. He couldn't go home. The spaceplanes were no longer flying. But even if they were, the chaos and animosity down below were such that if he did return, he would far too promptly die. He would accomplish nothing.

Now the Engineers themselves were telling him that even if the killing stopped, the dying would continue. It could not be prevented. The gengineers, and most of the biological infrastructure they had created to support civilization, were gone. The Orbitals had raw materials and energy and technical expertise in plenty, and they would surely be asked to help. He did not think they would.

If he wished to live, he could not go home again. If he wished to achieve anything at all in what remained of his life, he could not go home again. The Orbitals represented for now his—and humanity's—only path into a positive future.

He was fortunate, wasn't he? He had Donna Rose. He had Renny. He had lost everyone else many years ago. But what about Bert? And Jeremy Duncan?

They were down there, somewhere. He hoped they were still alive. He, himself . . . Hannoken had offered him a job. As soon as the Q-ship prototype had passed its tests, Hannoken had said, "We need to build more of these things. Bigger ones, for passengers and cargo. The ores will come from the Moon, just as they did for this." He had thumped the wall of his office to indicate Probe Station and all the other stations and habitats in orbit around the troubled Earth. "You can be the coordinator. Want it?"

He had agreed. He could not remain an idle, useless refugee. Nor could Donna Rose, who had already been working in the com center. He had drafted her for his assistant. And then . . .

Hannoken was growing her a daughter. The Q-ships would be ready soon. The *Gypsy* was being prepared, though precisely what it was being prepared for still seemed uncertain.

He sighed again, and Donna Rose heard him. "Do you think," she said, "there'll be anyone left to rescue by the time we can go get them? Or are we, my daughter and I, the last of the bots?"

Chapter
Sixteen

THE FLICKERING LIGHT of the flames gave the foot-thick trees that surrounded the clearing an air of cathedral majesty. The scents of smoke and pine resin and honeysuckle made one think of incense. That of hydrocarbons spoke of burning candles and ancient, leaky, oil-burning furnaces.

The smell of forest duff, the coolness of the night breeze, the sound of branches moving overhead, the awareness of the fact that the flames were not those of a ranked host of votive candles but of a small bonfire, all these weakened the illusion. Yet Sam Nickers still smiled dreamily. He had visited France once, he and Sheila, and they had visited cathedrals and chateaux and museums and more cathedrals. He clung to the illusion, to the memory it evoked of more pleasant times, of times when they had not needed to flee for their lives, scurrying like mice through dark corners and hollow passages.

He thought of the ancient right of sanctuary and wished that it still held in any form. But churches were weak things now. They still existed. People still believed in God or gods. People still prayed, confessed, rang bells, burned incense. But sanctuary? He looked up at the rough-barked columns that surrounded him. This was all there was.

He wished that were not so. What had happened to the Daisy Hill Truck Farm where he had grown up? What had happened to his father, retired, still living in a cottage on the farm? He had heard nothing. But the farm was prominent, visible, easy to find, and the mob had been destroying the trucks. Surely they would not have neglected the farm.

He stared at the tree-trunk columns and wished that he could pray. If he could, he would ask that his father's death had been quick.

Beside him, Sheila squeezed his hand as if she were sharing his thoughts, remembering the same things, wishing the same

183

wishes, and as unable as he to talk about it all. He turned his head toward her. The feathers that covered her scalp were not as sleek as they once had been. The decorative inserts over her cheek and jawbones were faded. Malnutrition did that, he thought. They could not, like the bots, sink roots into soil for the minerals they needed, nor use sunlight for more than a marginal gain of calories. Nor could they manufacture the vitamins plants could take for granted. They needed food, fresh vegetables and fruits, and there simply hadn't been enough of that. They—and the bots—had been hungry ever since the apartment building had fallen and they had gone into hiding.

His mouth watered. He stared at the edge of the fire, not far from his feet. They had food now, all they could use, and some of it was cooking now, under coals and ashes heaped in a dikelike ring around the flames. It would be ready soon.

He blinked and looked toward Jackie Thyme. She stood on his other side, rooted in the forest soil, smiling as she enjoyed the luxurious sensation of being embedded in the world to the full depth of her roots, as she had not been for so long. There had been more soil than food in the shelter, but there had not been much of either. And she too would be happy to eat.

Past Jackie Thyme he could make out Narcissus Joy, Cindy Blue, Garnet Okra, Lemon Margaret, more. All the bots who had survived the assault on their home and the months in the shelter and the long trek to this forest, over three hundred kilometers from the city. And there, further from the fire, stood the Eldest, oldest of these bots, representative of an earlier generation in their development. The moths the fire had drawn hovered over the heads of all the bots but were thickest around her.

The bots thought their Eldest more knowledgeable, more wise, better fit to cope with the catastrophes of history. They did not recognize, Sam thought, that this catastrophe was unique. Similar tragedies had stricken humanity in the past, but not recently enough for any bot to remember. For them, it was unique indeed. The Eldest might really be the wisest bot of all, but she could have no relevant experience.

Or could she? Sam had heard a little of their beginnings. There had, after all, been little else to do but talk and listen while they hid in the shelter. The bots had been the product of illegal gengineering, unlicensed, illicit. They had felt obliged to hide, to protect themselves as best they could.

And they had succeeded. Perhaps the Eldest was not irrelevant.

He sighed. The bots, half plant, had not thought of the fire. He had, and when he had it going, they had withdrawn their roots from the duff and moved closer. Once they had been used to working during the day, going rootless about their tasks in a civilization dominated by humans. They had rested, embedded in soil beneath bright artificial lighting, at night. The memory of that time had drawn them toward the light of the flames. Perhaps their more human half had also played a role, giving them a tropism for dancing flames, for a circle of illumination to bar the surrounding dark.

He sighed again. That dark was not just physical. They were surrounded by a night of the spirit as well, a night of savagery, of barbarism, of threat as vicious as anything that had ever darkened a Neanderthal's or Cro-Magnon's dreams. He wished, as his ancestral Neanderthals and Cro-Magnons must have wished, that the fire would indeed mean safety. Yet he had shed all his optimism many weeks before.

A fragrance rode toward him on an eddy of nighttime breeze. From the shadows beyond the Eldest, Eldest's Speaker spoke. "We are safe," she said. "Alone. No Engineers above our heads, behind our backs, seeking us. Now we can hide, stay hidden, live."

Cindy Blue stirred in a bot's shrug, the tips of her leaves unfurling just a little from her chest. "They will find us," she murmured, just loudly enough to be heard. "They are everywhere. They are many. We are few."

"But there are fewer of them every day," said Narcissus Joy. "My roots touch the honeysuckle, and I know. They starve. They sicken. They die. They even kill each other. What they want they cannot have. The day of their sacred machines is past, and without that . . ."

Sam got to his feet and stepped away from the fire to gather an armful of fallen branches. They had spoken like this before, he thought. As if the honeysuckle had senses of its own. As if it could see what happened wherever it grew. He sighed quietly. And it grew everywhere. There could be no secrets in a world that held such a thing, and with it people—bots—who could use it as if it were a corps of secret agents. If the Engineers only knew, they would be three times as eager to destroy the bots. They might even try to destroy the honeysuckle. He chuckled slightly, sourly. On the other hand, many of them did like the wine.

When he returned, he dropped the wood he had gathered beside his place and chose a stick to add to the fire. It caught with a crackle, bursting into flames and pungent smoke and bright sparks that soared into the air above them all.

"It's like it was soaked in oil," said Sheila. Her knees were drawn up before her, her arms wrapped around them, her eyes staring into the fire.

Someone said, "It would be even worse if that branch was fresh."

"Oil trees," said Tansy Dill, a bot with faded green blossoms on her scalp. "The originals came from Brazil. Then, when the petroleum ran out, the gengineers adjusted them to live in cooler places."

"The Greenhouse Effect," said Sam. "Things warmed up a little too. That must have helped."

Tansy Dill nodded. "I worked for a while on a plantation. We tapped the trees and shipped the oil to airports, for jet fuel."

"Every pore in the living wood is filled with oil," said Narcissus Joy. "It evaporates, but even long-dead branches still have enough to—"

"Do you think the Engineers still use them?" interrupted Jackie Thyme.

"They must," said Sheila. "It must be the only fuel there is for the few old trucks and cars and motorcycles they have."

"Are they that pragmatic?" asked Sam.

"If they didn't destroy the plantations," said Tansy Dill. "They had to realize they needed them, eventually."

"And what if they did destroy them?" asked Sam.

"Then they'll be looking for the wild trees. Plantations that were abandoned when the demand declined. Trees that seeded themselves in the forest, like these." Tansy Dill gestured at the forest that surrounded them. Most of the trees were not oil trees. Their wood burned normally, slowly, not explosively. Only a few were so soaked with hydrocarbons that they could make the fire flare.

"It's a wonder they survive," said Sheila. She was still staring at the flames. "A forest fire . . ."

A shudder ran through the gathering of bots as her words reminded them of what they had survived once already.

* * *

Only a few of the bots, fighters like Shasta Lou, had died in the ruins of their apartment building. All the rest—nearly three hundred, counting the children—had been safely hidden in the shelter of a subbasement that had once served as a parking garage. The ramps that had led to the outside had long ago been sealed off. For a time, its cavernous, pillar-studded space had been used for storage. But when the bots had acquired the building, they had left it empty except for a few piles of surplus soil and whatever mildewing cartons happened to remain. Only later, when the Engineers had begun to gain strength, had they reinforced the pillars, added more supports for the ceiling, and begun to move in more soil, lights, and tools.

When the building fell, the pillars shook. The injured, lying still on thin pads of fabric or even on bare dirt, cried out. The lights went out as electrical lines were severed. The roof creaked and groaned and cracked. In one spot, near the elevator, it had actually broken, and scorched bits of masonry, glowing coals, baked soil had tumbled through. More rubble had poured down the stairwell, and smoke and fumes had begun to poison their air.

But that had been all. The pillars, the ceiling, they held. Flashlight beams came on. Someone cried, "Water! Put that out!"

Someone else tried a heavy valve on one wall, a cabinet above it holding the rotten shreds of a fire hose. Water gushed, buckets were brought and filled and emptied, and soon the coals beneath the gap in the ceiling and in the opening of the stairwell were dark.

Smoke, heavy in the air, began to drift toward the stairwell and elevator, where cracks in the rubble let it rise, too slowly. Sam and Sheila crouched, their heads near the floor where the air was cleaner. Beside them was a manhole cover; a musty draft issued from the crack around its rim.

Someone said, "We need power for the lights," and Narcissus Joy began to shout orders. Two bots knelt beside Sam and Sheila to lift the manhole cover. Clear air blew the smoke aside, but brought a stench of sewage that made the humans gag. The bots did not seem to be bothered. Several promptly slipped into the tunnels that ran everywhere beneath the city.

By the end of the day, the bots had found and tapped several of the city's underground electrical cables. Their lights were on. A small bioform Bellows drew air from the tunnels, not fresh but still bearing the oxygen the refugees needed. The air found its own way out through the rubble overhead.

"Won't they notice the stink?" Sheila had asked. She was breathing through her mouth.

Sam had shaken his head. "If they do, they'll think it's us, rotting. And we'll get used to it."

Over the next few days, they had prepared their shelter as if they intended to stay for a long time, perhaps until the Engineers had vanished into history. They spread the small amount of dirt they had available into a layer just thick enough to give the bots a taste of root-ease. They positioned the bioform computers and the few snackbushes they had brought with them beneath the brightest lights. They began to dredge muck from the sewage tunnels and add it to the soil. They pulled honeysuckle vines along the tunnels until they reached their refuge, where the stems could be buried in soil to produce new roots.

The honeysuckle stretched over entire continents, its roots passing under rivers and canals and straits. In principle it could inform them of events wherever it reached. Yet its very pervasiveness was its greatest problem: The further away one wished to see, the more different things were going on, the more information was being funneled toward the observer. Only within a range of a thousand kilometers or so was there any practical hope of sorting out the signals and making sense of the wide, wide world. Within that range, through the senses of the honeysuckle, and through the eyes of those root-linked bots still at large in the world above, the hidden refugees could watch what happened as the Engineers established their dominance.

Unfortunately, the honeysuckle was not intelligent. It could not tell what was important and what was not. Bots had to link to its roots and filter the reports of its senses, looking for significance. Best of all, bots could use it to tell their fellows what they themselves had seen, and when there were many bots, the vines functioned much like a telephone network, passing messages instead of simple sense reports. Now that the number of bots was shrinking, the flow of information slowed.

The refugees mourned for the slaughter, and when their probes of the root network found their numbers dwindled from millions to thousands, hiding alone or in small groups, a few succumbed to black depression and killed themselves. Most, however, remained intent on survival.

The injured healed quickly, far more quickly than pure-animal humans. Within days, they were up and working beside the rest, though slowly. Within two weeks, there were few signs that any of the refugees had ever been damaged.

Only a few were not surprised when the power flickered and the lights faded. The rest soon learned that much of the world's electricity had long come from orbiting power satellites that converted sunlight to microwaves they could beam to Earthly antennas, and that the Orbitals had found other uses for the power. The refugees despaired, and then they rejoiced when the Engineers turned off street lights and forbade all but official, essential uses of electricity. What was left depended on the flows of water and wind and tide and sun, not the gengineered technology that had replaced the old machines and that the Engineers therefore hated and destroyed. Power was still there for the refugees to steal. They could still survive.

They did their best to pretend that they could hope for more than mere survival. Bot teachers, led by Mary Gold and Sam, used the bioform computers and the honeysuckle roots to hold classes for the children. Bot gengineers planted seeds and cultivated weapons. Groups met, drew maps, and planned.

Yet they did not forget that their time was limited. Even those benignly natural sources of electricity, unpolluted by human arrogance, renewable, eternal, even water, wind, tide, and sun, could be exploited only with the aid of machines. The machines themselves needed maintenance, repairs, expert personnel. And those personnel, those engineers, were suddenly scarce. A few, perhaps, had escaped to orbit. Most had been purged by the Engineers for their neophilic tendencies, for owning bioppliances or bioform houses, vehicles, computers, for being polluted by genetic modifications.

It was only weeks before the power they tapped began to weaken again. Their lights dimmed, brightened when the Engineers cut even some official demands for electricity, dimmed again, and finally stabilized at a level that barely let the refugees see each other in the murk. By then it was clearly time to leave their shelter.

They harvested what food and weapons they had been able to grow. They put the smallest of the bioform computers, loaded with Sam's programs and recordings, in a sack to carry with them. Then, one by one, they entered the sewers. The adults waded through slime and stench, carrying the youngest in their arms and on their shoulders, until they came to a gap in the masonry that let them enter a drier tunnel that had once carried underground trains. The tracks were still in place. They hiked on, and when this tunnel opened to daylight and the rails disappeared, leaving only the gravel roadbed, they stopped to rest.

After dark had fallen and the streets outside their hiding place had quieted, Narcissus Joy released a single botbird from the one plant they still had. Only when the picture it transmitted down its long fiber-optic umbilical revealed that no Engineers lay in wait for them did they begin to follow the long mound of gravel, still marked with rotting wooden ties, toward the suburbs. When dawn began to light the eastern sky, they saw that they were surrounded by stained brick walls, broken windows, ancient warehouses, tenements. They took refuge for the day in a burned-out hulk, and continued their journey when night came again.

They were lucky. No one saw them, or if anyone did, they did not recognize the straggling line of weary refugees for what they were. They, on the other hand, did see Engineers. Their first day out of the tunnels, hidden in the charred ruins of an ancient tenement, they watched as an equally ancient truck grumbled down the street, its stake-sided back filled with bound prisoners. A few showed signs of genetic modification—splashes of nonhuman color, nonhuman lines of arm and leg and even neck. Most did not. There were no signs of green.

On their second night, they could not travel. They huddled in their hiding place while gunfire raked the cityscape they had to cross. There were explosions, sirens, screams. The fear was palpable, a matter of odor, tension, vibration. Sam almost shrieked when a small figure appeared in the doorless opening that overlooked the roadbed.

The quick "Shhh!" was Jackie Thyme's. "I've been out there," she said. "Scouting. And they're all Engineers. Fighting each other."

They used the last of their botbirds long before they were out of the city and among the suburbs. Then they had nothing but their own senses and scouts like Jackie Thyme to warn them of the small bands of blue-coveralled Engineers that roamed the area, torching the few bioform homes that still remained. They watched from the shelter of a small copse of trees thickened by honeysuckle vines as one such band flushed a young girl from hiding in a pumpkin shell—perhaps, once, when her parents had been alive, or when they had been there, it had been her home—and ran her down. Only Sam had watched what happened then, wishing that he dared to interrupt the grisly proceedings, knowing that if he did more than one would surely die. He had not slept much, or well, that afternoon.

Eventually they reached the hillier country that rose toward the still distant mountains. The forest clearing in which they were now gathered was a kilometer or so from the greenway they had followed, and the forest ran on over the hills, pausing only occasionally where humans had interrupted its growth for their own purposes. They were a hundred meters or so from the weedy fields of an abandoned farm. Beyond the fields, visible from the edge of the trees, was a farmhouse, its paint all neatly white, its windows still showing the streaks of a springtime washing. It was empty of life though the cupboards held dishes and staples, and the closets clothes. The fields held potsters and carrots and squash and corn. Manure in the weed-grown barnyard spoke of horses and cows that had vanished with the people. The bones of a small Mack lay on the overgrown lawn. Honeysuckle vines, colorful with laden blossoms, thickened the fencerows and the borders of the forest and climbed upon the barn.

"Can we use the house?" asked Sam. He added another stick to the fire.

"They're gone," said Sheila. "They're dead, or they're slaves, and the Engineers stole their animals." She picked up a stick and poked at the ashes that covered their dinner. Wisps of steam rose into the air. She raked into view potatolike potsters, baked in their skins, and ears of corn in their husks. The odor of lobster brought saliva to their mouths. "They're done," she said.

The bots raked their own shares from the ashes, burned their fingers, tasted, sighed with pleasure. No one said a word for several minutes, until Sam nodded. "Do you think," he asked, "that they'll be back for the crops?"

"That's a chance we have to take, isn't it?"

"We've already planted the computer," said Mary Gold. The kitchen garden near the house had clearly been stripped of everything edible. Only weeds had still flourished. But honeysuckle roots had pervaded the soil, deep and dark, enriched by manure and compost. It had been a natural site for the classroom.

"We'll stay outdoors," said Alice Belle. "There'll always be someone plugged into the honeysuckle."

"We'll know if they come anywhere near these hills. And we'll keep watch for kilometers ourselves," said Garnet Okra. "You'll have plenty of time to hide."

Sam picked up another stick, stroked its dry surface and found it faintly waxy, peered at the large pores in the wood, sniffed its faint hydrocarbon fragrance. He tossed it into the fire and nodded in satisfaction when it burst instantly into flame.

"With luck," he said, "they'll leave us alone. Their numbers are shrinking, and they need fewer resources. Maybe they'll find food enough closer to the cities. Or maybe they'll have to abandon the cities. They'll fan out over the countryside looking for food. And they *won't* leave us alone."

"We are safe." A wave of odor and the soft voice of Eldest's Speaker identified the source of the words. "We will not be here long. We will be gone before the barbarians come again. Remember: One of us went into space to seek a place for us. She will find it. She will find a way to bring us there."

"So all we have to do is wait," said Sheila. Her tone was skeptical, but still a wordless fragrance suggested agreement. "To avoid the Engineers. To hide if they come close. To survive. And if we succeed, we will reach safe haven."

The sigh that followed seemed to express the hopes of every being who had heard her words. Safe haven. A place where they need not hide, nor flee, nor prepare against attack. A place where they could live as they wished, free, unhated, unfeared, unpersecuted.

Chapter
Seventeen

THE BLAST OF the labor camp's horn penetrated even the roar of the ancient front-end loader. A guard gestured, waving his hand over his head. The tractor's operator backed away from the wall of compacted garbage he was attacking, lowered his machine's bucket, and shut off the engine.

Jeremy Duncan did not know why the guards had interrupted the day's routine, but he had no objection. He looked at his fellow prisoners, fellow slaves. There were none of the surreptitious grins that once marked the faces of schoolchildren saved from a quiz by a fire drill, but there was a general relaxation of posture, a glancing toward the hovels they had so recently left behind. The early morning air was cool, and most of the prisoners would be quite happy to escape it. Certainly, they were not eager to start another day of scrabbling through the leavings of earlier generations, looking for metals and glass and plastic that could now be used as raw materials.

The door of the barracks slammed in the distance. Duncan looked, and a movement drew his eye to Looby's head emerging from his hovel, the largest of them all. Beside Looby appeared Amy. Both were peering toward the gate in the fence as it opened to admit a party of guards surrounding three new arrivals, their blue coveralls ashine with recent laundering, their fronts covered with bits of technological debris, every scrap polished to a metallic gleam. They carried swagger sticks, as long as their forearms, with brass knobs on their ends.

As the group came nearer, the three visitors moved forward, forcing the camp guards to the sides and rear. When they finally stopped before the slaves who had been waiting on the tractor's preliminary labor, they were at the front of the group.

The camp's inmates stared at the newcomers. They might have been envious of their freedom to go where they wished, of their clean clothes, of the simple fact that though they bore little spare flesh, they were clearly well fed. But no such feelings showed. The stares were stolid, patient, confident that such visits meant no good for them, waiting for the news to fall upon them.

The visitors stared back for a long moment. Eventually, the one with the most brass on his chest said, "We're looking for gengineers. Any here?"

Duncan did not volunteer. Indeed, thinking that this summons surely meant new torments, even death, he began to tremble and took one small step backward.

One of the guards noticed his movement. "You! Answer the man!"

He shook his head and tried to back up some more. His sandal came down on a bare toe. He lurched, leaned toward the body behind him, received an abrupt push, staggered upright.

One of the newcomers stepped forward and pointed his swagger stick at Duncan's side. "Those gills look like nice work. Who did them?"

He said nothing, but whatever shreds of pride he still retained betrayed him. He raised his head and stiffened his neck just enough.

The newcomer thumped him in the ribs with the knob on the end of his stick and said, "Take him."

The campus had once belonged to the Ginkgo County Community College. Now it was nameless, surrounded by chain-link fence whose barbed-wire top tilted inward. Once, like city streets and parks, the campus had been patrolled by litterbugs; now wind-blown rubbish was piled against the base of the fence. Every hundred feet, an open-sided kiosk held a pair of blue-coveralled guards who scanned the ground both inside and outside the enclosure. The lawns and playing fields had been neglected; wherever they had not degenerated to bare dirt under the pressure of feet and wheels, they were chest-high with ragweed and honeysuckle and other weeds. The honeysuckle crawled as well up the sides of the red-brick buildings and wreathed the windows.

The broad-armed chairs that once had filled the classrooms were now stacked in the gym, replaced by broad tables covered with jumbles of electronic equipment, test-tube racks and test tubes, microscopes, and more. Jeremy Duncan swore. "Sort it out," they had told him. "Make it work. We'll tell you what we want later."

He knew what they wanted. The equipment itself told him that, for it was precisely the sort of equipment he had had in his own lab. Or not quite that, but it was all equipment that had occupied labs much like his once upon a time. It was obsolete now, and it had been mistreated—cracked and dirty casings, unwashed test tubes and petri dishes and tissue culture flasks, scorched and tattered instruction manuals. He had put one of the petri dishes in the pocket of his white labcoat; from time to time, he grasped it tightly in his hand as if it were a talisman. Just as he had done before, in the days when life had seemed secure and settled, when the Engineers had seemed no more than a nuisance, he wore no shirt beneath the labcoat.

Across the room, Andy Gilman sorted through glassware. Long hair, dull with dirt and lack of care, hung from the rim of the man's skull. The bare top was crusted with old scabs. One side of his face was hollowed where a cheekbone had been broken and not repaired. His skin was wrinkled with both age and abuse. He had been, he had told Duncan when they were assigned to share a dorm room, a research director. Now he too was a slave, and folds of skin spoke of a plumpness his imprisonment had worn away. Unlike Duncan, he had no self-modifications that showed, even when he removed both his labcoat and the shirt he wore beneath it.

Duncan leaned over an antique DNA splicer. Its empty reagent magazine was supposed to hold two dozen small vials of nucleotides and enzymes and other biochemicals. He opened its dingy case and immediately noticed that the clock chip was missing from the mother board. He swore. Students, using the machine to learn how to produce small lengths of DNA, could have stepped it through its paces manually. For real gengineering, that would be insufferably slow. With its automatic timer, this primitive model from HPA, Hewlett-Packard-Apple, would be able to generate whole genes in a day or two. Later models would need only hours.

He straightened his back. There, on another table, was a

twin that might have the chip this one was missing. A glance was enough to tell him that its reagent magazine was not merely empty but missing. Another glance, and he spotted a plastic bottle of hand lotion. With a relieved sigh, he picked it up, popped its cap, squirted some of its contents into his palm, and reached beneath his labcoat to massage the edges of his gills.

"We'll have to cannibalize," he said a moment later, just loudly enough for Gilman to hear him. "Maybe then we'll get something that works."

"Maybe," said the other. He was reaching for the door of a laboratory refrigerator that stood against one wall. Duncan stepped toward him, as eager as he to see what its white-enameled shell might hide. When Gilman opened the door, both men grinned for just a moment. The refrigerator's shelves were crowded with a jumble of vials, many of them intact, their labels claiming that they contained the reagents the splicer would need to function.

"Litter," said Duncan. Far too many of the vials were toppled and broken, as if whoever had moved the refrigerator to this room had not cared what it held. But . . .

"No one plugged it in," said Gilman. No wave of cold had met them when he opened it. The refrigerator was at room temperature, and the reagents were surely spoiled. They did not keep well.

Duncan swore again. He pictured the Engineers storming the schools that produced the genetic engineers they hated. They would have smashed and burned, utterly destroying the laboratories, the libraries, the modern equipment. And then someone had realized that the Engineers might have to compromise their ideals, their principles, if they wished to survive. They had gone to the lesser schools that had trained only technicians, using outmoded equipment that had been abused by generations of students, schools that had so far escaped the Engineers relatively unscathed. Some would surely have turned in for destruction everything that smacked of forbidden technologies. Others would have stashed their battered DNA splicers in storerooms, hiding them against a better day. When the Engineers had recognized their need, the equipment had therefore been there, waiting to be ferreted out and seized. But it was useless without the vials of nucleotides, polymerases, and other biochemical reagents.

He surveyed the room once more. Before the rise of the Engineers, he might have felt wistful. The labels were familiar. HPA. Beckman. Eppendorf. Genesys. Zeiss-Nikon. Genentech. He had used some of these same devices when he was in school himself. He had used their faster, more efficient, more versatile successors in his work for the ESRP and Frederick.

But nostalgia was far from his mind now. He felt relief that he was no longer in the labor camp, pleasure at the white labcoat that draped his scrawny frame, more pleasure at the touch of the petri dish in his fingers, and anxiety whenever he wondered what they would ask him to make. Could he do it? Of course he could. *Should* he do it? *Would* he do it, when he hated them and all they stood for? If he refused, they would surely remind him of the punishments that could be his.

He and Gilman were not alone. Others, as emaciated as they from months of short rations, some of them nonetheless with the wiry muscles of forced labor, some weak from confinement and inactivity, all equally clad in the white of their profession, also roamed the campus's rooms and halls. Their faces too spoke of anxiety, and they too muttered and swore.

Duncan wondered if the Engineers knew how lucky they were. Gengineers were often like artists. They felt driven to their work, and the best thing the Engineers could do to make them cooperate was to give them back their labs. If they could make this ancient equipment work, if they could find or make the necessary reagents, they would.

Was that enough for him? He had chosen a job, running Freddy's clandestine lab for converting intelligent genimals to humans, that left him idle much of the time. He had used that time for some work of his own, but much of it he had been content to waste, reading and thinking. He was not as driven as many of his colleagues. Yet the work undeniably attracted him.

Gilman was standing by a dirty window fringed with honeysuckle leaves and blossoms, peering outward. Duncan joined him as the gate in the fence opened for a rust-splotched bus, salvage from some ancient junkyard. The bus creaked to a halt beside a dorm across the road, and a dozen ragged figures emerged.

The Engineers had collected gengineers wherever they could find them. They had brought them here, to this one-time campus and intended research center. Duncan had no idea whether there were other such places. Their captors were not saying, though they were still collecting. Each day saw new arrivals, much like these.

Another vehicle appeared in the distance. It was a horse-drawn wagon, its body packed with figures. More gengineers? But the guards were suddenly urgent, hurrying the new arrivals into the dorm, closing the gate, unslinging their weapons, taking up watchful positions. Duncan watched as the wagon drew nearer, stopped, disgorged a dozen Engineers in stained coveralls. One used a bullhorn to bellow, "NO GENES!" Others pulled weapons of their own from the bed of the wagon.

They never had a chance to attack the fence. As soon as the weapons were visible, the guards opened fire.

Duncan turned away as the first bodies fell. He had seen enough. The situation was plain. He was in the hands of progressives, Engineers who realized that some compromise was necessary. Out there were the conservatives, for whom all gengineering, whether it was essential to their survival or not, was anathema.

"In there. Siddown. No talking." The guards directed the gengineers into the lecture hall. Jeremy Duncan and Andy Gilman found seats together and tried to ignore the empty feelings in their stomachs. The food on the commandeered campus was not much more plentiful than it had been in the labor camp. The sweetish smell of severe malnutrition thickened the air of the lecture hall, at total odds with the image of civilization and prosperity presented by the sea of white coats that surrounded Duncan and Gilman and lapped against the walls of the lecture hall. Behind the lectern were several Engineers in clean, blue coveralls, their salvaged ornaments reflecting light from the ceiling fixtures.

Duncan thought of the Engineers who had pulled him from the landfill mine. These were not the same, but they had the same air of elite polish and carried very similar swagger sticks. He wondered if he and his fellow gengineers were about to be told why they had been brought to this place, what they were supposed to do for their masters.

Once all the gengineers were seated, one of the Engineers stepped forward and rapped the lectern with his swagger stick.

"You know why you are here," he said. He did not introduce himself. "We need you." He made a face as if to say he wished they didn't. "Our aim is to restore the Machine Age. But we must first rebuild the necessary infrastructure. And to do that, we must use genimals."

"Genimals." He said the word as if it were a curse. For him and his kind, it was. "Unfortunately, we do not have them anymore. Some of our more enthusiastic supporters hunted them down. They destroyed almost all of them."

His glare dared anyone to laugh or even smile at the irony that the Engineers should now need what they had destroyed. "We still have potsters and snackbushes. There are still oil trees, though we need more. We don't need goldfish bushes and Slugabeds and garbage disposals. We do need Mack trucks, Bioblimps, and box-turtle bulldozers. We need to restore the supercrops."

Someone in the audience muttered, just loud enough for all to hear, "What about cocaine nettles?"

The Engineer scowled at his audience. When he said, "We do *not* need them. They are quite properly extinct," Duncan snorted. He knew that not all Engineers shared that attitude. The guards at the labor camp had seemed quite happy to cultivate their drug-secreting plants.

The scowl intensified in the ensuing silence. Finally, the Engineer continued. "Humans were meant to *build* their tools, not grow them. That is why God gave us hands, to glorify Him with the work of those hands. Machines are the culmination of our nature and our destiny."

He paused to scan the room. Then he sighed theatrically. "And yes. It *was* our dependence on machines that exhausted the supplies of the ores and fuels that they required. But the answer was not to replace our mechanical technology with a biological technology! What we needed then, and what we need now, is a biological technology harnessed in support of our machines. We need plants that produce fuel. We need plants or animals that can filter minerals from sea water. We need trucks and bulldozers and cranes, biological if need be, to build the factories with which we will then build the machines to replace them.

"And we need *you* to make it all possible." He bowed his head for a second as if in apology. "Yes. In our first enthusiasm, we destroyed much that we should have preserved.

Now we need to rebuild it. And we are not gengineers. You are. We need you."

The room was silent, still. The pause lengthened, and then he said, "If you help us, you will once more be part of society. Honored parts. As valued and essential and honored as ever you were before."

"Do you believe them?" Duncan and Gilman were in their dorm room, squatting on the bare mattresses that were all they had for beds. The frames and springs had long ago been removed; eventually they would be melted down and turned into something the Engineers needed more than comforts for slave laborers, even if those laborers were now being promised honors and rewards. The layers of dust and dead insects in the corners and on the windowsill said that no one had bothered to clean the place before the gengineers had moved in, or after. Tendrils of honeysuckle vine pushed aside the sheet of cardboard with which someone had tried to patch a broken windowpane.

Duncan shook his head. He held one hand toward the room's locked wooden door. They were prisoners still, and . . . "As soon as they have what they want from us . . ."

Dinner had been a meager bowl of vegetable soup, served from a large kettle by a bored guard. They had sat at long wooden tables, where other guards had kept watch to prevent any attempts at conversation. The gengineers had had to content themselves with speculative glances at each other, surreptitious searches of the room for familiar faces, wary stares at the guards. After dinner, those guards had ushered the gengineers back to their rooms and clicked the locks behind them.

Gilman nodded. He scratched at the border of his scalp, stared at his fingernails, and pulled free the strands of hair that had come loose. "They need us," he said. "They're desperate. What were you doing before this?"

Duncan's own scalp itched. He resisted the urge to scratch as he described the landfill mine.

"They had me on an oil crew. They burned many of the plantations, and then they realized they still needed them. We were out in the woods, looking for wild ones."

"You find many?" asked Duncan.

"Oh, yeah. They seed themselves pretty well. Lots of volunteers."

"Think they'll make it work?"

"Even with our help?"

Duncan nodded.

Gilman shook his head.

"But we can—"

"Sure we can. It's politics that will doom them. They're dominated by ideology. They'll cut each other's throats."

"The protestors," said Duncan. "They're already arguing with each other."

"And we're in the hands of the losers," said Gilman. "The extremists always win, at least in the short run. They may lose in the long run—hell, in the long run, these Engineers will reinvent gengineering on their own—but we won't be around for that."

"How bad can it get?"

"We'll be shot. Every sign of gengineering will be stamped out. Maybe even every sign of selective breeding. Pets and house plants and traditional crops. They'll be back to hunting and gathering."

Duncan hoped his roommate was wrong. But he did not think he was. The fear of new technologies had been rising ever since the twentieth century, when the pace of change, of population growth, of urban spread, of occupational obsolescence, of the appearance of new devices and methods and risks, of technological progress, had grown too fast for minds that depended on a sense of tradition and stability to accept. The forces of reaction were now ascendant, and they would not fade until the conditions of life had grown worse than the fears that impelled those forces. Perhaps, as Gilman said, humanity would have to drop all the way back to savagery before it could rise again.

That thought was no comfort. It would not help them.

"But we have to try, don't we?"

Many of the obsolete instruments the Engineers had salvaged proved useless. Some, however, could be made to work, and within a month, Jeremy Duncan and Andy Gilman had a lab that could perform simple genetic engineering, at least in principle. Yet, in reality, it could do nothing. The two gengineers, like their fellows in the other makeshift, make-do labs on the Ginkgo campus, were spending much of their time at the window, staring toward the fence, watching the protestors arrive and be chased away and return, every day more numerous, more determined to close the campus down.

"What's the problem?" asked their supervisor. He was an Engineer who knew nothing of gengineering and, when they tried to explain even a little of how the technology worked, waved their words away. He wore a nametag that said simply "Calloman." He did not carry a swagger stick, perhaps because his rank was too low, but from time to time he did slap his thigh with the flat of his hand.

Calloman flicked a DNA splicer on. Its LEDs glowed red and green. Its motors hummed. The small display panel above the keyboard blinked patiently: "COMMAND?"

"The machines work," he said. "What else do you need?"

"Restriction endonucleases," said Gilman. He was seated at a computer that had been one of the few things to survive the destruction of the General Bodies research and development lab. The company's logo decal still decorated the side of the veedo unit. Better yet, the databases in its polygig memory had proved intact. "Ligases and gyrases," he added. "Oligonucleotide primers, polymerases, nucleotides."

"Chemicals," said Duncan. "Biochemicals. The same ones every cell uses to replicate its genes."

"There's a ton of them in that fridge." The Engineer pointed and his ornaments jangled lightly. "I saw them yesterday."

"No good," said Gilman. "They have to be kept cold, and that thing wasn't even plugged in when we got here. They're rotten."

"And we can't get more," said Duncan. Patiently, he explained that once, when they had been free, gengineers had been able to order every chemical they needed from a host of suppliers.

As Duncan spoke, Gilman summoned a list of corporate names and addresses onto the veedo screen. "All gone now," he said. "You destroyed the industry, the infrastructure."

"Then make them," said Calloman, slapping his thigh. "You can do that, can't you?"

Gilman nodded. "That's what the first gengineers did. But it takes time. It'll slow us down."

"Not too much." The Engineer frowned and turned toward the window. It was open, and the odor of honeysuckle wine was strong. "We need those genimals now. We have to be able to show them . . ." He pointed. "We have to be able to show them a success, the equipment for building factories and machines, the machines themselves."

"You won't," said Duncan. "You can't."

"We have to," said Calloman. "*You* have to." He flicked off the splicer, turned, and left the lab.

After a moment of silence, Andy Gilman looked up from the keyboard and screen before him. "We have the same problem they do," he said. "Don't we? No raw materials."

"We'll have to make them," said Duncan. "And *we* don't have any slaves to help us out."

Both men knew that their technology had started out with less than they now had. They could—they would, just as had the founders of their field—find bacteria that made restriction endonucleases, grow them, and extract what they needed. They would then be able to gengineer other bacteria to make the protein tools in greater quantity. They would gengineer bacteria to make other enzymes, and nucleotides in quantity, and copies of genes.

"At least," said Gilman, "we know what to do. That's a start. And we have the equipment we need. It should only take us a few months, not decades. And then we'll be able to try making a Mack. That's simple enough."

Duncan stepped toward the window. There were protestors outside the fence again, though they were quiet, not threatening, not drawing fire. Beyond them a scatter of small tents showed where they slept at night. A few wisps of smoke said how they cooked their meals.

"I hope we have a few months," he said. "If they run out of patience . . . Or if those . . ." He pointed. "If the conservatives take over . . ."

"Then we go back to the labor camps. Or we're dead."

Duncan shook his head. He didn't wish to see the landfill mine ever again. He didn't want to die. Nor did he want the Engineers to overcome their problems.

He slid his hand down his side, feeling the ridges of his gills, and thrust it into the pocket of his labcoat. His petri dish talisman was still there, waiting for his fingers. He clutched it. The protestors, he knew, were not likely to stay as quiet as they now were. He might live longer at the mine. Helping the Engineers, no matter whether he was doing what he loved to do, felt like licking the hand that beat him.

He wished there were some way to return to the past. Or . . .

He bent his gaze upward, but there was nothing visible except blue sky and scattered clouds. No sign of orbiting stations and habitats. No sign of Frederick. No hope of joining him, of escaping Earth entirely.

Chapter
Eighteen

THE DOOR SLAMMED open, and a familiar voice barked, "Gilman! Duncan!"

Jeremy Duncan and Andy Gilman jerked their heads up from the array of culture flasks they were studying. "Calloman," said Duncan. "No, we don't have a Mack for you yet. We're still working on"—he gestured abruptly at the flasks—"enzyme factories. That's all anyone is working on."

"You're too damned slow." Calloman stood aside from the doorway, and a pair of Engineers carried in a bot, her leaves ripped to reveal her breasts, her pale green scalp blossoms torn away in patches, her arms and legs bound. The bulb between her thighs looked bruised. "It *says* it knows a little gengineering. Maybe it'll make a good assistant."

The bot said nothing as she was dumped unceremoniously on the floor between two tables covered with glassware. Two more Engineers appeared with a wooden crate filled with dirt. They set their burden down more carefully, near the window, and left the room.

"It's time we need, not hands," said Gilman. He stared at the bot; her eyes were open wide, scanning the room as if searching for something familiar.

Duncan knelt and began to struggle with the knots that held the bot's legs motionless. "I thought there weren't any left," he said.

Calloman shrugged. "Some kids found them. Just half a dozen, on an island in the river, in a thicket. There's bound to be more out there somewhere. And time you haven't got. We need progress, now." He pointed toward the window. "There's more of *them* out there than ever."

Gilman glanced toward the small tent city and the forest of placards beyond the fence. The protestors were quiet but, yes, their numbers grew every day. The armed guards, and perhaps the sense that it was Engineers who governed what had once been the Gingko County Community College, kept them from storming the campus. "You think a Mack will help?" he asked. "Show it to them, and this place will be rubble in a day."

"Show it to the government, and we can get the troops to clear them out." Calloman said nothing more as he turned and left, closing the door more gently than he had opened it.

Duncan leaned back on his heels and stared at the mute solidity of the door. "Do you think we'd feel any safer?" he asked bitterly, even though he knew the Engineer could not hear him.

Eventually, he turned back to the bot and undid the last of the ropes around her arms, grunted sympathetically at the vicious redness of the marks the bonds had left, and helped her to her feet. She staggered, steadied, shook off his hand, and stepped toward the crate of dirt. "No one's safe," she said in a husky voice. "Not anymore." She leaned over the crate, felt the dirt, and added, "It's dry. Water?"

Andy Gilman brought a large beaker and poured its contents over the dirt. The water promptly disappeared. The bot stepped into the crate, root tendrils unfurling from her calves and palping the surface of the soil like so many slender tentacles. They worked their way into the soil, and the bot sighed. "They killed them all," she said. Her voice choked. "I'm the only one."

The two men looked at each other awkwardly. Both were familiar with the Engineers' attitude toward the products of gengineering. "I'm surprised," said Duncan. "I'm astonished that even one survived. What's your name?"

There was a long pause while the bot reached one hand toward the window. The marks around her forearms were already fading. She found a honeysuckle tendril and drew it toward her, bent, and tucked its tip into the soil near the edge of the crate. Finally, she said, "Chervil Mint."

"And are you . . . ?"

"A gengineer?" She managed to produce a faint smile. Her voice remained husky. "Not really. I was too young to work when . . ." The ragged tops of her leaves parted from her chest. Then, as if she realized she had nothing left to conceal, she let them unfurl, tilting them to catch the sunlight that entered through the window. "But I know the techniques. I know what to do." Then, as if in afterthought, she added, "There wasn't any honeysuckle on the island."

Deep blue sky arched over the old farmhouse's weedy garden. Burdock and honeysuckle sprawled. Trees strained to intercept the sun with leaves and needles. Clouds hovered on the southern horizon, hinting of the distant Gulf of Mexico and suggesting rain in the coming hours or days.

Sam Nickers sat on an upturned bucket in front of the keyboard of the bioform computer they had brought with them. The leaves that formed the computer's screen were tilted toward him, displaying the lesson of the moment. Around him were scattered two dozen young bots, their roots embedded in the soil, meshed with the roots of the honeysuckle, ready to receive what the computer would send them as soon as he issued the necessary commands. Nearest him was Jackie Thyme. Three teachers, including Mary Gold, stood ready to monitor the flow of information and soothe any students who could not absorb it without pain. The pain was less likely than it had been before Sam had learned how to use the computer, but it could still strike, and there seemed no way to predict who the victim would be or what lesson would cause the most suffering.

Other bots stood nearby, their roots too touching the honeysuckle, but in watchfulness, scanning the landscape with honeysuckle senses for signs of intrusion, invasion, threat. More than once since the refugees had found this farm, these sentinels had alerted the rest to hide while horse-drawn wagons passed on the road. Once a young couple, walking, had paused at the end of the weed-choked drive, stared at the house, asked each other, "Do you think they're alive?" and shaken their heads. They had not approached the house; if they had, they could not have missed the signs of occupancy.

The refugees had food. They had soil and water and sunshine. They had distance from the Engineers. They even retained some hope, though that grew more difficult day by day as the few bots who still survived outside of their small colony lost their connections to the honeysuckle net. They knew that the Engineers still hunted for prey, and that they still found it. It seemed more and more likely that it was only a matter of time before the Engineers found them, and then . . . There were no signs of rescue.

Sam was reaching for his keyboard when the image on the screen broke into static. "Litter!" he said as he rebooted.

"Wait!" said Mary Gold. A distant look spread over her face. "It's a message . . . A bot, imprisoned . . . They finally put her where she could reach the honeysuckle."

The details followed: The honeysuckle tendril Chervil Mint had put in the dirt of her pot had rooted. By then she had learned what the Engineers wanted of their captive gengineers. She knew the threat of the surrounding conservative Engineers. She knew where she was. And as soon as the honeysuckle roots had been ready for her touch, she had cried out upon the net. Against all hope, she had found others of her kind. But could they, would they, help?

No one spoke until Jackie Thyme said, "We have weapons, and Ginkgo County is not far away." She pointed south and west. "We can do it. We should."

"No!" said Mary Gold, the tips of her leaves opening and closing in a fearful flutter, her scalp blossoms trembling. "They'll find us then. And we'll be—"

"They'll find us anyway," said Jackie Thyme. "Eventually."

Sam thought of the human gengineers being forced to help the Engineers rebuild enough infrastructure to support a mechanical technology, of what would surely happen to them once they had succeeded, of what seemed all too likely even sooner, as soon as the faction outside the fence was sufficiently enflamed. "A meeting," he said. "We need to consider what to do."

The decision had not been quickly reached, but many of the bots had had enough of hiding safely while their kind, their creators, and their allies were all exterminated. And, as Jackie Thyme had pointed out, they did have weapons. A new crop of grenade plants, both gas and shrapnel, had ripened and their fruit was ready to use. New botbird plants had grown too. And the bots themselves had regained their strength. Two nights of steady marching on country roads would get them to the college. They could do it, if they only would. And with luck, the Engineers would not be able to follow them.

"I'm coming too," said Sheila Nickers. She was wearing a pale blue coverall, armless, its back a cross of straps. Her green skin glowed in the sunlight. "You can't leave me behind."

"I'm the medic," said Sam. "They'll need me with them. And I need you here, safe, even if that makes me a fatuously overprotective male. I want to be sure my mate will survive even if I don't."

"Be careful then," was all she said to indicate her acquiescence. Her arms tightened around his chest. Her head pressed beneath his chin. Her feathers tickled his nose. He tightened his own grip on her.

The first night of the journey passed without event. Sam marched near the head of the column, a sack of seed-case grenades heavy on his back. There was no moon, and clouds made the night so dark that when he turned, he could see only the few bots nearest him. Toward dawn, when a greying sky sent them looking for a grove of trees in which they could lie concealed till dark returned, it rained lightly. Sam did not find that comforting, though the bots smiled and spread their leaves.

The second night was as dark as the first until they topped a rise and, through scattered trees and empty buildings, made out the sparks of the campfires that ringed the Ginkgo County Community College campus. They were flickers, dying unfed while the Engineers slept. The small army concealed itself and readied its weapons. Botbirds flew, feeding images through their fiber-optic umbilicals to the leafy screens of their parent bushes. Sam and his companions searched those images carefully but saw no sentinels among the fires. Only then did they split into small teams and dare to approach.

The campus lay quiet, its surrounding fence dimly visible in the light shed by the nearest fires and spilled from the pools of orange cast by sodium-vapor lamps mounted on scattered poles. Once there had been more such lights in lines that traced the campus's roads and walkways but replacements for broken bulbs had been unavailable for many months. Once perhaps there had also been phosphorescent shrubs and hedges, but if so the Engineers had exterminated them. They had left intact the shadows from which classrooms and dormitories loomed, windows reflecting sparks, their red-brick sides hulking ominously.

Sam was surprised when Narcissus Joy poked a finger into one end of a gas grenade and capped the resulting hole with a thumb. "They don't have to explode," she murmured quietly. "Watch . . ." He and Jackie Thyme followed her as she approached a makeshift tent and carefully, for just a moment, vented gas over each sleeping face. Around them, other bots were doing the same. "They won't wake up till morning," she said, still murmuring.

There *were* sentinels around the campus, patrolling just within the fence. To silence them, the bots ringed the campus just beyond the reach of the lights and, nearly simultaneously, lobbed gas grenades to burst with emphatic pops near their feet. As soon as the guards had fallen, wirecutters made short work of the fence.

"There's Chervil Mint." Sam followed the pointing arm and saw a figure clinging to the honeysuckle vines that covered the side of a classroom building.

Bots headed toward the dorms to wake and free the captive gengineers and lead them too to safety. Unfortunately, not all the guards had been on patrol. Later, Sam would tell himself that they should have known, that they had been luckier than anyone deserved to be. But for all that he was a historian and he had read much of past military actions, he had no actual experience at all of such things.

He was watching a building when someone inside opened a door. Light spilled onto a walkway and revealed a bot in unmistakable detail. Sam swore. There was a cry of alarm, and interior lights flicked on. Guards tumbled out of doors, crying, "It's bots! Look at 'em! What are they doin'? Stop them! They're heading for the dorms. It's a break! Shoot 'em!"

Grenades arced through the darkness overhead and popped. Guards fell. Bots seized their guns. Other guards cried out more loudly, and more guards appeared in windows and doors. As the uproar grew quickly louder, lights came on in the dorms. Bot voices cried out in explanation, announcing freedom, urging haste. Gengineers ran from their buildings clad in coveralls, jeans, pajamas, nothing at all. Bots guided them toward the holes in the fence. Shots rattled against the night. Gengineers, bots, and guards fell, dead or wounded. Loud bangs announced that the shrapnel grenades had been unlimbered. The screams among the guards fell silent as more gas grenades were thrown.

As they withdrew, Sam could see faces at the dormitory windows. They had not rescued everyone, he thought. And of those who had tried to come with them, a few lay still on the ground behind them. So did a few of his companions, the bots. He was glad Sheila had stayed behind.

Was Chervil Mint with them? He hoped so, for she was the one prisoner whose plight had impelled them to come. Who else were they leading to their forest hiding place? Had they saved enough to make the deaths worthwhile? Or would they have done better to leave well enough alone?

At least, he told himself, the gas grenades had silenced all the guards in the end. No one was following them. They would not lead their enemy to the rest of their group.

By dawn they were ten kilometers from the campus, hidden in a line of trees between two fields of waist-high corn. Most of the bots had sunk their roots in the earth. The humans, the gengineers they had rescued from the campus prison, were gathered near Sam Nickers as he worked over those wounded bots who had managed to keep up with the flight from the campus. From what he gathered, only the dead had been left behind or abandoned on the way. The rest, if they lived, had made it, though some had had to be carried.

The bots were silent. The gengineers were not. Some of them were cursing the long hike and the prospect of more. Some, the leaner ones, those who had been toughened by forced labor in landfill mines and oil plantations, seemed less worn by the flight. All wanted to know, "What next? Where do we go? Will they pursue us? Capture us again? Punish us? Kill us?"

Sam faced two of the most insistent. They had introduced themselves as Andy Gilman and Jeremy Duncan. "You're free," he told them. "For a while, at least. We're taking you away from the Engineers. To a place where the rest of us are waiting. Where we've been hiding, where we've been safe so far. We hope we'll stay that way. But, yes, they're bound to pursue us. We'll try to keep them from catching us. And yes, we'll fight."

"With what?" asked Duncan. "You just threw those guns away."

"We had no more ammunition for them."

"But you could have . . ."

Nearby, Narcissus Joy was bending over the display screen of a botbird bush. Three of the birds, tethered by their hairlike umbilicals, hovered high above the trees, watching the path the group had followed. "They're looking for us," she said. "There are gangs of Engineers on every road." She moved aside to let Sam, Duncan, and Gilman see the screen. The aerial view showed the landscape like a map, green-turfed roads twisting like snakes across the surface between the fields and woods. "The campus is over there." She pointed toward one edge of the screen. Each road that crossed that edge swarmed with Engineers, milling, running, darting into the brush to either side, clearly looking for signs of their passage.

"It looks like an anthill that someone stirred with a stick," said Duncan. "They're not making much progress."

"They will," said Sam. "We'll have to stay off the roads. That'll slow us down."

"That's not just our guards," said Gilman. "Too many of them. The protestors are after us too."

The day wore on, and the flood of Engineers searching for them made little progress. But near the end of the afternoon, the botbird screen showed that small groups of Engineers with dogs were appearing ahead of the crowds on each road. Within an hour they had found the greenway the refugees had followed, and their movement began to show a sense of direction.

"We can't wait for dark," said Narcissus Joy. "We have to go now. And we have to hurry."

"Through the fields," said Sam Nickers. "Send a team ahead to gas whoever they find. Watch out for the farmhouses."

They did what he said, and by the next dawn they were far from their last resting spot. The hills that were their goal were visible ahead, the ground was rising, and the Engineers were still on their track, though they were somewhat further behind than they had been the afternoon before.

"Split up," said Andy Gilman. "Scatter to give them too many tracks to follow. Give us each a bot for a guide."

They followed his suggestion, and by noon they were home.

But they were not safe.

As each small group reached the farm, it was greeted with the news, picked up from the honeysuckle that grew everywhere, that the Engineers had not given up when the track they were following had split. Nor had they tried to follow every subtrail. They had split into just five groups, each with a small pack of dogs. Then they had chosen trails as if at random.

"They must," said Narcissus Joy, "have been sure we all were going to the same place."

"We were," said Sam Nickers.

"They'll be here soon."

"Are we going to fight again?" asked Jackie Thyme.

"We have to," said Narcissus Joy. "We don't have anyplace else to go."

"There's a road, a greenway, down the hill a kilometer or so," said Lemon Margaret. "It cuts their path. They'll have to cross it. And some of us are already there, with grenades."

The initial skirmish left dead on both sides of the greenway, and there matters rested for hours. This time there was no basement shelter in which to hide. There was nowhere to go. There was, it seemed, no hope.

"What's happening?" asked Sam Nickers. He sniffed as if that could tell him what he wanted to know, but all he detected was the scent of greenery. It was the smell of quiet, of peace, with only the aromatic scent of oil-tree sap suggesting civilization and its conflicts.

Jackie Thyme roused herself, furled her leaves, and blinked. "If you were a bot," she said, "you'd know. We're all plugged into the honeysuckle, and that's all we're talking about."

"So tell us," said Sheila. She stood beside her husband, her hand gripping his, green on green except on their whitened knuckles. "Let us in on it."

"They're waiting," said Jackie Thyme. "Some of them have turned back. They say they're going to call for reinforcements, soldiers."

"What for? Aren't there enough of them out there now?"

"They say they don't have enough guns." Her expression turned distant. "Now someone is saying they don't need them. They've noticed the oil trees. They're saying . . ."

As she fell silent, Sam shuddered. He remembered the branch he had once thrown into the fire and how it had burst into flame, even though most of its flammable sap had long since evaporated. How vigorously would a living tree burn, its flesh permeated with that sap? How hot and fast and deadly would the woods around the farm burn? How long did they have?

Chapter
Nineteen

RENNY LAY ON the carpeted floor near the station director's desk, his head resting on his crossed wrists, watching. Donna Rose reached toward her daughter, eyes bright with tears. Frederick Suida stood behind her, hands clenching and unclenching.

"No!" Alvar Hannoken's cry was panicked, desperate. "Don't touch it, Donna Rose!"

"But it's my daughter!" She spoke as desperately as he, her tone distraught, her face a grimace of disgust and anger and shame. "We uproot these things!" she said, but she backed up against Frederick, into the arms that grasped her shoulders, away from the pot full of black, moist soil. Behind it, the office's broad window admitted a flood of sunlight and showed, rather than the usual skeletal radio telescope, the shiny globe of the construction shack, its litter of Q-ships, most of them still under construction, and the fuel depot.

"But it's the way I want it," said Hannoken placatingly.

"You shouldn't do that," said Frederick.

A small beep and a flashing light on his desk announced an incoming call. "Athena, privacy." Hannoken turned back toward Donna Rose, ignoring Frederick. "And it was in you. In your genes. I just removed the sentience, the brains. I wanted something more decorative than the kudzu. I—"

"Decorative?" said Frederick, frowning. His hands gripped Donna Rose as comfortingly, as reassuringly as he could. "I suppose it is, but—"

"Freddy!"

He fell silent, remembering that Donna Rose did not want him to intervene. She had told him so earlier, saying Hannoken had gone too far. "He has stolen a piece of me," she had told him in their quarters, the tips of her leaves twitching convulsively about her chest. "I let him have the tissue sample, but

215

he didn't ask if he could do that with it. He went too far, Freddy."

Frederick had remembered how he had felt when he realized what a cruel prank intelligence could be. He had been shaped to be a garbage disposal. Yet some gengineer had chosen to give him brains he could never use except to go mad from boredom and frustration. "It must feel like rape."

"No." She had shaken her head. "No, not like that. Sex isn't quite so personal for us. But still . . ." He had thought then of pollen and wind and bees and thought he understood. "More like a burglar, perhaps?"

The purple-flowered kudzu was gone now, replaced by the scion Hannoken had grown from Donna Rose's tissue sample. That child of her flesh was over half a meter high now. Its central stem was thick and pale, much like Donna Rose's own, its surface sculpted into feminine curves and hollows. Long, tapering leaves fanned out from the bulb that bulged from the soil. But where a bot had a head and face, this plant had only a cluster of thumb-sized blossom buds and palm-sized flowers, deep red and blazing orange. There was no hint that the plant's trunk would ever split to form legs. Nor was there any sign that arms would grow.

The plant was indeed decorative. But the bots prided themselves on the nearness of their approach to humanity. They prized their brains, their faces, their ability to withdraw their roots from the soil that nourished them and walk about, and he was not surprised to hear that they aborted what, to them, could be nothing other than the most severe of birth defects. From Donna Rose's reaction, such deformities could not be rare. The gene complexes that made bots bots could not, perhaps, be stable. They must rearrange themselves spontaneously, reasserting the configurations of their ancestors, whose botanical portion had come largely from amaryllis plants. Hannoken must, he thought, have found it easy to gengineer her cells into this throwback.

"Kill it," said Donna Rose. Her voice was anguished. There were tears on her cheeks. "I won't have it. I can't stand it. Kill it!"

"No," said Hannoken. As she moved forward once more, her arms reaching toward the pot where her child basked in the mirror-channeled sunlight, he stepped in front of her, his own arms spread as if to block her advance. One elongated, black-clad foot tapped nervously against the floor. "It's not a bot," he said. "Not anymore. It's just a plant."

"But . . ."

Renny snarled at him. His hands clenched against the floor. Hannoken's face took on a pained, "You, too?" expression, but he did not move. "No," he said again.

Frederick thought of how the gengineers had once been accused of arrogance, of shaping life to their whims, of failing to respect the integrity of each being's nature which eons of evolution had painfully established. It was that arrogance that had once given intelligence to a brainless pig, shaped to fit under a kitchen sink and endlessly reduce vegetable peelings and other garbage into slush that would flow through a house's pipes. He had been rescued from the madness of boredom when a small boy had discovered him, alone behind the cupboard door. The same arrogance had provoked the creation of the bots' ancestors, and Renny's intelligence, and now . . .

The gengineers, he thought, had done the world—humanity—a lot of good. They had given it the resources it needed to stay civilized when fossil fuels and ores had been near exhaustion. They had given him a human body and Renny his hands. They were giving Lois McAlois her legs. But, yes, it was no surprise that they had antagonized so many people, that the Engineers had grown in numbers and vehemence and eventually had seized the reins of power on the Earth below Probe Station.

"But it's mine," said Donna Rose. "You cloned me. It's me, and it's deformed. You *have* to pull it up."

When Hannoken just shook his head and refused to budge from his guardian stance, Frederick finally said, "You have a responsibility. Gengineering isn't for making toys. You should be trying to maximize potential, making Donna Rose's child more intelligent, not less."

"You sound like a BRA bureaucrat," said Hannoken.

"And you," said Renny. "You sound like a selfish, self-centered pig."

A knock on the door interrupted the argument before it could develop any further. "Come in," said Hannoken, and the others turned to see a young man in a grey coverall. On his shoulder was the patch of the Station's communications staff. In his hand was a single photograph.

"We tried to call, sir," he said. "But . . ."

"What is it?"

"The spysats. We've been using them to monitor the surface, and . . ." He hesitated. "It looks like a war."

"What do you mean?" asked Frederick.

The clerk held out the photo. "The Engineers," he said. "Their troops are massing, around this area."

Frederick took the photo and stared at it for a long moment. "That looks like my town," he finally said, pointing one finger toward the picture's corner. "My city. Where are they?"

"Right here." The clerk pointed to an area of woods and scattered fields a couple of hundred kilometers away. Puffs of cloud obscured the landscape in scattered patches. A broad plume of what looked like smoke trailed southward. "It's hilly, and they're on the roads, here and here and here. They seem to be surrounding . . ."

"What are they up to?" asked Hannoken.

The clerk shrugged. "We don't know. We think they must have found some refugees."

"Bots?" asked Donna Rose.

"Maybe. We have more, sir, but . . ."

"Athena, open," said Hannoken. His desk promptly beeped again. "Answer it."

The wall screen came alive with the face of another communications clerk, who promptly spotted her colleague in the station director's office. "Sandor?" said the clerk.

"What have we got?" said the com tech who had invaded the director's office.

"Here. Live."

The picture changed to show the surface of the planet below. The smoke plume was larger. "Infrared," said Sandor. The colors shifted, and the source of the plume glowed red. "It looks like a forest fire," he said.

"They're burning them out," said Donna Rose. Her leaves constricted visibly about her torso, and her shoulders slumped.

"Can we get more magnification?" asked Frederick.

In answer, the picture shifted back to normal light and rapidly enlarged, zooming in on the edge of a patch of cleaned farmland, a farmhouse. Tiny, moving figures became visible, though it was impossible to tell whether they were human beings or bots.

"There," said Frederick. He pointed at a patch of bare soil near the farmhouse, a garden, where a group of smaller figures didn't move. "Bots. Those must be the kids."

"Can't we do something?" asked Donna Rose.

Frederick laid one hand on her shoulder while Hannoken shook his head. "We have spaceplanes, but there aren't any landing strips near enough to let us land. And we don't have troops or weapons."

"Just where is this?" asked Renny.

Behind the screen, Sandor recited coordinates and added, "But we don't have time. That fire's growing fast. There must be oil trees down there."

Renny did not answer. He was running toward the door as fast as his hands and feet could carry him.

"Where's he going?" asked Sandor.

"He's a pilot," said Frederick. "And a Q-ship . . ."

"Might be able to land," said Hannoken. "But he shouldn't try. No one's done it before, and we can't afford to lose it."

Donna Rose glared at the director. "At least he's trying. Not *playing.*"

The clerk turned to leave. Hannoken sighed and turned toward the plant he had gengineered.

"Tear it up," said Donna Rose.

He nodded. "I'll try again," he said. "I still have some of that sample."

"Just so you don't . . ." She gestured toward the pot.

"To her," said Frederick, "that's a monster. *Add* to her genes. Don't subtract."

"I'll try." The station director faced the bot. "Maybe you'd help with the design?"

She snorted, but her face relaxed.

Two of the new, larger Q-ships had been completed and were fully fueled. The other four were nearly done. All six floated outside the construction shack a few kilometers from Probe Station, tethered to a metal-framed, fabric-skinned sphere already full of lunar dust. Not far from the fuel depot floated a pod of dust waiting to be transferred to the sphere.

Renny deliberately took a route to the station's airlock that passed by the training simulator. As he expected, the simulator was occupied by one trainee, with a second awaiting a turn. "Buran!" he said to the latter. "Who's in that thing? Stacey?" When Buran nodded, he added, "Get her out of there. We've got a mission."

It took Renny only moments to don the suit that had been tailored to his nonhuman frame, thanking whatever gods might be that he had decided to trade his forepaws for hands, cursing the awkward tail that he still retained. He thanked those gods again as he rode a gas-propelled scooter toward the *Quincy*, his ship. On the way, he used his suit's radio to tell Buran and Stacey what he wanted them to do: to grapple the *Quentin* to the waiting dust pod, to take the three workers floating there, in suits, near the larger depot, to collect the necessary pumps and hoses, and to follow him toward Earth. They would stop at Nexus Station while he went on, and when he came back, if he did, they would refuel him for a second descent.

He wished Lois McAlois was back from her long journey. She was better than he, and he knew she would easily, quickly, almost instantly adapt her skills to the new, larger ships. But she was needed where she was. This job was his and no other's. He hoped desperately that he would succeed.

There would be nothing to delay his departure. The *Quincy's* dust tanks were full. He had already test-flown it. He knew it needed a crew of no more than one, that its capacious cargo bay could hold over a hundred passengers. He knew that it had no wings and that it was only minimally streamlined for atmospheric flight but that it had the brute force to land successfully. The designers had included a ladder for boarding from ground level, just in case the ship ever set down on a planet such as Earth or Mars. There were no seats for passengers, but nets could be pulled down from the ceiling and attached to the floor. They would serve to cushion the multi-gee strains of acceleration, and if they were not quite as good as proper acceleration couches, he was sure that injury was preferable to certain death.

He vented gas and stopped the scooter beside the *Quincy's* hatch. He did not need to undo the belt that would have held a human's thighs to the scooter's saddle, for he did not bend that way. He grasped the recessed handle of the hatch and used his legs to push the scooter away. He used his radio to say, "Get going now! I'll need that fuel." He did not watch to see whether the trainee pilots obeyed. He was sure they would.

The *Quincy's* cabin was just as he had left it the last time he had visited. He strapped himself into the pilot's seat that had been shaped for his body—notched for his tail and curved for his still-canine back and hindquarters—and activated the ship's systems. He did not take the time to run through all the many steps of the standard pre-launch checklist. It was enough that the indicator lights for the Q-drive were all green and that the tank gauges all said "Full."

He sighed with relief when the ship's rear-view cameras showed that no one was in the way. He switched on the com and said, "*Quincy* launching. Earth descent and return." His fingers—marvelous things! How had he ever done without them?—danced across a keypad to activate the Q-flux generator.

"Wait a minute!" was the immediate reply from Probe Station's communications center. "You can't—"

"Ask the director." He flipped off the com as thrust began to push him gently against his seat. With agonizing slowness, he maneuvered free of the other ships and positioned himself for a powered dive from the lunar orbit that was home to Probe Station. As the Station fell away behind, he swore at the great distance he must cross. He fed the ship's computer the coordinates of the landing site he wished, told it of his wish for utmost haste, and grinned wolfishly when it indicated that he could have what he wanted. He pressed the keys that gave control of the ship to the computer. The vibration of the drive did not falter.

Only after he had fastened the passenger nets into place did he try to relax at last, to luxuriate in the hours of waiting. But he could not help thinking of the raging fires coming closer to the refugee encampment, of time running out. He hoped his utmost haste would be fast enough, and he wished that he could increase the thrust of the seat against his back, speed the wheeling of the stars across the port as the ship neared Earth. But at last the *Quincy* did turn to present its tail toward the planet. He had only minutes now before the ship would begin to spout its greatest torrents of plasma against the planet's gravity.

He watched the play of indicator lights across the panel in front of him. He knew when the computer increased the power of the Q-flux, producing from the uncertainties of the very vacuum a flood of mutually annihilating particles, a flood of raw energy, the wherewithal to vaporize the dust that was entering the thrust chamber, generating plasma hot and wild and roaring to be free. He caught his breath just as the *Quincy* began to roar beneath him, thrust grew greater, greater, weight pressed him into his seat, and the ship tipped and began to slide down the gravity well toward whatever was happening far below.

He labored for breath. The root of his tail began to complain as his weight ground it into the now-hard padding of his seat. He had flown the *Quincy*, yes, but only in space. He had never used it to fight a planet's gravity well, never put so much weight and strain and pain upon his body. Nor had he ever felt such pain before; the spaceplane he had first ridden to orbit had been a gentle thing by comparison, and besides, he had not been on his back then. A bone snapped, agony stabbed through his hindquarters, and he tried to scream. He managed only a twisted moan against the weight of thrust.

Earth's air shrieked against the *Quincy*'s hull. Glowing plasma billowed outside the port but still he thought he could make out wisps of cloud and bluing sky. The altimeter's numbers grew ever smaller, their flicker slowing, the weight upon his chest and broken tail diminishing. Earth weight finally, the numbers steadied, and he steeled himself against the agony of his broken tail. He was hovering half a kilometer above the ground, held upon a pillar of fiery plasma. He activated once more the rear-view cameras, scanned the ground, saw the farmhouse and the field, and recognized the match with the spysat photo he had seen in Hannoken's office.

He saw the crowd of refugees, the smoke and flame of forest fire far too close, too close by far, the bursts of shellfire, the Engineers' troops strung out along the roads that bent around this patch of forest. The fire was closest to the refugees *there*. He aimed his hammer blows of thrust at the heart of the fire and slammed flat the trees, smothered the flames. He lowered, let the ship drift, used more blasts of plasma to clear away long lanes of fuel. He winched when he saw the flying debris burst into flame from the heat of his exhaust and tried to angle his thrust to throw the burning twigs and leaves and vines toward the larger fire the Engineers had set. His jaws parted grimly when he saw refugees seizing whatever flew the other way, toward virgin fuel and toward the crowd, and hurling it toward and across his fire lanes. He picked a landing spot a safe distance from the crowd—most of them were green, he saw, bots as flower-topped as Donna Rose, and among them the paler figures of human beings—and set down.

The drive quieted, and he groaned with pain. He could hear the crackle of flames. He told the computer to open the hatch to the passenger compartment and let down the ladder. Then, ignoring the microphone and loudspeaker he could have used to speak to those outside, he unstrapped and opened his own hatch.

Hot wind, heated by frictioned hull and blazing flames, pummeled his face. The hull rang as a spent bullet glanced off its metal. The refugees—bots, humans, a pair of greenskins— were flowing toward him like water returning to fill the hole left by a falling rock. Someone was in the garden beyond, digging up a computer. Others were moving young bots, too young to walk on their own, into tubs and pots and buckets. They knew what he was there for, and it did not bother them a bit that his head in the hatchway was not that of a human being.

He sighed. He took a deep breath. He shouted, "Come on! Let's go! But I can't take you all this trip."

They stood quietly aside while the computer and the children were carried aboard. Then, almost as if they had established a diplomatically formal protocol in advance, they filed aboard, bots and humans alternating, until the ship was full. Well over half the initial crowd of refugees remained on the ground, still bots and humans, the greenskins to one side.

"I'll be back as soon as I can," called Renny. He shook his head sadly as he closed the hatch. He hoped that would be soon enough.

As soon as the *Quincy* was in free-fall and he had recovered from the renewed agony of gee-pressure on his broken tailbones, Renny called Nexus Station in low Earth orbit, much, much closer than Probe Station.

"Yes," they said. "We can take them, for a while at least."

"Just transfer them to the *Quentin*. I'll take the last load all the way to Probe myself," said Renny. His voice tailed off into a low whine.

"You sound . . . Is anything the matter?"

"You might have a medic meet me."

"Will do."

When he finally opened the short passageway between his cabin and the passenger compartment and pulled himself through, he was met by silence. Green bots and fleshy humans, all alike suspended in the nets, held there by rootlets, hooked fingers, toes, stared at him as if they were one.

"We'll stop at Nexus Station," he said. "They'll sort you out and ship you on. I have to get back down there."

"You're going back? You'll get the rest?" Renny did not recognize the human who pushed forward, though his smell seemed almost familiar.

"As soon as I can," said the dog. "And I'll try, if the Engineers haven't—"

"I'm Duncan. Jeremy Duncan. Andy's still down there. I hope . . ." He paused and swallowed. "Is Freddy . . . ?"

He was interrupted by a gentle chime from the controls behind the pilot. "Excuse me," said Renny. His tail tried to wag once, involuntarily, within his suit. He winced at the pain, said, "Yes, he's here. Out at Probe Station," and turned abruptly away.

Minutes later, a passageway had snugged over the passenger hatch and the refugees were filing into Nexus Station's receiving area. A medic was carefully inserting a needle into Renny's lower back and saying, "This will kill the pain. I'd rather put you to bed."

"Uh-uh. I've got to . . ." Renny was staring out his port toward the *Quentin*. It had arrived safely. It had the dust pod with it. But . . .

"I know." She was young, pale blonde, boyishly slender, clad in a lime-green coverall. "You'll need a lot more than this when you get home."

"I'll cut it off."

"You bang it up much more, and that'll be your only choice."

A voice from the Nexus com center was saying, "We have them on the spysats. They're surrounded, and they can't run. The fires are spreading. The troops are firing more heavily. The farmhouse is in ruins and burning. You'll have to hurry."

"*Quentin*? Buran? Stacey? Where's my dust?"

"We've got some trouble here. Those workers . . . They want to talk to you. Chuck?"

Static crackled on the com line. "We're on strike."

"Say again?" said Renny.

"One load of those mechin' bots is more than enough. We don't need any more."

Renny snarled and hit the keys to focus his screen on the

pod to which the *Quentin* was attached. The three workers were visible. He snarled again, louder, baring his fangs even though he knew they could not see them. "I'll rip your suits," he said.

The Nexus com tech's voice broke in. "Why don't you just take them back to Earth? Drop them right in the middle of a labor camp. We'll get a crew out there to handle the hoses."

"Wait a minute!"

"He needs that fuel *now*! If he gets there too late . . ."

Renny watched as the three workers finally began to move, freeing a long hose from the side of the pod and snaking it in his direction. There was a clang as it hit the side of the *Quincy*, and he winced. There were more noises, the hum of the pumps came on, and the gauges began to indicate his tanks were filling.

What had Buran called one of them? Chuck, and they had met a Chuck on their first visit to Probe Station's dining hall. The two were surely one, for that first Chuck had not wanted to share space with bots either. Renny wrinkled his nose as if smelling something foul. He had met no other examples of that sentiment on the station, but they plainly existed. There were three out there, and all had tried to strike. There had been no sign of disagreement.

The Engineer troops had actually withdrawn in the face of the forest fire they had set to raging, but they were still within artillery range of the refugee encampment, or what was left of it. Puffs of smoke issued from the mouths of what Renny could now see were antique mortars and field guns, museum pieces from another age. Explosions cratered the earth. The farmhouse was flaming rubble. The bots and their human companions huddled in small groups in the open. As he watched, a shell landed in the midst of one such group. The bodies flew.

Renny clenched his teeth and ignored the pain in his tail. The medic's spinal block had worked for a while, but that second round of heavy gees . . . The anesthetic had settled out or been flushed by accelerated blood flow. Or the area was now so abused that anesthetic was not enough.

The fires had leaped the lanes he had swept before. They were nearing the refugees, while the hammerblows of shells came faster, eager to prevent escape, perhaps to destroy his ship.

He swore and swept his plasma tail across the troops and their artillery. He swept again and forced the fires back, at least for a moment. He landed, popped the hatches, and screamed for the refugees to board. They ran and climbed and entered, humans, greenskins, bots.

Then the ship was full, and there were still refugees on the ground. They stared at him, silently, bleakly. He said, "I'm sorry. There won't be time for . . ."

A bot with soot-streaked orange blossoms raised one hand. "Thank you," she said.

As he lifted off for the last time, a mushroom cloud of flame and greasy smoke was lifting skyward not far away. The fire had reached a grove of oil trees, and their sap had burst into flame all at once.

Chapter Twenty

A BEAM OF filtered, reflected sunlight came through the small porthole in the wall of the compartment Frederick Suida and Donna Rose shared, illuminating the trough of soil in which she spent much of her time. She was kneeling before it, patting dirt into place around the roots of a small shoot of honeysuckle. "Someone brought it with them," she said. "Someone took the time to pull it up and tuck it in their leaves and keep it safe."

On Earth, Frederick had lived and worked in old-fashioned buildings of masonry and steel. But he had been surrounded by living things as well. There had been trees and grass outside, honeysuckle vines around the windows, potted plants inside, bioform computers and snackbushes and a myriad more. Here the walls were as hard as ever. They had to be, steel walls and ceiling, steel floor beneath the carpet, all to keep the vacuum at bay and contain the air and warmth that living things required. There were none of the curves and softnesses of Earth's organic reality except in the people that surrounded him and in the few fragments of Earth they had brought with them. Plants existed only in pots and . . . He stood behind Donna Rose, a bot, half plant, half human. He stretched out one hand and gently touched the yellow blossoms of her scalp.

"I remember now," he said. "I met your ancestors when they were new. Even before the Eldest's generation. When I was still a pig. That's when I first found out how special the honeysuckle is to bots. They designed it, and you must have missed it more than I could possibly miss grass and trees."

He wished someone could bring him what he had lost, even a sprig, a shoot, a seed. "Bert's dead," he said. "Jeremy Duncan was in the first load, and he told me."

"Who was he?" Donna Rose did not look up from her gardening.

"A friend. He worked at BRA. Jeremy ran a lab for me in the suburbs. He gave genimals like Renny human bodies, when that was what they wished. He went through hell."

The bot looked up at him then. "They all did," she said. "You got me out just in time. Then you came too, and we missed it all."

He nodded, though he did not think he had missed it all, at all. He had seen his hell years before. After a moment of silence, he told her the little he had learned of Duncan's story.

"He must be angry."

"He didn't say that. But yes, of course he is. When he told me how Renny used the blast from his Q-drive against the Engineers, he seemed very satisfied."

Renny was the first to arrive, his fur askew as if he had not yet, in the hours since he had returned from his rescue mission, found a chance to brush smooth the marks left by his suit. Letting his tail jut out to one side, its base wrapped in a stiff bandage, he sat on one haunch near the pot that had had Donna Rose so upset, noting that it was now empty, and stared at Probe Station's director. Alvar Hannoken was behind his desk, muttering to his computer, glaring at screens full of reports and faces and views of rooms—the library, the game room, the dining hall—crowded with the refugees the dog had brought to orbit. Renny said nothing, seeming content to stare and smooth his fur with his hands, contorting himself from time to time to use his tongue.

When Frederick Suida and Donna Rose entered the room, Hannoken looked up from his screens and said, "We'll have to ship them out soon. We have the room to handle some of them. So do Nexus and the other stations. The Hugin and Munin habitats could take them all but say they won't take more than fifty each. But they will take more, eventually. They'll have to."

Frederick gestured for silence and glanced toward the corridor behind him. "Don't alarm them." As his words died, Walt Massaba appeared in the doorway. Behind him, ushered by two of the security chief's aides, Corlynn and Tobe, came a human, a pair of greenskins, and several bots. Two of the bots were carrying a wooden tub containing a few tiny sprigs of honeysuckle and a plant somewhat like the one Donna Rose had made Hannoken destroy so recently. This plant differed in that she was taller and her head and face seemed sculpted from a single massive flower. Beside her scurried a smaller bot whose disproportionately swollen bulb hinted that she had larger brains than her kin.

"Jeremy Duncan." Frederick indicated the human with what was almost a smile. "I knew him when . . . He's a gengineer."

"A colleague, then." Hannoken came around his desk and offered his hand.

"Sam and Sheila Nickers." Hannoken eyed the feathers on the greenskin woman's scalp and the inserts on her cheek and jaw but said nothing. They were, perhaps, too routine, too common, to provoke his professional interest. "I understand," said Frederick, "that they were living with the bots in the city, helping out their teachers."

Sheila Nickers held one hand toward the bots. "Narcissus Joy. She's a gengineer too. And Mary Gold. Lemon Margaret. Jackie Thyme." Each one, as her name was spoken, nodded her flowery head. "Chervil Mint. She's the one who called for help. They raided the campus to free her, and that's what started . . ."

"It's been lonely," said Donna Rose. "I'm glad you're here, all of you."

"Thanks to the dog," said Jackie Thyme, and Renny winced as his tail tip twitched against the carpet.

Hannoken turned toward the bot in the tub and her smaller attendant. "And . . . ?"

"The Eldest," said Narcissus Joy. "And Eldest's Speaker."

"Aahh!" sighed Donna Rose. Her tone was awed, almost worshipful. "I knew of you. I never thought . . ."

Acrid, pungent scent filled the room as the Eldest bent her head and trembled. A keening cry burst from Eldest's Speaker.

Sam Nickers explained briefly that the Eldest could not talk in words but only in odors, perfumes. The Speaker was her translator.

"I remember." Frederick had to raise his voice above the noise. A wary expression crossed his face. "She's much like the very first bots. They couldn't walk, and they used their perfumes to make men do their bidding."

"A later generation," said Mary Gold. "After we lost that ability. She is no threat to anyone here. Nor are we."

Hannoken looked skeptical. "I hope you're right."

The keening turned into words. "We once were many," said Eldest's Speaker. Frederick wondered if the neural circuitry necessary for translating odor to speech accounted for the greater size of the Speaker's bulb. "We now are few. A remnant only of a mighty people. Greatly oppressed, winnowed by fate. Escaped the slaughter."

Narcissus Joy nodded sadly. "So many of us," she said, "died when the Engineers took over. We thought we were the only ones. And some of us had to stay behind."

"To burn," said Jackie Thyme.

Sheila Nickers looked at her husband. "Alice Belle was one of them. I saw her waving."

"Ah, no." Sam's voice choked, and he bent his head for a long moment before he could speak again. "A friend," he finally explained to the others. His face said that he had not known the bot had been left on Earth.

"There are others down there," said Hannoken. He spoke to his computer, and the wall screen to the right of his desk showed satellite photos. "Surveillance found some in the tropics." He pointed to the broad region surrounding the Amazon River. Patches remained of the region's once thick cover of jungle, rainforest. The rest had vanished to feed lumber and paper mills, to provide farmland and pasturage for the urban poor of half a continent. When the thin tropical soil soon played out . . .

Gengineers had reclaimed the desolation with oil trees; deep-rooted, broad-leaved paper plants, whose bark unrolled in snowy sheets a kilometer long; sugar trees, whose sap was syrup; grains that could make their own fertilizers and pesticides; potatoes that grew as purple ten-meter snakes atop the soil and needed no digging for their harvest; and more. But then the Engineers had destroyed much of the nonmechanical technology they hated. Now there were vast expanses of burned field and orchard and forest, bare red dirt, soot-streaked, charcoal-studded, as hard as rock, eroded gulleys, brushy scrub, and abandoned homes, towns, factories. There was no one to argue possession, for the land was once more derelict. That was what made it safe for refugees.

Hannoken pointed again. "And mountains. It's hard to tell the bots from humans, except that they spend long periods standing still, outdoors. There's a labor camp. They're there, though it's hard to say how many."

"I haven't been able to find Andy," said Jeremy Duncan. When Donna Rose looked puzzled—Andy was hardly a bot name—he explained, "A human."

Hannoken had the computer produce the latest view of the area from which Renny had brought his guests. "If he didn't get on the ship . . ." He indicated the broad expanse of smoke-shrouded landscape. A shift to infrared cut through the haze and showed blackened earth. There was no sign of the Engineer troops, nor of life on what had been the farm.

Duncan's voice choked. "We met when they pulled the gengineers out of the labor camps. They wanted us to . . ."

Sam Nickers looked especially thoughtful when Duncan had described the crowds of Engineer protestors outside the Ginkgo County Community College campus. "Factionalism," he said. "It happens with every revolution. They may wind up tearing themselves to pieces."

"Will they leave anything for us to reclaim?" asked Frederick.

Sam shook his head.

There was another wave of scent, less acrid, more flowery. "What kind of ship?" asked Eldest's Speaker.

Briefly, Renny explained what the Q-drive did. "We can land again," he said. "We'll rescue all we can. And then—"

"We're building a larger ship," said Hannoken. "An asteroid, the *Gypsy*. When it's ready, we can leave. Perhaps we can find a world that's all our own."

"How many ships do you have now?" asked Narcissus Joy.

"The *Quincy* and the *Quentin*," said Renny. "Four more are nearly done, and their pilots are being trained. There's also the *Quoi*, a small test ship, but Lois took it on a supply run."

"The *Gypsy* project," said Frederick. "And Chryse Base, and Saturn. She'll be back in a few days."

"Then it's fast," said Sam Nickers. "Much faster than—"

Duncan shook his head. "Not fast enough to save us all. With just two ships of any size, it will take too long, and the Engineers will—"

"Buran and Stacey flew the *Quentin*," said Renny. "They did fine, and we'll be using all six ships."

"And where will you put the refugees?"

"New quarters can be built," said Donna Rose. "We're already expanding the stations and habitats wherever we can. We'll build new ones if we have to."

There was another wave of scent, imperative, demanding, and Eldest's Speaker said, "We can help. We too have minds and hands, and we too can build."

Over the next days, Probe Station's communications center used the spysats that orbited the Earth to pinpoint certain sites in the wastelands of the Amazon and Congo basins, in the vast emptinesses of Australia and northern Canada and central Asia, in New England and the Yucatan Peninsula, wherever bots and others had found temporary safety in isolation and distance from the Engineers, who concentrated in the cities.

Frederick and Donna Rose were in his office in the construction shack. She was searching databases for whatever solutions she might find. He was striving to accelerate the effort to finish the last four Q-ships and to find the necessary materials to build living quarters for the bots Renny had already rescued and the greater numbers yet to come. "We need more ore," he said. "More metal. More of everything."

"Then send them to the Moon," said Donna Rose. "Turn them into miners. Build quarters there as well."

He was nodding and saying, "They could dig trenches, roof them over, seal the walls," when Renny coasted through the doorway and growled, "Mechin' litterheads! Won't let me go. Won't let me fetch them up here. Hannoken says we need places to put them first."

"We do," said Donna Rose. "We don't yet have enough." When he stopped beside her, one hand clutching at the edge of the seat to which she was strapped, she scratched behind one of his doggy ears. For a second he closed his eyes and let his tail wag, but then he growled again. "And they're dying down there."

She touched her keyboard, worked her mouse-glove. "Freddy? Look at this." The screen before her showed an array of what looked like transparent globes interconnected by tubular passageways. "I've found an old scheme for a quick-and-dirty space station. Plastic balloons, inflated by air pressure."

Frederick turned toward her and stared with interest at the screen. "But we don't have the plastic."

"We could make it. And then we could use the same material to seal the lunar trenches."

"What would we make it from?"

"Vegetation. Renny could land on Earth with a few bots and cut trees. Or they could raid oil depots."

Renny laughed. "Yes!"

Moments later, Hannoken's face was on the screen and they were laying the proposal out for him. He in turn was asking his computer whether there were any chemical engineers on the station who could set up the factory they would need to turn whatever organics Renny might bring to orbit into plastic. When the answer was positive, he gave Renny the go-ahead.

He had barely finished speaking when something caught his attention. He stared to one side of the screen in which they saw him. He looked pained, frustrated, angry.

Finally, he turned back to them and said, "We'll need the space very soon. Look at this. Athena, play it again. Put it on the com." New images filled the veedo screen, showing troops surrounding labor camps. A campus much like that where Jeremy Duncan had been enslaved was being razed, its residents marched off to a field of barracks surrounded by heavy artillery.

The image on the screen changed to show a broad, polished desk with a wooden nameplate that read "Arnold Rifkin." Beside it rested a brass-knobbed swagger stick. On the other side of the desk sat a stern figure wearing a blue coverall bedecked with bits of polished metal.

A blare of martial music echoed throughout the construction shack to reveal that Athena had obeyed her master. The same pictures would be on every com terminal in Probe Station. The sounds would bellow from every outlet, with or without a screen.

The music fell silent, and then there were words:

"Orbitals! Come back to Earth! You are needed here more than you can possibly know! Bring back the machines, the resources, the assets you have stolen from us. Bring back the scientists and technicians who might replace them. Bring them back, and we will forgive your crimes.

"We demand your help in recreating the technology of the Machine Age. If you dare to withhold
it . . ."

The screen showed a scene of ragged prisoners, both bots
and humans, many of the latter modified in some way. They
were surrounded by blue-clad soldiers holding leveled weapons. The sound of gunfire began. The prisoners fell in ragged,
bloody heaps.

"We will kill them all."

There was silence. Then the station director said, "That just
came in. Now . . ." The screens in Frederick's office subdi-
vided to show a dozen, twenty, thirty faces wearing expres-
sions of shock, outrage, fear. Several the computer had sub-
titled with "Nexus," "Hugin," "Munin," "Moon," and other
labels. Most were marked "Probe," and some of these were
familiar: both the Nickerses, Narcissus Joy, Jeremy Duncan,
Walt Massaba. Hannoken's own face remained at the center
of each screen.

"We need . . ." Donna Rose's voice was anguished.

"An all-out rescue effort?" Hannoken nodded soberly, his
heavy jaw grimly set. "I agree. We've begun, and we have to
continue. But there are some—"

"We can't save them in any other way," said Massaba, Probe
Station's security chief. "We can't *make* them tolerant. We
can't even conquer them and take away their guns. We don't
have the troops to take over a whole world."

"We cannot intervene!" said a Nexus face. "It will mean
war!"

"What can they shoot at us with?" asked Renny.

"Look," said Hannoken. A screen blossomed with spysat
photos. "They've found a few undamaged spaceplanes. And
we've intercepted messages that make it clear they know where
to find the rockets, the missiles, that the world mothballed a
century ago. They can do it."

"War is inevitable," said Frederick. "We already have it."

"And we're right up front," said the Nexus face. "In low
Earth orbit, the easiest for them to reach."

"No!" cried a Hugin face after a moment's time delay. "It's
all your fault! You and Director Hannoken. If you hadn't let

that creature, that dog, of yours go down there . . . Mechin' cavalry to the rescue! Nothing would have happened! The gengineers would be safe."

Renny snarled. "Bots too," he said. "The killing had already started, long before I ever met Freddy. Even before Dr. Hannoken made me."

Frederick nodded. "Long before," he said, remembering his own first encounters with the Engineers' rabid attitudes. "And they're clearly ready to bring it to us, if they can."

"They are mad," said Narcissus Joy.

"They will not stop," said Sam Nickers. "Until everyone who does not agree with them is dead."

"Can you stall them?" Frederick asked Hannoken. "Buy us time, while we . . . ?"

"Freddy!" said Donna Rose. "No! You can't . . . !"

"That is not enough!" cried Jeremy Duncan. "We have to rescue all of them, all the slaves, as many as we can. We cannot afford to stall! Every moment of delay means more deaths."

"Yes!" said Donna Rose. "We can't afford to stall. If we might have saved them, then all those deaths must be on our conscience. If we let them die, then we are just as much their killers as are the Engineers."

"But we cannot save them yet," said Frederick. "We have no room. The ships aren't ready. And if we try, the Engineers *will* begin the slaughter."

"We have to try," said Donna Rose. "We have to threaten them . . ."

"Hit them," said Duncan. "Hit them as hard as they hit us, or their slaves."

"With what?"

Narcissus Joy was nodding in agreement with her kin. So were others, while those few fell silent who objected to any rescue effort, who thought it would lead to war as surely would an attempt to invade and force peace upon the Engineers.

"I know." Hannoken hesitated briefly. "We have to do what we can. But first, we do need more places to put those we rescue. Frederick? Can you coordinate the effort?"

Frederick nodded. "We'll need that plastic."

"Then go ahead. Send Renny after it. Even if it starts a new bloodbath."

"No!" cried Donna Rose.

"We have to," said Hannoken. "Lois McAlois is almost home, and she can fly the *Quentin*. The other pilots should be ready as soon as their, ships."

"A week at most," said Frederick. "Maybe ten days. How many can they slaughter in that time?"

"I'll stay away from them," said Renny. "I'll land in isolated areas. Where refugees have hidden. The Engineers may not even see me, and I should be able to bring back a few bots at the same time, while the rest get the next load ready."

"They'll see you," said Frederick.

"What about those missiles?" said the Hugin face. "What can we do if they launch them at us? What if they send up troops in the spaceplanes? We have no weapons."

"Of course we do," said Walt Massaba, Probe Station's security chief. "Weaponry is easy. We get most of the raw materials we need from lunar rock and gravel. We already mine it, package it, and use mass drivers to send it into orbit where we smelt it with focused sunlight. We can use the same material to make large lumps, artificial asteroids of many tons. We can equip them with small Q-drives. Then, if we have to, we can crash them into missile launchers, airports, armies. They will do more damage than nukes."

"Yes!" cried Duncan. "I'll work on that!" His eyes widened, almost glowing at the prospect of fighting back.

"Director?" asked the security chief.

"You can have him, Walt." The look Hannoken sent Massaba might have meant he hoped the security chief could keep Duncan reined in.

Frederick shook his head sadly. The idea seemed likely to be both economical and effective. It would divert materials they needed for other things, but the Q-ships were nearly done and the quarters they would have to build for the refugees would need more plastic than metal. Worst of all . . . "Won't using these things endanger precisely those we wish to save?"

"That's a chance we'll have to take," said Massaba. "We can't do any good if we can't protect ourselves."

"We'll need more miners," said Frederick.

"The bots, Freddy," Donna Rose reminded him. "They can dig trenches as they mine, and then line them with the plastic to make new quarters."

"They'll be barracks," someone commented. "Cheerless places. Prison camps. As bad as those on Earth."

"No," said Jeremy Duncan. "Not that bad."

Narcissus Joy's nose wrinkled as if scent had just billowed about her. A voice was a mutter behind her screen. "The Eldest agrees," she said. "Here we are not slaves, for here we work for freedom."

When Frederick returned to his quarters the next day, he found Donna Rose once more bent over her pet honeysuckle shoot. Yet she was not planting, cultivating, or fertilizing it. Instead, she held a small jar in one hand, and she was digging with the other.

"You left early this afternoon," said Frederick. "What's up?"

She froze. After a moment, her hands resumed their motions. She did not turn to look at him. "I've found a replacement for me, Freddy. Narcissus Joy—you've met her—will be in tomorrow."

"What?"

"I'm leaving, Freddy. Leaving you." The tendons on the backs of her hands were rigid with tension. "Look," she said. "It's already begun to branch out, from the roots. I'll leave you a piece." She had the shoot free of the soil now and was packing it into her jar. A second shoot, smaller, still sprouted from the pot.

"But . . ." He could not speak. He could not move. He could only feel anew the paralyzing shock of loss. At the zoo, all the friends he had ever had, almost. Again, when he had found his road home, back to BRA, cut off behind him. And now . . .

"You want to stall," she said. "You're a temporizer, an appeaser. You want to let my people die."

He managed to speak one line: "What else can we do, until we're ready?"

"Jeremy wants to fight. He'll force them to stop the slaughter, and he'll save everybody. At least, he'll try."

"It won't work."

"Of course it will. The Engineers are human, aren't they?"

Almost reluctantly, he nodded. "That doesn't mean much. Make them mad—worse, scare them—and they'll . . ."

"Then we'll kill them. Kill them the way they're killing us."

"You'll kill bots too."

"Eggs and omelets."

"You'll kill more than would die if you waited for us to prepare new quarters."

"At least we'll be doing *something*."

"But we're doing *something* too," Frederick told Renny later. The German shepherd had often come to visit since Lois McAlois had left on her long flight. Sometimes he had even stayed the night.

Frederick was sitting on the edge of his bed, his elbows on his knees, his chin in his hands. Renny squatted on his haunches, bandaged tail still. Both were facing Donna Rose's trough of soil, now empty of all but that single sprig of green she had left behind.

"She wants action," said the dog. "She has to know we have to prepare the ground first, but that doesn't satisfy her or Duncan. She's as human as he in that way."

"She's a plant," said Frederick. "A mechin' flower!" A murderous flower, he thought, and he almost laughed at the oxymoronic irony, the inherent contradiction, of the phrase.

"But human too," said Renny.

"All too human," Frederick agreed. He stared morosely at the trough. Eventually he spoke again: "Going to stay tonight?"

The German shepherd heard what Frederick had not said, that he wanted company, but he shook his large head. "Uh-uh. Lois is docking."

He needed to say nothing more. His tail was as eloquent as words could ever be, even though pain and bandage kept it from moving as vigorously as it might.

Later, waiting in the docking area, watching through a porthole as Lois's little *Quoi* slid out of blackness into visibility, Renny made out a pair of cargo pods held away from the ship on the ends of a long boom, like buckets on the ends of a water-carrier's shoulder pole. Each one carried *Gypsy* workers rotating home on leave. The ship's Q-drive spouted glowing plasma, and it slowed. It released the pods and nudged them within reach of the station's docking tubes.

The dog ignored the people who flooded out of the tubes and past him. He ignored the spacesuited workers who drew the emptied pods to one side and anchored them to the station's structure. He had eyes only for the *Quoi* and the pilot it concealed, and his hands grew sweaty when he saw the ship approach its own docking tube.

Why hadn't he told Frederick that he had been looking forward to this night for weeks? He knew the answer. He was as excited as any man who had ever been about to reunite with a traveling lover, but his friend was in no condition to hear such news. His feelings were as bruised as feelings got, and hearing of Renny's joy would not help.

There was the sound of hands touching the wall of the docking tube. His hindquarters began to quiver, and suddenly he realized that Frederick must have seen exactly how he felt. He was not always conscious of his tail, even when it hurt.

He dropped the thought as Lois came into sight. And yes, she had legs, short ones, childlike, useless still anywhere but in space. And yes, she was grinning to see him. And yes, his hands were on her shoulders, hers on his ribs, his tongue on her chin, her laughter in his ears. And yes, and yes, and yes . . .

PART 4

Chapter
Twenty-one

NUCLEAR WEAPONS HAD lost their appeal as weapons of war not long after it was generally realized that they destroyed far more than their targets. However, it was not the threat of radioactive fallout and death by immediate radiation poisoning or later cancer, nor even the threat of mutant children, that removed the missiles and bombs from the world's arsenals. Rather, it was the discovery that even a small nuclear war would have enormous effects on world climate, filling the air with so much dust and smoke that sunshine could not reach the surface, causing a nuclear autumn or winter, a months-long, crop-killing chill that would starve many who survived the actual explosions. A similar event—not nuclear, but the geysering of dust and smoke and steam that followed the impact on the Yucatan peninsula of a meteorite some ten kilometers across—had extinguished much of life on Earth, including the last of the dinosaurs, some sixty-five million years before.

Yet the sense of vulnerability that accompanied these discoveries did not lead to the destruction of all nuclear arms. The bombs were dismantled, yes. The submarines and ships and airplanes and other vehicles that had carried missiles were scrapped or converted to other uses. As for the missiles themselves, wiser heads prevailed, pointing out that the asteroid or comet that destroyed the dinosaurs was not the only one to strike the Earth. Such impacts had happened before, and since, and there were a great many more potential cosmic cue balls orbiting the sun. It was only a matter of time before fate once more took aim. When that day came, humanity's only hope would be to have the wherewithal to ward off the blow.

Today it would be a relatively simple matter to install a Q-drive and steer the asteroid or comet away from Earth, or even to park it in a convenient orbit for mining or other uses.

But then that option had not been available. The nations had
stored many of their rockets and warheads away. Their leaders
swore they would be used only in time of direst need.

No one was sure that war would not bring the warheads back
into play. Perhaps because of that uncertainty, wars stayed
small and local. But now Earth's leaders had identified an
external threat. It was not an asteroid or comet. It was not
even attacking them. But it denied their dreams and defied
their power.

The missiles came out of storage. Silos were reopened.
Rockets were inspected, and where the Engineers had the
necessary technicians, slave or free, some were refurbished
and refueled. Heavier warheads were replaced with lighter
ones the rockets could carry all the way to lunar orbit. Older
warheads had their tritium refreshed. Guidance computers were
reprogrammed with celestial targets.

Jeremy Duncan wore nothing except a pair of bright red shorts.
He was bare above the waist, the pink slits of his gills plain to
see along his sides, the skin now as healthy as it had ever been,
free of sores and bruises though still tender to the pressure of
overlying cloth. A small squeeze bottle of lotion jutted from
one of the pockets in his shorts.

He hovered before a bank of veedo screens. One showed
the rock factory in lunar orbit, where lunar soil was melted,
shaped, cooled, and fitted with Q-drives. Others showed the
small—too small!—clusters of finished rocks near the Munin
and Hugin habitats, near Probe and Nexus and other stations;
more rocks were scattered in low Earth orbit, waiting. Still
other screens showed spysat views of Earth, of silo mouths
in North America and Siberia and China.

Duncan's Orbital Defense Center was a metal bubble floating in space a few kilometers from Probe Station. The idea
was that if a missile destroyed the station, the ODC would still
be there, still be functioning, still be able to coordinate the
defense of all the other Orbitals and their homes. There was
no porthole, not even a small one to admit sunlight, filtered and
reflected, for Donna Rose. There was only a wall screen aimed
toward the station, showing its can-within-a-can configuration,
the bulb of the construction shack to one side, the cup of the
radio telescope beyond, the idle *Quoi,* the larger *Quiggle* and
Quimby. The rest of the Q-ships—*Quincy, Quentin, Quito,* and

Quebec—were gone, on their ways to or from Earth, fetching biomass and whatever refugees could fit around their cargos.

A bell rang to summon attention to the screens. "A launch," said Donna Rose. Her leaves were parted slightly from her chest as if to intercept a little more of the control room's artificial lighting. The lights were brighter in the ODC's living section, though not as bright as she had enjoyed in Frederick's quarters. Yet she could not leave in search of better light. The demand for workers elsewhere was so great that there was no one to relieve her. She and Duncan had to be there all the time, in case Earth tried . . . "The first one today. Near Yeniseysk."

"Thor," said Duncan. "Estimate target." He had named his artificially intelligent computer system after the Norse god of thunder and strength, the defender, the one with the magic hammer that went where he willed and then returned to be used again and again.

"No target." The computer's voice was much more obviously synthesized than those of Hannoken's Athena or Frederick's Minerva. The screen that had revealed the Siberian launch flashed for their attention. As they watched, the rocket's exhaust plume suddenly ended in a billow of white.

"They didn't replace the fuel on that one," said Donna Rose.

"They must have thought it hadn't deteriorated enough to matter."

The bell rang again, activated as before by the ever-watchful computer. "Minnesota," said the synthetic voice, and they turned their attention to another flashing screen. Blinking circles surrounded the mouths of three newly opened silos. From two of the gaping mouths, missiles erupted, rapidly accelerating, climbing toward space atop pillars of smoke. From the third, a flash, a billowing cloud, a rising mushroom viewed aslant.

"The fuel's not all that deteriorates," said Duncan. "Thor, estimate targets."

"Nexus Station. Nexus Station."

"Both of them?" He touched the keyboard before him. Donna Rose worked her mouse-glove. Two of the rocks near the target station began to move, their Q-drives spitting plasma. They accelerated, and a screen showed their projected courses intersecting those of the still-rising missiles.

An instant before collision, one of the missiles burst like a Fourth-of-July skyrocket into a cluster of subsidiary warheads. Several remained in the path of the Q-driven rock long enough to be destroyed with the rocket itself. A few escaped.

"Litter!" said Duncan. "It was mirved." Already Donna Rose was commanding the rocks that remained near Nexus Station to position themselves between the station and Earth.

The warheads reached the resulting barrier as a loose cluster. Most struck the rocks and were reduced to shrapnel, harmful enough to structures in space but benign compared to the threat they had been. One detonated, and the resulting electromagnetic pulse made the ODC screens flicker. There was no damage. In space, all electronic circuitry was routinely hardened against EMP effects. The precaution was necessary not because anyone expected to have to cope with nuclear attack but because solar flares could be nearly as damaging.

Duncan showed his teeth in a predatory grin and said, "Thor. Use two LEO rocks to hit the Minnesota silos. Use another to hit the Yeniseysk silo. Then . . ."

When he hesitated, the computer assumed he had finished his message. "Executing," it said.

The rocks were much, much smaller than the juggernaut that had destroyed the dinosaurs, but they still weighed several tons apiece and, driven by their Q-drives, arrived at high velocity. They were more than adequate to the task of obliterating the silos, leaving nothing behind but craters and clouds of dust.

"Thor," said Donna Rose. "Restock immediately. We can't afford to leave holes in our shield."

The next rocks to emerge from the factory in lunar orbit would set their courses for Nexus Station and low Earth orbit. Once there, they would replace the rocks Thor had expended to defend the Orbitals and punish the Engineers.

"They're not really trying very hard," said Duncan quietly. "We have to do more than plug the holes. They have thousands of missiles down there. If they launched them all at once, and if half of them were functional, they'd overwhelm us. We need more rocks."

"Can we hit the silos first?" asked the bot.

He shook his head. "We don't know where all of them are, and they're hardened well enough to withstand near misses. There's no way we can get them all. And even if we did know where they are, we don't have enough rocks in place."

They needed more rocks. But the factory was already producing them as quickly as it could. Did they need another factory, then? There was no time to build one. But time alone could help, if the factory would not break down, if the Engineers would hold off on a full-blast assault just long enough, or if they at least would not launch their missiles faster than Duncan and Donna Rose could stop them, or until they were out of rocks, if he could restrain himself from exhausting his stony armament in a vain effort to hammer the Engineers' silos into uselessness.

If time failed, the Orbitals were doomed. No bots would survive on Earth or elsewhere. Civilization would die, pulled down by the forces of reaction, conservatism, and fear.

Renny could see the *Quentin* not far away, its bulb-nosed image eclipsing the array of mirrors, chambers, flow tubes, pipes, and presses that the Hugin workers had assembled for producing sheets of plastic. He could not see Lois McAlois at its controls, any more than she could see him. But he could imagine her, strapped into her couch, her still-too-small legs loose in the legs of her suit. He had seen them every night since her return, slender, weak, the feet and toes like a baby's, still undeveloped but growing, eventually to be again what the accident had cost her. He now slept beside her, not at the foot of the bed, one arm awkwardly around her shoulders while she petted his furry side and stroked—gently—his injured tail.

"It gets in the way," she had said. "Doesn't it? You could have it removed." He had whimpered under her hand, growled quite involuntarily, and shifted his position. "I should do more than that," he had said, and she had laughed.

She had been as glad to see him as he had been to see her once more. They had missed each other. He still did, though he knew she was there, just within the walls of the *Quentin*.

Her cargo was bladders of oil Congo bots had filled by tapping trees. He carried oil as well, but unlike her he also held refugees, giving them freedom as a reward for their labor, though without that labor there would be no freedom—no room—to give them.

The bladders deformed easily under gees, fitting snugly against walls and into corners, turning any compartment into a tank. They were made of the same plastic that was also lining lunar trenches and forming the first of the new habitats just behind the factory in its orbit. The bubblesat was a cluster of ten-meter globes distended by air pressure, their walls and connecting tubes translucent enough to show the workers who were fitting cabinets, environmental controls, wiring, and plumbing into place. When they were done, the workers would assemble more globes and tubes into still more bubblesats. They would continue until it was time to fill them with refugees. Everyone hoped they would have enough of them.

The first trips to Earth had fetched only wood, which had then been vaporized with the heat of focused sunlight, exposed to catalysts, condensed, polymerized, and formed in sheets. Those sheets had made the first bladders, which were then delivered to whatever refugees happened to have gathered near oil trees. Oil was much easier to process than wood.

Yet oil was not all the refugees were instructed to collect. While Lois brought her ship close to Hugin's satellite factory, Renny approached the habitat. Like its sister Munin on the other side of the Moon, one hundred twenty degrees away in its orbit, it was a broad disk, spinning slowly to give its many decks a sense of gravity. One flat face of the disk was a maze of girders and metal plates expanding into space, extending the habitat's volume, turning the disk into a stubby cylinder with room for hundreds more inhabitants. The other face turned endlessly about a motionless hub studded with accordion-throated docking tunnels.

He positioned the *Quincy* and stopped. When the docking tube's flexible mouth had fastened to his hull, he opened the hatch. Only then did he leave his controls to watch those he had brought from Earth debark, drifting in the air quite helplessly, unused to zero gee, clutching at each other and the walls, grinning with relief when the catchers Hugin's crew had deployed grabbed their arms and legs and propelled them onward. They were bots and humans, modified and unmodified, gengineers and greenskins and ordinary people who had once owned gengineered devices or chosen to be decorated with tattoos and inserts. They were farmers and truckers, store-keepers and office workers, women and men and children. Everyone carried something, young bots in pots, sacks of seeds gathered against the day when they might be planted aboard the *Gypsy*, dolls and books and suitcases full of clothing and mementoes.

When the *Quincy* was empty of all but those few bladders of oil Lois had not been able to fit into her ship, he returned to his controls and moved toward the factory. There, while he waited for workers to remove the bladders, he scanned the sky toward Earth. A glint of light was one of the other Q-ships, on its way not from the great basin of the Congo, but from the Amazon valley, or the Yukon, or . . . He touched a key, and his computer magnified Earth's image. There, a spark as a warhead blew. There, a cloud of dust and smoke, surely a mushroom when seen from the ground. There and there and there, the craters Jeremy Duncan's rocks had pounded into the Engineers' forces. Everywhere, a growing haze of dust. If the Engineers kept up their attempts to attack the Orbitals, if the warheads kept betraying their age and instability, if Duncan kept on throwing rocks, food, water, and air would be contaminated with radioactive fallout. The atmosphere would grow opaque, and the air would cool.

Renny wondered if the Engineers knew or cared what the consequences could be for them.

"A launch," said Donna Rose.

"Africa," said the computer's electronic voice. "The Congo site." Thor recited coordinates, and Duncan swore. "They still have the old defense radars, and they've managed to track our ships. They want to hit whatever we're after."

"They must know we're picking up refugees."

He touched his keyboard, spoke to the computer, and an LEO rock began a full-power dive toward Earth's surface.

"It's on track," said Donna Rose. "Impact . . . Just as it leaves the atmosphere. Over Odessa."

They watched their screens as the rock and its target approached each other, merged, and vanished. Another screen showed the bright spark of a Q-ship's plasma plume against the broad expanse of central Africa. "Which one's that?" asked Duncan.

"The *Quiggle*. It's safe now."

*   *   *

Earth, white-mottled, blue and tan, sliced through by night, hung above the grey lunar surface. The long line of the railgun stretched toward the distant peaks, jagged and black-shadowed.

To either side of the railgun, the surface was scarred by the tracks of vehicles and workers and by the trenches from which the shattered regolith, lunar soil plowed by eons of meteoritic impacts, large and small, had been scooped. Near the railgun's loading station, Sam and Sheila Nickers occupied a metal pressure hut, a ten-meter half-cylinder covered over with regolith. This was their living quarters and the office from which they oversaw the labors of the Orbital workers and their refugee helpers, but they were not often there.

At the moment, Sam was seated in a balloon-tired mooncar, watching as a crew sprayed liquid plastic over the walls and floor of a trench, stabilizing it against movement even under the occasional prod of a moonquake, sealing it against any possibility of leaking air. They had already installed an arching framework of metal girders and an airlock that for the moment led only from vacuum to vacuum. Shortly they would spread plastic sheets from the Hugin factory over the girders, seal their edges with more liquid plastic, and bulldoze lunar soil over the whole as insulation against heat and cold and as protection against the smaller stones that fell from space. Soon after that, the plastic would have given up its solvents to the lunar vacuum. They would pressurize it, and another barracks would be ready.

Beside him sat Jackie Thyme, who never seemed to wander far away. She was staring not at the workers but down the length of the railgun, pretending to watch as the steel launching buckets zipped invisibly fast down its single superconducting rail, propelled by the electromagnets that looped over it at precise intervals. At the gun's far end, the buckets were diverted onto a return track while the lunar soil they carried flew onward toward the catcher nets in lunar orbit. There, where sunlight and energy were continuously available, interrupted by neither the two-week night of the Moon nor the twelve-hour night of Earth, metals and other materials had long been refined for the Orbitals' use. Now, much of the lunar soil was simply melted and cast into rocklike shapes for Jeremy Duncan's use.

"Why don't they use the Q-ships?" asked the bot.

"They could," said Sam. "But the ships are busy with other jobs. And this system works just fine. They've had it going since long before they invented the Q-drive."

"Of course." Jackie Thyme shifted her attention to where Sheila Nickers was using a bulldozer to shape the walls of another trench, pushing excavated regolith into a heap from which an auger loaded the conveyor that stretched toward the loading station. Workers in bulky vacuum suits waited nearby, standing beside the stack of curved girders that would become the framework of still another barracks. Others bent over molds that turned a mixture of liquid plastic and regolith to chairs, tables, beds, soil troughs, and other furnishings.

Other trenches, soil heaped beside them, awaited finishing touches, while heavy equipment scooped out still more in the distance. Just three barracks had already been completed and partly occupied. They would not be filled until many more were ready and the final, full-scale rescue effort could begin. In the meantime, more bots did arrive each day, adding their hands to the labor and accelerating the digging and sealing of more trenches.

Atop one of the finished barracks, several suited workers were pacing back and forth, inspecting the shielding layer of regolith. "Sam?" The radio crackled. "Over here, on Number Two." He looked, and one of the workers was waving both arms.

"I see you. What's up?"

"We need more light inside here." The voice was feminine. That and her comment told him the workers were bots. "Can we expose the plastic?"

Another voice, male, broke in. "Keep some patches handy, or you could wind up with more ventilation than you like."

Sam grinned as he recognized the truth of the recommendation. He had not been in space long enough to think of such a thing himself. "You've been here awhile."

"Years," said the voice. "And I'd keep that ceiling just as thick as I could. I've seen blowouts."

The bot's voice returned: "Then what can we do?"

"Make a plastic cylinder?" asked Sam. "Embed it in the dirt?"

"That should do," said the veteran. "Though it won't help at night."

"Of course not," said the bot. "But we're used to that."

"Night's two weeks long," said the veteran.

After a moment of silence, the bot said, "I'd forgotten that." Her voice, even over the radio, sounded sheepish.

"Go ahead and do it," said Sam. "You'll have light half the time, anyway."

He then looked toward his wife. She was backing her 'dozer away from the trench she had prepared and turning toward another. Suited workers were already lifting girders into position. His own spraying crew was beginning to move in that direction, ready to seal and stabilize the walls.

They were making progress at last. It had taken time to get the plastic factory running, to design and make girders and airlocks for the barracks, to train the refugees and volunteers in new tasks. But that time was past. Their barracks machine was rolling, even as the habitats were being expanded and bubblesats were beginning to take shape in space. They would soon be ready for all the refugees the Orbitals could deliver.

Not for the first time, he thanked fate—or God, or fortune— that the Orbitals had found the Q-drive. Without it, he would still be on Earth. He would, in fact, be ash and smoke. So would Sheila and their bot friends. In time, so would all the other bots on Earth, and every human who did not share the ideology of the Engineers.

"There hasn't been time to think of . . ." Alvar Hannoken stood behind his desk, gesturing toward the pot that still stood empty before his office picture window. Its soil was dry, cracked, sterile. "I have her cells in storage, but she's out there with Duncan, in the ODC. We haven't had a chance to talk of a new design."

Frederick Suida sighed and slumped in his seat. "I miss her," he said softly. "Narcissus Joy is a good assistant, but—"

"You were happy with Donna Rose," said Probe Station's director.

He nodded. "We had our differences. That's why she left. But still . . ." He had people around him, friends, perhaps more than he had had before he met her. But he was far lonelier now, as lonely as he had been just after the massacre at the zoo, as lonely as he had been just after getting his human body. "And Renny . . ."

"Lois is back. So he's with her when he isn't flying the *Quincy*."

"He visits, but it's not the same."

"You're doing good work," said Hannoken. "All of you. The new quarters are shaping up rapidly, and Duncan saves us every day."

A chime sounded from Hannoken's desk. The Director said, "Athena, I'll take the call."

The face of a com center technician appeared on a small screen on his desk. "Sir? There's a call from Earth."

"Put it on."

Arnold Rifkin once more appeared on the screen, his desk invisible below his blue collar. His expression was sterner and more unforgiving than it had been the first time they saw him. Metal dangled from his ears. Copper wire was threaded through his hair. His cheeks were hollowed as if by asceticism or hunger. His voice was abrasive.

He said, "Director Hannoken. We've asked for your help. You've refused it. Worse yet, you have chosen to attack us. You steal both oil and people. You bomb our farmland."

When he paused, Hannoken replied sharply, "You did not ask, sir. You demanded, and you threatened the prisoners you have taken. Now you launch missiles at us, and you dare to complain that we try to stop them."

"We still need your help. And we have many more missiles. You cannot stop them all."

Frederick stepped into view of the com's vision pickup. "Don't you care that so many of your missiles explode by themselves? That using them poisons your world?"

The Engineer's glare was cold. "Your saboteurs are skilled. But that will not stop us. We will prevail."

"I don't see how," said Hannoken.

"We no longer want just your help. We insist on your unconditional surrender." When Frederick snorted, the other added, "We have not yet cleansed this world of all our opponents. We have many thousands of prisoners."

"Slaves, you mean," said Frederick.

"They expiate their own sins, and yours. But we will not contaminate our souls with them much longer. If you do not surrender . . ." He turned aside and drew a veedo set beside him. "We held this cleansing yesterday."

The picture was small and grainy, but the scene was clearly a labor camp. Beneath the guns of Engineer soldiers, several hundred bot and human prisoners labored with shovels to excavate a broad, shallow bowl. When it was prepared, they emptied drums of oil into the bowl until the soil glistened with fuel. Then the Engineers forced their prisoners to march into the bowl, arranged them in ranks of almost military precision, and threw a torch among them.

"Athena, off." Hannoken's voice shook with rage and pain. "But put it on the com. Let everyone see that."

"They're mad," said Frederick.

When the recording ended, Jeremy Duncan put his hands over his eyes. He ignored Donna Rose's sobs, thinking only that he might have been there. He might have been one of the shoveling slaves, pouring oil around his own feet, standing still under the threat of the guns while the torch was readied, knowing all the while that he was about to die.

He wished he could believe that he would have screamed and struggled, led his fellows in a desperate fight for life. They hadn't. They too rarely had in all the history of humanity's stay on Earth. He thought of what the Germans had done to the Jews, herding them into cattle cars, taking them to camps, lining them up for "showers" that even the victims had to know—they could see the heaps of bodies, smell the stench of burning flesh, hear the rumors—were devices of efficient, mass extermination. They had not fought because they had prayed for last-minute reprieves, that their oppressors would change their minds, declare it all a monstrous practical joke, that they would, perhaps, be singled out and removed from the doomed mass, even that they would be rescued by some other force. It had not happened then. It had not happened now.

He thought of the Moslem terrorists of Lebanon. Like the Engineers, unlike the Nazis, they had thought to play upon the sympathies of their opponents. They had kidnapped innocent passersby and held the passengers of planes and ships at gunpoint, threatening their deaths if the world did not give the terrorists what they wished. It had taken many years for the world to learn that giving in did not end the problem. The terrorists would take their prizes and then refuse to surrender their prisoners.

He knew that he too would have hoped, right up until the moment when the torch hovered in the air before his eyes, tumbling, arching into the oil at his feet, and the flames burst up around him to sear his lungs and eyes and very life.

"We have to do something," he said.

"We can't," cried Donna Rose. "We don't have enough ships to save them all. We don't have the places to put them yet. We don't have time." She wailed.

"I know," said Duncan. "But we can . . . Thor. Give me the coordinates for Washington, Chicago, Denver, Moscow, London, Beijing, New Delhi, Paris. For every missile control center that we know of. For every Engineer military base. For labor camps and industrial centers."

"You can't!" cried Donna Rose.

He ignored her. He could. Of course he could. He had to. It was the only way to end a terrorist threat. The world had proved it with the obliteration of Lebanon. "Thor. How many is that?"

"Two hundred and sixty-seven."

He thought while Donna Rose tugged futilely at his arm. He did not dare to use the rocks that waited in low Earth orbit or around the stations and habitats. Nor did he dare to divert all the rocks being produced to those targets. He had to continue to strengthen the Orbitals' defenses. But . . . "Thor. Set aside half of the next thousand new rocks. Park them in low orbit. Program them with those coordinates."

"This will take ten days," said the computer.

"Don't worry, Donna Rose," said Duncan. "We can't do anything yet. But if they continue with their cleansings . . ."

"I left Freddy. I came to you because you seemed more willing to fight. But this! This . . . If you do it, you'll be no better than them," said the bot.

"But they have it coming," he said. "We do not. *You* and all the other bots and gengineers and people who accept modern technology. You, they, we do not. Our only sin is that we are different. We look forward. We embrace the future. While they—"

She nodded. "But we don't need to destroy them."

"They destroy themselves."

She nodded again, her hand heavy on his arm. "All we have to do is save . . ."

"As many as we can, yes. But they will destroy what they do not want just so we cannot have it. We have to stop them."

Donna Rose abandoned the ODC's control room for the living quarters she shared with Jeremy Duncan. There, beneath a bank of bright lights, stood a trough of lunar regolith mixed with compost, well watered. She sank her roots into the rich, black soil, closed her eyes as a wealth of nutrients rushed into her system, and briefly wondered why they used no regolith on Probe Station. Long ago, in the 1960s, when the first astronauts had brought samples of the Moon to Earth, researchers had discovered that plants of all kinds loved lunar soil. It had not been sapped like Earth's by eons of biological activity.

She missed Frederick. He had suffered as much as Duncan, and for far longer. But he was not vindictive. He was patient, willing to wait while he prepared the scene, like her more intent on saving what could be saved, not on destroying.

She wondered, Did he miss her? And what was he doing with Narcissus Joy?

Chapter
Twenty-Two

LOIS MCALOIS LAY naked on her bed. Her thighs tapered abruptly toward her knees, the skin shading to pink and hairless smoothness. Below the knees, her calves and feet were small and thin, yet they did not seem shrunken with atrophy like those of a paraplegic. They were clearly functional, aquiver with life and potential, the limbs of a child, or of an adult who had been treated with the viruses gengineered to stimulate regeneration. The bulk of her thighs had gone to feed the process of regrowth, to match the thick muscles near her hips to the new and slender bones below.

The rest of her body was that of a mature woman. Her belly swelled above a triangle of pubic hair a little darker than the close-cropped auburn that topped her head. Her ribs made visible lines beneath the skin of her torso, and her breasts, barely affected by the light gravity of this level of Probe Station, were nearly perfect cones, their nipples erect.

Renny sat beside her. His tongue lolled, he panted lightly, and then he winced as his tailtip twitched. He had involuntarily tried to sweep the whole organ from side to side over the sheet.

"Poor boy," said Lois. She gently touched the bandage that held the broken bones immobile. "The pain-killer just isn't enough. Will you be able to fly?"

"There's only six of us," he growled. "And six ships. I have to. Besides, a pilot doesn't need a tail. And they'll block the nerves anyway. Or try to."

"It needs to heal. You'll ruin it."

"It won't matter much longer, will it?" He shifted his hind-quarters out of her reach and leaned over her legs, one hand supporting his weight. The other touched her shin, stroking, patting, exploring.

"They won't stay this way," said Lois. She was using the fingers of one hand to knead the fur of his shoulder. "They're

257

still growing. But they're already better than stumps."

"I know," said the dog, his voice revealing just a hint of canine whine. He pointed his long German shepherd nose toward her belly. "I wish you were a bitch."

"I can't smell right to you."

"You would then." He sniffed ostentatiously and ran his tongue along one side of his mouth. His hand moved upward. "And then . . ."

"No," she said. Her voice was as turgid with yearning as his own. "Not now. I want to too. But it wouldn't be right."

He touched her breasts, her throat, her lips. "People have done it before."

"It still isn't right."

"We may never have another chance."

"I know." The fuel depot, that great fabric bag that had filled with lunar dust while the Q-ships were being finished, had been moved. It now waited in low Earth orbit, next to Nexus Station, while another swelled, nearly full, near Probe Station. Finished bubblesats had also been moved nearer Earth, ready to serve first to free the Q-ships for their rescue missions; they had their own small Q-drives, and as soon as they were filled with refugees, they would depart for lunar orbit. The new sections of the LaGrangian habitats were ready, waiting for their tenants; so were the barracks on the Moon.

Renny and Lois and their fellow pilots had hauled up from Earth their last loads of oil and wood. They were done with bringing to safety those pitifully few bots and gengineers and others who could squeeze into whatever cracks their cargos left. Tomorrow they would fly the first missions intended to bring only refugees. They would save as many as they could before . . .

"They'll be shooting at us. They'll be trying to drop missiles on our landing zones, and Duncan won't be able to stop them all. Some of us will—"

"I know," she said. He touched her again. Her hand slid across his side and found . . . "You're too excited."

He whined and grimaced.

"I wish . . ."

"There hasn't been the time. We've been too busy. But if we make it through this . . ."

"No! Don't!"

"I'll let them Freddyize me."

"What?"

He held his free hand between their faces and twisted it back and forth. "I'll let them make the rest of me match this. I won't have a tail then."

"Oh!" she said. "I'll like that! We'll . . . Stop that!"

He stretched his length beside her, his head on her shoulder, his nose beside her ear, his breath warm against her cheek and neck. One hand moved from breast to breast to . . . She stroked his side, his arm, his . . .

Eventually, they slept.

"Facing the Future with Frank Fogarty"
Veedo panel discussion, security fibercast,
transcribed from GNN (Government NewsNet):

Fogarty: Tonight, our veedo audience wants to know the answer to a vital question: Is it true that the government is asking those who live in the stations and habitats above our fair planet to help us reestablish the Machine Age?

Alan Sakherji, Secretary of State: No, Frank. We're not asking. We're demanding. The genetic engineers are directly responsible for our current difficulties. Years ago, they stopped public spending on maintaining roads and improving efficiency and finding new sources of energy. They deliberately allowed the old infrastructure to deteriorate. They forced us to subsidize genimal trucks and airplanes and other . . .

Fogarty: But it's the government that chooses what to subsidize.

Secretary Sakherji: Be careful, Mr. Fogarty. We know what the truth is. The government at the time was under *intense* pressure from the gengineers and their environmentalist allies. It had very little choice.

Fogarty: But why are you asking the Orbitals for reparations?

Senator Cecil D. Trench (DemSoc-NC): Because they *owe* us! They stole every little bit of mechanical technology the gengineers didn't destroy. They took it right away from us, and now that we need it they won't give it back.

Secretary Sakherji: I have reliable information that they are even landing their ships in remote areas to loot stands of oil trees. They are actually stealing fuel that we need desperately.

Fogarty: Fuel? What would they need fuel for?

Senator Trench: How else do you run machines?

Fogarty: I see. Can you tell us how you plan to force the Orbitals to cooperate?

Secretary Sakherji: First, quite frankly, there are still a great many botanicals, half-humans, and gengineers here on Earth, and we have told the Orbitals that how we treat them depends on how they respond to our demands.

Senator Trench: We're holding them hostage.

Fogarty: What will you do if the Orbitals refuse to cooperate?

Secretary Sakherji: I understand that your network's broadcasts of our mass cleansings have enjoyed quite high ratings.

Fogarty: That's true.

Senator Trench: But we're keeping the gengineers themselves.

Secretary Sakherji: We have set them to restoring the basic genetic technology. We don't have the mechanical infrastructure we need, and if the Orbitals continue their selfish obstinacy, we'll have to have the genimals. Of course, we'll only need them temporarily. As soon as we have the factories running again, we'll—

Fogarty: You'll let them go? Perhaps to join the Orbitals?

Senator Trench: That's what we're telling the Orbitals.

Secretary Sakherji: But the Orbitals won't be there. We still have a great many of the old missiles in storage, and we will—

Fogarty: Is there any truth to the rumors that you've already launched some of those missiles? And that the Orbitals have destroyed them?

Secretary Sakherji: They have no weapons! How could they possibly destroy them? By throwing rocks?

Fogarty: Will you be sending troops into space?

Secretary Sakherji: I can't say. But the gengineer saboteurs did not manage to destroy all the spaceplanes. If we decide to seize the Orbitals' technology, we do have the means.

"Minerva, how many barracks on the Moon?" asked Frederick Suida.

"Seventy-two," said the computer.

"Do we have enough air?"

"Check."

"Water?"

"Check."

"Food?"

"Insufficient data," answered the machine.

"Depends on how many we get," said Narcissus Joy.

"Bubblesats?" asked Frederick.

"Fifteen," answered the computer.

"They'll be crowded in their transfer mode," said the bot.

"How many refugees have we got already?"

"Six hundred and seven," said the computer.

"How many more can we take?"

"Four thousand six hundred."

"That's two dozen loads," said Narcissus Joy. "Four apiece."

"If the loads are full. If there are enough refugees at each stop. The ships aren't Bernies. They can't make more than one stop."

"And if we don't lose any ships."

"We should have more, and more pilots, in case of injury."

"At least, we have the fuel."

Frederick and Narcissus Joy were running over their checklists one last time, making sure that none of the necessary preparations had been skipped or scanted. Their voices were stiffly formal, Frederick's distant, the bot's cool and hurt.

She had done her best to fill Donna Rose's place in his life. She had taken over the other bot's job and done it well. She had moved into Frederick's quarters and occupied the soil trough that Donna Rose had left before the window. And the night before, when Frederick had been lying on his bed, she had sat beside him.

"She meant a lot to you," she had said. "She wasn't just an assistant."

Frederick had thrown an arm over his face as if to block her from his view. "How could you know?"

"The honeysuckle that she planted. It's small, but it remembers . . ."

He had sighed wordlessly. Then he had glanced toward the trough where it sat in its bright puddle of illumination. The sprig of vine Donna Rose had left had grown in the days since she had gone. It now hid a quarter of the soil with green, and buds were forming. Soon it would hold to the light blossoms full of self-fermented wine, of euphoric alcohol and drug. If he chose, he could . . . But he had never before wished to dull his pain in that way.

"I could . . ."

"No!" He had rolled abruptly from the bed, avoiding her reaching hand, and left the room.

When he had returned an hour later, she had been in the trough, leaves spread to the sunlight. She had turned her head to watch as he knelt at her feet to pinch away the honeysuckle buds but she had said nothing more. Nor did he as he rose and drew the curtain that walled off his bed.

Now Minerva, their computer, said, "Two scooters closing."

Narcissus Joy touched her keyboard and spoke into a microphone. In a moment, she said, "It's the Eldest, her Speaker, and . . ."

Frederick turned toward the window that overlooked the construction shack's work area. Here Arlan Michaels and his crews had built the drives for the Q-ships and Duncan's rocks. They were still building the small rock drives and working on the large ones for the *Gypsy*. But the design work was finished. Now Michaels and three of his physicists floated over a workbench to one side, leaving the routine assembly work to others while they concentrated on . . . Frederick did not know what they were working on, except that it looked more or less like a standard Q-drive from a distance and that Michaels and his colleagues covered it with a Velcroed tarp when they were not there.

"Let them in," he said. He sighed. He did not know what the bots might want with him. The ones Renny had rescued had been a significant help. Their hands had indeed hastened the construction of the lunar barracks, the bubblesats, and more. But now there was nothing more that they could do. Nor could he do any more than he had already done to help them, to build safety for their kin, to give the refugees a refuge.

Yet they had not come to ask for more. That much was plain very soon after the Eldest, propelled by the hands of her companions, floated into the office of the construction shack.

"You have a soil trough there," said the first to speak. She was a tall bot whose scalp blossoms were yellow with dark centers. Narcissus Joy had introduced her as Shasta Button. "Is that for your aide?"

"She uses it," said Frederick. "But . . ."

"It was for Donna Rose," said Narcissus Joy.

The Eldest bent her amaryllis-red head toward the trough and a wave of scent spread through the air of the office.

"Where is she?" said Eldest's Speaker.

"She left me," said Frederick. "She thought I wasn't willing enough to fight, to save the bots—and others—still on Earth."

The scent that issued from the Eldest's flowery head turned soothing. "She misunderstood," said Eldest's Speaker. "You and she have done just what you must. Saved us all. We expected no more, and we are grateful."

"Where is she?" asked Shasta Button.

"With Jeremy Duncan."

"The weapons master," expanded Narcissus Joy. "She helps him in the Orbital Defense Center."

Frederick nearly choked on the richness of the next gust of perfume. "Call her, please," said Eldest's Speaker.

Narcissus Joy immediately spoke to the computer, "Minerva, get Donna Rose."

A veedo screen promptly lit with Jeremy Duncan's face. "Hey, Freddy," he said. His eyes were red, his cheeks unshaven and, showing beneath his unbuttoned labcoat, the lips of his gills were puffy. "We've been working flat-out for the last thirty hours, but we're ready. We should be able to stop whatever they throw at us tomorrow, and then—"

"Is Donna Rose there?" asked Narcissus Joy. As she spoke, Eldest's Speaker pushed the Eldest in her pot a little closer to the screen.

Duncan stepped aside, and his bot assistant, her face drawn and her blossoms limp with weariness, appeared. "Eldest," she said.

The Eldest's perfumes billowed effusively, chokingly. The hitherto subliminal hum of hidden ventilators became audible as the fans strove to clear the air. "We thank you," said Eldest's Speaker. "You have done well. You could have done no more. It does not matter how tomorrow ends. We wish success, but the effort counts."

She turned toward Frederick. "When you first offered sanctuary, she used the honeysuckle. She told us of you, and then of that potential refuge here in space. We instructed her, told her to go if chance but offered. She did, and so did you."

Frederick was puzzled. "But how could you know we would try to rescue you? No one knew about the Q-ships. No one knew that the Engineers were about to take over the world, or that they would try to exterminate—"

"Donna Rose told us immediately. We knew near as soon as you about the ships. We had clues as well. About the future. We were everywhere. Where we weren't, there was honeysuckle."

Duncan abruptly pushed Donna Rose out of the veedo screen's field of view. "Then why?" he cried. "Why didn't you do something?"

"We were powerless." Narcissus Joy did not wait for a perfumed message from the Eldest or for words from her Speaker. "We could only prepare as best we could."

"We used the honeysuckle," said Eldest's Speaker. "It grew everywhere. Even in the pots of BRA's computers. And it could talk to them root to root. Through them then, through wire-net not root-net, connecting everywhere, we canceled job and ticket, cut your roots, cut you free."

Frederick grimaced awkwardly. "You manipulated me, marooned me here."

"Would you rather have stayed on Earth, Freddy?" Donna Rose had edged back onto the screen.

Frederick hesitated only briefly before he shook his head. Only a fool, he knew, could answer otherwise. "But why couldn't you manipulate others? Why couldn't you stop it all from happening?"

"No," said Shasta Button. "There were too many Engineers. Their voices were too strong."

Another burst of odor prompted Eldest's Speaker to say, "We could only stimulate and catalyze. Put you where you might help. Where your natural sympathies might create a home anew. Where those who might escape might go. Where at worst a single bot might live."

"And tomorrow . . ." said Narcissus Joy.

"Tomorrow," said the Eldest through her Speaker. "But you have fulfilled already many of our hopes. If tomorrow fails, our race still lives."

"So does ours," said Frederick. He did not mean the race of pigs or genimals or even genimals who had been given sentience and human form. Rather, his few words embraced all those who looked toward the future for their destiny, all those who loved the new, the unknown, the uncertain. If the Orbitals' six Q-ships succeeded in their attempt to fill the new living spaces they had built with refugees, if they failed, shot down by Earthly missiles, enough were safe already to ensure the future.

For a moment, he thought that Donna Rose looked at him more kindly.

Alvar Hannoken was facing his picture window, staring out at whatever he could see of Q-ships and bubblesats and more. Segments of the glass seemed to warp and flow as the computer, following his commands, enlarged fragments of the view, shifted far to near, near to far, projected even images of things the window did not face.

"We're ready," he said at last. Instead of his usual coverall, he was wearing a short, pale green tunic over grey shorts and his usual black stockings. His hands were clasped behind his back, twining restlessly, and Frederick could see his goat-bent, goat-hairy legs more clearly than ever before. They too were restless.

"And just in time," he added. "If we wait much longer, there won't be anyone left to rescue. They'll all have been 'cleansed.' " He paused, and his feet brushed against the edge of the pot that had been intended for Donna Rose's child. "Everything depends," he said. "On the ships, the pilots."

"They'll do fine," said Frederick. His face showed his impatience. There was no need for talk. There was only waiting, until Renny and Lois and the other pilots could do their jobs and the Engineers could finally be abandoned to whatever they might make of Earth.

He had left his office in the construction shack not long after the Eldest and her retinue had departed. He and Narcissus Joy had been on their way to the quarters they shared, as he had once shared them with Donna Rose, when the communicator had summoned him to the Station Director's office. He had tried to ignore the call, but Athena's voice had followed him from com to com down the corridor. At last, he had given in, knowing that he would have no peace, no rest, no time to worry about the morrow or at the hole Donna Rose's departure had left in his life.

"If they don't get shot down. That's what worries me.

The com center's picking up a lot of traffic, and it's coded. Military. They're planning something."

"We could destroy the comsats," said Narcissus Joy.

"No, we use them too."

"Then turn them off. We could do that."

Hannoken turned away from the window, shaking his head. "Then we wouldn't know what they're up to."

"We don't know anything now," said Frederick, "if they're using code."

"We know they're keeping secrets. We know they're up to something."

"But what?"

The station director made a sour face. "Probably something nasty. Like a mass launch of every missile they've got."

"Duncan says he can stop even that."

"I hope he's right." Hannoken looked Frederick in the eye, seeming finally to see the man he had summoned to his office. "You're tired, aren't you? And tomorrow will be a long day. You'd better get some rest."

Chapter
Twenty-three

THE FIRST TARGETS of the rescue missions were the prison camps where barbed wire and armed guards surrounded thousands of bots and gengineers and humans who had been genetically modified or who had demonstrated approval of gengineering or disapproval of the Engineers and their tactics. These were the prisoners who awaited "cleansing" or assignment to research and development squads such as the one Jeremy Duncan had escaped.

Renny and his fellow pilots knew that they would never be able to rescue everyone. They would probably get only one landing apiece in the prison camps. That single rescue attempt might catch the Engineers by surprise, and it might succeed. But then the defenses would be alerted, missiles would be targeted, and any Q-ship that tried a second landing, or even a first landing in another camp, would be all too likely to be destroyed. Unfortunately, there were only six Q-ships.

Those ships that survived the camps would then pick up as many as they could of the bots and humans who had fled the Engineers' murderous affections. These refugees, like those who had rescued Duncan, had found temporary hiding places around the globe. But none of their gatherings was large. Nowhere was there more than a few hundred refugees. Most groups were no more than two or three dozen strong. The ships would return to orbit nearly empty. With luck they would be able to make enough trips to fill the quarters that had been prepared for the refugees. But they would at best leave behind as many as they saved.

Quincy, Quentin, Quimby, Quiggle, Quito, and *Quebec.* Floating in loose formation not far from Probe Station, the Q-ships were bulb-nosed spears whose shafts were bundled round by tanks full of lunar dust, reaction mass to be vaporized, made

267

into plasma and thrust and velocity. A coin collector might have fancied that they bore some resemblance to bundles of sticks surrounding axes, to the fasces on old U.S. dimes, once a sign of Roman authority, more recently an emblem of fascist tyranny, now far more a sigil of freedom.

The official voice of Probe Station's communications center spoke: "We'll let you know if they fire any missiles at you."

"Thanks," said Lois McAlois dryly. "We won't even hear you unless they miss."

"Duncan has his rocks ready. He says he won't let 'em get that close."

Frederick Suida's voice broke in: "Good luck, Renny."

One by one, Renny, Lois, and the other pilots activated their Q-drives. Plasma flames began to glow behind their ships, and they began to move, accelerating at first slowly, then more rapidly, out of lunar orbit and toward Earth. As they neared the planet, they began to separate, three pairs of flames pushing their fasces toward widely separate destinations. Renny and Buran, together, would strike the airport from which the dog had first left Earth; it was now one of the largest prison camps on the continent. Lois and Stacey were bound for what had once been a European army base. The other two pilots would land in China. Each one carried in his or her Q-ship's computer a list of secondary destinations, their coordinates and courses laid down well in advance. As soon as the armed camps became too alert, too unsafe, for landing, they could divert to other large concentrations of the Engineers' victims. When all the camps were barred against them, they would scoop up the smaller groups.

Renny grimaced as his Q-drive roared and gees pressed him into his seat. He turned off his radio and screamed. As he had expected, the anesthetic Probe Station's medics had injected into the root of his spine to block the pain quickly proved inadequate. But even as he voiced his agony, he kept his eyes on his ship's instruments and his hands on the controls. As soon as he could, he turned on the radio once more. He dared not miss a word that the observers in orbit above might have for him.

The computer could handle the entire landing, but only as long as nothing went wrong. And if something went wrong, he could handle it only if he knew what emergency he had to cope with. If the Engineers fired ground-to-air missiles or antiaircraft guns, it would be his reflexes, not the computer's, that would keep him alive to see Lois again. And hers that would keep her alive, though that thought lasted for no more than an instant before he squelched it. He could not afford to let his attention wander. Pain or no pain, worry or no worry, he must stay focused on his ship, his landing, the screen that showed the prisoners scurrying away from the blast of his descending ship, more prisoners emerging from sun-baked hangars, the Engineer troops turning rifles and machine guns in his direction, more troops unloading long cylinders from a wagon and struggling to erect what could only be a launcher.

The roar of the drive cut off with a suddenness that left his ears ringing. Yet the spang of slugs against the *Quincy*'s shell was clearly audible, a metal rain that made him hope the metal that surrounded him was thick enough, tough enough, not to yield.

It was only seconds before he hit the controls that opened the hatch to the ship's passenger compartment and deployed the boarding ladder. Another switch activated the loudspeaker, and he said, "The cavalry is here." He could hear his voice booming over the airport's turfed runways even through the *Quincy*'s hull. Through the port to his right he could see Buran's *Quito*, its hatch as open as his, the Engineers' prisoners already beginning to climb its ladder.

"All aboard," he cried. "We can hold two hundred. Lay back in the nets and hold on."

External microphones picked up the rattle of rifle fire, the sustained ripping of machine guns. The metal hull rang. All around the edges of the crowds that surrounded the *Quincy* and the *Quito,* prisoners fell, both bot and human, young and old. Others tumbled from the ships' ladders, and from the very edges of their hatches.

When the *Quincy* was almost full, Renny used the loudspeaker once more to say, "No more on the ladder. No more, please. Back off. I have to launch."

No one paid attention. Indeed, the prisoners began to club at each other with fists, shoes, whatever they had in hand, struggling for one of the last places to be had. Renny sighed. He had once seen a historical veedo, the evacuation of some southeast Asian city in the face of an invasion of revolutionaries. Helicopters had hovered over a white building, full of refugees with more, panicked, desperate, clinging to the landing gear and to each other. As the helicopters had lifted into the sky, they had fallen, screaming, to their deaths.

The German shepherd sighed again and activated the drive. If he did not, he knew, he would never leave the ground. *Quincy*'s belly would be too full for the ship to move. Better, he told himself, that he escape with his load of refugees, that some should live, even if he must . . .

Plasma flame billowed against the ground. The prisoners fell from the ladder, screamed outrage at his betrayal of their hopes, and tried to run. But even as the *Quincy*'s torch incinerated them from behind, the Engineers' bullets withered their ranks from in front.

Renny gritted his teeth and activated the controls that stowed the ladder and closed the hatch. Then he fed full power to his drive and boosted straight to space.

The *Quito* remained visible through the port, boosting in parallel, fleeing the Engineers, carrying its cargo of precious salvage, of no one knew what, bots or humans, scientists or janitors. Renny was trying not to scream when the radio said, "They've launched a missile."

A moment later, he saw the *Quito* explode.

"That was the only one." The communication tech's voice choked, raw with anguish. One ship, one of only six, was gone, together with two hundred lives or more. And gone on the very first landing. The numbers they could rescue were cut by a sixth, unless the others dared more landings, took more chances, exposed themselves perhaps too often.

Renny's only thought was that he hoped Lois made it.

Despite the com tech's words, the ground-to-air missile that destroyed the *Quito* was not the only one. Others chased the other ships but fell short or were destroyed when they entered the Q-ships' plasma plumes. Some simply failed to explode or detonated prematurely.

The few spaceplanes the Engineers had not destroyed in the first, violent days of their takeover were fueled and filled with troops. They took off from their airports, climbed toward space, and died as Duncan met them with his Q-driven rocks.

Silos opened around the globe, and larger missiles erupted from the ground, bound for the stations in orbit. Some exploded on ignition. Others detonated their warheads while still in the atmosphere. Many reached space and were hammered into uselessness. A few bent their courses back into air and descended on the prison camps, obliterating those prisoners who had survived the plasma blasts and gunfire, the guards who had slaughtered so many first, and surrounding country-side, cities, structures, sending vast clouds of radioactive debris into the air.

"Now," said Duncan, secure in the shell of his Orbital Defense Command post, and at his command Thor sent rocks falling toward Earth's cities, military bases, troop concentra-tions, empty silos.

"No!" cried Donna Rose. "They're helpless. Stop the mis-siles, but—"

"Yes!" And craters bloomed. More clouds rose to choke the air, to shade the Earth, to bring on untimely chill.

The remaining Q-ships descended on other prison camps, filled up again with the Engineers' prisoners, weathered the battering of slugs and mortar rounds, and escaped once more. But then the camps and their prisoners were no more, tar-geted by missiles launched too nearby, flying too briefly to be stopped by Duncan's rocks, destroyed by Engineers who refused to let anyone else have what they themselves des-pised.

The rescue ships turned then toward the smaller groups of refugees in jungles, forests, mountains, collected what they could, and delivered new cargos to orbit.

One of Duncan's rocks missed its intended target. The lucky warhead struck Nexus Station, exploded, and sent a blizzard of shattered metal storming through space. Many shards struck the bubblesats waiting to fill with human cargo, but the shards were small, so were the holes, and there were plenty of patches. The bubblesats, and most of those within them, survived.

Renny was on the ground in northern Canada when the com burst into life. "The fuel depots are nearly empty," said the tech. "Last trip."

The dog cursed the pain in his tail. He had swallowed far too many pain-killers on top of his injections, and his brain felt fuzzy. But he remained able to function. He looked at his screens. This group of refugees was small, less than forty, mainly bots with a sprinkling of greenskins and other gengineered humans. They had not panicked, not even when a mushroom cloud had erupted to the south, a missile that had been targeted on his landing but had fallen short or been hit by one of Duncan's rocks. They stood in line, singing enthusiastically, joyously, unafraid, "Swing low, sweet chariot." They climbed the ladder without struggling among each other, passing bot children, safely embedded in boxes and buckets full of dirt, from hand to hand. He wished he could land a second time—there were other refugees on his computer's list, many of them—but he could not afford the fuel. This would be a small load.

"How many have we got so far?" he asked the com.

"Not enough," was the answer. "They've wrecked the camps. And we get only one stop at each refugee group. Their radars pick us up, and the missiles hit as soon as we're gone. Duncan can't get them all."

He bent his head. The control board before him had, among its variety of sensors, a radiation detector. At the moment, it registered only a little above Earthly background. But he knew that if he were on Earth to see, then soon, in mere days, its readings would rise to dangerous levels. The Engineers were mad dogs that fouled their manger. Billions had died already. Millions more would join them. Surely, surely, millions would survive. Warheads had exploded, yes. But most of the murk in the air was mere dust, not radioactive. Its worst effects would be the lack of heat and sunlight, the death of crops, and later famine.

The Orbitals and the refugees they had saved would be above the poisoned world, safe. Before too long, the *Gypsy* would be ready, and they would leave. The Engineers and their heirs would be left alone to make what they would of their world, of what was left of what had once been Eden.

The last of the refugees, a human with no visible signs of genetic modification, was on the ladder. Renny waited until the woman entered the hatch and then withdrew the ladder and sealed the ship. Once more, he activated the Q-drive. Once more, he rode the plasma thrust toward orbit.

But he did not make it safely.

He rode his ship, grimacing with pain, his tail screaming inside him, straining to watch his screens and indicators, to listen to the voice of the com tech crying warnings. He knew when a missile rose out of the distance toward him. And he knew he responded too slowly as he pushed his thrust to dangerous levels, screamed with increased pain, and thanked whatever gods there were that this time his load was light, that he had some hope, even as doped as he was, of accelerating beyond the missile's reach.

When the warhead went off, he was still too close. His screens blacked out. The *Quincy* bucked, rolled, spun, and twisted as the shockwave hit. He screamed again, and then he lost consciousness.

The ship's computer struggled to maintain course. It knew nothing of Renny's damaged body, nor of the fleshy wreckage in the passenger compartment, though its microphones registered moans and screams and the fluid sounds of broken bodies. But it did have a program, a course to fly, and its structure was enough stronger than those of flesh that it remained capable. It attained orbit, and when it neared those bubblesats that still waited for their liberated cargos near where Nexus Station once had been, it took position precisely as it should.

Lois McAlois was already there in the *Quentin*. When Renny did not position his ship for unloading, she tried to call him. His com remained silent, and the tech at Probe Station said, "He took a close one."

She began to weep.

"Can you see him through the ports?"

She moved her *Quentin* closer, drifting it across the *Quincy*'s bow, and peered into the other ship's control room. "Yes," she said. Renny was there, but his head lolled and his eyes were shut. He did not seem to be alive.

She bit her lip. Tears flooded her eyes. He had insisted on flying despite his tail. He had insisted that the pain-killers would not interfere with his piloting. But they had. They must have. Fate could not possibly have struck him down without that help. Could it? But then fate had certainly claimed the *Quito*.

She had to fight to keep her voice calm when she answered Probe Station's repeated query: "He's dead," she said. "But the ship seems okay."

"Can you get a tow on him?"

"I think so." She had towed pods full of supplies and passengers to Mars and the Belt, after all, and with a smaller ship. The *Quincy* would be just another pod. Its cargo did not matter now, except to her.

Chapter
Twenty-Four

THE FIVE REMAINING Q-ships were safe in orbit. The refugees they had saved were in their new quarters in Hugin and Munin and on the Moon. The bubblesats had not been needed for residence after all. They had been invaluable for transport, freeing the ships for faster turnaround, more rescue missions, more lives saved. But not enough. The camps had too soon become unsafe to raid. The refugee groups in the wilderness had been too small. The *Quito* had been lost too soon.

Frederick had given Alvar Hannoken the numbers: They had had room for four thousand six hundred new refugees, added to the six hundred they had already yanked from the Engineers' jaws. They had saved barely three thousand. There would be no more.

And there had been, before Hannoken had first talked to Frederick, before he had been reunited with Renny, before the Engineers had risen up like a tide to smash the sand castle of civilization, millions of bots, billions of humans who had been genetically modified or who had owned or used the products of the gengineers or who had worked in the gengineering industry. They were gone, all gone. Or almost all gone. A few, a pitiful few, had reached space. Many fewer remained prisoner.

At Hannoken's command, Minerva magnified a picture-window view of Earth until he could see the puffs of dust that marked the appearance of new craters. Jeremy Duncan was expending the last of his rocks in a mad and vengeful orgy of destruction. The Engineers' own warheads, exploding in the silos and in the air, pulverized by mechanical impact, had already doomed the Engineers' version of civilization, such as it was. There would be survivors, but . . . Now the cities, the factories, the landfill mines, the dams and power plants, all were rubble. The Engineers would be many, many years rebuilding.

"I hope," said a voice behind him, "he's saved a few, just in case he missed some silos."

Hannoken turned on one black-stockinged foot. "Arlan," he said. "Yes, there's a reserve. What have you got? When you called, you said . . ."

The Q-drive physicist was grinning broadly. "We may have a way to beat the light-speed limit," he said. When Hannoken looked skeptical, he added, "We've managed to get macroscopic tunneling. We can warp probability enough to make a ship stop being *here* and start being *there*. It doesn't have to cross the space between."

"It's instantaneous?"

Michaels nodded. "As far as we can tell. The only trouble is the distance. Our record is 1.2 millimeters. But we're pretty sure we can get it up to a meter or so, and maybe more. And there's no limit on the mass we can shift, at least in principle."

"So we'll be able to move the *Gypsy*." Michaels nodded even more happily than before. "A meter at a time, if you improve it that much."

"And if we can cycle the drive fast enough . . . Once every three nanoseconds, and we beat the speed of light."

Now Hannoken grinned. He didn't understand how the probability warp worked—in fact, it felt much like magic to him—but he knew that many devices operated on nanosecond cycles. What Michaels suggested seemed easily achievable. The implications were obvious.

"Have you tested it?" he asked.

"Just on the bench." Michaels nodded. "But we'll have something to try in the *Quoi* in a few days."

"So many dead!" cried Donna Rose. "So many! And we, we . . ."

Her head leaned against Frederick Suida's chest, her tears soaking his coverall, her yellow blossoms fragrant beneath his nose. His arms were wrapped around her chest, his hands gently patting the leaves that covered her back, and his face wore a smile at last. It was a sad smile, for she was grieving and what had made her grieve was more than enough to make Frederick—or anyone else—grieve as well. But it was a smile. It said that his heart was at peace for the first time in many years. Something he had lost had returned to him. A void in his life was full once more.

Ah, Donna Rose, he thought happily. My Donna. But all he said aloud was, "Yes. We did. The Engineers shot them and burned them and bombed them. And so did we. When the Q-ships took off. When the rocks struck."

"So many bots," she moaned.

"So many people," he murmured. "We'll carry the guilt for the rest of our lives. So will our children, and theirs."

"But we did save some." She looked up at his face, blinking. He used the tip of one forefinger to sweep the tears from her cheek. "We did."

"We did."

"I understand why . . . why Duncan . . ." She took a deep, shuddering breath and paused. "That's why I couldn't stay with him. I had to leave, to come back."

"I'm glad you did." His smile broadened, turned silly, fatuous, and his arms tightened around her. "Very glad."

"You're a builder. You'll be helping to get the *Gypsy* done. I want to build too. Not destroy."

While they kissed, and later, he thought that, yes, what remained was building, creative work, life-affirming, future-oriented. What they had done on Earth, to Earth, to the Engineers and to the bots and others they had been unable to save, had been essential. So was completing the *Gypsy,* preparing it for its long voyage and . . . But no one knew what else they were preparing the *Gypsy* for. No one knew what they would find on the worlds that swung around the hearths of other stars.

Sam Nickers sat before the bioform computer, stroking keys, studying the lessons that appeared on the screen. Over him arched metal ribs, plastic sheeting, a layer of lunar regolith pierced at intervals by solid plastic cylinders to admit the sunlight. Covering the floor and climbing the curved walls was a jungle of honeysuckle vines, the flowers already open, holding out their wine to all.

No one accepted the offer. Sam was surrounded by a garden of young bots, rooted in lunar soil, linked to each other and the computer through the honeysuckle. Mary Gold, the official teacher of the class, stood to one side, watching as he selected a lesson on plumbing and activated the download to the students' brains. Other bots paced purposefully past the class, erected plastic partitions, and arranged furniture.

As the lesson proceeded, Sam looked for his wife, scanning the tunnellike structure from one end—occupied by an airlock that opened into a trench that sloped toward the surface—to the other, where stood the Eldest, quietly rooted, protected from the hubbub by a low wall built of lunar boulders. Within her enclosure were several other boulders, artfully placed and linked by the single branch of living honeysuckle allowed to twine across the raked soil. From the Eldest and the vine drifted faint floral perfumes that spoke of contentment and an end to conflict. The overall effect was that of a Japanese garden, serenely peaceful, all-accepting, eternal.

The traffic shifted, and he saw Sheila not far away at all from him. She and Jackie Thyme and several other bots leaned over a table spread with plans for sections of the *Gypsy*. In just a few more weeks, some of them would board once more a Q-ship and travel outward to work on the great ship. Eventually, when the *Gypsy* moved Earthward, the rest would move as well, for the last time. Then they would have to be computer engineers, systems analysts, life support experts, and much, much more. They would even have to be carpenters, electricians, and plumbers. If they were not, progress would be excruciatingly slow.

He smiled as he decided not to interrupt her. They were safe, at least until the *Gypsy* left Earth's neighborhood and found other terrors among the stars.

In the long moment before he dared to open his eyes, Renny tried to remember what had happened. There had been agony. There had been the muzziness of drugs meant to call a halt to pain. There had been a missile and more pain and . . . Where was he? He should have been dead. He deserved it, after the way he had taken off, destroying the bots and humans, the prisoners of the Engineers, that he had meant to save. But the *Quincy* had been full. It could hold no more, and if he had let too many crowd aboard, he would not have been able to take off or to reach orbit and safety. Even more would have died. He had had no choice, not really. He had had to blast them.

But he wasn't dead. He lived, though the guilt remained and blood-warm fluid bathed his hands. He could tell that much. But he could not raise his arms. Straps bound them to his sides. Nor could he move his legs. He could not move his tail, but—wonder of wonders—at least it no longer hurt.

He managed to move two fingers, and his mind froze for an instant. They were not his. That was not his fur-covered side he touched. Bare skin—had he been shaved? For surgery? No. The ribs and curvatures and musculatures were not those he had grown accustomed to over the years. What, then?

He opened his eyes and blinked against the liquid blurs that filled them.

"Renny!"

He could see nothing clearly, but there was a figure leaning over him and the voice was familiar. "Lois? What happened?"

"You're okay! You're all right!"

His vision was clearing. He could see her hair, her auburn hair; her green coverall, the one with the chevrons, the one she had been wearing when he first met her, her face, her anxious, relieved, delighted grin. Beyond her, above her, hung a jungle of tubes and wires that he guessed must be plugged into his body. To one side were racks of intravenous bottles and the metallic casings and glowing screens and digital readouts of medical monitors. On the ceiling above him was a rectangular panel, mist-cloudy, blank.

Suddenly, he knew what had happened. He tried to indicate the overhead panel with his eyes. "Turn on the mirror."

"Uh-uh." She shook her head. "You're supposed to go back to sleep."

"Not yet," he said, though he could not help but blink once more, and yawn as well. "Please."

She obeyed, and he saw himself.

"Jeremy Duncan and Director Hannoken both worked on the design," she told him. "They thought you should keep a little of the old you. The way Frederick did."

"How long . . ."

"You've been in here a few weeks."

He was relieved to see that he did not have Frederick's upturned, flattened nose. His was smaller than before, and pinker, and as straight-bridged as ever, and it merged smoothly into his upper lip. His torso was hairless, but its shape matched his arms, and so did his legs. The hair on the top of his head was dark, nearly black; on the sides it was blond. His canines were a little long.

"I'm still a little doggy," he said at last. "The teeth."

"Gives you a predatory quality." She smiled at him approvingly. "Very sexy."

"Very oral." The moment of banter was not enough to keep him from yawning again.

Lois laughed gently. "You wanted this," she said. "And so did I. And when the medics said they would have to put you in the tank anyway, to regenerate, I told them . . ."

"Thanks," he said. "Though it'll take some getting used to."

"I'll help."

He stared at her deepening blush, wondered if he could do that now, too, and shifted his gaze to the mirror. He grinned then, a human grin, eager for whatever was to come.

The fatigue was suddenly worse. He had to struggle to keep his eyes open as he asked, "What about my passengers?"

"Most of them made it."

And some of them didn't. He sighed quietly. "Is the *Gypsy* on schedule?"

"No problems. By the time you're out of this tank, it might even be parked beside the station."

Renny struggled against the return of unconsciousness to see again the mirror on the ceiling. He was away from Earth, away from reactionary Engineers and animal-rights fanatics. And he wasn't just a dog anymore. Not that he couldn't have stayed a dog and been accepted here for what he was. But he had Lois. He looked at her and felt his body responding. She blushed again.

He fought to keep his eyes from closing. But his lids were heavy. He could not keep them open. The mirror and his new body, Lois, the new and promising future that awaited them all, everything within his view narrowed, darkened, and went out.

Yes, he thought just before his consciousness disappeared as well. Yes, and now he was human too.